RYDEVILLE HIGH ELITE BOOK THREE

SWEET

Retribution

USA TODAY BESTSELLING AUTHOR

SIOBHAN DAVIS

Printed by Amazon
Paperback edition © October 2019

ISBN-13: 9781697356076

Editor: Kelly Hartigan (XterraWeb) editing.xterraweb.com
Cover design by Robin Harper https://wickedbydesigncovers.wixsite.com
Photographer: Sara Eirew
Cover Models: Anthony Desforges and Hélène Bujold
Formatting by Polgarus Studios

DEDICATION

For Jennifer Gibson, critique partner extraordinaire and all-round amazing human being. This series, and this book, in particular, would not exist if it weren't for your support and encouragement every step of the way. Love you to the moon and back, lady. Thank you for always being in my corner.

AUTHOR'S NOTE

Although this book is set in a high school environment, it is a **dark bully romance**, and it is not suitable for young teens due to mature content, graphic sexual scenes, and cursing. The recommended reading age is eighteen+. **Some scenes may be triggering.**

CHAPTER ONE

Abby

"I need to use the bathroom," I blurt, interrupting the minister just before he reaches the part where we say our vows. My hand is clammy against Charlie's much larger palm as we hold hands while I prepare to do this. But a sudden bout of nerves has me second-guessing my strategy, and I need a time-out to ensure I'm doing the right thing.

"It can wait," my father snaps, narrowing his eyes at me.

"Abby." Charlie looks down at me. "What are you doing?" he mouths.

I press my lips to his ear. "I think I'm going to puke," I lie, clutching my stomach and contorting my face. I clamp a hand over my mouth, fake gagging, beseeching him with my eyes.

"Don't make me regret this," he murmurs in a low voice. "And don't try anything because your father *will* kill him." He jerks his head in Kai's direction.

"I know that, and I won't risk his life."

A muscle ticks in his jaw as he nods tersely. I step back, and my father roughly grabs hold of my arm. "You're not leaving this room until you're married."

1

"Daddy, I feel sick, and I'm liable to puke on myself. I'm sure no one wants to see that."

His face turns an unflattering shade of red. "What kind of idiot do you take me for?"

"Mr. Hearst." Charlie steps up behind me, placing his hand on my hip. "Abby can take five minutes to go to the bathroom." He purposely looks over at Kai. "Trust me, she's going nowhere."

The bastard glances at his watch, and his Adam's apple bobs in his throat. I'd have been halfway to the bathroom by now if he wasn't being such an ass about it. He slants me a look Satan himself would be proud of.

Don't worry, Daddy Dearest. The sentiment is shared.

But I keep a neutral expression on my face, shielding my true feelings from the monster who helped give me life.

"Maurio," my father barks. "Escort my daughter to the bathroom." Charlie's hand falls off my hip, and Father grabs hold of my arm again. "Don't delay or I'll come and drag you back here myself."

I stare blankly at the bastard. "If you hurt him, all deals are off." I cast a quick glance at my twin, ensuring he knows to watch guard over my man. "No one is to lay a finger on Kai." Drew cautions me with his eyes as I stalk toward the door, and I subtly nod. I'm not stupid. I'm not going to do anything that'll risk Kai's life, but I need to gather my thoughts. To ensure this is the right plan. Besides, Father needs me to return and say my vows, so he won't risk doing anything to my lover in my absence.

I slam the door to the bathroom in Maurio's face, locking it quickly, in case he has any ideas about standing guard inside. I sigh heavily as I plant my hands on the edge of the sink, staring at my reflection in the mirror.

My heart is on lockdown, and I reinforce the steel bars around it, unable to confront the latest revelation from my father. I squeeze my eyes shut as a barrage of emotion attempts to breach the invisible barrier I've erected. I cannot think about that now. If I do, I will charge out there and try to murder the bastard myself, and all that'll achieve is sure death for Kai and a lifetimes sentence for me.

In order to think about this pragmatically, I need to control my emotions. To lock them away and make decisions purely based on logic and fact. I grip the edge of the sink harder, and my eyes turn cold as I contemplate all I need to do.

Charlie has officially lost the plot.

That much is clear.

He cannot see over his stupid obsession with me. And I honestly believe that's all it is. I don't know when he started believing he was in love with me, but you don't treat the woman you love like this. Maybe his brain is so warped from all the shit they've done to him at Parkhurst. Or my father has brainwashed him, but I don't think Charlie is in love with me, and if he was thinking clearly, he'd realize that.

But I need to play on this fallacy. To keep Kai alive.

There is nothing I won't do to save the love of my life.

Because Kaiden Anderson is my everything.

And I will protect him till my dying breath.

Even if it means doing the unthinkable—becoming Charlie's wife and sharing a marital bed with him.

My stomach lurches violently at the thought, but there is no other option. If I refuse to continue the ceremony, my father will murder Kai.

But we can work this to our advantage.

My mind has been churning ever since the bastard dropped the hysterectomy bomb, and a clear plan is forming. I've always come up with my best ideas when I'm avoiding thinking about something and using a distraction to help redirect my thoughts. The way forward is clear now, and I'm itching to put my plan into action.

But first things first.

I need to get back out there and marry my newest enemy.

Then I've got to convince him and my father that I'm fully in.

That Kai is in my past.

And Charlie and the elite are my future.

Because infiltrating their world is the only way the plan will succeed.

I flush the toilet—purely for Maurio's benefit—and carefully wash my hands, smiling at my reflection as I visualize how this will go down.

By the time I'm through with him, my father will definitely wish I'd never been born.

Sounds of commotion drift out into the hallway from the burgundy room as we make our way toward it. My lips curve up at the corners as I wonder if the cavalry has arrived.

I don't know how long my father has had Kai, but the last I knew, he was traveling to New York with Jackson and Sawyer, so it's not inconceivable to think they were there when he was ambushed.

There's no way they wouldn't come for him, because those three guys are more akin to brothers. If something is going down, I'd wager it's Sawyer and Jackson to the rescue.

The smile falls off my lips as I contemplate a different scenario. One where my father hurt or killed Kai's two best friends, and rampant fear careens around my chest as my heart beats wildly behind my ribcage.

If he hurt them, I'll—

"Hold back, Ms. Abigail," Maurio says, cutting off my thoughts. He whips his gun out, pushing me back with his other hand. "Stay here and wait for me to return." Without waiting for my reply, he races toward the door, barreling inside.

I frown as I listen to the choking, coughing sounds trickling out into the hallway. A gun shot rings out, followed by a loud thud, and my heart rate spikes to coronary-inducing levels. I run toward the door, plowing into someone coming out of the room just as I reach it. The force of the impact sends me tumbling to the ground, and one of my heels flies off, skittering along the polished hardwood floor. Before the door shuts, I look into the room, spotting Maurio lying prone on the ground.

A scream rips from my mouth as a man wearing a scary mask looms over me. The mask is made of black rubber, and it completely covers his face. The glass lens hiding his eyes is tinted black, so I can't see who it is. His body is buff, encased in a black form-fitting shirt, black cargo pants, and black boots. A gun belt is strapped to his trim waist with a gun securely enclosed in the pocket.

I scoot backward along the hall as he extends his arm toward me.

In one fast movement, he unbuckles the mask, pushing it up over his head.

A string of expletives leaves my mouth as Jackson shoots me one of his trademark shit-eating grins. "Sorry, beautiful. Forgot I was wearing the mask." A large purple bruise paints his left cheek, and a cut on his lip is encrusted and sore-looking.

I kick off my one remaining heel, scrambling to my bare feet. "If you weren't here on a rescue mission, I'd knee you in the balls for scaring the hell out of me like that."

He pulls me into his arms, his cocky grin dropping off his face. "You okay?"

I shuck out of his hold. "I'm fine. But Kai isn't."

Jackson's eyes burn red. "I noticed." He cracks his knuckles. "I thought we'd get our chance to end your father today, but he ran off

5

before the sleeping gas could take effect."

My eyes bug out of my head as I look over his shoulder at the closed door, wondering what the fuck has gone down. "Sleeping gas?"

Jackson nods. "We didn't want to risk you, Drew, or Kai getting injured in a shootout, so we used the tunnel to get into the house, and we injected sleeping gas through the vents in the room," he explains.

"I heard a gunshot. Did someone die?"

"That asshole guard come rushing in with his gun. He shot at us, but the bullet embedded in the wall. He didn't have time to hurt anyone else, because the sleeping gas took effect then, knocking him out."

The door flies open a second time, and someone else comes out. He's also wearing a mask and the same black attire. I peek into the room, clamping a hand over my mouth as I count the prone bodies on the floor. Another few guys wearing masks roam the room, guns out and ready as they prod the unconscious forms with their booted feet.

The new arrival shoves a mask at me. "Put that on," Sawyer says, pushing his mask up on top of his head. His nose is swollen, and he has a large bruise on the side of his jaw. "We need to get out of here asap. Your father took off and even though this was prearranged with Atticus Anderson it doesn't mean he won't come back with reinforcements."

"Wait? What?" I say, taking the mask but making no move to put it on. "My father *knew* about this? *Agreed* to it? Why the fuck would he do that if he needs me to marry Charlie?" I'm totally confused.

Sawyer shakes his head. "Atticus made a deal so he could get Kai out, but—"

"What kind of deal? I thought they hated one another?" I ask, gripping onto Sawyer's arm.

Sawyer glances up and down the hallway. "Your dad needs to make this conflict with Atticus go away because it's damaging his reputation. With the Parkhurst vote only a few months away he can't risk it so he told him he'd give him back his company, his property, the money he took from him, and smooth the way for him to return to the elite and Parkhurst, in exchange for Atticus dropping his lawsuits, retracting his statements, and keeping Kai away from you."

Removing my hand from Sawyer's arm, I rub a tense spot between my brows. "So, you're saying my father knew you were going to show up here? Why would he agree to that?"

"Atticus made him promise not to kill Kai. He wasn't happy that Michael was using him to coerce you into going along with his plans, but it was a small price to pay to get what he wants." My lips thin and bile swims up my throat. Atticus Anderson is far too fond of throwing me to the sharks. Kai will go crazy when he finds out he's sacrificed me again. It's clear the agreement was only to rescue his son. That he doesn't give a fuck what happens to me.

"Michael doesn't want to look weak in front of the order, and there's no way he wants them finding out about this deal. Us busting in here to rescue Kai alleviates that concern," Jackson confirms. "And the only reason we are free is because Atticus needed our help."

"My father caught you both too?" I surmise.

"They were lying in wait for us at the private airfield," Sawyer explains. "We fought them, but we were outnumbered, and it didn't take them long to overpower us. They took Kai away, tied us up, and locked us in a shipping crate. Atticus showed up a few hours later and told us what he'd done, asking for our help. He also roped Maverick, Joaquin, and Harley into assisting, alongside some of his bodyguards.

That explains the other guys inside.

Kai will be so pissed his dad involved his younger brothers. Rick and Kai have done their best to shield them from this world, but

Atticus seems determined to drag them into it.

"But we have our own plan," Jackson says as Sawyer casts another glance along the hallway. "Fucked if we're leaving you behind to be forced into marrying that asshole."

"How did you know about that?" I inquire, dropping the mask onto the ground and wiping my hands down the front of my dress.

"Atticus explained. We were supposed to wait until after the ceremony to break in, and he's not going to be happy that we've ruffled your dad's feathers." Jackson smirks. "Stopping the wedding and taking you is really going to piss him off."

"Are we too late?" Sawyer asks, arching a brow as he looks at the discarded mask on the floor.

I shake my head. "No. We were only halfway through the ceremony when I asked for a bathroom break." I straighten my shoulders, because they won't like this, but no one is telling me what to do.

I'm in charge now.

They can like it or not.

"But I'm not leaving with you." I drill them both with a deadly look. "I can't. I'm staying here and marrying Charlie Barron."

CHAPTER TWO

"You can't be serious?" Jackson growls. "Kai will go fucking apeshit!"

"Kai will be a dead man walking if I don't go through with it," I calmly explain, retrieving my errant stilettos and slipping my feet into them. I stand up straight. "There's stuff you don't know. Stuff Kai can fill you in on. But right now, I need to get back into that room and let the gas knock me out like the others." Jackson's jaw slouches. "And you need to get the love of my life out of here before my father comes back and puts a bullet in all your skulls."

"Abby." Jackson recovers, gripping my face. "I'm not leaving you here. You can't marry him."

"But I can." My gaze bounces between the two guys. "Think about it. It's the perfect plan."

Sawyer and Jackson lock eyes, and I detect the moment they figure it out. A sly grin creeps across Sawyer's mouth. "What are you thinking?"

I glance up at the camera overhead. "Firstly, you need to contact Xavier to remotely hack into the security system and fuck up all the cameras. Father will expect that as part of your planning, so he won't be suspicious if all the cameras are out."

"Consider it done," Sawyer says, extracting his cell from his back pocket.

"Wait!" A thought occurs to me. "Tell Xavier to copy the feed for the last twenty-four hours before he does. Hopefully the camera was turned on and it captured my father murdering Charles Barron." That could be worthwhile blackmail material.

"What the fuck?" Jackson asks.

I nod. "Charlie sold his father out, and my sperm donor put a bullet in his head right in front of everyone."

"Fuck." Sawyer shakes his head. "What the hell has happened to Charlie Barron?"

"I think he's snapped," I admit. "And he's losing control. He thinks he's playing with the big boys, but I'm sure my father is only using him."

"All the more reason you need to leave with us and get the hell away from him," Jackson says.

I shake my head. "I'm going to marry Charlie and act like the doting wife. Within reason, or he won't buy it. And—" I place my hand over Jackson's mouth, cutting him off before he says one word. "I won't let him fuck me. You can reassure Kai of that."

"He's not going to stand by and let this happen," Jackson says, shaking his head. "You know that. He could end up getting killed anyway."

I poke my finger in his chest. "Do not fucking say that!" I hiss, jabbing my finger repeatedly against his firm chest. "When he hears my plan, he'll see this is the only way. No gain without pain, right?"

"And what's this great plan of yours?" Sawyer asks, bending down to pick up the gas mask.

"I'm not saying here. When it's safe, I'll get Drew to reach out and set up a meeting. Just keep Kai away for a few days."

"I doubt he'll be able to get out of bed for a few days anyway,"

Sawyer says in a clipped tone. "Atticus will be fucking pissed when he sees the state of him. I'm sure Michael was told not to hurt him too badly."

"That bastard makes up the rules as he goes along. No one tells him what to do. Atticus should know better than to trust him."

"Kai is going to go postal on our asses when he finds out we left you here."

"I know, but he'll just have to trust me. If we want to end this, end my father, we're doing this my way. I'm the one he has taken everything from, and I'll be the one calling the shots from now on." I plant my hands on my hips, daring them to challenge me. "Enough talking about it. It's time for action, and if you don't like it, fuck off back to New York."

Jackson bursts out laughing, reeling me into his arms. "Can we please find a way of cloning you because I need an Abby of my own."

"Lauder." Sawyer cautions him, and Jackson flips him the bird.

"Chill out, bro. I was speaking metaphorically." Jackson plants a light kiss on my forehead before releasing me. "Abby is Kai's. I know that."

"You need to leave," I say, glancing over my shoulder as all the tiny hairs on the back of my neck lift. "I'm getting nervous. If you've done this early, flouting the deal, Father won't be taking it lying down. Frankly, I'm surprised he hasn't returned with his guards by now."

Jackson winks, tapping his temple. "That's 'cause I'm not just a pretty face. It was my idea to gas the staff room too. Everyone is out cold, bodyguards included."

"He has guards manning the exterior perimeter," I confirm, wrapping my hand around the door handle.

"They were dealt with too," Sawyer says. "If anything, I'd say your father ran off to hide someplace until this is all over because he knows we've gone rogue and we're gunning for his ass."

"That sounds more like it," I agree, because there's no way Father would attempt to tackle them without backup. "But it still means he's around here someplace. I need you to get Kai to safety. Now."

The guys nod before securing their gas masks into place. I glance over my shoulder one last time. "Tell him I love him and that I'm doing this for us."

They bob their heads, and I open the door, barely reaching Charlie's side before I collapse unconscious on the floor alongside him.

"Those fucking bastards are dead," Charlie seethes, clutching his head in his hands and moaning. "And how did you end up knocked out beside me?" he asks, eyeing me suspiciously.

"I'd like an answer to that question too," the bastard adds. Briefly, I worry that he might have been watching the cameras while I was out in the hallway with Sawyer and Jackson. A cold sweat washes over me at the thought he might know what I'm planning. But I dismiss those concerns almost straightaway. Father doesn't know how to access the cameras, and he never steps foot in the security room.

"Maurio rushed into the room at the sound of commotion, and he told me to wait outside. But I heard a gunshot, and I panicked. I saw you and Drew unconscious on the floor," I say, eyeballing Charlie, "and I was terrified you were dead. I didn't stop to think. I just raced across the room toward you, only realizing it was sleeping gas when it was too late. Then I blacked out."

Charlie's expression transforms, and he looks like he wants to kiss me now.

My father coughs, and I redirect my attention to him. He's not buying it so easy. Time to deflect. "How did you manage to avoid it is an even better question seeing as you were in the room when they attacked?" I ask, risking his wrath, because I've zero fucks to give anymore. The guys got Kaiden away to safety and that's all that matters.

Charlie narrows his eyes at my father. "You seemed to know what was happening, and you rushed out of the room before the rest of us figured it out. How is that?"

My father's nostrils flare. "You dare to question me?" His deep voice is thick with unspoken menace.

Drew ambles over, rubbing at his temples as he listens to the conversation.

"We have a deal," Charlie spits out. "You shouldn't be concealing anything from me."

Daddy Dearest throws back his head, laughing. He slaps Charlie on the shoulder. "You, my boy, still have a lot to learn." All humor vanishes as he eyeballs him. "Don't challenge me in public, son. You won't like the fallout." His eyes dart to mine in an obvious threat, and shivers creep up my spine.

Drew stiffens, opening his mouth to say something, when I subtly shake my head. Drew is in enough trouble as it is. He came to my defense earlier, and Father will make him pay for that. I don't want him making things worse for himself.

Charlie slings his arm around my waist, hauling me into his side. "Do not threaten my wife."

"She's not your wife yet," Father says, annoyance washing over his features. "But we'll rectify that now." He clicks his fingers at the poor minister. The man is sitting cross-legged on the floor, clutching his stomach, looking dazed and confused. "Mr. Wittington. Stand," he barks. "We need to conclude the ceremony."

"I'm not feeling too hot, Mr. Hearst," the minister admits, dabbing at the beads of sweat on his brow with a handkerchief.

I can relate. I've the mother of all headaches and I'm feeling dizzy and a little nauseated, but so is everyone. Sylvia is still out cold, slumped along the couch where she was sitting. Christian and Trent have only just come to, and the bastard instructed Benjamin to carry his new fiancée, Patrice, up to his room until she wakes. I've no clue where Charlie's mom and sister disappeared to. He told them to leave before Father played the recording of Kai and me having anal sex. Anger bubbles up my throat at the recollection, but I shut it down fast.

My emotions will not serve me well now.

"Where are your balls, man?" Dad sneers at the minister, clearly disgusted.

Mr. Wittington wipes his brow clean, tucking his handkerchief into the inside pocket of his jacket. He nods once before bending down and picking up his book. He flips to the right page and clears his throat, lifting his head and leveling an impatient look in our direction. It appears he's now in a hurry to get the hell out of here. Not that I can blame him. I relate to that sentiment too.

Drew moves to my other side, linking his pinkie in mine in a way no one can see. Tears prick my eyes, for a brief, solitary moment, before an icy blanket sweeps over me, numbing me to everything.

Charlie keeps a tight hold of me as we stand in front of the minister to continue this charade.

I float off as the words are spoken, remembering a happier time, a few days beforehand with Kai, knowing I will need to rely on that memory to get through the weeks, and months, ahead.

"Mom, please." Charlie pleads with his mom as we stand at the side of his Land Rover outside the entrance to Chez Manning. Mrs. Barron has just discovered her husband is deceased, and she's inconsolable. In typical Michael Hearst fashion, he's blamed it on Atticus, saying one of his men killed Charles for trying to stop them rescuing Kai. I'm not sure if she believes it or if it matters. Lil, Charlie's sister, is already sitting in the back seat of the car, resting her head against the window, staring blankly into space. My heart aches for her. I know what it's like to lose a parent, and it's not something you ever recover from.

You find a way to survive.

To get out of bed each day and put one foot in front of the other, but you never forget.

Charles Barron was on my shit list of late, but I still wouldn't have wished for this. He was a good father and husband. He didn't deserve to die. And he didn't deserve to have his son betray him like that.

I'm sick to the pit of my stomach every time I think about it. What has happened to the Charlie I used to know and love? Because this new version is a piss-poor replacement.

A blast of cold wind lifts strands of my hair, blowing them across my face. My hand feels heavy under the weight of my engagement and wedding rings as I brush hair out of my eyes. Drew's mouth turns down, and his eyes are pained as he pulls me into his arms. "I'm sorry I didn't see this coming," he whispers in my ear, while keeping his eyes on Charlie. But Charlie is preoccupied trying to coax his heartbroken mother into the car, so he's not paying us any attention.

"I need you to do a few things for me," I whisper into his ear, not wanting to waste this opportunity. "Ask Rick to get me some sleeping pills, preferably in liquid form, and I need you to get me a new purse with a secret hidden panel. Xavier helped me order my last one, so he'll know what to do. Put a new cell and a small gun in there, and call over to the house in the next couple of days to give it to me. You can say it was my Christmas present."

"Please don't take unnecessary risks," he whispers, running a hand up and down my spine as I shiver.

I shrug. "I have nothing left to lose, Drew," I say in a quiet voice. "He's already taken it all from me."

"No." Drew forces my face up to his. In the background, Charlie is begging his mom to get in the car. "Use that to fuel your revenge, but *do not* believe in it." He kisses my cheek. "That's what he wants. For you to think you have nothing, but you still have a lot left to live for. Don't forget that, A." He kisses my other cheek. "And don't lose your fighting spirit, because we need it now more than ever."

Mrs. Barron drops to her knees, and a loud, painful wail filters into the silent night sky. Charlie glances at me, pleading with his eyes.

I owe him nothing.

He deserves to die for the part he's played in all this.

But Mrs. Barron is an innocent, and she needs my help.

I shuck out of Drew's hold. "Two days, D. Please don't let me down."

He pulls me back into his arms, hugging me tight. "I promised I'd never fail you again, and I meant it. Be safe, little sis. And call me if there's any emergency. I don't care what time of the day or night it is. And fuck consequences. If you need me, I'm there."

I circle my arms around his neck, clinging onto him. "I love you."

"I love you too. And I need you, so don't let anything happen to you."

I shuck out of his embrace with those parting words and walk toward Charlie and his mom.

"Elizabeth." I sink to my knees on the gravel, ignoring the way the sharp stones pinch my shins. I wrap my arms around her, and air whooshes out of Charlie's mouth in grateful relief as she falls against me, crying. "I can't begin to imagine how you feel, and I'm so unbelievably sorry for your loss, but can you try to pull yourself together? At least to comfort your daughter?" I smooth a hand over her hair. "Lillian needs you. She's grieving too." Her sobs falter for a second before starting up in earnest again.

Charlie's piercing green eyes lock on my face, and he's not hiding anything from me in this moment. Torment is the prevalent emotion shimmering behind his eyes. I can't tell how he feels about his dad, but the way he feels about his mom is transparent. It's killing him that she's hurting, and he wants to erase her pain.

Moments like these give me pause for thought. Perhaps all is not lost when it comes to Charlie, but I won't ever forgive him. Not as long as I live. There is nothing he can say or do that will ever make his actions okay. I suspect he's fucked in the head from all the sick shit he's seen and been forced to do at Parkhurst, but it's like my brother alluded to a while ago.

When does that responsibility transfer to the person performing the deed? You can't continue to hide behind the evil and do nothing. There comes a time when you need to step up and be counted. Like Drew is trying to do, I realize. But Charlie seems like he's tunneling deeper down the rabbit hole.

"Come on, Elizabeth." I hold her at arm's length, forcing her to look at me. Her red-rimmed tear-soaked eyes look half dead, and my heart hurts. Elizabeth and Charles Barron were the real deal. They truly loved one another. And I'm looking into the eyes of a woman who has lost half her heart and soul. A stabbing pain slices across my chest, and I'm struggling to breathe, as I imagine what it would be like to lose Kai.

It strengthens my resolve, and I pull her to her feet, gently placing her into her son's arms. Charlie holds her stiffly, with her back to his front, and I wonder if he's feeling any remorse, because he did this to her.

Every time he looks at her, for the rest of his life, he's going to be reminded of it. I wonder if he even considered that. I swipe under her eyes and tuck her hair behind her ears. "I imagine it feels like your world is ending, and I hate what you're going through, but your daughter needs you." Elizabeth turns around, looking into the back seat. Lil looks out at us, with tears streaming down her face. "Be strong for her," I whisper. "And we'll help you get through it."

Sniffling, she nods before opening the back door and climbing in beside her daughter.

"Thanks, Abby."

I shut the door and turn around, pinning hateful eyes on Charlie. "Don't thank me for cleaning up your mess," I hiss under my breath. I doubt Elizabeth can hear, because the windows are up and she's so consumed with grief she's barely cognizant of her surroundings, but you can never be too careful. "Because I did it for your mother. Not for you."

"I didn't know," he cries, as Drew comes up alongside us. "I swear, I didn't know he was going to kill him like that," he says in a low tone.

"Don't be so fucking naïve," Drew snaps in a cold voice. "What the hell did you think he'd do once you told him he was double-crossing him?"

Charlie hangs his head, and his lack of retaliation speaks volumes. He may not have been privy to my father's specific plans, but he knows exactly the kind of man he is.

And he knew.

Deep down, he knew my father would kill his father.

And he still went ahead with his plans.

CHAPTER THREE

"Is she okay?" Charlie asks, looking up at me from his place on the floor. He's sitting, with his knees raised, on the plush beige carpet in front of his parents' bedroom.

"Of course, she's not okay!" I say, quietly closing the door to the master suite behind me. "She's just lost the love of her life, and she doesn't know the half of it." A weariness sweeps over me, and I sigh. "They are both sleeping now. But we might need to call the doctor tomorrow and get some valium or sleeping pills for your mom. This is not something she'll get over easily."

He jumps up, nodding. "Are you hungry?"

"No. My stomach is still a bit queasy from the sleeping gas." I walk away from him, uncaring if he's following or not.

"Why didn't they take you?" he asks, keeping step beside me. I ignore him on purpose, picking up my pace as I stride toward my bedroom. He grabs my elbow, forcing me to stop. "I know you weren't in on the plan. You couldn't have known, so your little trip to the bathroom was a lucky break, but it also means you weren't unconscious when they were in the room." He pushes me up against the wall, caging me in with his powerful arms. "So, I'll ask again. Why didn't they take you?"

"Because I told them not to," I truthfully admit, lifting my chin and letting him see the honesty in my eyes.

"Why?" His gaze conveys nothing as he stares at me.

"Because I'm done fighting," I lie. "He has stolen everything from me, and I give up." Charlie eyes me warily, and he's right to be on his guard. "I love Kai enough to let him go. Staying with me will only get him killed, and that would destroy me, so I'm admitting defeat." I slip under his arm, glaring at him. "Congratulations, Charlie. Selling your soul worked. You have me now. I hope it was worth betraying your father and getting him killed."

I storm to my room, slamming and locking the door behind me. I expect Charlie to follow. To state it's our wedding night and he's owed a conjugal visit, but he stays away, and I'm grateful. Even if a part of me would've welcomed the argument because I'm dying to lash out at someone.

I wait a few hours, until it's the middle of the night, before tiptoeing out of my room in my robe and slippers. If Charlie catches me, I'll lie and say I was hungry after all. But as I walk past his bedroom, I notice the door is slightly ajar, and my eyes skim over the empty bed with curiosity. Either he's with his mom and sister, sulking somewhere around this vast mansion, or he's gone out.

With careful movements, I open the door to the master suite, checking the space to ensure he isn't in here.

Elizabeth and Lillian are still sound asleep, curled around one another in the bed. I sneak to the en suite bathroom, closing the door firmly but quietly behind me. Removing my burner cell from the pocket of my robe, I call Xavier. I want to call one of the guys directly, but I don't trust my father isn't tapping their phones. He could have a trace on Xavier too, but my gut tells me we've managed to hide Xavier from him so far and that he's the safest option.

"Fuck, babe. Are you okay?" Xavier says the instant he answers, not sounding sleepy.

"I'm fine. You heard?"

"All of it." His voice cracks, and intense pressure presses down on my chest.

"I need to know if Kai is okay," I say, choking over the messy ball of emotion clogging my throat. "Can you call Sawyer and find out?"

"He'll be fine," he says in a softer tone. "I'm with them now. We're at Lauder's place, and Rick has a doctor friend of his attending to Kai's injuries."

"I thought you went home for Christmas?"

"I did, but I came back as soon as I heard what went down."

My heart soars. I don't think it's going to take Xavier long to prove he is deserving of his best-bud status. "Thanks."

"You know I'd do anything for you, Abby. I promised I have your back, and I mean it."

"That means a lot, dude."

There's a rustling sound, and then a familiar voice speaks. "Did something happen?" Drew asks, and I roll my eyes even though I know he can't see me. He obviously just snatched the phone off Xavier, not even allowing him say goodbye. "I'm just checking on Kai."

"Is it safe to talk?" he queries, worry underscoring his tone.

"I think Charlie has gone out, and I'm using my burner cell in his mom's bathroom. I doubt there's any listening devices in here, and I triple-checked this cell for tracking devices and found none."

"Okay, but use it sparingly."

"Stop babying me, Drew."

A pregnant pause fills the air before he says, "Sorry. It's hard not to worry."

"I know, but I'm fine. Now put Rick on."

"Okay. I'll drop by in a couple days. Provided Father hasn't got me tied to a chair."

Acid crawls up my throat. "Talk your way out of it. I've watched Charlie stand up to the bastard, and he seems to respect it. Try the same, and it might work."

"Don't waste energy worrying about me. Watch your back, A. I've seen a side of Charlie you don't know. He's lethal. Don't push him too far." A shiver skates down my spine. I've always known that side of Charlie exists, but I've never seen it.

"I'll be careful."

More rustling erupts before Rick speaks. "Hey, you hanging in there?"

"I'm fine. How is your brother?"

"He's got a few cracked ribs, a dislocated shoulder, a mild concussion, and some internal bruising, but he'll pull through. He just won't be going anywhere for a while."

I hate he's so badly hurt, but at least he can't attempt any retaliation. I also think this might be an opportune time for Drew and me to tell him and Rick that we know it was their father who killed their mother. "Is he awake? Can I speak to him?"

"Sorry, Abby. He's all doped up and dead to the world."

"Shitty word choice," I say, chastising him. "Tell him I called and I love him."

"I'll pass that along. He'll be glad to hear you're okay. The few moments he was lucid he was panicking about you."

God, how I love that man. He's in a world of pain, but his only thoughts are of me.

"Did Drew ask you about the sleeping pills?" I inquire, needing to finish up in case Charlie catches me.

"Yeah, but there are different types, so I kinda have to know what you need them for?"

"I need something I can drug Charlie with so he passes out for at least a few hours."

Rick whistles down the line. "Wow, so married life isn't all it's cracked up to be?"

"Funny, ha, ha. Can you help or not?"

"I'll get something from Uncle Wes. I'll get it in liquid form, like you requested, but you'll need to be circumspect with it."

"I have a few tricks up my sleeves to enable me to get out of the house. This is just one angle, and I'll use it sparingly because Charlie is fucking smart and I don't want to make it obvious."

"Okay. I'll call Wes now and see if he can get a rush job on it. Either way, I'll hand Drew something to give you in the next couple days."

"Thanks, Rick. I've got to go. Tell everyone I said bye." I hang up without waiting for his reply.

I'm walking along the hallway, back to my room, when Charlie appears at the top of the stairs. He doesn't see me, and I tread softly as I walk toward him, watching him stare at my closed bedroom door with a whole host of emotions gliding across his face.

As I get closer, I notice all the telltale signs.

His hair is mussed up, the way Kai's gets after an energetic roll in the hay. His lips are swollen, his cheeks flushed, and his clothes are disheveled. But it's the scratch marks running up one side of his neck that give the game away.

He's too focused on my door to hear my approach or spot the disgust on my face. "You went out and had sex with someone else on our wedding night?" I hiss, making him jump as he snaps out of whatever daze he was in.

So, okay, it's not a real wedding, and I currently hate his fucking guts, and I've zero desire to sleep with him now, or any other night, but still. It's disrespectful, and he's now sunk even lower in my eyes.

I stand in front of him and rip his shirt wide open. Buttons fly everywhere as I yank the shirt off him. I examine his back. Long, red, raised nail marks trail up and down his flesh, confirming my suspicions. "You're disgusting." He stands rigidly still, not turning around to face me, so I put my face all up in his. "Thanks for making this easy for me." He sways on his feet, thrusting a hand out to hold himself up by the wall. I peer into his eyes, noticing how bloodshot and unfocused they are.

"Abby, please," he slurs, and his sour breath punches me in the face.

I take two steps back. "You're drunk."

"My father died today!" he blurts. "And it's all my fault." He falls to the ground on his butt, burying his head in his knees.

I slide down the wall, tucking my knees up to my chest, watching him carefully. Charlie is so erratic and unpredictable these days, and I can't tell what's real and what isn't anymore. I wait him out, watching his shoulders rise and fall. His body trembles all over.

When he finally lifts his head to look at me, tears cling to his eyes. "I'm sorry," he whispers. "I needed a release, and I know you won't let me touch you."

"Going out and screwing someone else guaran-fucking-tees it, Charlie."

"I wanted it to be you," he unhelpfully adds. "I pretended it was." My face twists bitterly as my stomach knots up. "Like I always do when I'm fucking any woman. It's always you in my mind, Abby."

"Wow. You just keep digging that hole deeper."

"I fucked up," he slurs, "and I promise I won't do it again." He crawls toward me, and I press my back into the wall. "I need you. Baby. Please."

I slam my hand into his chest, keeping him back. "Don't come any closer. You reek of whore and booze, and I want you nowhere near me. I don't care if I wear your ring and have your last name. You are not touching me with those filthy, disgusting, treacherous hands."

A mask ghosts over his face, and he rises to his feet, hovering over me with a thunderous look on his face. "I wouldn't have had to do it if you'd just give me a fucking chance." His voice is eerily controlled, and it's like the calm before the storm.

I scramble to my feet. "So, now, it's my fault? That's rich." I cross my arms over my chest, daring him to go there.

"I just needed someone to hold me. I wouldn't have asked for any more, but you fucking slammed the door in my face."

"With good reason." I tilt my chin up. "And you just said you needed the release, so how the fuck would spooning with me have helped."

"Because it's you!" He reaches out for me, and I jerk sideway out of his reach.

"Goddamn it, Abby!" He punches the wall, cracking the plaster, and dust and debris rain down on the carpeted floor. "I fucking love you, but you can't see past Anderson," he yells, slamming his fist into the wall again. "And I was thinking of you," he roars, hitting the wall again. A large crack forms in the plaster, splintering toward the ceiling. "Because I didn't want to stay here and end up hurting you if you rejected me!"

Wow, that's comforting.

Not.

The wall rattles this time when he hits it, over and over, without stopping.

"Oh my God! Charles." Elizabeth Barron comes running along the hallway toward us, and Charlie curses under his breath. "Sweetheart." She wraps her arms around him from the side in an awkward hug. "It's okay, baby. Shush." She lifts his arm from the wall, and tears roll down her cheeks as she inspects his torn knuckles. She looks over at me. "I don't know what's going on here, but he needs you."

I snort out an incredulous laugh. "I don't think it's *me* he needs." Charlie visibly stiffens.

"Whatever the argument is about doesn't matter," she says, her gaze bouncing between both of us. "You're married now." She levels me with a pleading look. "Your husband is in pain, and he *does need you.*"

Hearing that word, when it references Charlie, is like having a vat of hot oil poured over my naked body. It makes me want to scream from the pit of my lungs and claw at my skin. But I ball it all up and shove it into the innermost corner of my psyche.

I want to tell Elizabeth that her precious son is a monster, and partly responsible for her soulmate's death, but she's hurting enough, so I'll keep Charlie's secret.

For now.

CHAPTER FOUR

"What do you think you're doing?" I ask the next day when a burly guy with cropped reddish-blond hair climbs into the driver's seat of the red Lexus SUV before I can plant my butt in there.

The garage is packed full of cars, and Elizabeth said to take whichever one I wanted. I make a mental note to ask Drew to help me sneak my Kawasaki from the house and hide it someplace close by.

"Mr. Barron was very exact in his rules, Mrs. Barron," he says, instantly losing more brownie points. I want to lay into him. To tell him I'll castrate him if he refers to me as Mrs. Barron again, but I've a part to play, and there can be no missteps this time.

"And what exactly were those?" I ask, propping one hand on my hip.

"That I'm to go with you whenever you leave the house and I'm to drive you."

This is fucking priceless. I whip out my cell and dial Charlie's number. He answers on the third ring. "I can't really talk right now, darling," he says, and I puke a little in my mouth.

"Where are you?" I ask, because he was gone when I woke this morning.

After cleaning his wounds, I left him in the bathroom to shower, while I returned to my room. He didn't try to join me, and I'm glad to see he still has some modicum of sense left. Because I would've gone postal on his ass if he'd attempted to snuggle with me after spending the night screwing some other woman.

"I'm at the office."

"It's the day after Christmas. Surely, the office is closed?"

"It was, but I've had to call an emergency board meeting to decide how to run the business now my father is gone." His voice displays no emotion this morning, and I doubt I'll ever discover the truth behind his father's demise.

"I need to go to the pharmacy to pick up a script Dr. Wilson called in for your mom, but some goon won't let me drive myself."

The man in the ill-fitting suit narrows his eyes ever so slightly in my direction.

"You haven't driven since you passed your test, Abby." I can almost hear him smiling down the line.

"It's a fucking automatic! I think I can manage it. I did get a license after all."

"Not happening," he snaps. "You think I don't know you intend to run to him the first chance you get?" he adds in a lower tone of voice.

He'll need to grovel to get back into my good graces, and I intend to take full advantage of that, so this is fucking bullshit. "I married *you!* And I told you I've made my decision. I love him, but he's dead to me now."

I offer up a silent prayer for forgiveness.

"I want to believe you, but..."

"You're no better than my father. You realize that? You can't keep me like a prisoner."

"I'm not. You are free to go wherever you want, but Jethro will be your shadow until I know you can be trusted."

Fucking bastard.

"Until *I* can be trusted? Are you for real?" This is going to make things infinitely harder, and I'm not standing for it. The goon must go. "And do *you* have a bodyguard? Who's going to shadow you to ensure you don't cheat on me again?!"

Jethro's eyes perk up, and he's not fast enough to hide his reaction.

Charlie's heavy breathing echoes down the line, but it's clear he's not going to respond.

"I hate you," I spit out.

"We'll talk about this later. I'll see you at dinner." He hangs up, and I silently seethe as I climb into the back seat, instructing Jethro to take me to town.

When I return, Lillian has gone to her friend's house, Charlie is still AWOL, and Elizabeth is fast asleep on the couch with an empty bottle of wine lying on the floor at her feet and her wedding video playing on the big screen mounted to the wall. I turn it off, place a blanket over her, and tiptoe out of the room with the empty wine bottle and glass.

I sneak into her en suite bathroom and call Rick first, hoping to speak to Kai, but he's sleeping again, and I tell him I'll call later if I get the chance. I really need to speak to him. To hear his voice and know he's okay. But I won't stop worrying until I'm looking at him with my own eyes.

I call Xavier next. "Hey, babe. You doing okay?" he asks.

"I'm fine."

"Abby." His voice softens. "I know what he did to you. It's okay to not be okay."

Intense pain settles on my chest like a ten-ton truck just dropped on top of me. I can scarcely breathe over the pain ripping my insides to shreds.

I cannot think about it.

Not even for a second.

Because I will fall apart, and I need to be at the top of my game. "No," I whisper, hoping he understands I can't discuss it.

Xavier curses. "I'm coming over."

I open my mouth to object, but he's already hung up on me.

I've composed myself by the time he arrives, and I almost trip over my feet when I spot the sweet ride he showed up on. "Holy shit," I exclaim, stepping outside and deliberately ignoring Jethro. "Where did you get a Yamaha R3 from? And who owns it?"

"*I* own it. You converted me." Xavier puffs out his leather-clad chest, and I smother a giggle as I look him over. He's wearing a tight black biker's leather jacket and matching pants, with a Batman logo on both, with fitted elbow and knee pads, and heavy black biker boots. A Batman-branded helmet dangles off the handlebars, and I lose control of my giggle, full-on laughing.

Xavier runs his fingers through his fire engine–red hair, frowning. "What's so funny?"

"You," I splutter, pointing as I walk toward him. "You're like a walking cliché."

He plants his hands on his hips, pouting and tipping his chin up. "I'm Batman." He deepens his voice as he stabs me with a serious look. "Get used to it."

I crack up laughing, clutching my stomach in physical pain. He watches with amusement in his eyes. When I compose myself, I wipe at the moisture sitting on my cheekbones and straighten up. "Where the hell did you get all this gear?"

"A dude I know was selling it."

"I wonder why," I mutter before wrapping my arms around him. "You shouldn't have come here, but it's so good to see you."

"Why the hell not? Has Charlie boy decided you can't have friends now?"

I shrug. "I don't know. We aren't exactly on speaking terms."

"Come inside and tell Uncle Xavier all about it," he says, poking his tongue out at Jethro as we walk past him. Jethro slants a funny look at Xavier, and I arch a brow.

I think Jethro might have liked that.

I work hard to smother another giggle.

"Who's the scary dude?" he whisper-shouts.

"My new babysitter." I scowl. "But hopefully not for long," I add, leading Xavier into the house and down to the basement recreational room which Charlie refers to as a den.

"Shit. Dude's got some crib," Xavier admits with an admiring whistle, unzipping his leather jacket and flinging it on the L-shaped black leather couch.

"It's nicer than that mausoleum I grew up in, but it's still not home," I admit, moving behind the bar to fix us a drink. "Want one?" I shake the tequila bottle at him, and he nods.

Removing a small square device from his pocket, he walks around the room with it elevated over his head, and a look of fierce concentration on his face.

"Watcha doing?" I enquire, opening the overhead cupboard and removing two shot glasses. Xavier plops his butt down on a stool at the counter while I pour our shots and slice some lime. I've got to hand it to Charlie. He keeps a well-stocked bar.

"Checking the room for tracking devices but it's clean. We're good to talk."

"Could you check my room and bathroom before you leave? I've been sneaking into Elizabeth's bathroom to use my burner cell, but I'd prefer to know if my room is safe."

"Keep it." He slides it across to me. "You can hide it in the new purse Drew is bringing you tomorrow. The hidden panel has a decent amount of room."

"Cool. Thanks."

He pulls a square plastic sealed bag from his pocket. "Picked you up these tracking devices too. Open the sole of Charlie's shoe and slide one in. Use the glue tube to seal the heel back on. He'll never know." He holds out his hand. "Give me both your phones."

I pull my normal cell out of the back pocket of my pants. "I only have this one on me. My burner is hidden upstairs."

"Okay. I'll add the tracking software app to this one now and we'll go to your room so I can add it to your burner cell. I personalized it for you, so it looks like a girls clothing app, in case Charlie goes snooping."

"You really are a freaking genius, aren't you?" I hand him the salt container and he pours a little on his hand. "You think of everything."

He beams. "I do my best."

"You, my friend, are going to rule the world one day." I waggle my brows at him, fully believing it.

"I sure fucking hope so. Now, hurry up with those drinks, babe. I'm parched."

I slide a shot to him, along with a lime wedge. "So, those tracking chips and the app means I can see where he is at all times, right?" I ask, dropping some salt on top of my hand.

"Yep. It means if you are out of the house doing naughty stuff with Anderson you'll have enough warning to get your ass back here in time." We clink our shot glasses, lick the salt off our hands, and knock back the tequila in tandem. I hand him a lime wedge as I shove the other one between my lips, sucking on it to lessen the burn of the alcohol.

"Damn. That's good shit." Xavier slaps his chest. "Wish I could have another."

"I don't want your death on my conscience," I say, tucking the bottle away, even though I'd love another shot or ten myself. "God knows I've enough on my mind as it is."

His features soften as he reaches out to take my hand. "I couldn't believe it when Drew told me. Abs, I'm so sorry. I—"

I clamp my hand over his mouth. "I don't want to talk about it. I *can't* talk about it. If I do, it will all filter in. Everything I'm keeping at bay. And then I'm no use to anyone."

"You can't ignore it forever, babe." He squeezes my hand. "You've got to deal with it, or it will eat you alive."

"I'm not saying I won't deal with it. Just I won't deal with it *now.*" I come around the counter and lean against a stool beside him. "I thought my life was fucked up a few months ago but that was barely a blip, you know?"

He circles his arm around my shoulder. "You couldn't make this shit up," he agrees. "And the more I hear of Parkhurst, the elite, and the order, the more determined I am that we're taking them down."

My eyes burn with red-hot anger and dogged determination. "We're going to do it. Starting with my father, and then we'll tackle the rest." I sigh, finally giving up something I've spent a year dreaming about. "I can't escape Rydeville now. Too much has happened for me to turn a blind eye. There is so much more to this than just me or us."

I turn to face him. "You didn't see those girls in the dungeon. How many hundreds, *thousands,* of innocent kids has he destroyed? And Drew says there are towns like Rydeville, and men like my father, all over the country. Think of how many innocent lives have been ruined. We've got to do something to stop them."

"I agree, but it's a tall order even with our combined skills."

"I have an idea. One I think will work or at least it will cause uproar within the order and bring a spotlight on them that will force them to back down for a while." I hop up, offering him my hand. "I'm going to ask Drew to set up a meeting tomorrow night at

Lauder's house, and I'll fill you all in then. For now, let's go to my room and check for bugs, because Charlie could be home anytime."

After Xavier proves my room is clean, we sneak into Charlie's room, and he checks it for bugs first, confirming there are none, before we insert the tracking chips in some of his shoes. I hold one back to slip into the shoes he's wearing today when I next get the chance. I have a feeling Charlie will be spending a lot more time at the investment-slash-banking firm his dad owned and ran. It's been in his family for generations, so I expect a lot more responsibility is about to fall on his shoulders.

I hope it keeps him too busy to keep tabs on me.

I grab some chips, dips, and sodas from the kitchen and return to my bedroom. We sit cross-legged on my bed, munching as we talk. "Did you have time to look at the security footage from the house yet?" I ask.

His face contorts. "I didn't have to mess it up as your father had already tended to that."

I stop mid-chew. "What do you mean?" I mumble around a mouthful of cheesy nacho chips.

"The feed is all scrambled and unusable. I need to probe deeper to see if I can unscramble it. I can't figure out if it was still recording and the footage is just hidden or the scrambling was to hide the fact the cameras weren't recording on Christmas Day."

"Damn that conniving bastard." I thump my headboard in frustration. "I was hoping we'd caught the murder on tape."

"We might have," Xavier says over a mouthful of Pringles. "But I won't know until we examine it more closely. Hunt said he'd look at it tonight, so I'm dropping by their place after I leave you."

"You two are working very closely together these days. How's that going?" I plant my most innocent expression on my face.

Xavier smirks. "Ask what you really want to, babe." He waggles his brows.

My lips pull up at the corners. "Kai says I shouldn't interfere."

He arches a brow. "And when have you ever done what Kai tells you to do?"

My grin widens. "You raise a valid point." I brush chip crumbs off the side of my mouth. "Are you and Sawyer hooking up?" I bluntly ask.

He roars laughing. "I thought that's what you were hinting at. No, we're not hooking up."

I drill him with a look. "And?"

He pops a chip in his mouth, grinning as he chews, forcing me to wait him out.

"Oh, come on. Give a girl a break," I say when he reaches for the Pringles can again. "Put me out of my misery."

He leans forward, and I angle my head in closer. "Sawyer is hot."

"Tell me something I don't know." I roll my eyes.

"And I wouldn't kick him out of bed."

I rub my hands. "Now we're getting somewhere. Has something happened?"

"Nope, and I hate to disappoint you, chica, but it's not going to. He drives me fucking insane." He waves his hands about. "He's so pedantic. So structured. Way too fucking neat. I mean, the guy would blow his top if he had a hair out of place or if that crease in his dress pants wasn't exactly in the right spot." He scoffs, a look of distaste appearing on his face.

"Uh-huh. I believe you. Thousands wouldn't, but I do," I lie, and he throws a pillow at me.

"He's sexy as fuck, but it wouldn't be worth it. I can just imagine him now." He puts on a deep voice, wearing a serious expression. "Lift your hips five centimeters, spread your legs ten, and angle your ass so it's exactly in line with my cock." He grabs a handful of Pringles. "Fuck that shit. Sex should be messy and unplanned. And

Sawyer doesn't do messy and unplanned."

"There's always a first time for everything," I quip, grabbing the chips from his hand and smooshing them into his mouth.

CHAPTER FIVE

Dinner is a tense affair, and no one appears to have much of an appetite. Poor Mrs. Rose went to so much trouble preparing Lillian and Charlie's favorite spaghetti and meatballs dish with salad and homemade garlic bread, but it's being pushed around full plates instead of lining the insides of our stomachs.

"We need to discuss the funeral, Mom," Charlie says, when we've all given up on the pretense of eating.

I start clearing the plates away.

"I can't," Elizabeth whispers, and a fresh wave of tears pools in her eyes. "I just can't." A sob bursts free of her mouth.

"I can't do it alone, Mom." Charlie leans across the table, taking her hand in his. "I've got things to organize in the office, and I can't be in two places at once."

"I can help," I say.

Shock splays across his face. "You will?"

I nod, sliding his half-eaten plate out from in front of him. "I don't have much to do until school starts back. I've got time to organize it if you let me know what you want."

"Thank you, sweetie." Elizabeth squeezes my waist, and I press a kiss to the top of her head.

"It's the least I can do." *Because if your son wasn't obsessed with me, he might not have sold your husband out.*

"If you could call the funeral directors in the morning and arrange a meeting, that would be great," Charlie says, apprising me carefully.

"Okay. Sure."

I'm rinsing the plates in the kitchen when Charlie walks in. "You don't have to do that. Mrs. Rose will clean up in the morning."

I shrug. "It's not like I have anything better to do."

He comes up behind me. "Could we talk?"

"About what?" I ask, bending down and stacking plates in the dishwasher.

"About last night, I—"

"I don't want to hear more excuses, Charlie. I'm so sick of everyone lying to me."

"Abby." He holds my arm. "Come into the den." He looks over his shoulder. "It's not exactly private in here."

I close the dishwasher and follow him downstairs to the basement den, working out how I'm going to play this as we walk in silence.

"Want a drink?" he asks, closing the door behind us.

"Sure." I jump onto a stool, watching his long fingers work expertly as he fixes our drinks.

He hands me a vodka cocktail and takes his beer bottle, walking over to the leather couch. I sit down, keeping ample space between us. He takes a long drink from his beer, his throat working overtime, and I study him for a minute, remembering all kinds of stories from our childhood, wondering if everything has been a lie.

I sip on my cocktail, happy to let him start the conversation.

"Last night was unforgivable." His tongue darts out, wetting his full lips. "And I wish I could take it back."

"But you can't."

"Like you can't take back all the mistakes you've made," he coolly replies.

I settle back in the couch, eyeing him over the rim of my drink. "Like what?"

"Like hooking up with Kaiden when you knew it was going nowhere."

"That's a matter of opinion."

He leans forward, placing his half-empty bottle on his knee. "The only opinion that matters is your father's, and he'll never approve." He reaches out toward me, but I jerk back, and his hand drops to his side. "You need to let him go and give us a chance. I know we can be so good together."

He's starting to sound like a broken record.

"If this is your idea of an apology, it sucks."

He sighs, placing his beer down on the table and scooting over close to my side. He winds his hand through my hair. "I will make it up to you. I promise. But you need to make me a promise too."

The nerve of him to think he has the right to demand anything of me. Still, I'm supposed to be gravitating toward the doting wife impression, so I need to give him something. "What?"

"You will leave your old life behind. Anderson, Hunt, Lauder, and Xavier are a part of your past. I'm your future."

I stare into his eyes, honestly checking to see if there's some alien life form inhabiting Charlie's body. "I'm not giving Xavier up. He's my only best friend." Jane has moved away, and while I miss her, and I want to reach out to her, I've come around to my brother's way of thinking.

Rydeville is not safe for her.

Associating with us is not safe for her.

She is better off without us.

It kills me to admit that, but it's the truth.

I've got to let her go.

But I'm fucked if I'm letting Xavier go too.

"I'll be your best friend." He takes hold of my neck, pulling my face closer to his. "I will be everything you need."

Holy shit. He's batshit crazy. Like fucking certifiable.

"Xavier is nonnegotiable," I say, plucking his hand off my neck and moving away from him. Giving in would be out of character for me, so I can react naturally and still play my role to perfection. "And Jethro goes."

"You misunderstand, Abby. This isn't a negotiation. You're my *wife*. An elite wife. And it's not becoming to hang around that fucking freak. And Jethro stays, because you will not go near Kaiden Anderson."

"Do you even hear yourself?" I shout. "What the fuck did my father do to you?"

"He showed me endless possibilities, Abby. And we can make our own rules." He leans toward me, his eyes earnest and excitable. "No one is touching you or hurting you, and I will cherish you like a queen. All you have to do is follow my rules. It's not that hard."

Yeah, it is. Because I don't love you, you freaking nutjob psycho.

"You hurt me," I challenge, plastering a fake hurt look on my face.

"I know." He hangs his head, and I'm wondering who is playing whom.

"And forcing me to follow rules is hurting me too," I say, really driving the knife in.

He looks up. "It's for your own protection."

"Oh, Charlie. How little you know." I cup his face, shaking my head. "If you want me to come around to the idea of an us, then you can't clip my wings. It's as simple as that." I tap one finger off his temple. "Use the brain I know you still have, and think of all the things you know about me. I don't respond well to threats, and I hate being forced into doing anything I don't like."

"Don't patronize me, Abigail." He pushes my hand away. "I'm

not someone you can manipulate."

We'll see about that.

"I beg to differ." I smile sweetly at him as I stand. "This is the way it's going down, Charlie. I will stay away from Kaiden and do everything I can to be a good wife to you. I'll even consider making this real, but only on my terms."

He stands, grabbing my hips and pulling me to him. "You don't hold any cards, darling. You can't make demands of me."

"That's where you're wrong." My smile is smug in the extreme. "I know Mrs. Rose told you Xavier was here today. It wasn't just a casual visit." I purposely drop my smile, adopting a more sinister look. "He has the security footage from the house, and we have evidence of your father's murder." I run my hands up his toned abs and onto his broad chest.

"You're lying."

"I'm not. But there's an easy way to find out. Ask my father what happened to the tapes from Christmas Day." I'm bluffing, and it's a risky game, but I've got to try. "Tell him your new wife is already running rings around you, and see how well that goes down."

"He expects a rough start. He won't hold it against me."

"I do believe your arrogance will be your downfall, Charles," I say, stretching up and pressing my lips to the underside of his jaw. He shivers, and I smother my sly smile. "He will see you can't control me, and whatever deal you two have in place will be null and void. But go ahead," I say, pushing him off me. "Test me." I down the rest of my drink in one go. "If you breathe a word to my father, I will tell your mother what really happened Christmas Day." I prod my finger into his chest. "I will *show her* how it went down, and she will never speak to you again."

I will never show Elizabeth that tape if we even get our hands on it. Because it would destroy her. But Charlie doesn't know that. The threat of it should be good enough to win back some control.

I walk off, lingering in the doorway. I cast one last glance over my shoulder at him. "I want Jethro gone by morning, and you'll tell Mrs. Rose that Xavier is welcome here anytime."

"That's good, Abby," Drew says the following afternoon as we lounge in my bedroom, chatting. "Charlie adores his mom and sister. He won't risk approaching Father, because he doesn't want them to find out the truth."

"I seriously hope Xavier can recover the footage from the tapes, because it'd be nice to know I can substantiate my threat."

"Xavier and Hunt were working on it for hours last night. No success so far, but between both their nerd brains, I'm sure they'll figure it out."

"Can you set up a meeting at the house for tonight? I'm not sure what time Charlie will be home from work at, but I'll text you and tell you what time to get everyone to Lauder's."

"Everyone is hanging out there most nights anyway, so it's not an issue."

"Is Kai okay?" I whisper although there's no need. No one is around, and my room is clean.

"Well, his vocal cords are in full working order." He chuckles. "He's a fucking rotten patient." Drew smirks. "He is driving Rick insane with his bitching and moaning. And it's just as well he's injured because I doubt any of us would be able to stop him from coming for you. He's worried out of his mind."

"I'll reassure him tonight."

"He really loves you, Abby." Drew snakes his arm around my shoulders. "And I can tell you love him too. I'm happy for you, and I'm rooting for you guys."

I want to tell him so bad, but I want to talk to Kai about it first.

"Thanks, D." I lean my head on his shoulder. "I need you to do another thing for me. I discovered a way off the property from the rear garden when I was doing some snooping this morning. Can you park my Kawasaki halfway down the alleyway that runs on the other side of the house and message me the coordinates? I can't risk taking one of their cars in case Charlie notices something."

"I'll get it done."

"And one other thing." I worry my lower lip between my teeth. "I want to tell Kai and Rick what we discovered about their mother's murder tonight."

"Are you sure that's wise?"

I nod. "I hate that I've kept it from him. He has a right to know. *They* have a right to know. And Kai can't do anything about it while he's injured, so it'll give him time to process, and, hopefully, we can talk him into using it in a measured way to take his father down the same time we take ours down."

"Okay. You're right. They need to know, no matter how unpleasant that conversation will be." He kisses my temple before reaching behind him. I lift my head up, and he hands me a large rectangular package wrapped in glossy red paper. "Belated Merry Christmas, little sis."

I hug him. "Thank you." Drew is really coming through for me now, and it feels great to have my brother back in the fold.

"Everything you need is in the hidden bottom panel, but I'd still be careful to keep it away from Charlie. He's not some dumb schmuck you can manipulate with a bat of your eyelashes."

"I know how to handle him." I open my new purse, lifting the bottom panel and examining the contents. I hold the compact gun in my palm, loving how lightweight it is. I don't want to walk around town looking like my purse weighs ten tons. "I'll give him some fire and then soothe it with some loving," I add, checking the backup burner cell. My stomach twists unpleasantly at the thought, but needs must. "Starting with tonight." I extract the pack of glass vials, holding them up to the light. The liquid is clear, which is a bonus.

"Rick said to use one-third of a vial in a glass of water or juice. Based on Charlie's build, he reckons that buys you about five hours."

I remove one vial and place it under a book in my bedside table. "I guess we'll find out later tonight."

"What's this?" Charlie asks, walking into the formal dining room with a frown.

"Your mom and Lillian ate earlier. I wanted to wait up for you." I gesture at the two place settings, pulling out a chair. "Take a seat and I'll get our food."

He eyes me neutrally as he walks over, dropping into the chair. I place my hands on his shoulders. "You feel tense." It's not actually a lie. His shoulders are corded into knots. I start kneading his taut flesh. "I'll give you a back rub after dinner if you like." I lift the bottle of red wine. "Wine?"

He nods, eyeing me carefully as I pour him a glass. "Drink that, and I'll be back in a few minutes."

I load the hot plates from the oven onto a tray, along with the salad and bread, and head back to the dining room.

"I hope you still like lasagna," I say in a cheery voice as I return to the room. "I cooked it myself, using my mom's recipe. I remember you loving it." The lit candelabra on the table gives the room a distinct romantic nineteen-twenties vibe.

It's all so very Stepford wives.

I set his plate in front of him, loading some bread and salad on the side.

"What are you doing?" he asks, eyeing me with his sharp gaze.

I lean down and kiss his cheek. "I promised I'd try. Jethro is gone, so this is me trying." I walk around the table and sink into the seat across from him. I lift my glass filled with cranberry juice and a dash of red wine. "To a new future." I almost gag on my words.

He clinks his glass against mine, and I know he's suspicious as fuck. But that's okay. Because I'll thaw him out. I'll have him believing this bullshit is real. Even if it kills me to do it.

I tell him about the scheduled meeting I arranged with the funeral director and pepper him with questions about his dad's business and what he intends to do with it. When he informs me he'll most likely have to graduate early and drop out of school to attend to business operations, I have to work extremely hard to keep the grin off my face.

The more he relaxes, the more I top up his glass, and I don't think he realizes how much he's drinking. When he leaves to go to the bathroom, I empty one-third of the vial with the sleeping liquid into his drink, praying it works with wine. Drew only mentioned mixing it with water or juice, so I'm taking a risk. But I figure the wine will mask any taste better.

"Want to watch a movie in my room?" I ask, after we've finished eating.

"What are you up to, Abby?" His eyes narrow as he takes me in.

"If you're going to accuse me of ulterior motives every time I do something nice for you, we're not going to get very far." I invoke reverse psychology. "We've had a nice night. Maybe we shouldn't push it." I move my chair back. "I'll see you tomorrow. Goodnight."

I'm almost at the door when he calls out to me. "I'll grab a quick shower, and I'll drop by then."

Sucker.

"Okay." I toss a smile over my shoulder, wondering how long it will take for the drugs to take effect.

CHAPTER SIX

"Any issues getting away?" Drew asks when I arrive at Lauder's place a couple hours later.

"No. It went like clockwork. I left Charlie passed out on my bed, snoring his head off. I plied him with wine and a heavy dinner, and he worked a twelve-hour day, so hopefully, the fact he conked out won't raise any suspicions."

"Always one step ahead of the game, beautiful," Jackson says, approaching with his arms wide-open.

I fall into his embrace easily. "How's the patient?"

"He blew a gasket when Rick pushed his shoulder back into place. Thought he was going to murder him." Jackson chuckles.

"He's a fucking nightmare," Sawyer says, ambling toward me in a tight white T-shirt and loose-hanging gray sweats. His feet are bare. His hair wet from the shower.

"I see Xavier is rubbing off on you," I tease, gesturing at his casual style.

"Why does everyone assume I don't own sweatpants?"

"Maybe because you sleep in your dress suit?" Jackson jokes.

"Or because it's hard to imagine that stick up your ass fitting in a pair of sweats?" Xavier quips, yanking me out of Jackson's arms.

"Stop hogging the treasure." Xavier bundles me into his arms, and I close my eyes, allowing his warmth and his familiar smell to comfort me.

"Fuck off!"

My head jerks at the sound of his voice, and I pull away from Xavier without a second thought.

"Kai. You shouldn't be out of bed. You—"

"Screw off, Rick!" Kai roars. "I want to see my fucking wife!"

Kai appears in the doorway of the games room halfway down the hallway, and I take off running toward him. My heart is beating ninety miles an hour, and butterflies scatter in my chest as my stomach flips over. Kai clings to the side of the door, half-doubled over, and it's obvious Rick is right—he should not be out of bed. Cuts and bruises cover his face, but it doesn't detract from his gorgeous face. He is still every bit as beautiful to me.

His warm brown eyes are shining with a whole host of emotions, and I want to drown in their chocolatey depths. His dark hair falls over one side of his head, and my fingers twitch with the craving to feel the silky, smooth strands between my hands. One of my favorite things to do is put Kai in my lap and run my fingers through his hair and over the shorn sides of his scalp. He loves it too, and many of our hot fucking sessions have started with me worshiping his hair.

The stubble on his chin and cheeks is thicker than usual, but I guess shaving is low on his list of priorities right now. His lips are a little cut up but still plump and inviting, and I can't control my craving any longer.

It's been six days since my lips last tasted his. Six long days since I've felt his strong arms protecting me. Six days since I've felt him moving inside me. Yet it feels like six years, because even an hour apart is too long.

I want to throw myself at him, but I invoke restraint, because he's struggling to stand upright alone. I slow my run to a walk as I reach him, and tears well in my eyes. Summoning strength from somewhere, he straightens up and opens his arms. "Come here, firecracker."

A sob is birthed from my soul as I circle my arms around his neck and weld my body to his. His arms around me are like a comfort blanket. His scent is like the familiar scent of home. The way he affects me is something I thought only existed between the pages of a romance novel. All it takes is one look, one small touch, one fleeting eye lock, and I'm rendered to mush. My heart races and my stomach floods with butterflies just knowing he's in a room. And when I'm this close, all I want to do is suction myself to his side and never leave him.

It's more than just a temporary urge or a burst of liquid lust. It's an intense physical reaction that is only soothed when I'm locked in his embrace. When I'm touching some part of him, everything feels right with the world, and I know we can conquer mountains. All the pain and uncertainty and fear feasting on my insides disappears when I'm trapped in a bubble with my man.

I thought true soul-deep love was a myth.

But I'm happy to prove myself wrong, because what we share goes deeper than flesh. It's transcendental, and there will never be another man for me.

Kai is it.

For all time.

His mouth is on mine in a flash, and it doesn't seem to matter that he's hurt, because his lips and his tongue devour me with an intensity and a need that mirrors my own. He flattens his back against the side of the door, holding me flush against his rock-hard body as we ravish one another. And I can't stop kissing him. I need his kisses like I need oxygen. I suck in his scent and his taste, and I plunder his lips and his mouth, not knowing when we will get to do this again.

When we eventually pull our lips apart, it's only because we're both struggling to breathe. He places his forehead on mine, holding me firmly at the waist. "Baby. I've missed you so much."

I tighten my arms around his neck. "I've missed you too. I was so worried." I dust his face with feather-soft kisses, touching every place where my father hurt him. "I was so scared he was going to kill you." Tears pool in my eyes and I'm dangerously close to losing control of my emotions. "I'm so sorry he did this to you."

"Shush, sweetheart." He rubs his thumb along my swollen lower lip. "It's not your fault. We were too careless. We should've had a protection detail with us. We won't make that same mistake again."

"That's who those guys were out front?" I ask, remembering the four guys dressed all in black, blending into the shadows.

He nods, tucking me in under his arm, wincing at the motion. I try to shuck out from under his arm, but he holds me tighter. "Don't. I don't care that it hurts. I need you close."

"Okay, I'm all out of patience," my brother says, shoving Xavier out of the way and planting himself in front of us. "What did he mean, Abby?"

I know exactly what he's referring to.

"Can we do this in here?" Rick says, and I whip my head around. I hadn't noticed him perched on the side of the couch until now because I was so lost in his brother. "Kaiden needs to get his grouchy butt back into bed."

I cast a glance over the room, spotting the double bed in the center of the space, surrounded by a drip and some type of monitoring machine.

"I'll tell you but let me get Kai situated first," I promise my brother, wrapping my arm around Kai's waist. "Lean on me if you need to," I tell him as we slowly walk toward the makeshift bed.

"I'll manage," he says, trying not to put his weight on me. Little beads of sweat dot his brow, and his face contorts in pain with every step.

When we finally reach the bed, he flops down on it with a grateful moan. Rick props his pillows up against the headrest, lifting Kai's white sleep shirt and inspecting the thick layer of bandages covering his upper torso.

"How much pain are you in?" I ask as he reaches out, snatching my hand.

"It's nothing compared to the pain of being separated from you," he rasps, panting as Rick gently prods his side.

"Christ, Anderson," Jackson says, and I can almost hear the smirk in his tone. "Either the drugs have done a number on you or you're completely pussy-whipped."

"I missed my wife. Shoot me if that's a crime." Kai slants a 'fuck off' look in Jackson's direction.

"What the hell is going on, Abby?" Drew's gaze bounces between me and Kai as I climb into bed with him.

"There hasn't been time to explain," I truthfully reply. "It happened when you were at Parkhurst just before Christmas."

"We wanted to tell you," Kai adds, circling his arm around my back and urging me to snuggle into his side. I don't want to hurt him, so I carefully curl around him, watching how his body responds for clues, because it's clear Kai won't stop me even if he's in pain. "But there was no safe way to do that. I'm sorry, man."

"Are you saying what I think you're saying?" Drew asks, sitting down on the edge of the bed.

"Kai and I got married three days before Christmas," I confirm, gently placing my hand on my husband's chest.

"What?" Drew splutters. and I don't think I've ever seen my brother more surprised. "How?"

I look up at Kai with fresh tears in my eyes. "Kai proposed to me the night before you all returned from Parkhurst."

I'm not getting into the ins and outs of that conversation because it took some time before Kai was able to convince me his motives were the right kind. We'd been in bed at Lauder's place, and he'd suggested escaping. When I threw that out as an option, he brought up marriage. I turned him down flat at first, until he convinced me he wanted to get married for all the right reasons.

Not just to protect me from my father and to safeguard my shares in Manning Motors.

But because he loves me and wants to spend the rest of his life with me.

My heart swells as I recall that part of the conversation. I never thought he could be so romantic, but he swept me off my feet with his beautiful words. "Lauder's father sent his helicopter to bring us to New York early the following morning, and Hunt's father called in a favor. We got a license minutes before we were married at city hall."

Kai presses a kiss to the top of my head, pulling me in closer to his side. "We didn't even get a chance to celebrate. We knew you were due to return home from Parkhurst the same day, so we flew straight back, and we had literally only just arrived here when you called."

It broke my heart leaving him behind that day, and I sobbed all the way back to Charlie's house in the Uber. I should've known something was wrong when he didn't call me Christmas Eve night, but I'd assumed he hadn't had time during the party at Lauder's family home. I was an idiot not to suspect something. If I'd been smarter, I could've gotten Drew on the case, and he might have been able to discover the bastard had kidnapped Kai.

I stretch up and kiss him softly. "I love you," I whisper.

"I love you too," he whispers back, claiming my mouth in a

passionate kiss. Heat builds in my core, and a familiar ache throbs between my thighs.

I need him. Want him. We haven't even had time to consummate our marriage. But Kai is injured, and we've a room full of witnesses, so I reluctantly tear my mouth away from his.

"Were you there?" Drew asks, leveling a look in Xavier's direction.

"I was." He shoots me a tender look. "I'm glad I'd been staying here, or I probably would've missed out."

Drew averts his eyes.

"I'm sorry, D." I chew on the inside of my mouth, understanding why he's upset. If Jane and Drew had eloped and gotten married, without telling me or giving me an opportunity to attend, I'd be pissed. But our circumstances were different. If Drew had been in Rydeville, there's no question he'd have been there. But if he *had* been in Rydeville, there's no way I could've snuck off and married Kai. So, it was inevitable either way.

"When we end all this, we'll have a proper wedding, and you can give Abby away," Kai says, and I remember the conversation we had in the helicopter on the way back from New York.

I want to return to Alabama, where we met, and say our vows on the beach. It's on his Uncle Wes's estate, so there will be no issue in making it happen. We can hold the reception in the house or erect a marquee on the grounds.

It might seem weird to some to want to return to a place where I almost ended things.

But that's half the reason.

It's a reminder that life is precious, and I came very close to throwing mine away.

I also want to spend my wedding night in the cabin, having Kai make love to me sweetly and tenderly like he did that first night we met.

Drew lifts his chin. "I would love that." We share a look, and my heart is full. "And there's no need to apologize," he continues. "I understand. I wasn't here, and you couldn't wait." A surprised laugh bursts free of his mouth. "Now, I get it." He grins at us. "Charlie thinks you're married, but that wedding isn't legal."

"Exactly. And neither is the worthless contract Father made him sign," I admit, offering him a matching grin. "Because Kai already signed a legal document, right after we married, transferring the shares in Manning Motors back to me. Once I turn eighteen, those shares are *mine*. Not father's."

"And," Kai adds. "We put other provisions in place so that if anything happens to Abby or me, he doesn't get his hands on them either."

"Nicely played." Drew bobs his head. "But if Father finds out, your life will be in serious danger. Who else knows?"

"Only the people in this room and my dad," Sawyer says. "And he won't say a word. He knows how important it is to keep this quiet."

"Good, because both their lives are at stake. He will go ballistic if he finds out. This doesn't just affect his control in Manning Motors. It will impact his running for president at Parkhurst." He pins Kai with a somber look. "He won't just go after you. He'll go after Abby too."

"Then we just have to make sure he doesn't find out before we choose to reveal it," I say. I shuck out of Kai's embrace, sitting upright. "I have a plan of action, but it's complex, and it's going to take all of us working together to pull it off." I eye each man in the room one at a time. "Can I count on you?"

"One hundred fucking percent," Kai says. "Whatever you're cooking up, I'm all in."

A chorus of agreement rings out around the room as everyone, unanimously, confirms their support.

Adrenaline courses through my veins, and I just know this is it.

The pivotal moment where everything changes.

Where the power shifts and the people in this room are primed to take back control.

I cast a glance over everyone again, and powerful emotion swims up my throat. Before, the guys were fond of tossing out sentiments that they would kill for me or take a bullet for me, and I was skeptical. Especially when everyone in this room has betrayed me in some way.

But that's in the past.

Because I look at them now, and I know it's the truth.

I know they are in this with me.

That they want this as badly as me, and they will do whatever it takes to help me reclaim control over my life.

It's a surreal feeling.

To know I have such a formidable group of guys standing behind me, watching my back, and supporting my decisions. The feeling of empowerment is incredible. Indescribable. And exactly what I need to get me through the weeks and months ahead. It's not going to be easy, especially the part I have designated to play. But I know I'm up for the challenge with my crew at my side.

We will make it happen.

This time, the bastard *is* going down.

And there will be no getting back up.

CHAPTER SEVEN

"We're listening, beautiful," Jackson says, as Kai, predictably, gives him the evil eye. "Tell us your dastardly plan."

I stick my tongue out at him, and he chuckles. He hasn't once attempted to reach for a joint or a blunt, and it hasn't gone unnoticed. It's not long after the anniversary of his sister's death, and the pressure we're under is intense, so I'd expect him to be smoking his brains out most of the time. The fact he isn't warms my heart, and I hope it might mean he's turned a corner, because I want that for him.

But it's more than that.

If we're to pull this off and make it out alive, we need Jackson sober with his head fully in the game.

I make a mental note to discuss it with him at some stage.

"We need to approach this from several angles," I say, "because Father is a conniving bastard, and he always covers his tracks. But everyone fucks up. Everyone has a weakness, and I've discovered his." I pause for a second. "His penchant for recording people and using the evidence to blackmail them will be his downfall."

"In what way?" Rick asks, propping his butt against the back of the couch.

"You said he has lured senior and high-ranking elite members to the sex dungeon," I say, looking at my brother, "recorded them doing stuff they shouldn't be doing, and he's bribing them into supporting his campaign for president, right?" Drew nods. "So, the way I see it, we hit the bastard from two angles. We take Manning Motors away from him, and we take the vote and his status within the elite away from him."

"Okay. I think I know where you're going with this," Drew says, "but how do you plan to achieve it?"

"We need to find those tapes, and then we go to some of the men he's blackmailing and offer to let them"—I make little air quotes with my fingers—"'buy' them from us but the payment isn't cash, it's the removal of their support for his campaign."

"What if your father has backups?" Sawyer asks. "Because I'm pretty sure he will have."

"Then we find those and destroy them too." Confidence drips from my tone, even though I know finding one set of tapes will be challenging enough. "And if we can't locate them, we bluff. We'll tell them we have all copies. We can duplicate and triplicate the files if we need to, to make it look convincing. I don't really care if Father uses them against those men once we get them to remove their support for him first." I draw a deep breath. "Which is why we can only reveal all this the day of the vote. If the bastard tries to use the backups against the others after that, I'd consider that a win-win."

Drew nods proudly at me. "Because it would discredit them too and bring the whole institution into disrepute."

"Exactly."

"That should be part of our play," Xavier says, his eyes lighting up.

Sawyer nods. "We can set it up so that the tapes are revealed just after the vote goes against your father," he says, and I can almost see the wheels turning in his head. "We can make it look like it was your father's 'insurance' in case the vote went against him."

"That is fucking perfect!" Excitement bubbles up my throat. "Because that's exactly his M.O. No one would stop to question that it wasn't his work." Every nerve ending in my body is heightened, and I wish we could fucking get to work right now. I'm itching to set this in motion.

"It's a good plan," Kai agrees. "But it all hinges on finding those recordings. Do you know where he keeps them?" Kai looks at Drew. "Because this won't work if they are as well-hidden as the evidence your mom found."

"I know where they are," Drew says, his face turning to stone. "They are in the vault in the dungeon. He likes to bring his victims in there and watch the blood drain from their face as he shows them the footage on a big screen."

"I love it when a plan comes together." Xavier rubs his hands with glee. "Why didn't you think of this before?" he questions Drew.

"There were a few reasons. One, the vault is protected by a top of the line security system and armed bodyguards. It's virtually impenetrable. Two, I have no clue where he keeps the backup files, assuming he duplicates them, but as Abby has outlined, that's no longer a concern. And three," he looks pointedly at me. "I was focusing on another angle."

"Manning Motors?"

Looking at the floor, he bobs his head.

"Well, that one is pretty easy to lock up tight now we both have access to our shares when we turn eighteen," I say.

He lifts his chin, nodding. "I'll get working on that straightaway. I'll set up secret meetings with the board members, beginning with those I can trust not to run to Father. I've already built up good relationships with most of them. And I know a few of them regard you highly after your internship that summer, but to most, you're an unknown, and that might make a few of them nervous. We need to present a strong case, Abby, if we are to get them to support our position and vote the bastard off the board."

"I'm sure we can present an attractive proposition, and if not, I'll find dirt we can use to blackmail them."

Jackson chuckles, and Drew arches a brow. I sigh. "I know, D. And it's not the way I want to play it, but this is war, and it means we need to use whatever tactics are in our arsenal. I don't like playing dirty, but if we have to, I'm not going to lose sleep over it. The objective is to stop that bastard, and that's all that counts."

"I know we need to be smarter than him. I just hate seeing you with your hands dirty."

"We all know who Abby is," Kai says, winding his fingers through my hair. "And while it's not what I want for her either, the means will justify the end."

"Thanks, baby." I press my lips to his, hoping he still feels this way when he discovers exactly what I'm going to have to do to pull this off. "The other area we need to investigate is his background. Father's kept that hidden for a reason."

"Xavier and I have already started digging, but the records have been buried," Sawyer confirms.

"Not that that will stop us," Xavier says, biting heartily into a green apple. Little bits of juice spray around his mouth, and Sawyer looks at him like he wants to grab his face and dunk it into a sink full of water. "Batman and Robin are on the case," he adds, winking at me. "Have faith."

"I better be fucking Batman in that equation," Sawyer deadpans, glaring at Xavier for even bringing it up.

"There's only one Batman in this equation, and it's *not* you." Xavier grins before taking a massive chunk out of his apple. "I've got the leather getup to prove it," he adds, winking. "But don't worry," he mumbles while he chews, "I'll buy you some leggings." He flicks his eyes up and down Sawyer's legs, smirking as he savagely bites into his apple, spraying more juice over his face.

"Do you have to be so messy?" Sawyer looks personally insulted.

"Messy is good, dude." Xavier tosses the apple core into the trash can by Kai's bed. His tongue darts out, playing with his lip ring. "And I like to get messy." His eyes stick to Sawyer's. "A lot."

Jackson chuckles, and Sawyer glares at him. "Quit flirting," he hisses at Xavier. "And save your innuendos because they're fucking wasted on me."

"I've no clue what you're talking about," Xavier says. "I was only discussing my eating habits. What were you referencing?"

Drew rolls his eyes. "Enough. We have a lot to discuss, and Abby can't stay out all night."

I hate that he's right, and I've no clue how I'm going to wrench myself away from Kai when it's time to leave. "We're going to need more hands on deck, because we've a lot to do between now and the vote. I'm going to meet Chad and get him to reconvene the group I used to unearth the secrets on the students at school." I turn my head to Drew. "Can you compile a list of members Father is blackmailing and a list of board members too?"

"The board is fine, but I don't know all the names of the elite Father is blackmailing. I suspect he's been doing it for years, but he's only let me sit in on sessions this past year as I've been training to take over more responsibility."

"We don't need to know *all* the names. We just need some to work with so the team can start digging into their backgrounds. If Father has been doing this for years, the list is probably too long to approach every single person anyway. And we might not be able to get at that many tapes, so we need to find a few juicy candidates and target them."

Kai rubs his hand up and down my arm, and delicious tingles skate across my skin.

"If we can find the most powerful elite among that bunch and approach them, they should be able to get the others on our side. You said most of them don't know the blackmail is large scale because they are too embarrassed or terrorized to discuss it?" I ask, and Drew nods. "So, we make it known he is doing this to more than just them. There is strength in numbers. We need to get them to rally against him to stop the vote."

"Let's say we are able to get into the vault and get our hands on some of these tapes, which, by the sounds of it, is a tall order, and let's say we convince these elite to help, then what?" Kai asks.

I turn to face him. "We time it perfectly to go down the day of the vote. He thinks he is going to get elected, but the vote won't go his way. Then we disclose our wedding and tell him we have taken Manning Motors from him. He'll be kicked out of the elite for sure."

"But he'll still be a free man, and your father is resourceful. To get rid of him, we need him dead or locked up," Kai adds.

"If we release the recordings of the elite, they may well kill him for us," Drew cuts in.

"No." I shake my head. "No one is taking that justice from us."

"We need to find the evidence your mom collected," Rick says. "And get him arrested for our mother's murder."

"Or we just take him outside and put a bullet in his skull," Jackson says.

"That works for me," Drew says.

"That doesn't work for me." All eyes swivel in my direction. I've given this a lot of thought since Christmas Day, when I vowed to end his life. But that would be too fucking easy. I want to take everything from him, in the way he's tried to do to me, most especially his freedom.

I want to see him locked up.

Somewhere like Rikers Island with a reputation for violence. Not some cushy prison where you can kill yourself to avoid talking.

I want him locked up in hell on earth. Being beaten and fucked by hardened criminals in prison.

Sure, I want time with him before he's incarcerated.

And I *will* inflict pain.

But killing him would be too merciful.

I want him to suffer every single day for the rest of his miserable life.

Which means we need to find some evidence that we can use to get him imprisoned.

Because we can't pin Emma Anderson's murder on him.

Not when Atticus Anderson is the one responsible for her death.

I lock eyes with Drew, and we share a silent communication. He nods, and I'm glad we're on the same page.

I lace my fingers through Kai's. "Drew and I need to speak to Kai and Rick," I tell the room. "Can you give us a few minutes."

"What's this about, Abby?" Kai asks, cupping my face and forcing it to his.

"There is something I need to tell you both, and it can't wait."

CHAPTER EIGHT

"Okay," Rick says when everyone has left and the door is closed. "What's going on?"

"I need to tell you something Sylvia Montgomery told me about the day your mother died."

Kai stiffens beside me. "What did she say, and why are you only telling me this now?" His eyes darken, promising punishment, and my core pulses at the simmering violence in his gaze.

Kai's ability to turn me on with veiled threats is a rare skill, but there's no denying there's a twisted part of me that enjoys the possessive, dominant, alpha side of his personality. Even if I love his sweeter, sexier, more romantic side too.

Forcing my lustful thoughts aside, because hey, *audience*, and my husband is too injured for the kinds of things I want to do to him and have him do to me, I refocus on the conversation at hand. "I wanted to tell you that day in the warehouse, but I was afraid of your reaction. This isn't going to be easy to hear, and I don't want to break your heart." I rub soothing circles on the back of his hand. "But I was always going to tell you when the time was right."

"We agreed no more fucking secrets, Abby," he growls.

"I know, and I'm sorry. But I was also worried you'd ruin

everything we're planning, because when you know the truth, you're going to want to murder your father."

"Abby, what are you saying?" Rick's voice is laced with strain, and a muscle pops in his jaw. "Because my mind has wandered to some scary fucking places."

Time to rip the Band-Aid off. "Our bastard father drugged your mom and left her there to die, but he sent Christian Montgomery over later, on false pretenses, to ensure he had succeeded." Air whooshes out of my mouth, as I pin my gaze on my beloved. "When you found your mom, Kai, she was still alive. Barely, but she *was* breathing." He sucks in a sharp gasp, and Rick slumps to the ground on his butt, shock splayed across his face.

I wet my suddenly dry lips, hating to have to say this. "Christian watched your father suffocate your mother with a pillow after he got you kids out of the place."

"No! Fuck, no!" Rick's anguished cry echoes around the silent room, and he buries his head in his hands. His shoulders shake. Drew sinks to his knees beside him, placing a hand on his shoulder.

"Kai." I touch his cheek, because he's as rigid as a statue. The glazed look in his eyes confirms he's someplace far away. His chest heaves up and down as he stares into space. I snuggle into his side, carefully, circling his arm around me as I plant my hand softly on his chest. "I'm so sorry, babe." His arms tighten around my waist, but he still says nothing. His body trembles underneath me, and I can't even begin to imagine what he's thinking right now.

Rick's muted sobs filter through the air, and tears prick my eyes, but I squeeze them shut to ward off the incoming onslaught of emotion. I can't let myself feel anything, and tonight's reunion with Kai has been emotional enough as it is.

I don't know what else to do, so I just cling onto my husband, offering him physical support. After a few beats of silence, he finally cracks. "She was alive?" he chokes out in a voice barely louder than a whisper.

I raise my head, and my heart aches at the tormented expression on his face. "According to Christian, she was."

"That's if Christian is telling the truth," Drew quietly says. "We have no way of proving or disproving his version of events."

"I saw him there that day," Rick says, sniffling. He tips his chin up, looking at his brother with red-rimmed eyes. "He was walking down the hall, away from the room where Mom was, toward the front door." He swipes at the moisture under his eyes. "He gave me a hundred-dollar bill and told me not to tell anyone I'd seen him."

"All that proves is that he was there," Drew supplies.

"It's the truth," Kai says, his voice stretched tight. A lone tear rolls down his face, and I run my hand up and down his arm. "I thought she was trying to speak," he croaks. "I ran to Dad and told him, and he shooed us out of the room. When I asked him later, he told me she died in his arms." A bitter laugh bursts free of him. "Fuck me. He actually told the truth." His eyes blaze red, and he grinds his jaw. "He just left out the part where he was the one who killed her."

"That fucking bastard." Rick hops up and paces. "For years he made us believe Michael and Abby were at fault. Made us hate them. Coaxed us into following his plans for vengeance. Roped us into looking for evidence of Michael's guilt, when he was the guilty party all along!" he shouts.

Kai crawls out of bed on the other side, slamming his fist into the wall a couple times.

I climb over the bed toward him. "Baby, don't." I try to pry his hand away. "You'll only injure yourself further." He leans his forehead against the wall, and his entire body is a solid block of tense, corded muscle. I wrap my arms around him from behind, resting my head on his back, wanting so badly to take his pain away. He clasps hold of my hands with one of his, and I plaster myself to him, fighting tears the whole time.

Rick is still pacing, grabbing tufts of his hair. "He took everything from us, Kai," he says in a more controlled voice, but I'm under no illusion. He's seething with rage and primed to explode.

I thought Kai would be the one to restrain, but I've completely underestimated Maverick Anderson.

"Our mother, our brothers, our childhood." Grabbing a glass bowl off the sideboard, he hurls it at the far wall. It shatters instantly, raining shards of glass over the carpeted floor.

"Fuck." Kai straightens up, and I release him. With measured, slow steps he walks to his brother's side, careful to sidestep any broken glass. Kai grabs his brother into a firm hug, and an intense craving to hug my brother consumes me. I walk to Drew's side and circle my arms around him as I watch Kai and Rick holding one another, talking in hushed tones.

"What do you think they'll do?" Drew whispers in my ear, wrapping his arms around me and holding me close.

"I don't know," I murmur, "and it's their call to make, but we can't forget the bigger picture."

Drew pulls me over to the couch, and we sit down, giving Kai and Rick time to deal with the bomb I've just dropped. "Do you have any ideas on how to get into the vault?" he asks me, and I'm glad for the distraction.

I answer him, keeping one eye on Kai. "Are there any plans of the basement that might help us?"

"None that I'm aware of, but there must have been at one time. Whenever he constructed it."

"It wasn't long after Mom passed," I say, because I remember workmen traipsing in and out of the house for months on end.

"That's right. I'll talk to Xavier and see what we can dig up. But what then?"

"Then we need Xavier to locate the security software and hack into it. And we physically need to get down there to study the layout and the guard rotation."

Drew's brow puckers. Kai glances over his shoulder at me, and I mouth, "I love you."

"Love you too," he mouths back before returning to calming his brother down.

I glance at my cell, frowning at the time. I won't be able to stay much longer, and I need some alone time with my guy. I check the tracker app, emitting a relieved sigh when it confirms Charlie is still at the house, hopefully snoring happily on my bed where I left him.

Drew rubs his temples. "You don't mean that—"

"I do," I cut my twin off. "I have to attend one of the events in the basement." My stomach sours at the prospect, but there's no way around it.

Even if Xavier hacks into the software system and manages to disable it so we can sneak down in the middle of the night, we can't walk in blind. We need to have studied the layout in advance. Figured out the guard rotation and whether they patrol down there when the space isn't in use and if there could be any number of traps we fall into it.

Father cannot know we have those tapes until the day of the vote.

"Hell will freeze over before I let you go down there." Drew's tone is loud, and it's enough to capture the Anderson brothers' attention.

"Go where?" Kai asks, shuffling toward me in obvious pain.

I draw a brave breath. I don't want to fight with him, but I need to put this out there now. "I was just informing Drew that I need to attend a function in the basement so I can do some snooping."

"No fucking way," Kai snaps, maneuvering awkwardly onto the couch beside me. "I know you can handle yourself, Abby, but it's too dangerous."

"I'll have Drew." My tongue darts out to wet my lips. "And Charlie," I add in a quieter tone of voice.

Predictably, Kai's eyes burn with intense loathing and a muscle ticks in his jaw. "No, no, no." He shakes his head repeatedly. "This isn't going down like that."

"*It is*, Kai." I jerk my head up. "I know this is hurting you, but I have to convince Charlie our marriage is legit and that I'm willing to give the idea of *us* a try."

"No. Fucking. Way!" He grips my shoulders firmly. "I know you have to go back there. I can just about tolerate that, but that's it. It fucking kills me you have to do that because of me."

"It's not *because* of you!" I bark. "It's *not* your fault. It's his and my father's, but I must toe the line, Kai, or they. Will. Kill. You."

"They won't get near enough to try." Rage flickers under the surface of his skin.

"So, you're going to drop out of school and move away from Rydeville? Go into hiding?" I ask, "because that's the only way you can protect yourself from them."

"Abby's right," Drew reluctantly agrees. "And it's more than just protecting you. The whole plan impinges on Charlie being suckered in. He's obsessed about Abby for years. And it's reached a crisis point. He betrayed his father so he could have her. To him, she is the love of his life and his only salvation. If he doesn't have Abby, Charlie will self-destruct in a big way, and he could seriously fuck with our plans."

He shoots a sympathetic look at Kai. "I get that you hate it. Fuck, man, I hate it too. But he needs to believe she's falling for him. It will help keep him distracted, so he doesn't see what we are up to. It won't take her long to convince him, because he is blind when it comes to her."

"And he's mentioned that he will be graduating early and dropping out of school to run the family business," I add, hoping to soften the blow. Tentatively, I thread my fingers in his, relieved when he curls his hand around mine. "He's going to be crazy busy with the business, supporting his mom and sister, and elite stuff, so I won't see him that much, and at least we'll get to see each other at school."

"He'll never tolerate that," Kai grits out. "He'll put some asshole guard on you. Or have spies at school reporting to him."

"I've got it in hand."

Kai arches a brow.

"I'm going to remind the students at school of the shit I have on them. If any of them blab, I will fucking ruin them. I'll remind them what happened with Rochelle and Wesley, and that should put them in their place."

"And what about the bodyguard?"

"He put a goon on babysitter detail, but I've already gotten him removed. I've told him we have the tape from Christmas Day and that he needs to back off, and give me my freedom, or I'll show it to his mom. The last thing he wants is her discovering he sold his soul to the devil and got his father killed."

"Your mind is a devious place, Abby," Rick says, grinning. "But I fucking love how you think."

Kai growls. "Only because she's not your wife, and you don't have to worry about her being in the line of fire. Or picture that asshole touching the woman you love." Kai pulls his hand away, dragging it through his hair.

"I won't let him take it too far. I promise."

"God-fucking-damn it." Kai yanks fistfuls of his hair in frustration. "I can't do it." His tormented gaze guts me, and I understand, because even the thought of our roles reversed makes me want to hack up my dinner. "We'll find another way." He grabs both sides of my face. "We'll fucking run. Let's do it. Let's just go now and forget about all this."

Pain spears me, making mincemeat of my heart. "We talked about this before. We can't. He'll go after everyone we love."

Thick silence engulfs the room.

"Abby is right, Kai." Rick sighs, scrubbing a hand along his smooth jawline. "We need to take both those bastards down. And the only way we can do it is by playing them at their own game."

CHAPTER NINE

Kaiden

I need to fight. To release the tsunami building to epic proportions inside me. Except, I'm in no fucking condition to fight. I'm only in control because I don't want Abby to see the murderous intent racing through my mind.

I want to throttle my father until he's blue in the face.

And I want to punch Charlie Barron until he's a bleeding, broken, lifeless piece of shit at my feet.

I scan every inch of her beautiful face, vowing to do everything in my power to protect her. Not for the first time, I don't feel worthy of her.

How she is still standing, still fighting, is beyond me.

After everything that's happened, most women would, understandably, be a shell of themselves.

But the more her father pushes, the more determined my wife gets.

With every calculated move, he tries to break her spirit only to reinforce it. Abby is one of the strongest people I've ever met, but I see what she's doing too.

She's throwing herself into this battle full force so she doesn't think about the ultimate betrayal.

Murderous intent returns with a vengeance when I think back to Christmas Day. When he told her he'd stolen her womb. Stolen the experience of her carrying my child from both of us. I've spent the last few days in and out of consciousness, but any lucid moments were consumed with thoughts of Abby and all that we've lost.

Michael Hearst is going to suffer for the pain he's inflicted on his daughter.

I will fucking die to ensure it if I have to.

But he is not getting away with it.

Which is why I know I need to agree to this.

My ribs are on fire, and my body fucking aches, but it's nothing compared to the pain in my heart at the thought of what she'll have to do to save us.

I could live a million lifetimes and never be worthy enough of her.

I'm a lucky son of a bitch that she loves me. Still don't understand why. But I won't ever take it for granted. The only way I can get through this shit show is to remember all we have to look forward to.

"Okay." The word is like poison as it slips out of my mouth.

Abby's shoulders slump in relief, and I know I've done the right thing. Even if it will kill me every second of every day. I won't add to her burden. Especially when she's doing it to keep me safe. But we will be having words in private, because there are some lines she cannot cross.

"And that's the only reason we're not going to strangle Atticus with our bare hands," I add, giving Drew and Abby a glimpse into Rick's and my conversation.

"You've made the right call," Drew says, thanking me with his eyes.

"Abby and Kai are the only reason I'm not on a plane to New

York already," Rick admits. "I want to hang that bastard by his balls from the rafters."

"He's going to get what's coming to him," I say, as my hands clench at my sides.

Abby unfurls one fist, leaning down to press a kiss to the back of my hand, and I want to grab her into my lap and hold onto her for eternity.

But I know we're on borrowed time. She needs to leave soon. And I need private time with her. "I know we have a lot to discuss, but I need to speak with Abby alone," I tell Drew and my brother.

They stand. "Of course." Drew leans down and kisses the top of his sister's head.

I'd worried the elite and Parkhurst had changed Drew permanently, but it's obvious how much he still cares. Sending his woman away killed him, and I admire his strength. I'd like to think I'd do the same in his shoes, but when it comes to Abigail, I'm a selfish prick. I can't last five minutes without her, so there's no way I'd consider sending her away for good. Drew sent Jane away to protect her the only way he knew how, and he's going out on a limb for his sister, double-crossing his father even though he knows he's a dead man walking if he finds out.

I don't know how Drew has managed to hold on to himself in the midst of all that carnage he's grown up with, but he's certainly fared better than Charlie and that douche Trent, both of whom seem corrupted by the excesses of the world they inhabit.

I bite the inside of my mouth to stifle my painful moan, as I climb slowly and awkwardly to my feet. "Come lie down with me." I want to feel my baby in my arms, but my ribs are fucking throbbing like a bitch, and I need to be prostrate.

We clamber into the bed, and I pull her up tight alongside me, ignoring the stab of pain that shoots through my side with the motion. "Talk to me, baby. How are you feeling?"

"I'm fine." Her protest is too quick and too practiced to be real.

I tilt her stunning face up and drown in the depths of her gorgeous brown eyes.

Abigail Anderson is the most beautiful woman to walk the face of the Earth. Her natural beauty clings to her like a visible aura, and I'm in awe of her lack of awareness as much as I'm in awe of her inner strength.

But my girl is hurting.

Oh, she's hiding it well. But I see behind the mask, and she's in a world of pain. "Baby, it's me. You don't have to hide. I know it's killing you because it's killing me, and I—"

"Stop." She stiffens in my arms, and panic washes over her face. "Please don't go there, Kai. Please don't say it." Tears pool in her eyes, and her lower lip wobbles. I feel utterly helpless as I watch her struggle against her emotions.

Overwhelming pain shears a line right through my heart, and the physical pain of my injuries pales in comparison. My wife is in agony, and I'm fucking injured and can't do anything to help. I can't even fuck her to take her mind off it.

I dust kisses all over her face, holding her close, offering silent words of comfort, because the truth is, this is a minefield and I'm terrified of stepping in the wrong place. I don't know what to say. I can't force her to talk about it. I won't. Even though I want to talk about it. Because it impacts me too. But she comes first.

Always.

And I will always put her needs above my own.

"I love you, firecracker." I press a tender kiss to her lips, and I'm reminded of the first moment we met. When she was a broken, beautiful stranger prepared to end it all on a beach. She brought out a side of me I didn't know existed that night. And I need to reveal that side right now.

What I wouldn't give to be able to make love to her now like I did that night. But I'm physically incapable of it, and I won't do anything to jeopardize my recovery, because I need to be firing on all cylinders. I can't work behind the scenes to protect her if I'm only operating at half capacity.

"I love you too, caveman." She sniffles, burying her face in my shirt. I smooth a hand up and down her back, dotting kisses all over her hair, trying to ignore the fact she's bottling her grief inside, and just enjoy the feel of her in my arms, because I know she has to leave soon, and I don't know when I'll get to hold her like this again.

After a few minutes, she lifts her head. "I know we need to talk about it at some point," she whispers. "And I know it impacts you too, but I can't talk about it now, Kai, because I will self-destruct. And I can't lose this battle. I can't lose you."

"I'm worried about you." I brush hair back off her face. "You're so fucking strong, Abby. But you're human too. And you can't shut off your emotions forever."

"I know that." She plants her hand on my chest, and I feel her touch in every part of my body even through my shirt. "When we have dealt with our fathers, then we can deal with that."

I take a risk. "Can I just ask you one thing?" Rick put this idea in my head earlier. "What if it's not real? What if he just said that to mess with your head? What if—"

"It's true," she blurts, and I mentally kick myself in the butt when more tears appear in her eyes. "Apart from a little bleeding after the abortion, I haven't had a period." Her face pales, and I want to take a gun to Michael Hearst right this fucking second and end him for putting that anguished look on her face. "I should have had one. I … I stupidly thought that…" She shakes her head before burying her face in my shirt again.

"What, babe? You thought what?"

"That I might still be pregnant," she sobs. My eyes pop wide. Could she be? My brief euphoria dies as fast as it appears.

There's no way she could be.

Her father wouldn't allow it to happen because the vote is too important to him.

But hang on.

My heart thumps painfully behind my sore rib cage. What if Abby is right? What if she is still pregnant? What if Michael thought they could pass the baby off as Charlie's? He would also be guaranteeing himself her shares because he'd have stopped her from marrying her baby daddy.

Except we are married, and he's not getting his hands on those shares either way.

But that's of little consolation given our current situation.

"Rick says he can organize an ultrasound. That will—"

"No!" She jerks out of my arms, bolting upright, shaking her head vigorously. Panicked eyes latch on mine. "No tests."

"But, baby."

"No, Kai." A more determined look appears on her face.

"Don't you want to know if you are?" I want to place my hand on her stomach, to relive the experience even if it is a lie.

"And what if I'm not?" she whispers. "What if it's all true. The abortion and the hys—other thing."

Fuck. She can't even say it. She's in complete denial.

"Isn't it better to know?" I softly ask.

"No." She shakes her head repeatedly again. "It's not better to know if it's true. I will be a basket case. I will be a sobbing mess. Broken, damaged goods. I won't be able to drag my body out of bed, let alone do what I need to do to take these bastards down."

She runs her nails through my hair, and my cock twitches to life behind my pajama pants, as my libido fully wakens.

"Please don't take my revenge from me, Kai. Because I need to do this. I need to make them pay. Fooling Charlie and then revealing the truth will destroy him. My deceit and the reality of what he's done to his family is enough payback in his case. Taking everything from my father and putting him behind bars is what I really need to begin the healing process." She kisses my cheek. "Then, and only then, can I think about dealing with this." She peers deep into my eyes. "I know you're hurting over this too, and if you've changed your mind, if you—"

Now it's my turn to halt her. I clamp my hand over her mouth, trying to leash the rage pouring through my veins. "Do not fucking say that, Abby." I don't want to lash out at her, but she's making it hard. "I said my vows, and I meant them. I will love and cherish you every day for the rest of my life. That's all that matters to me. The rest we will figure out as we go along." I grip her chin hard, trying and failing to tone down my glare. "Nothing has changed. *Nothing*." I press a hard kiss to her lips. "You are still the fucking air that I breathe. The blood pumping through my veins. The only reason my heart beats in my chest."

I loosen my tight grip, relaxing my facial features. "You're the center of my universe, Abby. *You*. Only you. You hear me?"

CHAPTER TEN

Kaiden

She clings to me, and I wrap my arms more firmly around her. I can't say goodbye. I can't let her leave to go back to him.

But I must.

And she needs me to be strong.

Reluctantly, I ease her out of my arms, kissing her deeply one final time. "Go, baby. Be safe, and message me when you get there." Now that she has a new purse, and Xavier has confirmed her room and her burner cell are clean, we're going to start up our nightly calls again.

Unless that asshole Barron gets in the way.

The thoughts of him sleeping beside her, holding her in his arms, brings every murderous intent to the surface again.

The idea of killing him crosses my mind. As it has several times since Christmas Day. Hell, if I'm honest, those thoughts started long ago. When I first noticed how he looked at her.

I've wanted to murder Charlie Barron pretty much since the moment I returned to Rydeville.

"I love you." She stretches up, pressing her lips to mine, and I sweep my tongue into her mouth, savoring the taste of her. "And I promise I won't have sex with him. Like I said, the fact he *cheated* on me the night of our wedding is a good thing. It gives me ammunition to keep him at arm's length, and it's believable."

When she told me that, I couldn't believe it. What kind of fucking idiot is he? Or was he so wound up he needed the release and didn't want to take it out on her like he's claimed? I wish I knew the truth. But all I know is he's one fucked-up asshole, and I hate my wife has to pretend to be in love with him.

But this isn't about me, I remind myself, shoving those thoughts aside.

"I love you so much." I pull her head into my chest and squeeze my eyes shut as I cradle her against me. It's killing me to let her go.

She eases out of my arms this time, looking forlorn. "I should go." She's as hesitant as me to part.

"If anything changes, or your life is in danger, I'm your first call. You promised," I remind her.

She bobs her head. "I know, and if it's something I can't handle, you're the first person I *want* to call."

I kiss the tip of her nose. "Later, firecracker." We have a rule about not saying goodbye.

"Later, caveman."

I'm bereft the instant she steps away from me, and the churning storm in the pit of my stomach is the same one that's always there every time we are forced to separate.

One day, no one will be driving us apart.

I watch her hugging Drew and Rick but cast my gaze aside as she walks toward the door, already knowing she won't look back.

The door softly closes, and I drop onto my bed, exhaling heavily.

"It sucks, man," Drew acknowledges, sitting down beside me. "But at least you still get to see her. I don't even have that luxury."

I clamp my hand down on his shoulder. "When this shit is done, we'll get your girl back."

He shrugs. "It'll be too late by then."

I frown. "It's not like you to give up." The Drew I remember from my youth was like a dog with a bone once he got his teeth into something.

He sighs, scrubbing a hand along his jaw, looking world weary.

"What's up?" I harrumph. "Besides the obvious."

"I haven't told Abby yet, but Dad's found a new fiancée for me."

"What. The. Fuck?" Rick explodes, almost falling off the couch.

"We wants us both happily married and settled before the vote."

"He can't force you," Rick naively says.

"I had to agree," Drew says with a loud sigh. "It was that or endure another punishing beating because he's pissed at me again for defending Abby on Christmas Day."

Blood boils in my veins, and a red layer coats my eyes. When he told me Charlie had bugged Abby's purse and he'd seen everything that went down between us that weekend in my house, I wanted to shoot the bastard. Then he explained how Hearst had shown it to the room, on a large screen projector, and how everyone was witness to the first time Abby and I had anal, and I went fucking nuclear. Only the fact I was drugged up and in a shitload of pain stopped me from charging off and riddling Hearst and Barron full of bullets.

That and the fact I don't want to make my wife a widow so soon after our wedding, because there's no denying it would be a bloodbath with few survivors.

But I'm wracking my brains now for some way I can protect her. I know she's tough as nails, smart, and reactive. I know she can take care of herself. But she needs to realize that's my job now too. And I'm not going to let her do this without additional protection.

I just haven't worked out what or how I can make this happen.

Getting back on my feet is priority number one. Then finding a way to protect my wife will take precedence.

"I'm sorry, man." Drew took one for the team, and now, it's come back to bite him.

"You don't have to apologize. I was trying to help my sister and I'd do it all over again. It doesn't matter anyway. He'd have found some way of foisting it on me anyway."

"Who is she?" Rick asks.

Drew shrugs. "Who cares?" His Adam's apple bobs in his throat. "The only woman I want to marry is Jane, and she's gone."

Gloomy tension hangs in the air, and I'm grateful when Lauder bursts through the door without knocking.

"Abby's gone," he confirms. "Xavier has gone after her to ensure she gets back okay."

I nod, slowly warming up to the quirky tech nerd.

"What's going on?" Hunt asks, leveling us with his sharp, observant eyes.

"Hearst is forcing Drew into marriage too," Rick supplies, as two sets of eyes flit to Manning.

"Is she hot?" Lauder asks, and I roll my eyes.

"Have you been smoking again?" He promised he was going to lay off that shit. Because we need everyone with full working brain cells.

"No." He frowns.

"Then engage your brain, fuckwad." I jerk my head in Drew's direction. Lauder isn't known for his tact, but he could cut the poor guy a break.

Funnily enough, the strain that's been evident between Lauder and me since Abby appeared on the scene is gone now. Allowing him into our bedroom confirmed what I've known all along.

Abby is mine.

For now and always.

Deep down, I know Lauder knew that, but he needed something visual to confirm it.

It's weird that that broke the ice.

But it did.

I still can't fucking believe it went down.

I mean, we've done shit with chicks together in the past.

But Abby is different.

She has always been the exception to every rule. And I'm not sharing her with anyone. Ever.

My dick stirs in my pants, reminding me it's been six days since I was buried balls deep in my woman. At least I know that part of my anatomy is still in full working order.

"Manning knows I'm joking."

Drew slants him a deadly look that confirms he knows nothing of the sort.

Hunt and Lauder are still suspicious of him, and I know it's in part tied up with the renewal of our friendship. They still don't trust him one hundred percent and until he has completely proven himself to them, they will continue to hold back.

Can't fault them for that.

"Was anything else agreed with Abby before she left?" Hunt asks. He can always be counted on to refocus any conversation.

"No. We pretty much already agreed to the plan," I say. "You and Xavier will continue to dig into Hearst's background and work on hacking into the basement security system. Drew will get Abby those names, and she'll get her crew to start digging for dirt on the board members and the few elite members we target. Drew will set up meetings with the board members so him and Abby can get them on our side. And Abby will work on being the perfect wife, while manipulating Charlie into getting him to bring her to the dungeon."

Lauder arches a brow, and I shake my head. I'm not getting into another discussion about it because I'm liable to hit one of my friends if all this pent-up anger doesn't find an outlet soon.

"I'll repair my relationship with Charlie too. Pull the brother-in-law card." Drew's eyes flit to mine, as if it's only just occurred to him that that's what we are to one another now. "I need to stay close to him and that asshole Montgomery."

"Good call." If I can't protect Abby in person, I'm comforted knowing Drew can. An idea pops into my head. I can put a guy on Charlie. Someone to shadow him discreetly so I can see what he's up to. And who knows? Maybe we'll find some dirt we can use against him. While I'm at it, I'll put someone on Abby too. They won't be able to guard her too often because they won't be able to shadow her in school or at Charlie's house, but I like the idea of someone being close by in case I need backup, and he can tail her whenever she leaves the house.

I make a mental note to chat to Lauder about it in a while. His father has an expert team at his disposal. He got himself in deep with the wrong crew a few years back, and he's had to watch his back ever since. The Lauders are well versed with taking protective details with them whenever they step out into the public domain. Lauder's old man wanted to sic someone on him when we moved here, but it was too risky in case it gave the game away. I know Lauder has enjoyed not feeling someone breathing down his neck or watching him twenty-four-seven. Even though it would've come in handy when we were attacked at the airport.

"What about me?" Jackson asks. "I want to be involved."

"You'll act as back up to all of us, slotting in wherever you're needed." I'll ask him to keep tabs on Abby in school, because I can't risk being seen looking at her or engaging with her even if Abby threatens the other students into silence.

"In other words, you'll be our bitch," Rick jokes. Lauder flips him the bird, but he takes it in his stride.

"Rick and I will work on the plans for Atticus," I confirm. I refuse to call him Father. He lost that right when he murdered our mother, brainwashed me into believing Abby was the devil's spawn, and gave up our two youngest brothers for adoption.

Hunt shifts, his eyes narrowing. Dude never misses a thing. "What don't we know?"

"Atticus killed our mom," I say, forcing the words out of my mouth. "It wasn't Hearst; although, he set the whole thing in motion."

"What the fuck, bro?" Jackson's jaw slackens.

"What are your plans for him?" Drew asks, his gaze dancing between Rick and me.

"We haven't worked that out yet. We're still processing." Both our initial instincts were to end him, as soon as possible, but neither of us will do anything to jeopardize the main plan.

"Good." Drew straightens up, adopting a grave expression. "I know what you'd like to do, but you need to hold back. Your father is a necessary cog in the wheel. We need him to continue to exert pressure on my father. He's stressed with the upcoming vote, so let's give him something else to worry about. We need him distracted enough not to pay attention to us so we can get to his board and get into the vault. If he's preoccupied with other shit, we should pull it off."

"You want us to play Atticus," I surmise, and he nods.

"In what way?" Rick asks.

"You need to manipulate him. He thinks he's square now with Hearst because he's given him back everything he stole. You two need to convince him it's not enough. There should be compensation. He should suffer for all the years you've suffered." He smooths a hand over the top of his head. "Make it clear that Atticus has not gone away as a threat, so Father is looking over the other shoulder. I'm sure you get the gist."

"We know what we need to do." Rick and I exchange a knowing

look. I'll enjoy screwing over my father. He'll think we're completely on his side. When we'll be setting him up for a fall.

And when the day of the vote arrives, he'll see what happens when you cross family.

He will regret killing our mother.

And if he thinks he lost everything before, he'll realize it's fucking nothing compared to what we are going to take from him now.

Because he will have nothing and no one once we are through with him.

And D-day can't come fast enough.

CHAPTER ELEVEN

Abby

I tiptoe into my bedroom, holding my breath, almost collapsing with relief when the sweet, soft rumbling sounds of snoring tickle my eardrums. Charlie is still passed out on top of my bed, oblivious to the fact I've been gone for hours.

I sneak into the bathroom, shed my clothes, and grab a quick shower, trying to pretend like my heart doesn't feel like it's been cut up with a machete.

I love spending time with Kai, and I was relieved to see he was okay, but it was painful too. Because every time we part, it gets harder and harder.

The truth is, Kai makes me weak.

Because I can't shield my emotions around him. He knows me too well. Plus, I want to give in to them when I'm with him. I want him to cradle me in his strong arms, whisper reassurances in my ear, and let him carry some of the burden. But that is a luxury I can't afford to indulge, and it's the sweetest form of torment.

The other truth is, being with Kai makes me stronger. When I'm with him, I feel invincible. Like I can achieve anything with his hand in mine. With his infallible belief in my abilities.

And then he's ripped away from me, and doubts creep in again, when I can't allow them to. One false move is all it will take to bring everything tumbling down around me. And then we're all up shit creek.

So, in a way, it's best we're apart. Even if it feels like I've lost half of myself.

Until we win this battle, I need to act like I'm a lone island.

It's the only way I can harden my heart to do the things I need to do.

Doesn't mean I won't miss my husband like crazy, because I will. School doesn't start back for a week, and it will be at least that long until I see him again.

Turning off the shower, I get out, dry myself with a large, fluffy white towel, and slip into my sleep shorts and top. Then I brush my teeth, clean my face, and comb my hair back into a ponytail, staring blankly at my reflection in the mirror as I prepare to face my first test.

I tap out a quick text to Kai on my burner cell, confirming I got home safe, telling him I love him. I switch it off before he can reply and conceal it in the hidden bottom panel of my bag. Then, I ease out of the bathroom like a sneaky thief in the night.

Charlie hasn't budged in the last few minutes, and he's sprawled across the bed, taking up most of the space. I lift his arm, very carefully, hoping not to wake him, placing it across his stomach. Then I peel back the covers and climb in.

He's on the top of the bed, and no part of his body is in contact with me, but it still feels like such a betrayal to be lying in bed with another man. My chest heaves as I glance sideways at him.

He looks like a fallen angel in sleep. His jet-black hair has flattened out, falling across his forehead, brushing the tops of his strong brows. His full lips are slightly parted, and his chest rises and falls as he languishes in slumber. I watch him for a few minutes, still trying to figure out how we got here.

How someone I once considered one of my closest friends could seemingly switch personalities overnight.

Or has he always been like this?

Have those dark glimpses I've caught on occasion been the truth, and he's become adept at disguising his true self?

One thing is for sure—I'm about to find out.

For a brief instant, when I wake the next morning, I believe I'm protected in Kai's arms. Until reality comes crashing down upon me.

At some point during the night, Charlie must have undressed and climbed in underneath the covers with me, because his bare leg is sandwiched between mine, and his large hands are resting on the exposed skin of my tummy. My top must have ridden up in sleep. Acid snakes up my throat, and a sob rips from my mouth as I stare, horror-struck at the place where his hand is.

Memories of waking up with Kai's hand in a similar place return to haunt me, and it's no act when I wrench Charlie's hand away and scramble out of the bed, hitting the side of my head off the bedside table in the process. I cry out as stinging pain zips along my skull.

Charlie bolts upright, his wild eyes instantly alert as they latch onto mine. "Shit. What happened?" He crawls across the bed toward me.

I lift my hand up to halt his forward trajectory. "Don't fucking come near me." I wince as I dab at the sore spot on the side of my head, silently cussing when my fingertips come away red. Great, I've broken skin, and I doubt it'll be that easy to disguise in such a prominent place. If Drew or Kai see it, they will go fucking apeshit.

"Did I do something wrong?" he asks, his brow puckering.

"Who said you could strip to your boxers and get into bed beside me?"

And who said you could put your hand *there*.

You motherfucking asshole doucheface fucktard bastard.

"Abby." He swings his legs over the side of the bed, and I purposely avoid staring at his carved abs and broad chest until I remember it's what someone in my shoes would do—sneak peeks at the prick even though I'm still furious with him for screwing someone else. I'm coy about it, glancing quickly at his hot body before averting my eyes. But not before I see a glint of pleasure light up his eyes. "Darling." He sinks to his knees beside me.

"Don't call me that. Save it for your bit on the side," I hiss.

"You know there's no one but you. That was an error in judgment, and I already promised it won't happen again."

"As if your word means anything." I glare at him before deliberately softening my look and sighing. "Look, Charlie." Forcing back bile, I gently cup his face. "I'm trying, but you can't expect me to be happy about you sneaking into bed with me. You fucked someone else the night of our wedding. That's not something I can forget overnight. Or even in a week or a month. You have a lot to do to prove to me it was a onetime thing. To prove I mean what you profess I mean to you."

"Abby." He leans into my hand, rubbing his face against my palm, and he reminds me of a newborn puppy, nuzzling into his owner, desperately craving attention. If Charlie hadn't been brought up in a loving environment, with two parents who worshiped each other, and him, I'd say he was starved for affection.

But that simply isn't true.

"I mean every word of it. I love you, and I will prove it to you. Just give me a chance. Please."

I eyeball him without blinking as I pretend to think about it. "Okay. But we need to take it slow. And that means you don't sleep in my bed unless I tell you you can."

"Mom is going to think it's weird," he says, reaching out and pressing soft fingers to the sore spot on my head.

"Your mother is grieving. She won't even notice. And if she does, it's not any of her business."

"Let me attend to that," he says, purposely ignoring my comment. Evasive Charlie does little to reassure me he is sincere.

I nod, letting him help me to my feet. He walks me into the bathroom, keeping one arm wrapped firmly around my waist from behind, and I deliberately pretend I don't see the giant bulge straining his boxers.

He positions me on top of the closed toilet seat before he stalks to the large overhead cupboard, pulling supplies out. Kneeling in front of me, he cleans the cut with some water and cotton balls. Then he pats it dry with a towel and fixes a Band-Aid in place. "Does it hurt?" he asks, gently prodding the small lump.

"Not really."

"Why don't you go back to bed and I'll bring you some breakfast and a couple of pain pills."

"That actually sounds pretty wonderful," I truthfully admit, because I'm zonked after my nighttime expedition. "Thanks."

He takes my hand, leading me back into the bedroom and tucking me under the covers. I don't protest or fight when he kisses my lips briefly. I watch him pull on his wrinkled pants and creased shirt, fighting a smile, and I wonder if it is going to be that easy. I guess time will tell.

Charlie is true to his word, fixing me a tray worthy of a queen. He's showered and changed into a gray checkered suit with a pristine white shirt and charcoal-gray tie, and there's no denying how dapper he looks. "I've got to go into the office again. I'm sorry."

I'm not.

"It's fine. I understand. What about the meeting with the funeral director?"

"I'll be home in time to pick you up, and we can go there together."

"Okay." I bat my eyelashes and bite down on my lip, staring at him with my best wide-eyed innocent look. Then I sit up on my knees and stretch up and kiss him. "Have a good day."

He winds his hand into my hair, holding me in place at the back of my head. "Have you any idea how happy you make me?"

I shrug.

"I know this has been hard for you, Abby, but I promise I won't let anyone harm you ever again. I love you so fucking much."

Again, with the self-delusion. Doesn't he see how much *he's* hurt me? How much he continues to hurt me by forcing this on me?

He kisses me again, prodding at the seam of my lips with his tongue. I open for him, hating every second of it. When he pulls away, his lips are swollen, and his green eyes are dark with desire. "Just let me love you, darling. That's all I ask. Let me shower you with affection the way I've always dreamed of doing."

I can tell he means it. It radiates from his eyes.

Now is as good a time as any.

"I was thinking maybe we should have a party." He blinks, looking confused. "To celebrate our wedding. It was all so fast, and it's not really how I pictured my wedding day." I look at him through hooded eyes, praying I'm not pushing too far too soon. "Every little girl daydreams about her wedding, and I'm no different," I lie, because that's never been me. But he doesn't know that.

"I gave up on that dream when I became engaged to Trent because marrying a monster is the stuff of nightmares, not dreams."

94

I drag my lip between my teeth. "But when he was out of the picture, I started to dream again. To think it might come true when I married you."

He reels me into his arms, hugging me tight. "I'll give you anything you want, Abby. Anything."

How about my real husband, huh? Will you give him to me? Yeah, didn't think so. My snarky inner demon conducts a one-sided conversation in my head.

"Okay." I fake a smile, easing out of his embrace. "We can discuss the details later. You can't be late for work."

He totally pushes his luck, kissing me again. "I'm taking you out to dinner after the funeral meeting."

Oh yay, great. That is just what I'll feel like doing after such a morbid meeting. "That would be nice." I don't gush, because I don't want to overdo it.

"Wear a pretty dress. I want to show you off."

Blech. My stomach dips to my toes as I remember how often my father expressed similar sentiments. A shiver works its way through me at the thought that Charlie could end up being exactly like my bastard father. Imagine I'm stuck with him, and he turns out like that?

An icy chill creeps up my spine, and it's a struggle to mask my true emotions. But I do, slapping another fake smile on my face. "I'll see you later. Don't work too hard." I waggle my fingers at him, and he blows me a kiss.

Gag.

The instant the door closes, I flop down on the bed, rubbing at my mouth, wanting to erase the taste of him still lingering on my lips.

"If Father could see you working Charlie like a pro, he'd be so fucking proud," Drew says, later that afternoon as we walk through the expansive grounds at the back of the house.

"Please don't say shit like that. And don't talk about that bastard unless it involves our plans to annihilate him. Otherwise his name is mud. He's Voldemort. Got it?"

"Sorry, A." He pulls me into a quick hug. "I'm just proud of you for holding it together. I know it's not easy."

"It's not," I admit, cutting across him. "And it's infinitely harder when everyone keeps referencing shit I don't want to think about or talk about. I just want to focus on our plans, because the sooner we get this done, the sooner I can be with my husband and start properly living my life."

"I hear you." He kisses the top of my head. "I know you have something to say, but before that, there is something I need to tell you. Try not to get mad."

"Has anyone ever *not* gotten mad when someone says that?" I question, and a half smile graces his mouth.

"Father has found me a replacement fiancée," he blurts. "And you've been summoned to dinner on Sunday to meet her."

I slam to a halt, turning to my brother with my jaw trailing the ground. "No! He can't do that to you! To Jane!"

"Jane is gone, A," he quietly confirms. "And you know he can and will do this."

"Who is she?"

"All I know is her name is Alessandra Mathers, and she's from out of state."

"Weren't any of the girls around here good enough?"

"Apparently not."

"You can't agree to it, D." I clutch onto his arm, pinning him with panicked eyes. "What if Jane finds out? It will kill her!"

Anguish skates across his face, plain as day. "I hope that doesn't happen, but I can't say no. Besides, it doesn't matter. I'll try to stall it until after the vote and then call it off."

"What if he won't let you?"

"Then I'll go through with it and get an annulment after."

I hate my brother might have to do that, because he and Jane share this epic love, and it's not right that they can't be together. "I hate this for you."

"I'm not exactly enamored with it myself, A. But, right now, I need to be seen to cooperate. To make amends for my supposed betrayal. He's still pissed I jumped to defend you on Christmas Day."

"Well, then, my plan should help you out too."

"What do you have in mind?" he asks, looping his arm through mine and urging me forward.

We keep step as we walk farther from the house. "I've already planted the seeds with Charlie, now you need to do the same with the bastard. You need to tell him it's in his interests to publicly showcase my wedding. Tell him he needs to throw a lavish party and this time it should be downstairs."

"He will never go for that, Abby."

"Yes, he will if you choose your words carefully and manipulate him into it. You need to convince him that I'm on board and I've put my errant ways behind me. That his plan worked. Feed his ego. Let him believe he's broken me. Molded me into submitting. Tell him I've always secretly harbored a crush on Charlie and it's why I didn't protest too much. He'll push back, and that's when you tell him to test me. To bring me into that world and see how I behave. Tell him it's time I was indoctrinated and that I learned what is involved in being a respected elite wife."

I stop walking again, bracing my hands against my brother's forearms. "Blow smoke up his ass. Tell him whatever he needs to hear to believe it, and we kill two birds with one stone. You'll be back in favor, and we'll get into the dungeon to do our recon."

"And to think Father believes women are the weaker sex." Drew grins.

"I'm glad he underestimates me." A matching grin spreads across my mouth. "Because it means he won't see me coming."

CHAPTER TWELVE

"**A**re you okay?" I ask Charlie, as we leave the funeral director's office after a difficult meeting.

Air spurts out of his mouth. "I'm fine."

Liar.

It's as obvious as the nose on his face that he's anything but fine. Charlie is waging an inner war with himself, and I've no clue which side will end up victorious.

He takes my hand, linking our fingers. "Could we walk to the restaurant? I need some fresh air."

I'm not really wearing the right shoes, but I don't argue. "Sure."

The night air is brisk, but we're both wrapped up in warm coats, so I only feel the icy chill upon my face, reddening my nose and stinging my cheeks. Charlie emits little breathy cloud rings into the air as we walk in silence toward the most expensive restaurant in Rydeville.

The maître d' is effusive when we arrive, fussing over us in a way that's completely over the top. He takes our coats, and Charlies casts an appraising look over the navy-blue lace mini-dress I'm wearing. I've got stockings and garters on underneath and a pair of sky-high silver Gucci shoes on my feet. I took extra care with my appearance tonight, wearing a full face of makeup and styling my hair into soft curves, and from the way Charlie is eyeing me like he wants to ditch dinner and eat me instead, I'd say I've accomplished what I set out to.

He grips my hand, grinning appreciatively, and I swallow the bile forcing its way up my throat. The trek across the restaurant is an ordeal as well-meaning acquaintances and nosy busybodies stop us at every step, offering condolences and congratulations. Father placed an announcement in the local and national papers confirming our marriage, so every sniveling asshole is aware it's official, and they are tripping over themselves to lick Charlie's ass.

Charlie slides into the booth after me, sighing deeply as he rubs at the spot between his brows. The waiter hands us some menus, and Charlie orders the most expensive bottle of wine. It doesn't matter that we're not of age. People in Rydeville are used to turning a blind eye and bending the rules for the elite. Especially now Charlie is the patriarch of his family and the newly-appointed CEO of Barron Banking and Financial Investment Services Ltd.

"Fuck." He cricks his head from side to side, running his finger along the collar of his shirt.

"Hey." I pat his thigh. "It will be okay. Once we get through these next couple days."

"I'm worried about Mom," he admits. "She barely comes out of her room, and I hear her sobbing all the time."

I do too, and I've tried to help, but most times, she won't even open the door to me.

"She needs to speak to a therapist. I know the doctor is attending to her, but pumping her full of valium and sleeping pills isn't the answer. You don't want her to end up like poor Sylvia."

"Do not compare my mother to that woman!" he hisses.

Several heads turn in our direction, and I snatch my hand back, pissed. I grind my teeth to my molars, ignoring his outburst and focusing on the menu, because I can't be seen to have a blazing argument with him in public in case word gets back to my father.

"Shit, Abby." He reaches for my hand, but I tuck it under my butt, keeping it away from him. "I'm sorry. I didn't mean to lash out at you."

I quell my temper, purposely softening my look. "I know you're under a lot of strain, Charlie, and I'm trying to help, but biting my head off isn't going to help your cause." I eyeball him seriously. "You know how I get when I'm pushed."

A faint smile cracks across his lips. "I happen to like that side of you." In a lightning-fast move, he darts in, nipping my earlobe with his teeth. His breath fans over the side of my face. "I'm betting you're a real tigress in the bedroom, and I can't wait to find out if I'm right." He plants his hand on my exposed thigh, inching his fingers up higher.

Panic swims up my throat, and I'm ready to pry his fingers off when the waiter arrives with our wine.

Talk about perfect timing.

Charlie removes his hand, and I release the breath I was holding. He pours me a glass of wine, with a knowing smile on his face, and I'm growing uncomfortably hot as he eyes me up and down, his gaze lingering on my thighs and my chest. He clinks his glass against mine. "To us."

I can barely breathe over the lump wedged in my throat, let alone speak, so I simply smile and tap my glass against his, taking a healthy glug of the chilled, crisp New Zealand Marlborough Sauvignon Blanc. He presses his wet lips to my cheek. "You look stunning by the way, and I'm the envy of every man in here."

Considering the average age of the patrons is mid-forties, I don't doubt that. But it's still gross, and it sticks in my gut. "Thank you."

I kiss his cheek too, holding back my gag the whole time. "But enough about me." I smile coyly at him over the top of my wine glass. "I want to hear all about your day."

I pepper him with questions the whole way through dinner, asking him how things are going at the office, hanging off his every word like the docile, attentive little wife I'm aiming to be.

He finds numerous opportunities to touch me, and I'm squirming in the seat, growing more and more uncomfortable. From Charlie's smug grin, I can tell he thinks his attentions are turning me on. I get immense pleasure from knowing he's having the opposite effect. My gaze darts around the restaurant, half-expecting to see Kai sulking in the shadows, but that's ridiculous because I know he wouldn't do that.

Although he hates this as much as I do, we both understand what we need to do.

And now I'm thinking of Kai.

Wishing it was his hands all over me.

His lips teasing my skin.

His dirty words whispered in my ear.

A sharp pang of longing jumps up and bites me before I put a leash on it.

I'm glad when dinner is over and we leave even if I'm a little anxious about what Charlie expects when we return home. I told him last night I wanted to take it slow, but he seems to have forgotten the memo.

He plants his hand on my thigh, when we're tucked up in the Land Rover with the heating on full blast, rubbing circles on my thigh with his thumb as he drives.

"What are you doing?" I ask, when we are halfway home and his hand moves farther up my thigh, dangerously close to the hem of my dress.

He flashes me a saucy grin. "What does it look like?"

I slap his hand away. "Are you hard of hearing?"

He frowns.

"I told you I want to take it slow. This isn't slow."

"Come on, Abby. We're not eighth graders."

"When it comes to sex, you were never an eighth grader. You went from zero to ninety overnight."

He throws back his head, laughing. "True, but there's nothing wrong with sex, Abby." He pins, dark, wanton eyes on me, and I shiver all over. But not in a good way. "It's natural and healthy. And it's what married couples do."

"We haven't even been married a week," I counter.

"Most married couples have sex on their wedding night." He opens his mouth, to take it back, no doubt, instantly realizing his mistake.

"Yes. But we're not most married couples, are we?" I bark. "Because you were out screwing some whore." I pretend to fume, while I'm secretly smiling inside. This is a good way to keep his hands off me. I'll just start an argument any time he tries to get frisky. If I rile him up, he'll think twice about wanting to fuck me.

I hope.

"You're beginning to sound like a broken record, Abby."

"And you're beginning to sound like the stereotypical cheating husband!" I roar. "How fucking dare you say that to me! I have every right to be pissed, and you don't get to dismiss it like that."

He sighs, rubbing his hands down his face.

I'm fuming as I turn in my seat, faking a glare. "Who was she? I want to know who my husband spent our wedding night with."

Now, it's his turn to squirm uncomfortably in his seat. "She's no one. Inconsequential."

I cross my arms over my chest. "I still want to know who she is."

"No."

"No?" I pout. "I have a right to know!" I demand when I really couldn't give two shits.

"Goddamn it, Abby." He pounds his fists off the steering wheel. "I said drop it!"

Hmm. He doesn't want me to know who she is.

This is interesting.

I tuck this little nugget away for future reference.

"Fine." I sulk, glaring out the window, and Charlie drives us back to the house in complete silence.

When we walk into the house, we go our separate ways without speaking, and I lock my bedroom door, trying not to gloat as I grab my cell and head into my bathroom to call the man I love.

The following day, I insist we are having a family dinner. The funeral is tomorrow, and Charlie's mom and sister need to be aware of the arrangements. I get why they want to bury their heads in the sand, and pretend this isn't happening, but I need to at least try to prepare them. Tomorrow is going to be hell on Earth, and I'm already wishing I had a fast-forward button.

Normally, dinner is served at the formal dining table, but I've dismissed the housekeeper, and I've cooked a pot roast with all the trimmings and purposely set the kitchen table. Whether she likes it or not, Elizabeth Barron needs to face up to the fact it's her husband's funeral tomorrow, and she must put her best face forward.

I sent Charlie a text message earlier, telling him of my plans, and I got a curt acknowledgment in reply.

Suits me if he's still sulking. The more this goes on, the longer I get to keep him out of my bed.

Elizabeth and Lillian are seated at the table, and I'm plating our food when Charlie rushes into the kitchen, looking a little flustered. "Sorry I'm late."

"You're not," I say without looking at him. "I was just about to serve up."

He stalks toward me, producing a massive bunch of flowers from behind his back. "These are for you." He leans down and kisses my cheek. "A peace offering for last night. I'm sorry."

Could he be any more cliché?

"Thank you." I peck his lips briefly, taking the flowers and placing them in the sink. "I'll put them in a vase after we've eaten. I don't want our food to go cold." I place my hands on his chest. "Go talk with your mom and sister while I finish our plates."

Charlie and I single-handedly keep the conversation going over dinner, and it's awkward as fuck. We run through the plans for the ceremony tomorrow, but Elizabeth just stares blankly at us the whole time. Lil doesn't have much of an appetite, pushing food around her plate, appearing sullen and pissed off.

After dinner, I go upstairs with Elizabeth to find something suitable for her to wear tomorrow. She crawls onto the unmade bed the instant we enter her room, and I walk into her closet alone, wondering how she's ever going to bounce back from this.

Charles and Elizabeth lived for one another, and I don't know if she knows how to cope without him.

I find several black dresses that will work, walking out into her bedroom with them on the hangers. "What about either of these?" I ask, holding up the two most appropriate ones.

"Whatever," she mumbles from her place on the bed, not even looking up. She's curled into a fetal position on top of the disheveled covers, and my heart aches for her.

I return the dresses to her closet, picking one and leaving it out for the morning. I choose matching shoes and a purse before stepping out of the closet and walking toward my fake mother-in-law. Perching on the side of her bed, I brush knotty hair back off her face, caressing her cheek with a feather-light touch. Elizabeth Barron is a beautiful woman, and she usually takes pride in her appearance. But it's clear it's been days since she's showered, and she's a bit of a hot mess with her red-rimmed eyes, puffy cheeks, and blotchy skin.

Not that I blame her.

She's heartbroken. Taking care of herself is bottom of her list of priorities.

I lie down beside her. "I'm so sorry, Elizabeth." I take her hands in mine. "I can't begin to imagine how much pain you are in."

Her bloodshot eyes lock on mine. "It's never getting any better, is it?" she whispers.

"I haven't lost the man I love," I say, my heart spiking painfully as the stupid words leave my mouth, because even the thought of anything happening to Kai sends a rush of panic charging through me. My pulse throbs in my neck, and I force myself to calm down. "But I have lost my mom, and I miss her every single day." I don't mention the loss of my babies, because it's still too raw, but that pain is something I carry on my shoulders all the time.

"I miss him so much." Tears roll down her face. "And I don't want to go on without him." More tears cascade down her cheeks. "I know that's selfish. That Charlie and Lillian need me, but how can I be there for them when I'm so broken on the inside?"

I'm broken on the inside too. But I'm using it to fight back. If I didn't, I'd be a basket case in bed too. It sounds harsh when I put it like that, and I don't mean it to be, but it speaks to our environments. I've had to claw, bite, and fight my way through my life since my mother passed, whereas Charles Barron worshipped the ground his wife walked on and he went out of his way to shield her and keep her safe.

But his protection has weakened her, and she needs to pull herself together, or the elite will eat her alive.

I wrap my arms around her. "You are stronger than you think. And you know Charles would want you to be strong for your children. He wouldn't want to see you suffering like this." I don't really know if what I'm saying is helping or hindering, as I've no experience helping someone deal with their grief, but I'm trying. Sure, Drew and I leaned on one another after Mom died, but we were little kids. We just clung to one another without words, and somehow got ourselves through it.

"I don't feel, strong, Abigail. I feel utterly weak without him." She clutches onto me. "He was my everything. My strength. My hope. My joy. My purpose in life." She sniffles. "I don't know who I am without him."

I don't ever want to be that dependent on Kai. I want him to be all those things for me, but I don't want to have to rely on him to the point I can't do things for myself. I wonder if Elizabeth realized that is what was happening with her and she was happy to stay in blissful ignorance, or it just snuck up on her and she's only realizing now that he's gone.

Elizabeth Barron is a good woman, and she's not unintelligent, but her husband made her vulnerable and weak.

I worry about what will become of her now she doesn't have her husband's protection.

An icy shiver tiptoes up my spine as I contemplate what might happen within elite circles to the widow of a founding father.

Nothing good I'm sure.

There was a time I could bank on Charlie to safeguard his mom, but I don't know who he is anymore. Or what exact deal he has made with my father.

"You are still you, Elizabeth." I tilt her face up to me. "And your children need you to be that strong woman tomorrow." I press a kiss to her forehead. "You need to be strong for you, because there will be challenges ahead, and you can't ignore them no matter how much you may want to." I don't want to be blunt or appear harsh, so I'm hoping my subtle insinuation will sink into her foggy brain and force her to start taking control of herself. "Can I make a suggestion?" She shrugs. "Let me run you a nice warm bath. You'll feel a little better after. Please let me do that for you?"

I don't expect her to agree, but she does. "Okay."

"Just give me a few minutes, and I'll set it up."

I run the faucets in the tub, dropping some bath oil that I find in the cupboard over the sink into the water. I remove a couple of towels, placing them over the radiator so they are warm for her when she gets out. Then I help her into the bathroom and leave her to soak in the tub while I find a clean nightdress for her to change into and replace the covers on her bed with fresh linens.

When she emerges from the bathroom, in a cloud of steam, rubbing at her wet hair with a towel, it's good to see her at least looking like the woman I know. Propping her up on the bed, I gently pull a comb through her hair before blow-drying it.

I'm conscious of the form lingering behind the doorway, but I don't acknowledge him, and Elizabeth doesn't notice her son at all. I don't know how long he's been there or how much he heard.

I stay with her after she's tucked up and has taken a valium, only stepping out of the room when she's asleep.

The door has only just closed after me when Charlie reels me into his arms. "Thank you for taking care of her." He holds me tight. "I couldn't do this without you. You are my strength, Abby." He kisses the top of my head. "You make me want to be a better person," he adds, and I smother my snort of hilarity. "A better man. To be someone worthy of you."

What a pity he hadn't thought about that before he got his father killed and shattered his family beyond repair.

CHAPTER THIRTEEN

The funeral is every bit as horrific as I expected it to be. I insist that Charlie sits in between his mother and sister at the top pew in the church, and I'm sitting on the other side of Elizabeth. Drew is on my other side, and my father and Patrice—that emotionless bitch he's engaged to—are sitting on the other side of him.

The church is packed to capacity, and there are people standing outside too.

Elizabeth's quiet sobs can be heard throughout the ceremony and I bleed for her. My hands rest on top of hers in her lap, while Charlie has one arm wrapped around his mom and another around Lillian. Lil's eyes are red, and she's sniffling intermittently, but she's holding it together far better than her mother. Charlie is stoic, his face not betraying much emotion, but the strain is evident in the tense shape of his shoulders and the near-constant tick popping in his jaw.

We all breathe a sigh of relief when it's finally over.

After the burial, at the town cemetery, in the assigned Barron plot, everyone makes their way to the local hotel, where a lavish spread has been set up in the function room upstairs.

"Hey, little sis." Drew ambles up behind me, pulling me away from a boring conversation with neighbors of the Barron's that I'm only half listening to. "You doing okay?"

"I'm fine. But I'll be glad when this is all over."

Drew glances over his shoulder, his eyes locking on our father and Patrice. They are deep in conversation with the Montgomerys and not paying attention to us. "Come to the bar with me." Drew steers me away, over to the bar at the top of the room. He orders an old-fashioned for himself and a cranberry juice for me. "I've got those lists," he says under his breath, discreetly removing a small, sealed envelope from his inside jacket pocket.

I slide the envelope into my purse, ensuring no one is looking. "Thanks. I spoke to Chad last night, and he's in. He's already rallying the investigative crew."

"Good. I've also tentatively reached out to a few trusted board members. The two men and one woman who remember you fondly from your summer internship. I'll meet them alone first, throw out a few feelers, and see how they respond. If it's favorable, then we can both meet with them. These three are the most influential. If we can convince them, they will do most of the legwork for us."

I smile at an associate of my father's as he passes by with his new, much younger wife. "I can't imagine Father is all that popular with the board. He's not a very likable individual."

"True, but he has most of these people terrorized, so we still need to proceed with caution." He sips from his drink, his sharp gaze calculating. "Do you think you could get away Sunday night for a meeting? You're allowed to see Xavier, right?" I nod. "So, tell Charlie you're hanging with Xavier and meet us at the warehouse. We'll use the back entrance and hide our cars in the woods in case he's tracking you or has someone spying. No one will know we are there."

I lean into Drew, pressing my mouth to his ear. "Is he well enough to go there?" I whisper, not daring to say any more.

Drew angles his head, moving his mouth to my ear. "He's doing much better now. He'll be there. It's killing him being apart from you."

My heart races and butterflies swarm my chest at the thought of seeing Kai again.

A hand slides around my waist, and I jump, spilling some of my juice on the counter. "What are you two plotting over here?" Charlie asks, narrowing his eyes at Drew in a way that clearly betrays his suspicion.

My blood pressure shoots sky high at his choice of words and the wary look on his face. My palms are suddenly sweaty, and I subtly wipe them down the front of my conservative black dress. I'm opening my mouth to throw out some frivolous lie, when my twin beats me to it.

"Just the usual." Drew waggles his brows, sipping his whiskey. "World domination. How to eradicate poverty. How to oust Jeff Bezos from the richest man in the world position, etcetera, etcetera."

"Don't be glib," Charlie drawls. "It doesn't suit you."

Drew's gaze skims the room quickly before he moves in closer to Charlie. "We were discussing your predicament," he says in a low tone.

"What predicament?" Charlie coolly replies.

"Father promised Atticus he could return to the elite and return to Rydeville. It's happening next week. From what I hear, your mom isn't in a good place. How do you plan to keep her quiet? She can't go mouthing off about Atticus being responsible for your dad's murder," Drew says.

I jump on the bandwagon. "And it's not like you can tell her the truth, so what are you going to do?"

All the blood drains from his face, and in this moment, I almost feel sorry for Charlie.

Almost.

"I don't know, and I'm wondering why your father didn't forewarn me about this."

"He's been too busy boning his bride-to-be," Drew deadpans. "But I'm sure he plans to talk to you about it. I'm just giving you a heads-up. You need to have a solution. One that will appease him so he can keep Atticus on board, and one that will keep your mom's mouth shut."

"I'll think of something," Charlie says, not sounding as confident as he looks.

"What did you say to your mom?" I ask as we make the journey to Chez Manning for Sunday dinner. I'd woken this morning to the sounds of screaming and shouting coming from the vicinity of Elizabeth's bedroom.

Charlie exhales heavily, dragging a hand through his hair. "I told her Michael had investigated and that Atticus Anderson had not given any order to shoot. That he had specifically warned his men not to fire. I explained how the guard who took the shot did so in error. And that he's been punished for it."

I stare at him incredulously. "You expect her to buy that pile of crap?"

"What the fuck else was I supposed to tell her?" he snaps, clearly agitated.

"Maybe you should tell her the truth."

"You know I can't do that! Your father would put a bullet in my skull next if I did. And then he'd go after Mom and Lil." He glances briefly at me. "And you'd probably end up reengaged to Trent."

I snort. "Over my dead fucking body. Besides, he's engaged to Shandra."

"They'll both be here, by the way."

Interesting. I hope I get a chance to pull Shandra aside to feel her out. I'm on the fence about her allegiances, and I wouldn't mind discovering if she's a friend or a foe. We have always respected one another, but I can't say we've ever been overly friendly.

When we arrive at my family home, Charlie parks the car in the garage, killing the engine. "Do I need to remind you to behave?"

I turn a heated glare on him. "I'm not a fucking child, *Charles*. And I'm not a fucking idiot either. I know how I need to act."

He stares at me for a few silent beats.

"What?"

"Is that what you're doing?"

I frown as my heart starts picking up speed. "I don't understand," I lie.

"Is it all an act?" He points between us. "Are you just saying what you think I need to hear?"

"Give me a fucking break, Charlie. Have you forgotten what he's done to me?" I purposely let my voice crack. "Because I haven't," I croak. "And I can't take any more. I was stupid to think I could win against him, and I don't want to fight anymore. I'm tired of it. This might not be what I wanted," I admit, and he stiffens. "But it's the best-case scenario for me." I tilt my chin up, peering deep into his eyes as I lie. "I want to love you, Charlie." I touch his cheek. "Honestly, I do, but you can't expect miracles, and you've got to give me time to adjust to everything. I'm trying my hardest to keep everything together because I don't want to let you down. But this is all new to me, and I'm still processing, and yes, I'm still forcing some of it." I cup his face, pressing my lips to his. "But not this." I stare deep into his eyes, unblinking. "Okay?"

He bundles me in his arms and my cheek is pressed to his chest, his heart beating frantically under my ear. "I'm sorry. I just had to ask."

"It's okay. It's going to take some time for us to trust one another."

He helps me out of the car, taking my hand as we make our way inside the house.

Everyone is congregated in the formal dining room when we arrive. Sylvia and Christian. Trent and Shandra. Patrice and my father. Drew is in conversation with an unfamiliar man and woman and a stunning girl with long dark wavy hair, whom I'm assuming is his new fiancée, Alessandra Mathers.

I'm inclined to hate her on the spot, just because of my loyalty to Jane, but it's not fair to take it out on her.

"Aw, here are the newlyweds," Father says, walking toward us with a fake-ass grin on his face. He pulls me into a hug, and I nearly collapse in shock. "You look beautiful, Abigail. Marriage clearly suits you," he bellows, ensuring everyone heard him. When his hand wanders to my butt, and he squeezes, I almost throw up all over him. I have my back to the door, and everyone else is in front of us, so the only one who sees is my fake husband.

"Michael." Charlie yanks me away from my father, and the terse tone of his voice tells me he definitely saw my father groping me. "Thanks for inviting us," he says through gritted teeth. Drew has turned away from his conversation, watching us with a calm expression but I see the question in his eyes.

I wrap myself around Charlie, fighting a bout of intense shivers. Father has been a little handsy with me lately, and I don't like what it implies. I'm shaking all over as the magnitude of just how much danger I'm in hits me full force. Bile builds at the back of my throat, and my stomach churns violently.

"Abby." Shandra approaches me. "I haven't seen you to wish you congratulations." She leans in to kiss me on my cheek. "Are you okay?" she surreptitiously whispers, and I guess I'm doing a piss-poor job of concealing my fear.

"I'm okay," I whisper back as I kiss her cheek, carefully composing my features.

"Denton. Let me introduce you to my daughter and her husband," Father says, sounding every bit the proud father as he ushers Alessandra's father to us. He has dark hair and sallow skin, and his daughter clearly takes after him. He's handsome for an older dude, but he wears that same arrogant expression all the elite wear as he walks toward us with an elegant redhead clinging to his arm and I've already decided I don't like him. Alessandra's mother looks nothing like her daughter, but she's pleasant enough as she shakes my hand, offering us congratulations.

"Very nice to meet you, Abigail," Denton says, blatantly trailing his eyes up and down my body.

I cling to Charlie even tighter, and he's stiff as a brick against me, anger rolling off him in waves.

"Charles Barron." Charlie thrusts his hand out, slanting a warning look at the older elite. "Abigail's husband." Charlie holds Denton's hand in a hard grip, shaking it for longer than necessary, as he eyeballs the man without shame.

At least I know there is one thing I can count on Charlie for. As long as I'm with him, he won't let anyone hurt me. I'm convinced of it, and it goes a long way toward reassuring me.

Father chuckles, breaking up the tense standoff. "Charles is very possessive of Abigail."

"So, I see." Denton's grin is tight. "But he'll soon learn." He turns his gaze to me again, and he might as well be stripping me bare with the way he leers at me.

Fucking pervert.

I'm learning all the elite are.

The way he's looking at me reminds me of the way Christian Montgomery used to leer at me, and I'm beginning to realize this is a familiar trait.

115

I straighten my shoulders and meet his gaze dead on, refusing to cower at Charlie's side any more. "If you'll excuse me," I say, moving past him and pulling Charlie with me. "I would like to meet my future sister-in-law."

"Fucking asshole," Charlie whispers in my ear as we walk to where Drew and Alessandra are standing beside the long, mahogany sideboard.

"Hey, little sis." Drew pulls me into a hug. "He's a prick," he whispers in my ear.

"Aren't you going to introduce me?" I ask, smiling as I size up Alessandra.

She's even more stunning up close. She's tall, almost as tall as Drew, with knockout curves and legs that go on for miles. Her piercing blue eyes are much darker than Jane's lighter blue eyes, and that isn't the only difference.

It's as if Father deliberately went out and found a woman who is the complete opposite of my bestie.

I swallow over the lump in my throat, missing her more than ever and wishing she could be here even though I'm glad she's not.

"This is my sister, Abby," Drew says, forcing a pleasant smile on his face.

Alessandra's eyes travel over my green and black fitted dress with disdain. She trails her gaze up my body, smirking at my big boobs, which look ridiculous on my small frame, before skimming my face with disinterest. She fakes a smile. "Nice to meet you," she says, sounding like it's a chore to act polite.

"Same." I match her fake smile with one of my own. "This is my husband, Charlie." It's a miracle I get those words out without choking on them.

"Welcome to Rydeville," Charlie says.

"I haven't been all that thrilled at the idea of moving here," she drawls in a Southern twang, her eyes lighting up as she studies Charlie. "But things are definitely looking up." She wets her lips and bats her eyelashes at him.

What a fucking bitch.

It appears she isn't just different from Jane in looks.

She's about as opposite as you can get in every way.

"I suggest you pin those fuck-me eyes on your fiancé," Charlie says, looking like butter wouldn't melt in his mouth while his voice oozes menace. "Because I'm very much in love with my wife, and the last thing you want is to make an enemy of me and Abby."

"Oh, such promises." She winks, sliding up to Drew. "Now I'm even more intrigued."

A brief flash of irritation shimmers in my brother's eyes, but he disguises it fast. "I don't know what game you think you're playing, but try and make a fool out of me and see how well that works out for you." He smiles malevolently at her. "I dare you."

"Maybe you're not so boring after all," she retorts as the sound of heels clacking off the polished floor draws my attention to the door.

Two gorgeous girls enter the room with their shoulders back and chests thrust forward, oozing sophistication and confidence. "Who are they?" I ask, glancing out into the hallway through the open door to see if their parents are with them.

"Giselle is Alessandra's cousin and the woman with the red hair is Isabella, Alessandra's older sister," Drew confirms.

"I hope you found the bathroom okay, ladies," Father says, perving over them unashamedly.

"You have a beautiful home, Mr. Hearst," the tall redhead says, pawing at his arm as she sucks up to him.

From the corner of my eye, I spot Patrice narrowing her eyes at the girl. Perhaps she's not fully emotionless after all.

"When will they be here?" the shorter blonde asks. She's drop-dead gorgeous with long straight blonde hair falling to her butt and fabulous curves. She's wearing a clingy gold and cream dress I would kill for. Although, it's more suitable to go clubbing in than attend dinner in a stuffy mansion that's over a hundred years old.

The sound of approaching footsteps in the hallway summons the arrival of more guests. An ominous sense of foreboding washes over me and my heart accelerates wildly. All the tiny hairs on the back of my neck lift when Father swivels his head in my direction, treating me to one of his smug grins. "I do believe our final guests have arrived."

My eyes dart to Drew's, and he subtly shakes his head, letting me know he's as ill-informed as me.

My mouth is parched, my tongue almost glued to the roof of my mouth as I wait with bated breath to see who it is.

But deep down, in some subconscious part of me, I already know.

Atticus appears first, and the sight of his gloating face makes me want to commit murder.

Then two familiar forms darken the doorway, and my stomach lurches to my toes. Panic has a vise grip on my heart, and blood thrums through my veins as I stare horror-struck at Rick and Kai.

CHAPTER FOURTEEN

All the blood drains from my face as they step into the room, and I sway a little on my feet. Charlie's face doesn't betray any outward emotion, but he holds me tight, squeezing my waist in warning. I'm trying to compose myself, but I'm in a state of shock. What the fuck are they doing here, and why didn't Kai tell me in advance? Or maybe he tried to, but my burner cell has been off all morning because Charlie was around, and I don't risk keeping it on in case it vibrates in my bag and sets his spidey senses on high alert.

I can't fucking believe this.

As soon as I think things can't get any worse, they always do.

Now, it's obvious why the two girls are here, and murderous rage sweeps through me at an alarming rate. I'm primed to spill blood.

Isabella is older, so she's clearly meant for Rick, which means the knockout blonde is here for Kai. I dig my nails into my palm, fighting a host of competing emotions. I feel Drew's eyes on my back. Hear his words in my ear, and I know what I need to do. I cling to steadfast determination, reminding myself of everything that's at stake as I lock my emotions up tight.

I plant my game face on, praying I have what it takes to survive this dinner without betraying myself.

Or killing anyone in cold blood.

The bastard is introducing the guys to Alessandra's parents when I snap out of my inner rage. Kai looks briefly at me. It's a quick silent communication. A warning to follow his lead. I concede with my eyes, letting him know I'll play along.

I'm going to hate this.

I can already tell.

But I remind myself I'm doing this to protect him and to safeguard our future.

Acid churns in my stomach, clawing at my insides, and a sick feeling travels up my throat.

Father introduces the guys to the girls one at a time. Isabella looks mildly interested in Rick, but she's not gushing over him the same way Giselle is over Kai. I dig my nails even harder into my palm, wanting to gouge out her eyeballs with sticks and shove them down her throat so she can't eye fuck him ever again.

"Wow. That guy is seriously hot," Alessandra unhelpfully supplies, fixing her gaze on Kai. "I wonder if he has those tattoos all over his body," she muses, her eyes lingering on the tat creeping up Kai's neck.

"Show some respect," I snap at her. "Charlie and Drew have warned you what will happen if you step out of line." I coolly regard her, picturing her as a voodoo doll, imagining stabbing pins all over her stupid hot body.

"Do I look like I care?" She plants her hands on her hips, sizing me up.

"You should." I lean in closer to her. "Because you're in our territory, and we can make this easy for you or make you wish you were dead." She seriously does not want to mess with me right now.

"I hope there's no problem over here," Father says, creeping up on us.

"Why are they here?" Charlie asks, working hard to control his temper. For once, we are both on the same page.

"Atticus is returning to the elite and moving back to his house in Rydeville."

"I meant Maverick and Kaiden."

"Atticus's sons have a lot of catching up to do. They will be fully immersed in our society, and there's no more time to waste." Horror engulfs me. I know this is all part of our plan, but what exactly have Rick and Kai signed up for? There is no way I want my man anywhere near Parkhurst.

I consider it a good thing that neither Joaquin or Harley are here, and I know Kai and Rick did something to ensure they were kept away. But I wonder how long they'll be able to shield them from this life.

"I thought you said Kaiden was not to come anywhere near Abby," Drew adds.

"That was before your sister was married and before Kaiden came to his senses." Father bores a hole in my skull, and I hold myself rigidly still, afraid to even breathe in case I do that wrong.

This is a test.

The first of many.

He's waiting to see how I react to my ex-lover.

And I won't give him the satisfaction of winning this round.

"It doesn't matter," I tell my brother, glancing up at Charlie. "Kaiden is in the past. I'm with Charlie now."

"And Kaiden will be getting to know Giselle better," the bastard says, enjoying this immensely. "To see if she'll be a suitable bride for him." His eyes glint wickedly, and I steel another layer around my heart as I zone in on his neck, imagining my hands wrapped around it, squeezing the life from his treacherous body.

I don't know how I stand there without retaliating, but I summon restraint from somewhere. A line of sweat coasts down my spine, and I'm trembling with rage on the inside. On the outside, I'm Switzerland. Cold, serene, beautiful, and neutral.

The bell chimes, signaling dinner, and I'm grateful, because my legs are threatening to go out from under me, and I need to sit down. Father claps his hands. "Dinner is served. If you will follow me." He strides across the room, flashing a menacing look at Kaiden as he passes, grabbing Patrice's hand and leading her through the partition door into the other side of the room.

Charlie threads his fingers through mine, guiding me across the floor. I cling to his hand, needing to hold on to him to keep myself upright. Especially when Kai offers his arm to Giselle, and she clings to his side, giggling and staring at him like a lovestruck fool. "What the fuck are you looking at?" Kai hisses, shooting daggers at me.

"Nothing much, loser," I scoff, pulling my lips into a sneer, as we settle into a familiar pattern.

"I don't know what I ever saw in you," he says. "And I regret every second I spent with you."

"Touché, asshole," I instantly retort. Invisible daggers penetrate my flesh and bone, stabbing me all over, as pain suffuses my body, almost crippling me. I'm fighting tears, and the battle is real. I know he doesn't mean it, but it's hard to maintain the charade when his words cut me, slicing and dicing as if the sentiments were true. I can scarcely force one foot in front of the other, but Charlie is there, tugging me forward with a determined look on my face.

Of course, Father seats Charlie and me directly across from Kai and Giselle, and I eye my steak knife with longing, wondering how good my aim could be. If I picked it up and threw it at my bastard father, would it embed in his cold heart, plucking his lifeforce away?

As if he can sense where my mind has gone—he most likely can, because I'm an open book with him—Kai subtly kicks me under the table. It's a warning to get myself together and not be so transparent.

"Were you in an accident of some sort, Kaiden?" Alessandra's mother, Meredith, asks, casting a suspicious look over his bruised face. While his injuries are nowhere near as bad as they were a few days ago, it's still obvious something awful happened to him.

"Kaiden is into cage fighting," Father says before anyone can respond. "He's got quite the reputation in the underground circuit where he's undefeated."

That fucking asshole.

Everyone in this room, except the Mathers, knows how Kai got those injuries. Father is covering his tracks and testing Atticus at the same time, seeing how he will react.

Atticus levels a cool look at Michael, obviously displeased, but he does a decent job of disguising it.

"Oh." Meredith is definitely unimpressed.

"Come now, Meredith," Denton, Alessandra's father, says, from his seat beside me. He plants his heavy hand down on her thigh. "Look at the positives. He'll be well able to protect Giselle." He drills her with a warning look, and it's her cue to shut her mouth and focus on looking pretty.

I grind my teeth to the molars, schooling my features into a neutral expression.

"Kaiden has a four-point-oh GPA and he's expected to graduate top of his class. He'll be attending Rydeville University next fall, studying architecture," Atticus says, trying to paper over the bastard's sabotage attempt. "And Maverick is in his senior year at Harvard. He's studying to be a doctor."

"A very noble profession," Meredith says, smiling at Rick, more enamored with him than Kaiden.

"And what about you, Abigail?" Denton asks, turning in his chair to look at me. From this proximity, he can see down the top of my dress and he isn't shy about ogling me.

"I have a four-point-one GPA, and I intend to attend Rydeville University next year although I'm undecided on a program." I smile at Charlie before letting my gaze drift across the table to my father. "Unless my husband or my father has other plans for me, of course."

Kai leans back in his chair, sliding his arm along the back of Giselle's chair, smirking. "Look how far the mighty have fallen."

"Excuse me?" I act incredulous, although I'm seething inside, watching his fingers toy with her hair. She's mooning at him, looking seconds away from launching herself into his lap.

It's only an act.

He loves me.

I love him.

I tell myself this over and over, but it's fucking hard.

"I used to think you had balls."

"Kaiden," Atticus snaps. "Watch your language."

Kai ignores his father. "But you're just another weak female who can't think for herself. Pathetic. I'm glad I wised up before I made the biggest mistake of my life."

"You don't get to speak to *my wife* like that, Kaiden." Charlie straightens up, sliding his arm around my shoulders and pulling me into his body. "And I think you'll find it's Abby who wised up before ruining her life attaching herself to a degenerate like you."

"Now, now, boys." Dad thumps his fist on the table. "There's no need for a pissing contest." His gaze dances between Charlie and Kaiden.

"I don't understand," Denton says, frowning. "Is there something I should know?"

Father's jaw tightens. "Kaiden and Abigail dated for a *very* brief period. It wasn't serious."

Denton frowns again. "But I thought she was engaged to Mr.

Montgomery before she became engaged to Mr. Barron?"

I cast a quick glance over the table, and everyone is riveted, all eyes trained on Kai and me. Giselle and Alessandra seem especially interested in our drama, and that makes me all kinds of suspicious. Who exactly are these girls, and how come they were chosen for the guys?

Trent smirks at me from the other end of the table, while Shandra pins me with sympathetic eyes. "I broke off my engagement when she cheated on me with Anderson." Trent casually throws out an incendiary statement, and it goes down as expected.

Father slams his fist down on the table so hard it's a miracle the table doesn't break in two. "I will not have you spreading filthy lies about my daughter, Trent." He glares at Trent, and Christian shoots a warning look in his son's direction. Sylvia's vacant eyes meet mine, but it's clear no one is home.

"I apologize, sir." Trent is instantly chaste.

His big mouth and huge ego are going to get him in a world of trouble some day. Even the elite can't tame his recklessness. And he clearly hasn't gotten over my betrayal. Which is rich considering he was boning any female with a pulse.

I need to watch out for him.

He's still baying for my blood.

"My joke was in bad taste." Trent plasters a soft look on his face, as if he once held affection for me, which is fucking laughable. "Abby and I broke off our engagement because we realized we weren't right for one another. I'm happy for her and Charles." A wicked glint glistens in his eye as his gaze meets mine. "They wholeheartedly deserve one another."

Man, he's such an idiot. He almost recovered there. But everyone heard that insult.

"I couldn't agree more," Kai says, his lips pulling up at one corner.

He lifts his glass. "I propose a toast." I give him the stink-eye, and there's zero acting involved. "To the happy couple. May they have a long and happy marriage."

I know he's talking about us, and it helps erase my little burst of anger.

"To the happy couple," everyone choruses, but it's as fake as the tits sitting awkwardly on my chest.

Charlie is like a poker beside me, and I guess he's having murderous thoughts about Kai.

But, honestly, who the fuck knows what Charlie is thinking?

"Thank you, Kaiden. That means a lot to me." Charlie clasps my face gently, forcing my gaze to his. "Because I've loved Abby my entire life, and I've wanted this for a long time." He sends a surreptitious look at Kaiden. "Abby and I were always destined to be together." Then he claims my lips in a passionate kiss that is a deliberate F-you to both Kaiden and Trent.

I want to wrench my lips away, but I can't.

When we break apart, I force my gaze to Kaiden's, offering him a smirk, because that's how the game is played. I'm sick to the pit of my stomach, but I do what needs to be done. His glass is empty and he's gripping the side of the table so hard it's a wonder he has any nails left.

The rest of dinner continues along the same vein. Tension is so thick you could cut it with a knife. Kai and I trade barbs every now and then, but I do my best to avoid looking at him. I can't stomach watching Giselle paw at my man and listening to her giggling at whatever he's whispering in her ear. I've got nail marks in my thighs and a twisted knot in my stomach. I push food around my plate, barely forcing anything down. Every muscle in my body is strained, and I wish time would speed up instead of how it appears to be slowing down.

Alessandra has been remarkably quiet, but I'm watching her. And she's taking it all in. Building a profile of everyone, like I would do in her shoes, and that makes me nervous. I don't like her or trust her.

She's up to something.

As if we needed any other curveballs, but my brother's new fiancée is definitely someone we need to watch out for.

I make a mental note to add her and the other two girls to the list for Chad and the crew. I need to do some digging into their backgrounds.

When Kai starts feeding Giselle some of his dessert, I have officially reached my limit. My chair screeches as I abruptly stand. "Excuse me." I smile at the table, purposely ignoring Kai and Giselle. "I need to use the bathroom."

"Are you feeling ill again?" the bastard asks in a deliberate dig, and it takes colossal willpower not to launch myself over the table at him.

"No. I just need to freshen up."

"If you say so."

I want to ram my fist in his face and wipe that superior look off it.

"I'll come with," Shandra says, pushing her chair back and ignoring Trent's look of displeasure.

"I'll be back in a minute," I say, leaning down and kissing Charlie firmly on the lips.

"There's no rush." He takes my hand, bringing it to his mouth and planting a soft kiss on the back of my hand.

Rick coughs to disguise a snort while Kai gags, and Giselle predictably giggles. She's hanging off his every word, and I hate her with a passion unrivaled.

I ignore them, giving Shandra a tight grin as she joins me. We walk tall as we exit the room, but the instant I'm outside, my shoulders slump as all the stress I've been holding inside makes a bid for freedom.

"Oh my God, Abby," Shandra whispers, grabbing hold of my arm. "What the fuck is going on?"

I cast my eyes up at the camera, and she nods, understanding it immediately. Shandra Farrell is one of the smartest girls in school for a reason.

When we reach the bathroom, I pull her in with me. "Fuck my life." I shouldn't let my guard down around her. She is Trent's fiancée after all. But I honestly don't think she's into him. Anyway, even if she is on his side, I fucking need to vent. I plant my hands on the edge of the sink, looking at the strain on my face in the mirror.

"Abby." She grips my elbow, and when I turn to her, naked fear is written all over her face. "Please tell me we're on some crazy reality show and some dude is going to pop out and yell surprise at any minute, because if that is not the truth, if that"—she flings her hands in the direction of the dining room—"is actually our reality, then you might as well just kill me now."

"What has he done to you?" I ask.

Her lower lip trembles, and I know I've hit the nail on the head. "He's a psycho," she whispers. "Certifiably insane. And I know there's only so long I can hold him off." Panic dances in her eyes as she stares pleadingly at me.

It could be an act, but something tells me it isn't.

"You and I need to have a talk, Shandra. But not here." I pull out my cell. "Put your number in there." She adds her digits, and I call her. "Now you have my number too. Call anytime. I know how to handle Trent, and if I can help, I will."

"What about you?"

"What about me?" I'm instantly on guard.

"Don't do that." She frowns. "Don't be wary of me."

"Shandra, if you'd lived my life, you'd be cautious too."

She nods. "That's a fair point. And I only now realize how much I've been sheltered."

"What does Christian Montgomery have on your father? How is he forcing this engagement?"

"My father bribed a court official to acquire lands to expand his business. When the city came under scrutiny for awarding the land without it going to tender, he bribed a few more people, and it became a mess. He's not a founding father or a high-ranking elite, so he can't talk his way or buy his way out of it. Christian found out about it, approached him, and made this deal."

"Let me guess. Your father wasn't given any choice."

"He was told he had to agree to this engagement, or they'd hand over the proof and let him rot in jail."

And her father, being a typical man within this world, threw his daughter to the wolves rather than doing the right thing.

I add him to my list of bastards to take down.

"I'm scared, Abby." The truth radiates from her eyes. "Trent has been educating me on how the elite treat their wives, and how we are expected to act, and I can't do that. I *won't* do that."

I grip onto her forearms. "I'll help, but for now, you've got to continue doing what you're doing. Act like the dutiful fiancée in public. Continue to say all the right things to Trent in private but keep him at bay. The whole virginity thing is a big deal for the elite so play that card."

"I have been, but he's a horny fucking bastard who doesn't like the word no."

"You don't need to tell me. I've been in your shoes, and I hated every second of it. I wouldn't wish it on my worst enemy." Giselle pops into my head. "Screw that, I so would."

"She's pathetic," Shandra says, somehow guessing where my mind just went.

I arch a brow.

"Giselle." She pins me with a "don't even attempt to bullshit me" look. "And he has zero interest in her."

My hackles are raised again, and I pull back, folding my arms across my chest as I regard her.

I want to trust her. I really do. But I've been burned too many times to take anyone at their word.

"It doesn't matter. I'm with Charlie now. Kaiden is in my past."

"What have they done to you, Abby, that you trust no one?" she softly asks.

A sudden rush of emotion charges through me, and I gulp over the messy ball of emotion in my throat. "What haven't they done to me is an easier question to answer."

She grips my arm again. "I'm so sorry, and I know you think you can't trust me. But you can." Her eyes plead with me. "I need a friend, and I think you need one too."

"What are you suggesting?"

"Let's hang out. Get to know one another. I know I need someone I can count on to have my back, and I trust you. We have never been close. I'm not really sure why, but I have no beef with you. It seems like most women in this world are either submissive or numb." Fire dances in her eyes. "That will never be me. And that will never be you." I see nothing but the truth on her face. "You're a fighter, and I'm a fighter. Alone, we don't stand a fucking chance, but together, we just might find a way out of this nightmare."

CHAPTER FIFTEEN

I'm still fucking pissed when I arrive at the warehouse later that night. Charlie was in a funny mood when we got home. I think he's realizing he's bitten off more than he can chew. Or he's trying to figure out what's going on with me and Kaiden. I don't know, and I'm giving myself a headache trying to work it out.

He didn't put up any protest when I said I wanted to hang out with Xavier. When I left him at the house, he was watching a movie with Lillian, and he seemed lost in his thoughts.

"The others aren't here yet," Xavier says when I step into the warehouse after parking the red SUV. "But they are en route. Minus Rick. He had to return to Harvard to work on his thesis, apparently." He pulls me into his arms. "You look pissed." He gives me the once-over. "Hot but pissed."

I'm wearing a black skater-style dress over black leggings with black and gold stilettos and my red leather jacket. I left the house with my jacket stuffed in my bag and my sneakers on so Charlie wouldn't be suspicious, but I changed outside in the car.

I don't usually doll up to meet Kai, but my nerves are shot to pieces today.

And, okay, there's a teeny, tiny part of me comparing myself to *her*, which is ridic, because I know our charade at dinner was a total act, but I can't help how I feel.

And I feel threatened.

And a bit scared.

Father has the power to mess with my head, and I'm terrified of anything or anyone fucking up what Kai and I have.

"Earth to Princess Abigail." Xavier flicks his fingers in my face. "You completely zoned out."

"Sorry. I've a lot on my mind, and I *am* fucking pissed."

He slings his arm around my shoulder. "Oh, oh. What don't I know?"

I give him a cliff's note version of the dinner earlier.

He whistles under his breath. "Do you think your father is on to us?"

"I don't think so, but he's a naturally suspicious person, and he was always going to test me. Especially now Drew has planted that idea in his head." Although, it was *my idea* that Drew suggest I needed to be tested.

Talk about something coming back to bite you in the butt.

I flop down on the lumpy couch in the main section of the warehouse. "But it was a complete fucking shock seeing Kai and Rick there." I know the bastard said he was welcoming Atticus back into the elite, but I didn't think he'd move so fast or that he'd want the guys involved. Especially knowing how much he hates Kai. But understanding my father as I do, I know this is his way of testing both me and Atticus. He wants to push me to see if this act I'm playing with Charlie is real. And he wants to see if Atticus is truly back on board.

Or he's moved up a level in this twisted game he's playing.

He needs Atticus to play ball now.

But once he's elected president, I'm guessing all bets are off.

Atticus forced his hand, and he won't like that. I think he's doing what he needs to do to win him on his side, and then he's going to knock him flat on his ass again.

"They are working their father, and he's working your father," Xavier says, perching on the arm of the couch. "We should have expected this. And I hate to say it, babe, but you'll have to get used to it."

"I know." I pout, planting my high heels on the old coffee table. It's littered with empty pizza boxes and moldy coffee cups, but I find an empty space to rest my feet. "I know he's going to use Kai and Giselle at every opportunity to try and break me."

"You won't crack." Xavier's confidence bolsters my spirits.

But only a little.

"Please tell me you found something on the bastard we can use."

"We *have* found something interesting."

I sit up, slapping his arm. "You should've opened with that!"

"Let's wait for the others to get here because you know I don't like repeating myself." He glances at his watch. "They should be here by now."

"I hope nothing's wrong." I hate how my mind immediately goes there. But that's the kind of world we live in.

"Did you check your stuff for bugs?" Xavier asks, effectively distracting me from my worry.

I nod. "I check daily." I'm expecting Charlie to plant more tracking devices on me, so I use the device Xavier gave me to check my bag, my clothes, my shoes, and my cell every time I leave the house. I also check my room on the regular, paranoid about him planting a camera or listening device in there.

But so far, he hasn't.

And that makes me suspicious. I'm not naïve enough to think he's buying my act yet, so why isn't he trying anything? I'm hoping it's because I've been careful enough to cover my tracks, and that he's effectively distracted with his family situation and the business, but, when it comes to Charlie, I've learned he's unpredictable. So, I'm on edge, constantly looking over my shoulder, waiting to be found out.

"Huh." Xavier frowns, and his thoughts must mirror mine.

"There's a tracking device on the car, but that's because all the Barrons' cars are fitted with them."

"Why hasn't he tried to bug you again?" Xavier asks, tugging on his lip ring as his brow furrows.

"I've asked myself the same question, but I can't get a read on Charlie. I literally have no clue what's going through his mind. I—"

A loud noise from the rear of the warehouse cuts me off mid-speech. I stand, and a flurry of butterflies sprouts in my chest. Xavier leans forward on his elbows, watching the side door.

Kai appears first, and he stalks toward me like a marauding Viking intent on pillage.

An instant ache throbs in my core, and my legs turn to Jell-O. His eyes ooze danger as he charges toward me, and my heart speeds up to coronary-inducing levels.

A cavalcade of emotions assaults me, and I can't decipher how I'm feeling, because I'm all kinds of fucked up after today.

God, he's so fucking gorgeous when he's all pissed and angry.

I'm sick in the head.

I know it.

But this version of Kai never fails to arouse me.

I want him to take all that aggression out on my body, and I'm already quivering in anticipation.

He reaches me, grabbing my wrist and yanking me toward the secure office at the back of the warehouse. "No one follow us," he barks, tossing his command over his shoulder.

Drew scowls, looking at me with concern in his eyes. Jackson waggles his brows and blows me a kiss. Sawyer rolls his eyes, already looking bored.

Kai's hand is like a furnace in mine, and he's dragging me with him at a record pace. I totter on my heels as I struggle to keep up with him, but I don't complain because he radiates fury like a flashing beacon. He yanks the door to the office open, pulling me inside. The door slams as he kicks it shut, quickly locking it.

He turns to face me, and steam is practically billowing out of his ears.

My hand is raised before I process the motion. His head whips back as I slap him hard.

Darting forward, he grabs my ponytail, yanking my head back sharply. I cry out as a sharp sting rips across my scalp.

His mouth descends on mine in a brutal, harsh kiss that electrifies every nerve ending in my body. He grabs my butt, and my legs automatically wrap around his waist as he walks us backward toward the conference table, our lips never losing contact.

Laying me flat on the table, he takes my shoes off and tugs my leggings down my legs. All the while, his angry eyes pin me in place, and I barely risk breathing. Shoving my dress up to my waist, he slants a dark look at me before ripping my lace panties off. A cool breeze floats across my bare pussy, and a rush of liquid lust pulses deep in my core. He pushes my legs farther apart, parting my pussy lips with his thumbs, and stares at my most intimate parts. Lowering his head, he swipes his hot tongue along my slit, and a guttural moan escapes my lips.

"Fuck, yes." God, I need this. I need this so badly.

He devours my pussy, sliding his tongue in and out of my channel, while he rubs his thumb against my clit. My orgasm is already building, and I arch my back, lifting my legs and placing them on his shoulders, forcing his mouth even closer to my core.

I cry out when he roughly shoves two fingers into my pussy, thrusting them in and out in quick succession, coating them in my juices before ramming them into my ass. He pumps his fingers in and out of my tight hole, as his tongue returns to my pussy, doing wicked things to my hot flesh. My body bucks and thrashes, and my climax is building, building, building, almost reaching dizzying heights when he removes his tongue and his fingers and sets my legs down on the table.

I squeeze my eyes shut, caging the scream that begs to let loose.

He's punishing me. Stopping me from coming. And I want to rage at him. But I want to fuck his brains out more. "Fuck me now," I demand, glaring at him.

He arches a brow, not moving an inch, as he watches me squirming on the table, clearly enjoying torturing me.

"Fuck me now or I'll go home and fuck Charlie," I hiss. It's a *very* low blow, and I shouldn't taunt him. Even though we both know those words are a lie, it's still unforgivable.

A primal growl erupts from the base of his throat, and he rips his shirt off before unbuckling his jeans and thrusting them down his legs along with his boxers. His long, thick cock springs free, and I wet my lips in anticipation.

He strokes himself as he pins dark eyes on me. "I should leave you wanting for daring to say that to me." He pumps his cock harder as my hand slides down my stomach. "For daring to kiss that asshole in front of me."

"You don't want to play that game," I warn, moaning as my fingers circle my swollen clit.

"Push your fingers inside yourself, baby." His eyes are flooded with desire. "I want to see you touching yourself."

I slip my fingers inside my drenched pussy, but it's not enough. I need his cock filling me up.

"Fuck. That's hot."

"Kai, please."

He leans over me, continuing to stroke his cock. "Please, what?"

"Please fuck me!" I yell, frustration getting the better of me.

"How badly do you want my cock?"

I sit up, sliding my body to the edge of the table, and grab hold of his hips, tugging him toward me. His eyes are pitch-black as he stares at me. I grip his cock, and he jerks in my hand. I pump him quickly, rubbing my thumb over his crown, soaking up the precum beading there. "Badly." I guide his cock to my entrance, and he slams his hands into my chest, pushing me back down on the table.

He pins my knees to my chest, parting my folds and playing with my over-sensitized clit.

"Kai. Please, baby. Please. I need you inside me." I am not above begging. Tears prick my eyes, and he finally takes pity on me, slamming into me in one fast, hard thrust.

I scream, closing my eyes and pivoting my hips up as he slams into me over and over.

Yesss.

This is exactly what I need to release all these crazy pent-up emotions.

I'm grateful this room is soundproofed because the sounds ripping from my mouth are bordering on inhumane.

Kai leans over, continuing to fuck me without mercy, claiming my lips in a searing-hot kiss. Our tongues battle, and he bites down on my lip, not hard enough to draw blood but hard enough to sting. My body floods with heat, and I hug his cock tightly with my inner walls, grabbing hold of his ass and digging my nails into his taut butt cheeks. I don't touch his back, as he's still got a bandage strapped around his ribs, and I know he's in pain, because he's holding his body stiffly and sweat is pumping out of him.

He wraps one hand around my neck, applying just the right amount of pressure. Not enough to leave a mark but enough to send adrenaline coursing through my body at the implied threat. My eyes roll back in my head as my orgasm peaks and I come, screaming out his name as I feel him releasing inside me.

He didn't use a condom.

But there's no need to anymore.

The second that thought flits through my mind, a sob bursts free of my mouth. I'm not fast enough to smother it and he goes rigidly still. Then I'm lifted into his arms, and he's cradling me to his injured chest. "I'm sorry, baby. I was too rough."

I shake my head, forcing the tears to subside. "No." I press a fierce kiss to his lips. "You were perfect." I gently cup his face, completely at odds with the way we just attacked one another. "It's not that." I peer into his eyes, silently communicating what's on my mind because I can't voice those words.

"Firecracker." He winds his hands loosely through my hair. "I fucking love you so much." He kisses me with infinite tenderness, and it has the power to unravel me, rendering me into a mushy pile on the floor.

"I love you too." I press my forehead to his and our joint ragged breathing echoes around the room.

"I'm sorry," we both blurt at the same time, and then we smile. I love how in sync we are. How much we just get one another. I've never had this connection with anyone else.

I rest my head carefully on his chest, circling my arms around his waist. "Am I hurting you?" I whisper.

"Never," he whispers back, running a hand up and down my back.

We stay locked in our embrace for a while, before fixing ourselves up and putting our clothes back on.

Kai drops onto a chair and I curl myself around him, situated in his lap. "Today was fucking hell," he admits, kissing my temple. "I only found out at the last minute, and I tried to warn you, but your cell was off."

"It's okay. I know you would have if you could." I cup his handsome face. "I fucking hate her. I want to rip her apart with my bare hands. Gouge her eyes out so she can't give you those pathetic googly eyes and rip out her tongue so that incessantly annoying giggle dies an instant death."

"She's a stage five clinger," he agrees, his face contorting as he shudders. "And it killed me acting like that with her as much as it killed you."

"You hurt me," I admit. "When you said you regretted every second you spent with me." Pain dances in his eyes. "I know you didn't mean it, and I tried telling myself that, but it didn't matter. Seeing you whispering with her, and touching her, it ... it killed me."

"I took it too far." He holds my face in his larger palms. "I didn't intend to be that hurtful. I knew we needed to snap at one another, to sneer and pretend like we hated each other, but I wasn't planning on being so touchy with her."

His tongue darts out, wetting his lush lower lip, and I'm envious.

I want to be the one licking his lips.

Tasting how sweet and sexy they are.

"I let jealousy get the better of me," he explains. "He was all over you, Abby, and I was frustrated and fucking mad as hell."

"I couldn't stop him, Kai, because Father was watching us like a hawk."

"I noticed." Kai scowls. "And it wasn't just him. Everyone was watching us with bated breath."

"I'm sorry about the kiss." I drag my nails lightly through the side of his head, in the place where his skull tattoo starts, and he purrs under my touch. "I hated it. And I knew it was upsetting you, but I couldn't see any way out of it without making it look obvious."

"I know, baby." He rubs the underside of my wrist, sending delicious tingles shooting up my arm. "You have no idea how badly I want to end Charlie Barron." His eyes burn with anger, and he sighs heavily. "But I've been thinking about it ever since, and I can't deny how much he cares about you. And that's … that's a good thing."

My brows climb to my hairline. "What are you saying?"

"He's genuine in his feelings, Abby. I've always thought that, but he confirmed it today. Yes, he was all grabby hands to send me a message, but he loves you. Or at least he thinks he does."

"And you're pleased about that?" My voice is laced with disbelief.

"It's better than the alternative." His reaction shocks me into silence. "I hate him. I hate every look and every touch. But he won't let anyone harm you, and that is reassuring. I can't be there to protect you." His voice cracks, and his face contorts unpleasantly. "And I'm worrying about you nonstop. It helps that I know he'd die to save you. I still hate the bastard, but it's better he truly loves you than it being a lie."

I'm stunned speechless, and Kai knows it. He smiles, tweaking my nose.

Someone pounds on the door. "Open the fucking door, Kai," Drew shouts.

Kai's eyes widen. "I thought this room was soundproof? How can we hear him?"

"Xavier built it using this new technology developed by some Italian scientists. It's kind of like a one-way mirror for sound. They can't hear us, but we can hear them."

"Man, he really is a freak."

I thump him in the arm. "He's a freaking genius. And we're lucky he's on our side."

"Kai!" Drew roars. "I'm not fucking messing. Open the damn door before I take a sledgehammer to it and your face."

Kai laughs, and I roll my eyes. Now that we've both gotten that off our chests, it's like a weight has been lifted. I feel lighter and more reassured than when I arrived here. Kai moves to place me on the seat alongside him. "Wait." I cling onto him. I examine his face closely. "This is going to be infinitely harder than we thought." I bite down on my lip. "He won't stop testing us. Pushing us. Can we do this?"

His answering kiss is devoid of the recent tenderness and laced with resolve. "Yes, we can fucking do this." He grabs hold of my face. "We love each other, and we both understand what we need to do to protect one another and our relationship." He rubs at my cheek. "No other couple could handle this." Steely determination glints in his eye. "But we can." His eyes search mine. "Because we're one and the same, Abby, and there isn't anything either of us won't do to save the other."

Including kissing other people, it seems. My gut twists painfully at the thought of having to watch Kai kiss that fawning bitch. But if he can watch me kissing Charlie, I guess I'll just have to suck it up. I still live with the memories of Rochelle grinding in his lap and giving him head, and at least it's not as bad as that.

Plus, if Dad continues to involve him, then it means Kai and Rick will be at the wedding party in the dungeon, and more hands on deck is always a good thing.

I'll just have to focus on finding the positives in every situation forced on us rather than dwelling on the negatives.

I press my forehead to his again, ignoring Drew's latest round of insults as he continues pounding on the door, demanding we open up. "I would die for you, Kai." I mean it sincerely. "Nothing or no one means more to me than you."

His lips crush against mine again, and we are both panting when we break apart. "The only ones dying are those bastards who helped give us life." He sweeps his thumb along my swollen bottom lip. "But you and me aren't dying, Abby. We're going to do this. And we're going to live a long and happy life together."

I commit his words to memory, knowing I'll need them to keep me motivated, and sane, in the coming weeks.

CHAPTER SIXTEEN

"I still want to punch you," Drew says, glaring at Kai ten minutes later when we are all seated around the conference table, nursing steaming cups of coffee.

"Do I need to sanitize the table?" Xavier, unhelpfully asks, and Drew growls, his hands fisting into balls on top of the table.

"Chill out, Drew." I pin him with a cautionary look. "I've heard you fucking too many times to count. This room is soundproof, so at least you weren't subjected to that."

"With the way he fucking dragged you in here," he says, prodding his finger in Kai's direction, "it didn't take much imagination."

"I happen to like angry makeup sex," I admit, blowing on the top of my coffee.

Drew pales. "Not helping, A." He glowers at Kai. "Not helping at all."

"You have an issue with the fact your sister enjoys sex, or it's just Kai you object to?" Jackson asks, his eyes locking on mine in a way that lets me know he's thinking about what went down in Kai's room between the three of us.

"I have an issue with my sister being manhandled," he snaps.

"So, you've never had rough sex with Jane?" I ask, knowing full and well he has, because with the way Jane used to scream the house down, it couldn't have been anything else. I don't like bringing her name up, because it hurts my brother, but this needs to be put to bed. Kai and Drew have been renewing their friendship and I don't want this coming in the way of that. Now, more than ever, we all need to be tight.

His nostrils flare as he glares at me, purposely not answering.

"Are we done with this yet?" Sawyer asks, drumming his fingers off the top of the table. "Because I'm pretty sick of the way every conversation we have ends up in the gutter."

"Have we offended your delicate senses?" Xavier asks, smirking as he kicks his feet up on the table. I swear he's done that purely to mess with Sawyer.

Sawyer's eyes zoom to Xavier's feet and the layer of mud caked to the soles of his boots. "Someone has to try and keep things on track." He glances at Drew. "Drew is usually our guy, but someone seems to have removed his brain from his skull tonight." His gaze drills a hole in my brother's head. "Your sister has rough sex with her husband. Big fucking deal. Get over it."

Xavier grins, and Jackson chuckles. Drew flips Sawyer the bird, while Kai gloats like he's King Big Dick.

I sigh. Because he pretty much is.

Not that I'd ever tell him that. Kai's got a healthy enough ego as it is. No need to send it into orbit.

I squeeze my thighs together as my mind conjures up images of said big dick and my panties are flooded.

Man, I have it so bad.

I look sideways at him, and he grins knowingly. As if he has laser vision and can see how soaked I am for him.

I clear my throat and shake off my sex-obsessed thoughts. "Now that we've gotten that settled, what have you discovered about our father?" My gaze skirts between Sawyer and Xavier.

"Hearst Senior, the man who apparently *adopted* your father, was actually his biological father," Sawyer confirms.

Drew frowns. "But I thought his mother was a prostitute and her pimp was his dad?"

Xavier shakes his head. "Because that's the fake story he'd rather have people believe. It's better than acknowledging he's the illegitimate bastard son of a wealthy man who was screwing prostitutes behind his wife's back."

"I can't imagine that going down too well within the order or with the council," Kai says.

"It wouldn't," Drew agrees. "It's one thing to be a down-on-your-luck quasi-orphan and a ward of the state and quite another to be an illegitimate child and dirty little secret. If this was common knowledge, it would cast more doubt on his campaign."

"Maybe we should release that info anonymously," Jackson suggests.

"It could be a useful distraction," I admit, thinking out loud. "But he'll know someone is on to him then, and we risk exposure before we're ready."

"What if we pinned it on this other faction?" Kai says. "Whoever this guy is pulling my dad's strings?"

"We'd need to know who it was in order to set it up, so the blame falls on him," Drew adds. "Have you asked your father about him?"

Kai shakes his head. "Not yet. I've only started worming my way back in. If I start asking leading questions, he'll smell a rat. This has to be played carefully." Kai absently runs his thumb back and forth across the back of my hand, and it's enormously difficult to concentrate, because his touch does amazing things to my body.

"I don't think we can use it yet," I say. "Because that'll put the bastard on high alert, and he might increase his security, making it even harder to achieve our goals. I think we need to keep that in our arsenal and either we release it closer to the vote to put him on edge, or we include it in the big reveal on the day."

"Or we keep it in reserve in case we need to use it at some critical point," Drew suggests.

"Agreed," Sawyer says, turning his head to me. "What progress are we making on the wedding front?"

"Charlie seems on board," I supply. "But he hasn't set a date or anything. I intend to apply pressure this week, so it moves along."

Anger rolls off Kai in waves, and I kiss him quickly on the lips.

"I've mentioned it with Father. Presenting it as the ultimate test," Drew says, his mouth pulling into a tight line. He tugs at his collar. "His eyes actually lit up at the idea." He stares at me. "And it makes me unbelievably nervous. If he gets you down there, Abby, he could try *anything*."

I lean forward in my chair as Kai's hand wraps around my arm. "I'll be with you or Charlie at all times," I remind him. "I know how dangerous it is, and I won't risk going anywhere alone."

"I'm fairly certain Rick and I will be invited," Kai says. "We can help keep a lookout."

Sawyer pulls out his phone. "I'll get some earpieces from Dad," he says, not looking up as he taps out a message. "He has these new prototypes they're developing. They are tiny little buds that slot into the ear. Virtually unnoticeable unless you were looking. You can all wear them and keep in contact with one another."

"How can I score me some of those?" Xavier asks, his eyes glimmering with excitement.

"You can't." Sawyer gloats.

"Not even for sexual favors?" Xavier rests his elbows on the table, staring intently at Sawyer. "I'm up for anything in the bedroom. You can do whatever you want to me. Nothing is off-limits." He waggles his brows, and his tongue darts out, toying with his lip ring.

Drew spits coffee all over the table, and Jackson throws back his head, laughing, because the expression on Sawyer's face is priceless. It's a cross between wanting to throttle Xavier with his bare hands and wanting to test him to see if he means it.

I can't see Xavier and Sawyer on the same wavelength to ever start something permanent. But I wonder if they'll end up hooking up at some point. There is enough tension between them to suggest that's a possibility.

"Screw off, Xavier. Hell will freeze over before I let you touch my cock," Sawyer says, and Kai rolls his eyes.

"What about the security system in the dungeon? Any luck there?" I ask, not even attempting to disguise my deliberate change of subject.

Sawyer shoots me a grateful look. "Drew found some old plans from the time the place was constructed, and we're building a picture of the layout. My father has given me a couple of trustworthy guys, and they are working around the clock to infiltrate the firewall and to descramble the video footage from Christmas Day. Your father obviously hired guys who knew what they were doing to set the whole thing up, but my dad's guys are better. We'll get there."

"Great. I've had a few conversations with Chad, and the team is primed and ready to go but they need some place to work." I glance at Xavier. "Would you be willing to let them work from here? I was thinking we could clear out that space at the rear of the main room, put in desks, and you already have the technology all set up."

"Can they be trusted to keep the location secret?" Xavier asks. "Because I've spent a small fortune building this place and I don't want to risk losing it. *We* can't risk losing it."

"I'll drill that point home, but they won't say anything."

"Because you have shit you're blackmailing them with?" Jackson asks, grinning.

"It's more than that. They are loyal to me and Chad, and that's why they'll keep our confidence." The truth resonates from my words, and it feels good to know I have people who have my back, no matter what.

"I'll work with Chad and Xavier this week to get it set up," Drew confirms.

"Let me know when it's ready, and I'll ask them to meet me here during the day while Charlie's at work. I'll split up the targets and set them working on it," I add. We only have one more week left before school starts back, and we need to make the most of it.

"What else do we need to discuss?" Drew asks, casting a glance at his watch.

"Assuming our reconnaissance goes well, and we get the intel we need during the wedding party, how will we get rid of Father long enough to have an opportunity to break in and steal those files?" I ask.

"The annual Parkhurst meeting is the second week in February," Drew says. "It's an important meeting, because it's the last big one before the presidential vote in April. Charlie, Trent, and I will be expected to attend with Dad and Christian, so that gives you ample opportunity to break in and get the files."

"That's six weeks away," I grumble. "Do we really have to wait that long?"

Kai slings his arm around my shoulders, pulling me in close and pressing a kiss to my temple. "It sucks, but we'll need that time. To plan the party and the surveillance and the break-in."

I'm just thinking of our lengthy separation and how challenging it'll be keeping Charlie out of my bed, and my panties, for that period of time.

"Will my father be invited to the annual meeting?" Kai asks.

Drew taps a finger off his chin while he thinks about it. "Most likely, but I think it's doubtful you and Rick will be included. If this is the first time Atticus is attending a meeting after being exiled from the elite, he will be required to attend several interviews with the existing council members. If they approve him to return, then you and *all* your brothers will be added to the training and induction program."

"Over my dead fucking body will I allow my younger brothers to be brought anywhere near that place," Kai seethes.

"You won't have much of a choice, Anderson," Drew says, shooting him an apologetic look. "You are all sons of a founding father. There will be no exceptions made."

"Your father must know this," I softly add.

"He does," Kai says, in a clipped voice. "Rick and I had to threaten to walk away for good in order to get him to agree to leave Harley and Joaquin at home today. He's determined we will all be inducted into the elite way of life."

"You'll just have to deflect and defer as much as possible," I say. "But it might be no harm if you get access to Parkhurst. You might spot shit Drew has become immune to."

Drew jerk's his head up, scowling.

"No offense, D. But you have been brainwashed to some degree. Having some fresh eyes around the place can't do any harm." Not that I want Kai exposed to that, *at all*, but it could be advantageous.

Drew sighs, scrubbing a hand across his jaw. "I suppose that's a fair point. I'm pretty much immune to the shit I see now," he admits, looking apologetic. "But I can remember what it was like at the start." He shudders, pinning Kai with a somber look. "It's going to be ten million times worse than you imagine. And there will be a lot of eyes on you and Rick, so I'm not sure how useful it will be." He slouches in his chair, staring up at the ceiling, looking like he's drowning under the weight of all his sins.

A sixth sense prods me in the back, and I just get the feeling something else is going on.

Drew and I aren't as close as we once were. There was a time when we could finish each other's sentences and we always knew what the other was thinking. As we've gotten older, that has faded somewhat, but the twin connection is still there, simmering away under the surface.

And it's prompting me to pry.

"Drew."

He lowers his eyes, turning to look at me. "Yeah?"

I examine his face carefully. "Is there something you're not telling me? Telling us?"

His Adam's apple jumps in his throat. "Why are you asking me that?"

I tuck my hair behind my ears, maintaining eye contact. "Call it intuition." I shrug. "My gut is telling me something is going on. That you're hiding something."

He exhales heavily, sitting up straighter, shooting me a shy smile. "I never could keep anything from you for long."

I stand, walking to his side and crouching in front of him. "We agreed no more secrets."

"I've kept this one for a reason, A." He tenderly cups one side of my face. "Because I didn't want to say anything until I was sure. I didn't want to get your hopes up only to dash them."

"But?" I prompt.

"But I can't do this alone." He looks at Xavier.

A light bulb flashes in Xavier's eyes. "This is something to do with that research you had me doing on Parkhurst employees?"

Drew nods. "I was hoping to find something, anything, I could use, to blackmail one of them into helping."

"But they are all squeaky clean," Xavier adds.

"Why were you digging into Parkhurst employees' records?" I ask.

"And why was it confined to staff working in the medical facility?" Xavier asks.

Every nerve ending in my body is on fire, and bile travels up my throat, as my mind works overtime. "Drew?" I whisper. "What's going on?"

He hauls me up into his lap, locking his arms around me. His breath oozes out in spurts, and he looks anxious as fuck. "Please forgive me, Abby. I was going to tell you when I had proof, but I haven't found that yet. Other than assumptions I've made based on things I've heard and seen over the years, and my gut instinct, which tells me I'm correct, this is still supposition."

"Spit it out, D." He's killing me here, and I'm wound as tight as a ball of yarn.

"I don't think our mother is dead, Abby. I think the bastard locked her up in Parkhurst and he's been hiding her there the entire time."

CHAPTER SEVENTEEN

Drew's arms tighten around my back, and that's the only reason I haven't slumped to the floor. "What?" I blurt, sure my ears must be deceiving me. "Why?" I croak. "Why would he do that?"

"Think about it. She's insurance. In case he loses control of us."

My brain is grappling with a hundred different strings, and I can't form words.

"Because if your mom is still alive," Sawyer says, following his train of thought. "Then he is still in charge of Manning Motors. No shares will transfer to you when you turn eighteen if your mother is alive and they are still married."

I turn it all over in my mind, because it's confusing as fuck at the best of times. Mom's shares in Manning Motors transfer to Drew and me on our eighteenth birthdays unless I'm married, and then, my shares automatically go to my husband, thanks to elite bullshit sexist rules. However, if I'm pregnant and I don't marry my baby daddy, then the shares are forfeit and my father automatically retains them. Dad "marrying" me off to Charlie was supposed to seal the deal for him. Charlie has already signed a legal contract transferring those shares to my father upon my birthday. However, if my mother is still alive, then the bastard automatically still retains them.

I'm giving myself a headache trying to figure this all out.

Drew vigorously nods his head. "Exactly."

"But why is he engaged to Patrice then?" I ask, emerging from the confusion in my mind.

"To look good in front of the council," Drew says. "If he was in such a hurry to marry her, he would've set a date *before* the vote, but they've set a date for the end of the year. I'd be surprised if that wedding ever goes ahead. She's a means to an end right now. That's all."

"But if she is … if she's alive, what's he planning to do? It's not like he can just roll her out after all this time? How would he explain it?"

"It wouldn't be easy, because to the outside world, she is gone. But he can't contest that will unless he brings her forward."

"Do you think the council knows?"

He shakes his head. "The council doesn't hold women in high regard, but Mom is the daughter of a founding father, and Dad is only in his position by virtue of marriage. If they discovered he faked her death, and locked her up without any real justification, they would not be pleased. But he's clearly been planning this for years, and he needed a backup in case it went tits up. Which is why I think he's kept her alive," Drew explains.

"How is he getting away with that?" Sawyer asks.

Drew shrugs. "My best guess is she's in there under a false name. That few, if any, know who she really is."

"And no one gets visitors," I confirm, because I didn't see anyone getting visitors during my time there, and Wyatt mentioned how most of the patients are signed over and basically forgotten about.

"Oh my God." Tears well in my eyes, and I clamp a hand over my mouth as the memory hits me full force.

"What is it?" Drew gently takes my wrist, pulling it away from my mouth. A chair scrapes behind me.

"I think you're right." My voice wobbles, and tears stream down my cheeks as Kai firmly lifts me out of my brother's lap, holding me against his warm body. I fist my hand in his shirt, clinging to him, my heart beating ninety miles an hour. Resting the side of my head against Kai's chest, I face my brother. "I think she came to me. When I was there."

Shock splays across my brother's face, and you could hear a pin drop in the room.

I swipe at the moisture under my eyes, lifting my head up, but keeping my arms wrapped around my husband. "I thought it was a dream," I recall. "Because the bastard had just given me that letter—" I gulp over the painful lump in my throat, momentarily squeezing my eyes closed as remembered heartache assaults me. Kai runs his hand up and down my back, pressing soft kisses to the top of my head.

I box up my emotions and soldier on. "I was upset. I'd cried myself to sleep, and at some point during the night, she came to me." I lock eyes with my twin. "You remember how I used to conjure her in my mind's eye when she first passed? Whenever something sad or painful happened?" He nods. "It hasn't happened for years, but I was so consumed in grief I thought it was my mind's way of helping me cope."

I shuck out of Kai's hold, leaning down over my brother. "But what if it wasn't? What if it was her? If she'd somehow snuck into my room?" I remember how real her touch felt, and hope swirls and churns in my gut. "And something else weird happened." I cast my mind back. "Fuck. I'm such an idiot." My eyes widen as I lean onto the arms of Drew's chair. "There was an incident with some woman in the psych ward when I was going to breakfast one morning. Cryptic comments were made, and I had a gut instinct about it." My stomach is throwing somersaults. "I think that was her, Drew." Butterflies are going crazy in my chest. "I think you're right."

"If I am," he says, a fresh layer of pain contorting his handsome face, "then we need to get her out of there before it's too late. If Dad is elected president, and you turn eighteen, and he believes your shares are his—"

"Then he has no further need of her," I say, finishing his sentence.

Heavy silence engulfs the room as everyone understands the enormity of what's been left unsaid. If Mom is still alive, it may not be for much longer. Her life is at risk unless we get to her first. We need to act fast. "What were you planning in relation to the staff investigations?" I ask.

"I was hoping to find some dirt on someone and use it to blackmail him or her into talking or at least giving us access to the system so Xavier could search their records to see if she was there."

"If she's there, she's enrolled under a pseudonym." We've already agreed we think that's how it went down. "She's not on some computer system," I say, shaking my head. "That's far too risky for Father." I prop my butt against the edge of the desk, blown away at the prospect she might still be alive. But I won't allow myself to believe it either. Because my heart can't sustain any more blows. For now, I'll allow myself to tentatively hope. But that's as much as I can permit.

"There is one person who knows the truth," Jackson says, his eyes darting briefly to Kai's.

"Christian Montgomery," Sawyer says.

"You think I haven't thought of that?" Drew says. "I wanted to ask him, but the truth is he'll say jack shit, and it's too dangerous. He'll tell Dad, and God knows what he'd do then. We can't take a chance, because if she *is* still alive, we can't jeopardize her safety."

"Jesus, Drew." I press my palms on my knees and lean forward, looking right into my brother's eyes. "Has she been alive this whole time?" He clasps my hands. "And what have they done to her in that Godawful place." A tremor wracks my body as I recall how they violated me, and I was only there for five weeks. If we're correct, she's been there over ten years.

Imagine the horrors inflicted on her in ten years.

A sob flees my mouth, and my lower lip wobbles as tears pool in my eyes again. "I can't bear to think about it," I choke out. Warm arms wrap around, me and Kai pulls me into his chest again.

"Don't do this, baby." Kai hugs me fiercely. "Right now, we don't know anything. I hope she's alive, and if she is, we'll help her deal with the aftermath."

"I shouldn't have said anything," Drew says.

"No! You shouldn't have kept your suspicions from me this long," I cry out.

"You've been through so much already. If I'm wrong…"

I swipe at the hot tears coursing down my face. "Let's just investigate the staff. There has to be someone we can get to."

"We'll need all hands on deck," Xavier says. "Even with Hunt's father's guys, Chad and his crew, and us, we are swamped."

"We've got one week left of Christmas break. If we divvy up tasks between us, we can make good progress."

"It's not going to be enough. We're talking about investigating board members, elite members, Parkhurst employees, and trying to hack into the security system in the basement, plan a wedding and a break-and-enter, and we've all got school. You're working Charlie. Drew's working your father, and Kai is working Atticus. It's too much in the timeframe we have to work with."

He's right, and I'm wracking my brains trying to think of a solution when Sawyer speaks. "Leave it with me. I'll talk to my father about setting up a special project team. He has thousands of employees in his company with the kind of skill set we need. I'll get us more bodies."

I cock my head to the side. "Why does your father help us?"

"There are many reasons," Sawyer says before clamming up.

"You should go," Drew says. "You don't want to make Charlie suspicious."

"Just one more thing. Shandra and I had an interesting talk in the bathroom today."

"I thought that might be the case," Drew says. "And?"

"And she's not on board with the whole arranged marriage, and she hates Trent." I snort. "Not that that's in any way hard to believe, but she indicated we could be allies. What do you think?" I ask my brother, as he's the only one here who has any real knowledge of her.

"I've always liked her," Drew admits.

"Me too. She's smart and she doesn't ruffle feathers. She avoids drama and divas and she's always seemed super focused."

"What's your gut telling you?"

"That I should explore it but stay sharp."

"Then do that," Kai says. "She seems genuine, and she knows how to play the game. You would never know she hates Montgomery from the way she conducted herself today."

"That's not necessarily a good thing. She could be playing me."

"It doesn't seem likely," Kai says. "I think you should give her the benefit of the doubt."

"She also told me what Christian has on her father." I proceed to fill them in. "You could make that go away fast, right?" I ask Xavier.

"A few keystrokes and the evidence would be kaput," he says.

"Maybe I can use that to keep her on our side," I muse.

"I wouldn't do that," Kai says. "It might set the relationship off on the wrong foot if she's sincere."

I shrug. "Or maybe, I tell her when she's proven herself we give her the evidence as reward for her loyalty. She can use it to screw over Trent and his despicable asshole father." I loop my fingers in the band of his jeans. "I need to go." I look up at him, hating the thought of leaving him again.

He kisses me slowly, uncaring we have an audience. "I hate this part," he whispers over my lips.

"Me too," I whisper back, yanking him in closer to me, my body heating again. One round with Kai is never enough, and I wish I could go to bed by his side and wake up with his heavenly arms around me.

"One final thing, Abby," Xavier says. "I created that dossier file we discussed before, and I have everything set up. If anything happens to any of you, it will be sent to the leading local and national TV and radio stations."

"Thanks, Xavier. You're the best."

"I helped," Sawyer says, pouting a little.

"Aw, you're the best too, Sawyer." I mess up his hair, knowing it will freak him out. Sure enough, he scowls, swatting my hand away and attempting to tame the errant strands of his dark hair.

Xavier is right. Sawyer is wound up too tight, and he needs to loosen up. Not for the first time, I wonder what his story is.

The guys leave first, and it's as if Kai has taken half my heart and soul with him. I drop onto the lumpy couch, psyching myself up for returning to Charlie.

"I know it sucks, babe," Xavier says, flopping down beside me and circling his arm around my shoulder. "But it won't be forever."

"It doesn't make the goodbyes any easier. It kills me. Every time."

"I'm happy for you, Abby. I don't think I've said that. Me and the caveman haven't gotten along in the past, but I'm fully Team Kaiden now." He twirls a lock of my hair. "He loves you, girl. Like really loves you. Don't let your bastard father come between you, because then, he's really won."

The next week flies by way too fast. New Year's Eve comes and goes, and it's the dawn of a new era. Or that's what I tell myself. Because this is the year I will free myself from the chains my father has kept me in. This is the year he will finally get what's coming to him.

It's a flurry of activity. Setting Chad and the crew up in Xavier's warehouse. Digging into our investigative work. Keeping Charlie happy without letting him get too close. Trying to coax Elizabeth into coming out of her room. Trying really hard not to get too excited over the idea Mom is still alive, but the more I think about it, the more I'm convinced she was in my room. That it wasn't a figment of my imagination.

And if she was, she must have had help.

That bolsters my spirits.

If we can just find out who, we might have our way in.

Father gives the wedding party his stamp of approval and a date is set for the end of the month. Charlie gives me free rein on the planning. Telling me to do whatever I want. No expense spared. He's working crazy hours, and I don't usually see him until nine or ten p.m. each night. Which makes it easier to sneak out a few times to meet Kai.

It's Sunday night, and it's the night before we return to school. I told Charlie I was catching a movie with Xavier, but I'm in the warehouse with Kai, both of us sprawled across the couch, naked, with only a flimsy white sheet covering us, wrapped around one another. Xavier left, giving us privacy, and I love him for it.

"Are you still in pain," I ask, lifting my head up from Kai's chest.

"Now, she asks," he quips, winding his hands in my hair.

"I probably should've asked before I attacked you," I admit, grinning as I remember how I jumped all over him the second he arrived without giving a moment's thought to his injured ribs.

"I like how you attack," he murmurs, nipping at my earlobe. "Feel free to jump me anytime."

"I *will* take that literally, you know."

"I'm counting on it." He smiles, hauling me up his chest and capturing my lips in a slow-moving kiss. When he kisses me like this, like he has all the time in the world, I feel like the most cherished woman in the world. No measure of time will ever be enough with this man. I will love him to infinity and beyond. "And it barely hurts anymore. Rick knows his stuff."

"He's going to make a great doctor," I agree.

"I have something for you," he says, leaning down and pulling a package from the inside of his jacket.

"It's not my birthday," I say, taking the pink package from his hands. It's a small rectangular shape and semi-heavy.

He sweeps my hair off my shoulder. "I don't need a reason to give my wife a present."

"I love it when you say that," I whisper, pecking his lips.

"I love saying it," he admits with a smile. "And I only wish I could say it more."

"Soon, hon. Soon." I sit upright, and the sheet pools at my waist. I scowl at my naked breasts, still hating the sight of them. They are way too big for my slim frame, and they just look ridiculous on me, like two big melons planted on my unsuspecting rib cage. And they are so obviously fake, which only makes me hate them even more.

Kai notices my scowl and he pulls the sheet back up, tucking it in under my arms, and I fall in love with him all over again. "Fuck, I love you," I say, my eyes brimming with emotion.

"Love you, too, firecracker. Now open your present."

I tear at the pretty wrapping, unveiling the brown leather album inside. I open it up and gasp. "Is this what I think it is?" I ask, fighting tears as I flick through the first few pages.

"I wanted you to understand how much you mean to me."

"There are so many," I say, flicking through his drawings of me. Some of them are familiar, from times I went snooping in his sketch pad. But most are new. "When did you draw all these?" I ask, running my finger over the drawing of me standing beside Kai at the office in city hall where we got married. The look of euphoria on my face perfectly sums up how I was feeling that day. We didn't take any photos, because we couldn't risk any evidence, so I know he's drawn this from memory. "It's beautiful." I tip my chin up. "You are incredibly talented, and I'm so lucky you're mine." I lean into him, kissing him passionately.

"Thank you," I say, holding the album to my chest, embracing it like the precious gift it is. "I love it."

He caresses my cheek. "I wanted you to have a physical reminder of our love. For the times when I'm not there, and you need to feel the strength of my feelings for you." He looks a little sheepish as he continues explaining. "Those sketches represent everything I'm feeling deep inside. I poured my heart and soul into them, and drawing helps me feel connected to you, especially when we're apart."

He pulls me back into his lap. "When I need to see your face, and I can't physically be with you, opening up my sketchpad is the next best thing. It helps me visualize you from a happy memory or imagine a future one. And it gives me hope." He kisses my cheek. "I want it to give you hope too. To help reinforce our love at times when we're tested, because it is going to be tested, but I never want you to doubt my love." He kisses my other cheek. "I want you to always remember how much I fucking love you, because you are all I see. Always."

He always knows what I need to hear, and this is perfect, because I've been stressing out over him being forced to bring Giselle to my wedding party as his date. With this gesture, he has allayed all my fears. Now, I'll just need to find some secret hiding place in my bedroom to keep it, because there's no way I'm not taking it home with me.

"You have no idea—" I cut my words off when I see the alarmed look on his face. "What is it?" Panic bubbles up my throat.

He looks down. "Abby," he chokes. His panicked eyes meet mine. "You're bleeding."

"What?" I look down, and my stomach twists and turns. A bright red circle stains the sheet in my lap, growing wider.

I climb off Kai, letting the sheet drop to the floor, standing on wobbly limbs as I examine the streaks of blood running down my thighs with disbelieving eyes. My panicked gaze darts to Kai's, and I sway on my feet as a multitude of questions flit through my mind. He stands, grabbing hold of me before I tumble to the floor. My mind is churning over possibilities, as hope simmers under the surface of my skin. I stare at the blood, wondering if I'm imagining it. "Can you see it?" I whisper, peering deep into his eyes. "The blood between my thighs. Is it really there?"

He nods, looking worried. I clutch onto his arm. "It's not real," I whisper, as tears pool in my eyes.

"It's real, baby," he says in a soft voice. "I see it."

I shake my head. "I meant what my father said," I clarify. "About the hysterectomy. It's not real. The bastard lied to me again."

CHAPTER EIGHTEEN

"Baby." Kai's tortured eyes meet mine. "We can't be sure of anything, and right now, I need to know that you're okay. That this—"

"Isn't a sign that something's wrong. That I haven't healed after the operation," I say as my brain catches up to his.

He nods, brushing hair back off my face, trying to mask his concern.

"But it could just be my period," I whisper, wanting so desperately for it to be that.

Another flash of pain sweeps across his retinas, but he composes himself fast. "I think we should call Rick." He holds onto me with one arm while bending over to grab his cell from the coffee table. "Are you in any pain?"

Only emotional, thanks to the maelstrom building in my mind. I shake my head, existing in a dazed state of shock. "I feel fine." I don't even feel a twinge.

"Did I hurt you?" he whispers as he waits for the call to connect, confirming his mind is tossing out ideas too.

"What? No!" My stomach twists painfully at the thought that something might've ruptured inside me when we were fucking, but

Kai wasn't rough with me tonight, and I honestly don't think it's that.

Or maybe I'm just delusional because I want this to be my period so badly.

"Rick, we need your help," he blurts into his phone, holding me tight to his chest. "Abby is bleeding, and we—" He hands the phone to me, putting it on speaker. "He wants to talk with you."

"Hey." I barely recognize my voice. Kai snatches the sheet, folding it over and concealing the bloody patch, before wrapping it around my body as I shiver against his naked form.

"Talk to me. Where are you bleeding? Are you in pain?" Rick asks. "Do you have a temperature or feel unwell?"

"No. Nothing like that. I'm fine. I … I think it's just my period."

He sucks in a sharp gasp. "Are you sure?"

I snort out a laugh, even though this is no laughing matter. "I've had enough of them to know, but we're not sure." I swallow over the lump in my throat, locking eyes with Kai as I speak. "Could it be something else? Like what if they botched up the job at Parkhurst and something is wrong inside me?"

Kai's face pales, and he runs a hand up and down my back, keeping me close.

"How heavy is the blood flow?" Rick asks.

"It's not that heavy," I confirm, feeling a tiny flow trickling down my thighs. I should really get cleaned up.

"Then it probably is your period, but you need to get checked out. Can you come up to the city tonight? I have a good doctor friend we can trust. He already offered to run tests. I'll call him now."

I shake my head even though he can't see me. "Not tonight. I'm due home soon, and Charlie will only get suspicious."

"Fuck Charlie." Kai fumes. "Your life could be in danger. We'll think of something to tell him. Set it up, Rick. We'll be there as soon as we can." He doesn't give me a chance to argue, ending the call and wrapping his arms around me. Not that I'd protest. I didn't want the tests before, because I was scared. Scared to confront reality, but now, in the face of new hope, I sure as fuck want them.

Tears prick my eyes, but I hold it together. I can't celebrate just yet. Not until I know it's not something else. Blood trickles down my legs, and I wriggle out of Kai's loving embrace. "I need to use the bathroom." I snatch my clothes off the floor, hugging them to my chest.

He nods, pecking my lips. "No matter what it is, I'm in this with you. You feel me?"

"I feel you," I whisper. He plants a feather-soft kiss on my lips. "Love you."

"I love you too."

"Go." He gives me a gentle nudge. "Do what you need to do, and I'll call your brother."

I stop my forward trajectory. "I don't want to worry him."

"He'll go apeshit on your ass, and mine, if he finds out we didn't call him. Besides, we need him to drive us. You've got to leave your car here, and we can hardly go in mine. And I want to hold you. I can't do that if I'm driving."

Be still my beating heart. Seriously, this guy. He slays me. In the best possible way.

"Okay. Call Drew," I agree. "And ask him to stop at the store on his way and grab some pads." Drew has done it so many times for Jane or me that I know he won't bat an eyelash at the request except for what it might mean.

"Got it," Kai says, shucking into his jeans as I walk toward Xavier's small bathroom.

I emerge ten minutes later, fully dressed and cleaned up as best I can. Kai is on my cell, wearing only his jeans, with the top button open, and my libido notices. Fuck. He's so damn hot with his ripped, toned abs, that carved V-indent at his hipbones, broad shoulders, and the magnificent ink painting his arms, chest and neck. I lick my lips, trying—and failing—not to drool. I wipe the dried blood off Kai's lower stomach with the warm washcloth I found in the bathroom as he ends his phone call.

"You have an alibi," he says, and I arch a brow as I pat his stomach dry with a hand towel. "Hope you don't mind, but I got Drew to call Shandra. He told her we have a bit of an emergency without going into the deets. She agreed to tell Charlie, or anyone who asks, that you were hanging at her house tonight."

I chew on my lip. "That's still kinda risky. If I'm not back at a reasonable hour, Charlie might come looking for me."

He tugs his shirt down over his head. "Shandra will cover it." He sits down, lacing up his boots. "It will be a good way of testing her. You don't need to tell her where you're going or with whom, just that if anyone asks you were at her place."

"Okay," I concede, because I need answers, and it can't wait.

Reeling me into his arms, he peers deep into my eyes. "Stupid question, but are you okay?"

"I don't know," I truthfully reply. "I'm scared to hope too much."

"I know, babe," he whispers. "I'm feeling that too."

"I'm pretty sure it's my period. I'm just afraid to hope. Plus..." I sigh, averting my eyes.

He tips my chin up with one long finger. "Plus what, sweetheart?"

My chest heaves, and slicing pain rips through me. "If it's true, it means the babies are truly gone," I whisper.

During the day, I work hard not to think about all the shit that bastard has put me through. But, in bed at night, alone and missing Kai, my mind wanders. To avoid confronting reality I like to imagine different scenarios. Especially the theory where I'm still pregnant and

Father was planning on passing it off as Charlie's. But that's completely ruled out now if this is my period.

Meaning the bastard *did* abort my twin babies.

Pain does a number on me, and a sob rips from the back of my throat, as I relive the agony all over again, but I hold it together. Just about. I'm an emotional cripple right now, and it won't take much to set me off, but I try to keep my emotions at bay. At least until we know exactly what is going on.

Drew picks me up from Shandra's after I dropped off my car and had a quick chat with her. She let me use her bathroom, and I grabbed a few tampons. She asked me if everything was okay but didn't pry beyond that, and I'm really starting to like her a lot.

I climb into the passenger seat beside Drew and wave at Shandra as he reverses, beginning the journey back down her driveway. Drew hands me a paper bag, and I kiss his cheek. I try not to stare at the back seat where Kai is lying on the floor, staring at me with that intense look of his, and it's damn hard, because I need to wrap myself around my husband and get lost in him so I can't think about shit until we reach Boston.

Once we turn out of Shandra's driveway, he sits up, wiggling his fingers in a come hither gesture. I vault over the console into the back seat, throwing myself into his arms and kissing the shit out of him until Drew loudly coughs.

"Seriously?" He eyes me through the mirror. "How do you expect me to concentrate on the road when I have to listen to those slobbering sounds?" He fakes a shiver. "Gross."

"I happen to like slobbering all over your sister," Kai retorts, pressing his lips to my collarbone, eliciting shivers all over my skin.

"I've noticed," Drew deadpans.

"He's helping distract me," I say, rushing to Kai's defense. "Unless, you want me bouncing off the seats the entire journey."

"Are you okay?" Drew asks, his attempt at humor drying up as he runs his eyes over me from head to toe, checking to make sure I'm okay.

"I feel fine, honestly. I don't think this is anything bad."

"I hope you're right," he says.

Silence engulfs us for a few beats until I break it. "If I'm right, it means he lied. Why would he do that?" I rub at a tense spot between my brows. "I mean, I know he's a sick fuck, and he's not above toying with me, but what does he have to gain by this?"

A dark glare crosses Drew's face. "Maybe he's hoping you'll stop using birth control and that Charlie will get you pregnant?"

Kai growls. "If you want to get out of this car in one piece, I suggest you don't repeat that statement." He tucks me in under his side. "Although it sounds like something your twisted father would dream up, I think we should keep our theories on hold until we find out what we are dealing with."

"Relax, Abigail," the good-looking doctor says, rubbing the gel-like substance all over my flat tummy. "I won't bite." He glances at Kai. "Unless you ask nicely."

"And I won't beat you to a pulp if you stop flirting with my wife and get to it," Kai says, sounding like butter wouldn't melt in his mouth as he delivers his threat.

The doctor friend of Rick's chuckles. "Rick told me you were possessive. Just wanted to test it for myself."

The doctor runs the handheld device over my stomach, squinting as he stares at the monitor. Kai has a tight grip on my hand, and we're both barely breathing. "Well?" I rasp, unable to stand it any longer.

He turns to me with a smile. "Everything looks perfectly normal."

"You mean?"

"You still have a womb and ovaries." He wipes the gel off my stomach, and Kai pulls my shirt back down, looking as shell-shocked as I feel.

"What?" I rasp, sure my ears must be deceiving me.

He pats my hand. "Everything is as it should be. In full working order." He smiles. "You can conceive and carry as many children as you like."

My lower lip wobbles, and the tsunami is growing in strength inside me, building and building until it explodes, ripping through me with violent energy. Everything I've worked hard to contain releases in a rush, and I burst out crying, trembling, and shaking as powerful emotion takes control of me.

CHAPTER NINETEEN

Sobs wrack my body, birthed straight from my soul, and I fall apart in Kai's arms. I can't speak over the tightness in my chest and the anguished cries emerging from my mouth. It's too much. I can't deal. Emotion overtakes me, and I can't stop crying—it oozes out of me, like a river overflowing its banks, bursting forth in welcome relief. My chest heaves, and I cling to my husband, needing him now more than ever.

Kai holds me, whispering soothing words, and running his hand up and down my back, as the doctor discreetly exits the room.

"He lied," I sniffle, staring at him with tears pumping out of my eyes. "That fucking bastard lied."

"For once, I'm glad he did," Kai admits, smiling through a haze of tears.

A tingle starts at the back of my skull, expanding as the thought grows. I run my fingers up my arm and I feel it. "Kai," I rasp, taking his hand and placing it in the same place on my arm. "Do you feel that?"

He frowns. "What is it?"

"I felt it once before in the shower, but I didn't pay much attention to it." I remember thinking it was probably something they did to me at Parkhurst, related to one of the surgeries they performed on me, and not being overly bothered by it. If I'd thought to consider it more carefully, I might have pieced it together. I stare at him, confused as to what the actual fuck is going on. "I think it's the hormone implant." He looks puzzled so I elaborate. "It's a form of birth control," I explain.

His brows knit together. "I don't understand."

"I don't either," I admit, "but something is definitely off."

The doctor pops his head back into the room. "Is it okay to come back in?"

A goofy smile graces my mouth as I let the full magnitude hit me. "Sure," I choke out, my throat almost closing with emotion.

"This is the best news ever," Kai says, leaning down to kiss me. I hold onto him, grinning like a loon, and I pinch myself, because I'm struggling to believe this is true.

The doctor approaches, holding a different type of handheld device. "I'd like to examine your cervix," he says, "but I'll need to do that via a vaginal ultrasound if that's okay?"

A growl leaves Kai's mouth, and I squeeze his fingers as I nod at the doctor. I'm not leaving here until he's checked me thoroughly to ensure there are no more surprises.

He works quickly, avoiding looking at Kai, which is a smart move, because he looks like he wants to shove him out the window and watch him go splat on the sidewalk below. After he's taken blood, a urine sample, and checked my blood pressure, I ask him about the little lump under my arm. His warm fingers press down in the exact spot. "That is definitely a birth control implant. I'd put money on it." He smiles reassuringly. "Have you had any nausea, headaches, mood swings?"

"All of the above. And I was incredibly tired for a few weeks."

"I'm not surprised," he admits, removing his gloves and tossing them in the trash. "Your body has been in a heightened state of trauma after the abortion, the breast augmentation surgery, and being constantly drugged for a couple of weeks would've altered your body's natural rhythm and zapped your energy too for a bit." Rick obviously clued him in on stuff, but I can't fault him for being thorough, because I know he was doing it in my best interests. "Everything you have felt has been normal."

"So, Abby hasn't had a hysterectomy and she's protected from pregnancy?" Kai clarifies, and I'm glad to hear he can actually form words, because all he's done is growl at the doctor since we came in here.

"That is correct." The doctor's face falls. "I don't know the specific circumstances, because Rick explained it was safer that I didn't know, but I was shocked when he told me someone had done that to you. I'm embarrassed for my profession, because no doctor with any moral code would even consider something so heinous. Especially to a young woman with her whole life ahead of her."

He has no clue about the world we live in. And how that violation isn't as heinous as some of the stuff being doing to those poor young girls in that dungeon.

"Well?" Drew asks, when we step outside, having thanked Rick's doctor friend. Rick looks to his brother.

"The bastard lied," I confirm. "They didn't perform a hysterectomy on me."

Drew pulls me into his arms. "Oh, thank fucking God." He hugs me close. "I'm so happy for you, A."

Rick has Kai in a bear hug when I shuck out of Drew's embrace.

"At last, some good news," Rick says, bending down to kiss my cheek. "God knows it's overdue. I'm over the fucking moon for you, Abby."

Kai tucks me in under his arm. "We are too." He looks into my eyes, kissing the tip of my nose. "But I'd really like to know what's going on. What does Hearst have to gain from lying?"

"He's been trying to break her spirit," Drew says. "But she keeps fighting back. He needed her to marry Charlie, so maybe it was just a threat to ensure it happened."

"He knew I'd marry Charlie to keep Kai safe. He didn't need any insurance."

"Maybe, we won't ever know," Rick says.

"We all know he's a twisted fuck," Kai adds, as we start walking along the hallway toward the elevator. "So, maybe, it was just a mindfuck to him. Maybe there is no reason for it."

There's no denying Father is cruel for cruelty's sake, so Kai's assertion could very well be the truth.

As we drive back to Rydeville, my mind churns endlessly, trying to figure it out. Something the doctor said has stuck with me, and I can't get it out of my head. Something is just out of my reach. Something poking and prodding at the back of my mind, silently screaming at me to wake up and realize it. It's frustrating the hell out of me, and I'm wracking my brains to work it out.

"You okay?" Kai asks, tilting my face up to his, and a ping echoes in my mind as it finally dawns on me.

I twist in the back seat, glancing between him and Drew, as I scramble to decipher my thoughts. "I'm trying to figure it out," I admit. "And I'm wondering if Father was telling the truth."

"I'm not following," Kai says.

"What if he said it because he genuinely believes it to be true?" Drew's eyes widen as his train of thought aligns to mine. "What if he demanded that of the doctor at Parkhurst, but instead of fulfilling his wishes, the doctor didn't perform the surgery and implanted the birth control implant in case I accidentally got pregnant, to hide what he'd done?"

"Why would he do that?" Kai asks. "They are all monsters."

"Maybe this guy has a moral compass. Maybe not all of them are monsters." I sit up, poking my head through the gap in the two front seats. "Maybe we've just discovered a way to identify the ally in the medical facility we've been looking for."

There's a new spring in my step the next morning, and I can't describe how ecstatic I am to know I haven't lost the ability to carry children. That I can someday look forward to nurturing Kai's baby in my belly. That I can experience pregnancy with all its pros and cons, just like every other woman.

I'm also buoyed by the thought there might be someone with a conscience in the Parkhurst medical wing, and if we can find out who this person is, he may be willing to tell us whether our mother is incarcerated there or not. I remember a couple of male doctors attending to me, but it might've been the same guy. So much of those first few weeks is a blur because I was doped up, and we can't rely on my memory.

Xavier and Sawyer are already on the case, because Drew and Kai met with them late last night. I wanted to be there, but I had to get home before Charlie sent out a search party. He was waiting up for me, and he gave me his version of the Spanish Inquisition, but I got out of it by letting him sleep in my bed and spoon me under the covers.

Shaking off that gruesome memory, I switch back to last night's meeting and the subsequent messages Kai sent me after. Xavier and Sawyer are working to infiltrate the IT system in the medical facility to see if they can find any records of doctors who treated me. If that information is not on file, they can pull up a list of all the doctors listed as employees at Parkhurst, and we can start checking their backgrounds.

It's a hell of a lot easier than doing background checks on every single employee who works in the building, and it should deliver more immediate results.

So, yeah, I'm in a good mood.

And Charlie notices.

"You seem happy?" he asks, sipping his coffee and eyeing me circumspectly over the rim of his mug.

"Is that a crime?" I tease, pouring a cup for myself while I wait for my toast to pop.

"Not at all. I'm just curious what's put that big smile on your face?"

"I'm going wedding dress shopping today," I say. It's not a lie. While I was waiting on the guys to pick me up last night, I asked Shandra to come with me after school. She attends yoga downtown at the same time I attend ballet, so it suits both our schedules. We also discussed meeting up after our respective classes, as a standard agreement, to get to know one another better. It was her suggestion that we remain aloof at school, so Trent doesn't suspect we're talking behind his back, and I liked it, because it's exactly what I would do.

Charlie stands, walking to my side with a huge smile on his face. My toast pops, and I yank it out of the toaster, yelping as the heat singes the top of my fingers. He presses his body up against me from behind, and I force myself to remain relaxed. Brushing my hair aside, he plants a kiss on my cheek. "I'm happy you're happy." He runs his fingers down the side of my neck, and my breath stutters in my chest. "And I can't wait to see you in it."

"I asked your mom if she wanted to come," I truthfully say. "But she passed."

He sighs, stepping away from me, and I release the breath I was holding. "I'm worried about her," he says. "It's been almost two weeks, and she's getting worse."

"There's no time line on grief," I say, buttering my toast and taking my plate and mug with me to the table. "And she's hurting. You need to be patient and gentle with her."

He takes the seat across from me. "I know. But I'm worried about Lillian. She's floundering too. And she needs someone. I wish I had more time to spend with her, but I can't leave the business until it's on a more secure footing, and things are still a hot mess."

"I can hang out with Lil, and I've offered several times, but she always turns me down." I take a big bite out of my toast, noticing the time on the wall clock behind Charlie's head. I need to get my ass in gear, or I'll be late for school on our first day back.

"She's a little shy around you, because she's always looked up to you." Surprise splays across my face. "And she doesn't know how to act around you."

"She told you that?"

He nods. "I told her to just break the ice, but I think it'd be nice if you could maybe ask her to go to the salon with you or something."

"I'll see if she wants to do something this weekend. I can book a spa day." I smile sweetly at him. "I need to start beautifying myself for our big party."

He stretches his hand across the table. "Thank you. And you don't need to do a thing. You are already the most beautiful woman I've ever known."

"It's no biggie," I say before stuffing the remainder of my toast in my mouth so I don't have to respond to the second half of that statement.

Romantic Charlie scares the heck out of me. Because it makes me believe the Charlie I knew is still in there somewhere, and I worry he's doing it on purpose to try to draw me out. I'm on tenterhooks around him all the time. Constantly on edge. Terrified in case I say or do the wrong thing.

I can't ever forget what he's done.

If he can get his father killed, Kai would be no skin off his back.

My stomach heaves at the thought, and I hope I'm not about to be reacquainted with my breakfast.

"I love you." He rubs circles on the back of my hand with his thumb. "And I got you something," he adds. His lips curve up at the corners. "I left it in your room."

"You don't need to buy me stuff, Charlie." It's getting a little ridiculous. Every day, he returns home with a bouquet of flowers, even though I've told him it's not necessary. And he's the one who rang up Madam to inquire when ballet classes were starting up again.

I don't want him doing nice shit for me, because it fucks with my head and makes me feel guilty.

He moves my hand to his mouth, planting a kiss on my knuckles. I work hard not to scowl and wrench my hand away even though my body is screaming at me to do that. "You're my wife. If I want to spoil you, I will."

He doesn't get that I don't need or want expensive gifts.

Kai's album of drawings means more to me than all the flowers and gifts in the world.

"I've got to go," I say, removing my hand from his and standing. "I can't be late."

"Let's meet for dinner after your appointment," he says. "I should be able to sneak away early, as I don't have any late meetings scheduled today."

"I can't. Ballet starts back, and I arranged to meet Shandra for a bite to eat after."

He leans back in his chair, arching a brow. "I didn't know you two were close."

"We're not, but she'll be marrying Trent in the summer, and considering we're all part of the elite and going to be spending more and more time together, I figure I should get to know her better. I've always liked her anyway."

"I can't imagine Trent is happy for you two to spend time together."

I walk to the sink, placing my dishes on the counter. "What he doesn't know can't hurt him."

Charlie rises, grabbing his suit jacket from the back of his seat. "Be very careful, Abby. And don't tell her anything she can use against you."

I cock my head to the side. "Why do you say that?"

He walks to my side, running his hands through my hair. "Because Trent has a long memory and he hasn't forgiven you. I wouldn't put it past him to use Shandra to try and get to you. Watch your back."

CHAPTER TWENTY

"What are you doing?" I ask, as Charlie steers me toward the door.

"I'm giving you a ride to school because I haven't had my fill of you today." He grabs me to him, kissing me passionately, as is his usual style. Guilt smacks me in the face, like always, but I keep my guard up, smiling softly at him when he breaks our lip lock. "Fuck, I love kissing you."

"You're an amazing kisser." It's the truth, and I try to be truthful where I can, especially if it gets me out of admitting stuff I don't want to admit.

Like how I fucking hate kissing him because it feels like a betrayal every time.

But I don't have to enjoy it to know he's got a skillful mouth. Although I don't like thinking about how he learned to use his mouth so effectively. Because then, I'll definitely hurl my breakfast.

"I'll have someone drop your car into the parking lot during lunch. The keys will be left for you in the secretary's office."

"That's really not necessary," I protest, already knowing this is a bad idea.

"We hardly get to spend any time together," he pouts, doing his best impression of a sulky teenage girl. "I want to drive my wife to school."

I smile, shrugging. "Okay. If you insist." I let him lead me outside to the garage with a pool of dread building in my stomach.

"Have a great day, darling," Charlie says, pulling right up to the curb at the front entrance of Rydeville High. I know he's done this on purpose, and any goodwill I was feeling toward him earlier evaporates.

My heart plunges to my toes when I look out the window, spotting Kai, Jackson, and Sawyer watching us from the top step. I quickly turn around before I'm accused of staring at them. Charlie cradles my face between his palms as he leans in, kissing me deeply. I want to die, over and over, with each brush of his lips, and I'm praying Jackson or Sawyer had the good sense to drag Kai inside. I don't want him seeing this shit, because I know what it'd do to me if I had to watch him locking lips with someone other than me.

It would fucking destroy me.

Charlie pulls back, and I want to pound my fists into his chest, and scream in his face, but I give him my best doe-eyed look instead.

"Enjoy your dress shopping and dinner with Shandra. I'll see you tonight." He glances over my shoulder—at Kai, I'm guessing, and my heart lurches at the thought he witnessed our kiss—as he winds his hand into my hair, pulling me toward him and kissing me even more enthusiastically.

Pain infuses my chest, making breathing difficult, and I'm close to losing control. In my mind, I visualize myself slapping him away, but it does little to help. "I'm going to be late," I murmur over his lips, unable to stand it anymore.

"I will never get tired of kissing you, Abby," he says, pecking my lips again, and he's really fucking overdoing it. "And I'm glad you're giving us a chance." He looks behind me again, and his eyes narrow as he pins me with a dark look. "But if I find out you've had anything to do with him, I won't be responsible for my actions."

I shove him away from me. "Are you threatening me?"

"I'm just reminding you of your promises."

"I don't need a reminder," I hiss, curling my hand around the door handle. "Do you?" He doesn't answer, and I'm instantly suspicious.

Climbing out of the car without uttering another word, I wonder if Charlie is really working late in his office every night or if he's up to some extracurricular activities. I know he's at the office, because the tracker Xavier put on my phone shows him there every night. But if he has somehow discovered the tracker chip, it wouldn't be difficult for him to leave his shoes there and go someplace else in other footwear.

Everything is a mindfuck, and I long for the days when life is simple. When all I have to worry about is what I'm cooking for dinner or whether I need to put another load of laundry in.

Mundane sounds absolutely blissful, but it's a long, long way off.

Especially with Charlie acting in a way that makes him unreadable.

And that worries me.

He still refuses to tell me who he was fucking the night of our wedding, and I'm sensing there's more to this story. If we weren't already too freaking busy with everything else, I might try to investigate it. But, unless it becomes a necessity, it will have to remain on my "like to do" list.

Slowly, I climb the steps, as Charlie drives off, glad the new elite have vanished into the building because I can't look at Kai after that blatant PDA in the car.

"Do you always let him maul you in public like that?" Alessandra sneers, standing alongside my brother and fixing me with a derogatory look. "Or was that just for shits and giggles?"

"Why don't you do us all a solid and fuck off back to whatever shithole you crawled out of," I retort. Unfortunately, Alessandra has transferred here now. She is also staying at my old house and doing her best to infiltrate our lives. She's a Class-A bitch, and Drew says she's all up in his business, and it's driving him insane. "It's not as if any of us want you here. Least of all my brother."

At least her annoying cousin has gone back home, and I don't have to stomach her every day. If I had to show up to school and see Giselle draping herself all over my man, I'd be up on a murder charge in next to no time.

"You'd better get used to me, *sister*," she drawls, tossing her dark hair over her shoulder. "Because I'm going nowhere."

Drew steps right up into her face. The neutral expression he's wearing gives nothing away, but the lethal chill in his voice even scares me a little. "You will speak respectfully to my twin sister, or I'll be forced to show you exactly how the elite ensure females toe the line."

All the blood drains from her face, and she takes a step back. "You can't threaten me."

"Oh, honey," Drew says, his lips curving into a smug smile as he leans casually against the door frame, looking like an angel while spewing venom from his mouth. "That wasn't a threat. It was a promise."

"Get over there and bend over the desk now, firecracker," Kai commands while locking the classroom door and pulling the blinds down. Sawyer and Jackson are keeping watch out in the empty hallway. This part of the building is usually like a ghost town during lunch break, but we can't take any chances even though I issued a warning this morning, through my network of trusted crew, reminding everyone I hold their dirty little secrets in the palm of my hand.

If anyone spills anything to Charlie, they are going down.

And I'm not afraid to make an example of someone to prove my point.

I think about fighting Kai on his demands, but he's hurting, and I want to help ease his pain. I knew that shit this morning would be playing on his mind all day, so him grabbing me in here wasn't completely unexpected. I saunter toward the desk and lean over it, like a good little wifey.

He pulls up my skirt and yanks my panties down. "Kai, I…" I start to say, remembering my period when he cuts me off mid-speech by yanking the tampon out of my pussy and tossing it in the trash can. My mouth hangs open, and shock splays across my face at the casual way he did that. Honestly, I have no words.

His hand comes down, slapping me once across the ass, and pure liquid lust floods my core. That's the only warning I get before he's thrusting inside me with his bare cock, slamming into my pussy repeatedly, reminding me I am his. Not that I need the reminder. But I think he needs the reassurance, and I won't deny him that. He plunders me, drilling me with all his pent-up rage, and I take it like a dutiful wife, pressing my ass back, urging him to go harder and deeper.

My orgasm creeps up on me out of nowhere, and Kai holds his hand over my mouth, stifling my screams of pleasure. He grunts when he comes, and I feel his hot cum filling me up, cranking my arousal to new heights because there is something so fucking hot about feeling him release inside me with no barrier. He cleans me up with some tissues, and I grab a fresh tampon from my purse, locking eyes with Kai as I turn around, splay my legs, and let him watch me pushing it up inside me.

"I'm a sick bastard," he admits, "because that seriously fucking turns me on."

I grab some wipes from my bag, sterilizing my hands and watching as Kai cleans my blood off his dick before tucking himself back inside his pants. "I guess I'm a sick bitch, because watching you wipe my blood off your dick fucking turns me on," I say, pulling my panties back up and fixing my skirt into place.

He laughs, and it's so rare to see these days that it warms all the frozen parts of me. My stomach flip-flops, and my heart starts beating to a new rhythm. "Sounds like a match made in heaven," he purrs, opening his arms. "Come here, Mrs. Anderson. I need to kiss you."

I swoon at his words and float into his welcoming arms. His kiss is tender, and I melt against him, closing my eyes and savoring his taste and his touch. He must have vanquished his demons with our fast, hard fuck because he's taking his time kissing me, making love to my mouth, and I'm drowning in him, never wanting to come up for air.

But we do. Because we know our time is limited.

"I'm so sorry about this morning."

"Shush." He places a finger over my mouth. "Don't apologize. I should have left the instant he pulled up." He rests his forehead against mine. "We both know what we signed up for."

I ease back. "I was just thinking this morning how fantastic it would be to just have normal mundane shit to worry about."

He nods slowly. "Like bringing the car in for an oil change or getting the furnace serviced," he says.

"Like anything normal," I say, rubbing my thumbs against the side of his neck.

"We will have that one day soon. I promise." He dots little kisses all over my face.

"Where do you think we'll be this time next year?" I ask.

"Living in our own house together. Going to bed wrapped up in you and waking up with your scent all over my skin," he says without hesitation, and I melt again.

"God, I want that so bad."

"I will give that to you. That's a solemn promise."

"Where?" I ask.

He shrugs. "Wherever you like. Here. Another part of the US. Abroad." He shoots me a wistful smile. "We can go anywhere, and I don't care where it is as long as I'm with you."

Tears spill out of my eyes. "I can't believe this big old softie lives underneath this rugged exterior," I say, trying to laugh over the messy ball of emotion in my throat, as I run my hands up and down his impressive chest. "I'm so proud to be your wife, Kai." I clasp his face in my minds. "And I can't wait to shout it from the rooftops."

A rap sounds on the door, and we both sigh in unison. He presses a firm kiss to my lips. "Love you, baby. Be safe."

"Love you too." I fling my arms around his neck, clinging to him, not ready to let him go. "You'll always be my caveman, and I'll follow you to the ends of the earth. All you have to do is ask."

CHAPTER TWENTY-ONE

"You look absolutely stunning, Abby," Shandra says as I peer at my reflection in the mirror during my scheduled appointment at the haute couture wedding store. I run my fingers along the tight corset top and full-bodied skirt. This dress is not something I would ever pick for my wedding day. But it's perfect for what I have planned.

"I agree." The store owner appears on my other side, beaming. No doubt, dollar signs are flashing before her eyes.

"I'll take it," I confirm.

Her grin expands. "Excellent."

"But I'll need a few alterations."

Shandra quirks an eye. "What are you up to?"

I sway my hips, twirling in the dress, watching the slow smile spread across my mouth in the mirror. "Ensuring my gown is elite-worthy."

"Do I want to know?"

My lips tip up. "The less you know, the better."

The run up to the wedding party flies by, because I'm crazy busy organizing it with the wedding planner I hired, supervising Chad and the team as they build dossiers on our targets, sneaking time with Kai behind Charlie's back, attending school and ballet classes, hanging out with Shandra, bonding with Lillian, and worrying about Elizabeth, who has become a virtual recluse. Charlie is going out of his mind, and it's cruel to say it, but at least it keeps him distracted.

I nearly puked when I opened his gift to discover three flimsy silk and lace nightgowns, and my stomach roiled at his subtle way of trying to move our relationship forward. I suppose I should consider myself lucky it wasn't lingerie, because the thought of Charlie shopping for bras and panties for me breaks me out in a cold sweat.

But it's getting harder and harder to hold him off. I'm still playing the betrayed wife card, but I can only get away with that for so long.

It's the night of the party, and I'm seriously on edge. Because there's a lot riding on tonight. And I fucking hate being back in this mausoleum. Hate being back in my childhood bedroom where the memories are more bad than good, and I detest being back under *his* roof. At least I'm not staying the night although it's of little consolation, because I'm also scared of what Charlie expects when we get home after the party.

He's been dropping hints about tonight being our proper wedding, and I know what he's implying. The only way I can think of getting out of it is to drug him again, and it's most likely what I'll end up doing.

I stare at my reflection in the mirror, happy I at least appear composed on the outside. All eyes will be on me tonight, and I want to really give them something to stare at. My hair is in a classic chignon, and it's the only part of my outfit that could be described as traditionally elegant. My scarlet lips match my black and red dress, and they give me a much-needed boost of confidence. The makeup artist gave me heavy smoky eyes rimmed in lashings of thick, black mascara. I have naturally long lashes, and they frame my eyes perfectly. None of those fake spider-web lashes for this girl.

I run my hands down over the black and red taffeta of my dress, smirking as I think of Father's expression when he sees me. I'm sure he expects me to turn up in virginal white.

But fuck that.

I'm going into the lion's den, and I need to show them I mean business.

Showing up like the virgin bride would only have them frothing at the mouth.

I'm not naïve. I know what's going to happen tonight.

Father is testing me.

And I fully expect to see doped-up girls in cages and men old enough to be their fathers abusing and debasing them.

I rub a hand along my stomach, fortifying it, because I can't break tonight. Otherwise, arriving like this has all been for nothing.

I need to show up there like a boss. To show them I belong in this world. But not as a puppet on a string.

I'm the daughter of a founding member, and I know that gets me automatic special privileges.

But I know it doesn't protect me from evil.

There are men gunning for my father. Men he doesn't know the identity of, so it's quite likely some of them will be in that room.

None of them will think twice about using me to get to him.

Which is why I have my small handgun strapped to my left thigh and a pen knife strapped to my right one.

If any of those men dare come at me, I *will* fight back. I'm quick on my feet, thanks to years of ballet and self-defense lessons, and no one is putting their hands on me tonight. I don't care about the consequences.

The bastard will be furious.

He'll want to discipline me.

And Charlie might be willing to go there again.

But it will be worth it.

To claim this one small victory

A rap on the door rouses me from my inner monologue. "Come in, Drew." I know it's my brother because he's escorting me to the dungeon. This isn't a traditional wedding ceremony because we've already said our vows. This is just the celebration part although I use that word in extremely loose terms, because there is zero to celebrate.

Still, we have roles to play.

Drew will escort me to Charlie in the dungeon, and we will then be announced into the room.

The party kicked off an hour ago, and everyone should be in attendance by now. My black, red, and gold gothic-themed décor downstairs might have already given the game away, but I guess I'm about to find out.

Drew sucks in a sharp breath. "Abby," he whispers, as I turn around to face him.

I jut my leg out, planting my hands on my hips as I strike a pose. The slit in my dress runs to just above my knee, so it's not indecent, and it hides the weapons I'm concealing, yet it gives me easy access to them too. The bottom half of my dress is made up of layers and layers of black and red taffeta, with subtle applique accents. It swishes around my legs as I sway my hips, grinning at my brother. His eyes drop to the wide blood-red sash tied at my waist, drifting quickly over the fitted black corset-style top with the slightly plunging neckline that showcases the hideous melons on my chest.

If I'm regretting anything, it's that I didn't get the neckline moved up higher. The point of this is not to have the men tripping over themselves but to demonstrate I'm a force to be reckoned with and not one to be pushed around so easily.

I know how to conduct myself, and I'll be the epitome of the well-brought up young lady.

Unless I'm crossed.

And then my claws will come out.

"Holy fuck. You look magnificent." He kisses my cheek. "That dress is … wow, and you look beautiful, but he's going to blow a gasket when he sees you're not wearing white."

"I know. But I'm not walking down there in sheep's clothing."

He nods. "I get your point, but I'm not sure it's wise." Little beads of sweat form on his brow. "Keeping the elite away from you is one of our biggest challenges tonight, and you've just made that harder.

"Don't." I lift my hand. "Don't ruin my mojo. I did this for *me*, Drew. To take back some control. And even if I'm punished for it, it will be worth it. No one will come near me, because I have you, Kai, Rick, Charlie, and Chad, and some of the others there, watching my every move, and I know how to protect myself."

There is safety in numbers, and I managed to convince Father to let me invite a couple of the guys from the inner circle to the party. It's not the done thing. Events in the dungeon are usually reserved for the higher-ranking elite, but Charlie supported my call, staying true to his word to give me whatever I wanted. I did a number on him with my whole dream wedding bullshit, and he fell for it hook, line, and sinker.

Of course, I couldn't get Father to agree to let the girls attend. Sexist pig. I'm betting he only declined because he knows he can't touch any of them. Not without causing a backlash within Rydeville, so he has no use for them.

But they are all here tonight anyway—the girls from our investigative crew. Working as part of the catering company staff. Xavier falsified paperwork and got them hired, much to my relief. I feel more secure knowing we have eyes and ears dotted around the room.

Drew steps closer. "It's not too late to call it off. We can say you have food poisoning or make up some other excuse."

I cup his face. "I'm not backing out of this. It's too important. We have planned this well, and you and I are the only ones who stand a chance at getting into the back offices to snoop. Going it alone is too risky. We all agreed it takes two. One to snoop and one to take point guard." I tweak his nose. "Stop worrying. I've got this." I realize it's the truth as the words leave my mouth, and a layer of anxiety flitters away.

I'm on edge, yes, but a lot of it is adrenaline. And I'd think there was something wrong if I wasn't feeling antsy.

"It's not you I'm worrying about," Drew says, sighing. "It's all those other fuckers."

"You won't let anything happen to me."

He nods, breathing heavily. "Here." He pulls a small plastic pouch from his inner jacket pocket. "I almost forgot about this." He takes out a small egg-shaped thin silver object. "This part goes in your ear." I take it from him, fitting it in easily. "And this part needs to be concealed somewhere on your upper torso so we can all hear you," he adds, holding out a flat round silver disc.

I slip it in under my corset top, pressing it down, and it instantly adheres to my flesh. "At least these boobs are good for something," I mutter.

"The ear bud is active, but you need to press the communication chip if you want to speak or you want others to hear the conversation you are in. It will feel warm against your skin when it's active and cool when it's not."

"It's warm," I say, feeling a little heat spot on my boob.

"You activated it when you were putting it on." Drew chuckles.

"What's so funny?"

"Atticus is trying to give Kai a pep talk about how to conduct himself tonight except it hasn't gone down too well."

My lips tip up. "What did he do?"

"He punched him in the face."

I grin. "That's my man."

"Thank you, baby." Kai's dulcet tone filters through my ear like warm chocolate.

"I can hear you!" I exclaim.

Kai quietly laughs. "At least we know it's working."

"I can't believe you punched him. Or, actually, I can. He's long overdue a punch or ten."

"He's overdue a lot more than that, and if you'd heard the shit he was spouting, you'd have wanted to punch his lights out too."

Bile swims up my throat. "Is *she* there with you?"

"She's over the far side of the room. I'm here with Chad, pretending to talk."

I draw a long breath. Tonight is going to be challenging in more ways than one.

"We can do this, baby," Kai says. "This brings us one step closer to our goal. Just keep thinking that. And I'll keep her at arm's length. I promise. I don't want you distracted worrying about her. Trust me to handle her."

Which is more than I can do for him. Tonight will be torture for Kai, and I can't be selfish. "I'm fine. Do what you have to do. None of us can afford to lose sight of the end goal."

"I love you, Abby."

Drew smiles, not even attempting to hide that he's listening.

"I love you, too, babe."

"If you two lovebirds are done," Rick says, his deep voice tickling my ear. "You better get this show on the road. Charlie is getting an ear bashing from your father over why you aren't down here already."

"We're on our way," I say. "See you in a few minutes."

I loop my arm through Drew's, watching as he taps out a message to Charlie, telling him our ETA. He guides me out of the room, closing it behind me. "Ready?" he inquires.

I pick my head up, thrust my shoulders back, and plant my game face on before eyeballing my twin. "Let's do this."

CHAPTER TWENTY-TWO

The trek from my bedroom to the underground dungeon takes longer than usual, thanks to my voluminous dress. But eventually, we reach the end of the dark passageway, stopping in front of the last door. Noise permeates through the wood, confirming the party is in full swing on the other side.

"You sure about this?" Drew asks me again.

"I'm sure." I hold onto his arm tighter, ignoring the wild fluttering in my chest. "Let's do this."

He opens the door, and Charlie is there, standing in front of the black curtain, which is the last barrier to breach. Heavy pulsing beats reverberate in the air, joined by the loud chorus of voices laughing and talking.

Shock splays across Charlie's face as he stares at me. His jaw is slack. His eyes widen, as he rakes his gaze over me from head to toe. "Abby," he whispers, stumbling as he takes a step forward. "You look ... incredibly beautiful. I ... I seriously have no words."

"You're not disappointed?" I coyly ask, swirling the dress around my hips as I look at him through hooded eyes.

"Disappointed?" he chokes, recovering and walking toward me with confidence. "I will be the envy of every man out there." Before

I can say a word, he sweeps me into his arms, dips me down low, and kisses me until I see stars.

Fuck.

I hate when he does that.

Because his lips are the wrong lips.

And I don't want them touching me.

It's going to be a freaking long night.

"You'll ruin her makeup," Drew deadpans, effectively breaking Charlie out of whatever lust-fueled fantasy he's in.

Charlie straightens us up, pulling his lips from mine. "Fuck." He stares at my lips, and I'm guessing my red lipstick is smeared halfway across my face. Taking my purse from Drew, I open my mirror and do a quick repair job.

"We can't let any of them near her," Charlie says, his voice laced with concern.

I close my compact, sealing it in my purse.

"Agreed." Drew nods. His plan to worm his way back into Charlie's good books hasn't happened because Charlie is always working and there has been little opportunity for them to spend time together. Drew has purposely hung around the house after visiting me, to catch Charlie for a few minutes, but things are still strained between them. Except when it comes to my safety, where they are always on the same page.

Drew looks down at me. "You stay with me or Charlie at all times."

"I understand the situation I'm walking into. I'll behave." Charlie looks skeptical, and I can't blame him with my track record. I lace my fingers through his. "I don't want any of those assholes touching me, so trust me, I'll be sticking to your side like glue."

He leans down, pressing a feather-soft kiss to my lips. "Thank you, darling. I can't bear the thought of anything happening to you."

He gently pulls me to him, careful to keep my face away from his chest so he doesn't ruin my repair job.

Drew watches us, locking eyes with me, and I can tell what he's thinking. He sees how much Charlie loves me. How it's not even a hint of a lie. I swallow back bile, reminding myself of the things he's done. It's the only way I can hold the guilt at bay.

Chad pokes his head through the curtain. "Your father is about to lose his shit." His eyes pop wide. "Holy fuck, Ab—"

"What the hell is the hold up?" my father hisses from somewhere behind Chad.

"Get rid of him," I plead, because I want him to see me for the first time out in the room.

"They are ready, sir," Chad says. "You can tell the orchestra to start."

"He's gone," Chad whispers a second later. "See you out there." He waggles his brows at me. "Fucking love the dress. You own it, girl."

I blow him a kiss.

"He's going to freak," Charlie whispers in my ear. "But I'm guessing you already know that."

"He wants me to be a part of this world, Charlie," I say, peering up at him. "So, this is what he gets."

"I respect you so much, Abby," he says, and I barely manage to hide my snort of derision.

Yeah, he respects me so much he fucked someone else the night of our wedding.

What a load of bull.

Sad thing is, Charlie believes his own press.

"I'm sorry your mom isn't here," I say, squeezing his hand.

"I'm not." A muscle clenches in his jaw. "She's far too fragile, and I don't want her surrounded by vultures." He hurriedly composes himself as the music starts. "It's better she's not here."

"It's showtime," Drew confirms, moving to the curtain. "I believe that's your cue." I nod, and Charlie loops my arm in his as we start walking. "Knock 'em dead, little sis," Drew whispers, and I cling to his words as the butterflies in my chest turn circles. Adrenaline courses through my veins as the announcer introduces us to the room.

I helped plan the setup, yet it's still a visual assault on the senses as we round the bend, halting at the top of the room while everyone gets to their feet, clapping. The walls have been covered with sheer red drapes, and the bulbs in the chandeliers have been replaced with red-tinted ones. Circular tables, seating ten, are artfully arranged in the center of the room, around the rotating bar. Black silk tablecloths cover each table, and all the place settings are in red and gold except for the smattering of white rose petals tossed abstractly over the top. Tall rose bouquets, consisting of red and black roses, look darkly elegant as centerpieces.

The stage at the back of the room is also decked out in red and black silk drapes, and a row of candelabras in different sizes line the front of the area. Lighting has been deliberately turned down low at that side of the room, and the soft flickering of candles adds an eerie quality to the ambiance. A twelve-piece orchestra is playing my music of choice. A fantastic rendition of "All I Ask of You" from *The Phantom of the Opera*, complete with a male and a female singer who are nailing the powerful emotion of the piece. I've little doubt Father is seething as he listens to the words, especially when he locks eyes on me and all the blood drains from his face.

His eyes trail down my body, his lips pursing, and when he lifts his head back up, the look he gives me is so evil it sends shivers all over me. Gulping, I eyeball him, not backing down from the silent face-off. His eyes burn with quiet rage, and he pulls Patrice in closer to his side, digging his nails into her waist and doing little to disguise it.

Panic bubbles up my throat, but I force it back down.

I knew I'd get this reaction, so there's no point freaking out about it now.

Shocked gasps ring out around the room as Charlie leads us forward. I don't know where Kai is, but I feel his eyes burning a hole in my back as we walk along the red carpet, greeting our guests.

"You are my every dream brought to life, Abby," Kai whispers through my earpiece. "You are exquisite. I could live a thousand lifetimes and never be worthy of your heart."

I want to tell him he's wrong.

That it's I who would never be worthy of him, but I can't speak because it's too dangerous.

We continue down the line, proceeding slowly, shaking hands, and accepting congratulations. My handshake is firm, my smile is wide, and my eyes meet every stranger dead on. Apart from my friends, hidden around the room, I know none of these people. I don't know who is a potential ally or who is a foe.

Eventually, the procession ends, and we make our way to the head table. It's strategically positioned close to the stage, so we have an excellent view of all of tonight's entertainment, with the small dance floor at our rear. At least that's what I told the planner. Truth is, it's close to the side door that leads to the back area, and it'll make it easier to slip through to the bastard's office later.

This is a much larger, circular table, for family and close friends only, so I'm instantly aggrieved when I spot Father leading Kai and Giselle, Atticus and some blonde, and Rick and Isabella toward us.

"What the fuck is he doing?" Charlie hisses under his breath as he holds my chair out for me.

"I'd like to know too," I murmur, gripping the armrests of my chair painfully. This was already going to be difficult without having to face my love across a table while I'm pretending to be in love with the man who thinks he's my husband.

How the fuck did I end up here? Seriously. My life is one epic clusterfuck after another.

Dinner is a tedious affair. But at least the loud entertainment means there is minimal opportunity to talk. The orchestra is booked to play throughout our meal, which means conversation is limited to the person directly beside you.

I work hard not to look at Kai, sneaking the odd glance when no one is looking. Giselle is doing her best to drape herself around him, but he keeps removing her hands, pinning her with a dark glare. Alessandra is making minimal effort to talk to Drew, and he looks happy about that fact. Isabella is spending more time fawning over my father, instead of paying attention to Rick, much to Patrice's disgust.

Father is quietly seething.

Oh, he looks like he's having the time of his life, stuck between two women fighting for his affections, but the murderous looks he shoots my way, when he thinks no one notices, say otherwise.

Along the other side of the table, Sylvia is knocking back champagne like it's water, while Trent glares at me instead of paying attention to his fiancée. Shandra shoots me alarmed looks every so often, and the tension is so thick you could cut it with a knife. I take a tiny sip of my champagne, only to look polite. I'm not risking drinking because it's too fucking dangerous to let my guard down around here.

Even Atticus, who is usually so arrogantly assured, looks on edge, smiling weakly at whatever his date is saying. The only two people who look at ease at our table are Denton Mathers—Alessandra and Isabella's father—and Christian Montgomery. Deep in conversation, they are ignoring their wives, having swapped seats, and their heads are huddled together.

Kai spots where my attention has wandered. "They are up to something," he whispers. I subtly nod. "I'll keep eyes on them."

As if they heard us, both men pick their heads up at the same time, pinning wicked eyes on me. All the tiny hairs on the back of my neck lift, and I shiver uncontrollably.

"Cold, darling?" Charlie says, pressing his mouth close to my ear as he circles his arm around my shoulders, pulling me in closer.

"Nervous," I say, smiling shyly at him, while trying to ignore the eyeballs latched to my back. Kai is suspiciously quiet. "It's a lot to take in. Although," I say, lowering my voice as I look over my shoulder. "I'm surprised there are no girls in cages. What happened to the stalls at the end of the room?"

Charlie presses his mouth closer to my ear. "Your father wouldn't risk having that on display tonight. There are too many outsiders here." He trails his fingers up my arm. "He moved the action to the private corridor over on the other side of the room. Only elite with the code can access it. You'll notice people slipping out of the room after dinner, and that's why." His warm breath fans over my face, but I just feel cold all the way through to my bones. "Whatever you do, do not go near that side of the dungeon."

"It's time," Jacqueline—the wedding planner—says, coming up behind me. "Are you sure you still want to dance to this piece?"

"Absolutely." I stand with a flourish, holding my hand out for Charlie.

I know he's a good dancer, because we were all made to take lessons years ago, and it's just as well because this song isn't going to be easy to slow dance to.

The orchestra kicks off, and Charlie sweeps me into his arms, twirling me out into the center of the dance floor. People get up from their tables, surrounding the floor, watching us. I feel the heated eyes and lustful looks from several of the men, and a shudder works its way through me. Charlie plants his arm around my lower back, pulling me in close to his body as he directs our moves. He's a smooth dancer, and we glide naturally across the dancefloor.

"What song is this?" he asks as he twirls me around.

"It's called "The Rains of Castamere." It's from the red wedding in the *Game of Thrones*," I innocently explain, knowing he has no clue because he's vocal in his dislike of the popular show.

"Ah," he says, "I see. That's where you got the red theme from?"

"Sort of." I bury my face in his shirt to hide my smirk. Little does he know the red wedding was a blood bath with few making it out alive. I thought I was being tongue in cheek choosing this music for our first dance, but as my fake husband twirls me around the dance floor, and I feel the dark heat from copious sets of eyes, I wonder if it isn't ominous.

CHAPTER TWENTY-THREE

An hour later, the dance floor is hopping with drunken couples dirty dancing. The goth band I hired is rocking it out onstage, and the crowd is loving it. If I'd wanted the actual wedding to be a success, I could be slapping myself on the back right now for a job well done. But I'm too wound up to celebrate. We were banking on Father and his cronies leaving the room at some point so we could sneak out to his office to snoop, but he hasn't moved from the room all night.

"Please, Kaiden." Giselle's whiny voice bores through my brain. "I really want to dance."

"For the last fucking time, I don't dance," Kai snaps.

"I'll dance with you," Trent says, sidling up alongside her.

She considers it for all of five seconds before ditching Kai for his arch nemesis. Drew snorts as we watch them make their way to the dancefloor, disappearing into the middle of the crowd. "Doesn't your cousin have any sense of self-worth?" he asks a bored-looking Alessandra.

"About as much as your sister," she retorts, giving him the evil eye.

"What the fuck is that supposed to mean?" Drew pins her with a sharp look.

"It means Goth Barbie has bitten off more than she can chew."

"Christian," Drew bellows. "Alessandra was just mentioning how much she'd love to dance with you."

Christian's lips tug up on one side. "Well, I'd hate to disappoint such a pretty lady." He stands, rounding the table and extending his hand toward my brother's fiancée.

Alessandra's smile is pinched as she rises, looping her arm through Christian's. She shoots daggers at Drew as they walk off.

"Poor Drew," Charlie whispers in my ear. "She's a fucking weapon."

"Tell me about it."

"Michael," Rick shouts over the music. "Surely, you're not going to leave Isabella wanting?" He smirks at his date. "She hasn't been flirting relentlessly with you all night to leave without at least one dance?"

Isabella and Patrice both glower at Rick, and I fight a lip twitch.

Father stands, grinning at Isabella, with dark eyes full of nefarious intent. "I can assure you," he says, eyeballing Alessandra's sister. "You will have the pleasure of my company in due course, but right now, I think it's time I took my daughter for a spin on the dance floor." He infuses his fake tone with light laughter, but no one is buying it. Kai stiffens, and Drew clamps a hand on his leg in warning.

"Charles." Father approaches, tapping him on the shoulder. "If you'll excuse us." He extends his hand to me, and I almost puke my dinner up all over myself.

Charlie drags a hand through his hair, slanting alarmed eyes at me. I know he wants to tell him to fuck off, but he can't.

A father asking his daughter to dance at her wedding party is not unusual.

Unless your father is a fucking psychopath named Michael Hearst.

Then anyone would understand wanting to run for the hills and hide.

But we don't have options here.

"Some time this century—if you don't mind," the bastard drawls, barely concealing his annoyance. Patience has never been his strong suit.

I stretch up to kiss Charlie, discreetly pressing the communication chip to activate it. "Interrupt us after one dance."

He nods. "Be careful."

I walk ahead of my father, out to the edge of the dance floor, where we are in full view. But he grabs my wrist, subtly twisting it as he guides me through the middle of the crowd and over to the other side, where it's darker and less packed. He nods at some man as we pass, and a shiver works its way through me with the way he's leering at me. Out of the corner of my eye, I spot Chad steering some girl out onto the dance floor beside us. My heart rate calms a smidgeon. But only a smidgeon.

Father yanks me in close, holding one of my hands up while placing his other hand way too low on my back. I'm forced to loosely hold onto his waist, and touching him, even over his clothes, breaks me out in hives.

We dance awkwardly for a few beats. It seems dancing, as well as sports, is not in his repertoire. He stands on my toes, several times, but I know better than to complain. Little beads of sweat roll down my back the longer we dance, and he makes no attempt to strike up a conversation. His eyes pierce mine before dropping to my cleavage. Bile swims up my throat as he looks down the front of my dress, and I curse myself for not getting the neckline adjusted. The hand on my back edges lower, and my heart is banging against my rib cage in fear.

My eyes dart to Chad's, and his dark frown tells me he notices.

"I don't know what the hell you think you're playing tonight," the bastard says, finally speaking, "but you aren't fooling me with this charade."

An icy cold chill sweeps over my body. "I don't know what you're implying." Forcing my mounting terror aside, I look him dead in the eye. At least he's looking at my face now.

"Do not play this game because it will only make things worse for him."

Fear has my heart in a vise grip, and I can barely breathe.

"I told you what would happen if you disobeyed me," he continues.

"I haven't disobeyed you," I blurt, acting confused. "Charlie told me you want me to accept this lifestyle, and he told me to adapt so you'd see I'm embracing it," I lie. "Why else do you think I planned all this?" My brows knit together. "I don't understand what I've done wrong."

He stares at me so long I wonder if he's lost the ability to speak.

"Please, Father. Tell me what I've done wrong, and I'll fix it." I purposely glance around. "The party is a huge success. I don't understand." I'm praying my acting skills are holding up because he's been stewing all night, and this won't end well for me if I can't convince him this is me trying to toe the line. "I'm behaving at school. I'm looking after Charlie's mom and sister, and I'm being a good wife. What else do you want me to do?"

His hand moves around my waist, along my hip, and down to the top of my thigh. My breath stutters in my throat, and acid churns in my stomach.

"I've always believed Drew was my only option. That you were weak, just like your mother," he spits out, and I want to snatch my knife and bury it deep in his cold heart.

I seriously contemplate it.

I'm close enough I could do it.

But there are too many witnesses, and I know he has cameras in some parts of this room, so it's too fucking risky.

I'm not going to prison for him.

And I want *him* to rot in a jail cell. Death is too easy.

That thought helps calm me down.

His hand moves lower, and he tugs up my skirt, sliding his hand under the slit and onto my bare flesh. My stomach dips to my toes, and nausea travels up my throat.

"But I think I made a grave mistake." His hand inches higher, and I drop my arm, grabbing hold of his wrist and digging my nails in. It's a risky move. One that will ensure I'm punished. But I'm fucked if he's going to move his hand any higher.

He's not touching me there.

And I can't have him finding my weapons.

"You have more balls than your brother, and I see a lot of myself in you," he continues, leering at me.

I want to scream that I'm nothing like him, but I've still got a role to play.

And where the fuck is Charlie? Because this is longer than one dance.

He pushes against my bare thigh, and I hold onto his wrist with a firmer grip, ready to inflict pain with my talons if I need to. In my periphery, I see Chad preparing to make a move, and I glare at him, warning him to stay back. I do not want him mixed up in this. So far, he's a friend from school. The offspring of a well-respected inner circle member and that's it. I don't want him on Father's radar, so he needs to protect me from the shadows.

"I *am* a lot like you, Father," I say, and I'm amazed how calm my voice sounds when I'm fucking trembling inside. "Meaning I take no prisoners." I dig my nails into the underside of his wrist, knowing I've broken skin. "So, take your hands off me. Because I believe my husband made a deal with you, and he made himself very clear. No. Sharing."

"Abby!" Charlie pants out from behind me, and I glance briefly over my shoulder. "Fuck off, Christian," he hisses, shoving Trent's father away from him. Coming up to my side, Charlie looks at the standoff between me and the bastard with an obvious scowl.

Father had ample time to remove his hand from under my dress, but he's left it there on purpose. He wants Charlie to see.

It's a threat.

A warning.

And my stomach sours, understanding exactly what he intends to do with me.

"Get your hands off my wife." Charlie doesn't hesitate to defend me, shoving my father in the chest before pulling me behind him, shielding me with his body.

Kai and Drew appear behind my father, whispering with Chad, and I use my eyes to plead with all three of them to back the fuck down.

"She was insubordinate tonight, and she needs to be punished," Father says.

"I'm responsible for her," Charlie calmly replies. "I'll take her punishment."

"What? No!" The words leave my mouth before I've questioned the wisdom of it.

"Stay out of this, Abby," Charlie warns.

"This is elite business," Christian adds, sharing a conspiratorial look with my father. "And I believe we should take this upstairs."

Father nods. "Come with us, Charlie, and we'll settle this like men." He sends me one last dark glare. "Do not do anything in my absence to make the situation worse," he warns before stalking off.

Even though this is the opening we've been waiting for all night,

I didn't want to achieve it like this. I don't want anyone sacrificing themselves for me. I grab hold of Charlie's arm. "You don't have to do this!"

He kisses me fiercely. "I promised to protect you. This is me doing that." He jerks his head toward Drew. "Stay with your brother. Remember what I told you."

I nod, and a heavy weight presses down on my chest. "I'm sorry."

He shakes his head. "Don't be."

"It's better to not keep your future president waiting," Christian says, smirking at Charlie before turning his beady eyes on me. "You're looking especially ravishing tonight, Abigail," he adds. "But I suspect you know that." He grabs hold of Charlie's arm. "Save a dance for me," he tosses over his shoulder before escorting Charlie off the dance floor.

Over my dead fucking body, perv.

Drew approaches as Charlie and Christian walk away. "This could be our only chance," he murmurs, pulling me into his arms and swaying us to the beat of the music. "The decoy will go off in a couple minutes, and then we'll make a dash for it. Kai and Rick will watch the room for any signs of them returning."

"Are you okay, Abby?" Kai asks in my ear.

"I'm fine."

Out of the corner of my eye, I spot Trent watching us. "Shit." I look up at Drew. "We forgot about Trent."

"No, we haven't," Kai says, and I watch him stalking across the floor toward Trent and Giselle, followed by Chad.

Trent has his hand up the front of Giselle's dress, and he's doing nothing to conceal the fact he is fingering her in front of everyone. I think she must have drunk too much champagne because she's slumped against him, letting him do whatever he wants to her. Or else he drugged her. That thought just pops into my mind, and I seriously hope I'm wrong. I don't like the girl, but I don't wish that on anyone.

Kai storms up to them, yanking her away and quickly passing her to Chad. Then he thrusts his fist out, punching Trent in the face. The crowd automatically parts, and the two guys start swinging at one another just as our decoy kicks off.

Lights spark and sizzle overhead, and a snapping, crackling sound has everyone looking up at the ceiling in initial alarm. A fake starlight night sky washes over the ceiling, and oohs and aahs echo around the room.

It's amazing what some sound and light effects can do. We couldn't risk anything more elaborate as it might draw Father back into the room. This was Xavier's idea, and it's worked like a charm because everyone's attention is riveted on the ceiling.

Drew grabs my hand and we race toward the side door while everyone's attention is diverted. He taps in the code, pulling me behind the door before anyone spots us. Drew lifts his finger, silently warning me to stay put. Stretching up, he places a thin chip on the underside of the wall-mounted camera, waiting until the little red light turns on, confirming the camera is scrambled. Xavier got a whole bunch of new gadgets courtesy of the safe-cracking guy. Apparently, he's kept in contact with him, and he's a mine of information when it comes to tech gadgets and covert ops.

Drew takes my hand, and we walk down the long corridor toward the main door. We know there's at least one guard back there, but we're acquainted with all my father's guys, even the new hires, and we're confident we can talk our way in. Thoughts of guards remind me of Oscar, and I make a mental note to call Julie again. I've been calling her weekly for progress updates, but it's been so busy lately I haven't had time. I'm sure she would have left me a message if there was any change in his condition.

Drew punches in the code on the second door. "Ready?"

"As I'll ever be."

He steps through first, and I follow directly behind him, because I will always have his back.

CHAPTER TWENTY-FOUR

"Mr. Manning." Freddie nods at Drew, frowning when he spots me behind him. "Miss Abigail." He nods again. I breathe a sigh of relief that it's Freddie and not Benjamin or Maurio, because they would be naturally more suspicious. Freddie is all brawn and no brains, and it's no secret the bastard keeps him in his employment purely for the muscle power.

"Father asked us to retrieve something from his office," Drew says. "He's gone upstairs for a meeting."

Freddie folds his arms and purses his lips, removing his walkie-talkie. "I'd better check with the boss man."

I quirk a brow. "Do you want to get fired?"

He visibly swallows, pausing with his finger over the button. "You didn't see how angry he was when he pulled my husband out of the room. I really wouldn't risk getting on his bad side. Besides, it's only us." I throw my hands in the air. "It's not like we're here to steal from him or trash his office." I roll my eyes. "We're his children. I think it's safe to let us through."

He scrubs a hand over his jaw, frowning as he thinks about it. "I suppose it's okay."

I stretch up, kissing his cheek. "Thank you, Freddie. You're one of my favorite guards. You've always been good to me, and Drew, and I remember these things. We both do. Don't we, Drew?"

"I think someone has a bit of a soft spot for you, Freddie." Drew nudges him in the elbow, playing along, and the man is completely flustered. He's trying to work out if we're yanking his chain or genuine. Bless him. He actually is like a big soft teddy bear. Although I've no doubt those beefy arms have inflicted a lot of pain in the Hearst-Manning name, and I'm under no illusion where his loyalty lies.

"That's kind of you to say, Miss Abigail," he splutters.

"Don't mention it." I shoot him a saucy wink and sashay my hips as we walk past him.

Drew is sniggering under his breath. "I cannot believe they fall for that shit."

"It's shocking," I agree.

Drew stops in front of the only door back here, tapping in a code. "I hope he hasn't changed it," he whispers, and we share an anxious few seconds waiting with bated breath until a small click resounds and the door swings inward. "Jackpot!" he whispers.

I slide out of my heels the instant we're inside, racing around the large desk and dropping into the leather seat. I power up the desktop computer as Drew rushes to the mahogany cabinet behind me, sliding back the doors.

I slip the USB device Xavier gave me out of its little hiding place at the side of my corset top. The boning in both sides was a perfect place to stitch a little pocket. The bridal store owner gave me serious side-eye when I requested those alterations, but the extra two grand I gave her ensured she asked no questions and she built in two little pockets, one on either side.

Inserting the USB stick into the side of the computer, I pray it works. The guys have been struggling to hack into the system remotely, but this device should be able to break through the firewall from the inside. While that's doing its job, I swivel around in the seat, watching Drew scowling at the row of TV screens.

"I assumed they would always be on, but they must be linked to his computer."

A pinging sound chimes, and I turn back around. "Yes! Xavier, you freaking genius," I murmur as the screen loads before me. The device cracked the firewall and unearthed Dad's log-ins as Xavier predicted. He hoped Dad had put all his efforts into the external firewall, not expecting an attack to come from the inside, and he was right. I remove that device and slip the second USB key inside. This one will copy everything on the hard drive and should give us everything we need to hack into the system from the outside. We're also hoping to find some useful shit among his personal documents.

"The screens are powering up," Drew says, and I get up, watching as the images load on the TVs. There are six different visuals in total. Two are of corridors that lead to the vault, and the other four screens flip through different angles of the steel room built somewhere underneath us. "Shit. Look."

I lean in, my eyes narrowing, as I stare at the thing Drew is pointing at. "What are those?" A bunch of red lights crisscross along the bottom of the floor.

"It's an infrared alarm. You know like in *Mission Impossible*."

"Aw, fuck. Didn't you know he had that?"

He shakes his head. A noise resounds from outside, making both of us jump. "Freddie is getting jumpy. Is that nearly done?" he asks, nodding at the computer.

I glance over my shoulder. "Only twelve percent left."

"Mr. Manning. Ms. Abigail." Freddie's booming voice is muffled. "Are you okay in there?"

"We're just trying to find it," I shout. "We'll be out in a minute."

Sweat dots my brow, and my hands are clammy as I yank at the drawers either side of Father's desk. But they're both locked, and I didn't bring my pick with me.

The mission was simple.

Get into the system, copy the hard drive, and check out the screens to see what kind of security is protecting the vault. Then get the fuck out before we're caught.

"How do you access the vault anyway?" I ask as the thought occurs to me.

"Through here." Drew pulls open a door to the right of the cabinet, revealing a hidden elevator.

"He thinks of everything. I doubt the freaking CIA or FBI are as well protected."

The computer pings, confirming the download has completed, and I yank it out, tucking both USB keys back into the sides of my dress.

Drew grins. "I think Father may have been right earlier. You're every bit as smart as he is." I'm opening my mouth to protest when he places a finger to my lips. "But he lacks the one thing you have in spades. *Compassion.* You use your smarts for the right reasons, which is why you could never be like him."

A pounding on the door brings a halt to our conversation.

"Mr. Manning. I must insist you come out here right now."

I power off the computer, and the screens die out behind us. Drew pulls the cabinet doors closed, while I put my shoes back on, grabbing a book off one of the shelves as an afterthought. Then we open the door and face a rattled-looking Freddie.

"I thought you said you just had to get something for the boss. What took you so long?" His dubious gaze dances between us.

I wave the book in his face. "He asked us to get this, but have you seen how many books are on those shelves?" I roll my eyes, trying to make light of it.

"Heads-up," Kai says in my ear. "Christian Montgomery has just returned, and it looks like he's looking for one or both of you."

Drew's eyes flit to mine, as Freddie peers at the book. "Mr. Hearst asked you to get *The Seven Habits of Highly Effective People* in the middle of a party?"

I laugh. "We told you he went upstairs for a meeting, silly." I pat his broad chest. "Maybe he's loaning it to someone." I shrug, and I know it's lame, but I'm trying to avoid using what I know against him. Because if we play the blackmail card, he'll know we were up to no good.

"I'm calling Mr. Hearst," Freddie says, and it's clear I underestimated him. He's not as dumb as a bag of hammers after all.

"He's fucking going toward the door," Kai hisses. "I'll try and head him off, but get the hell out of there now."

"I don't think so, Freddie," Drew says. "And I really wish you'd kept your mouth shut."

"No, Drew!" I shout, watching in horror as he whips out a gun with a silencer, pointing it at Freddie. He pumps two rounds into his skull before I can even blink. The lights go out in Freddie's eyes instantly, and he falls to the ground with a resounding thud.

"What the fuck is going on?" Rick shouts in my ear.

"Nothing you need to be concerned about," Drew calmly says, pushing Freddie's leg off his foot.

"You need to get out here," Rick adds. "Kai just punched Christian, and all hell is breaking loose."

"We'll be right there," I hear myself say as I stare at the dead bodyguard on the ground.

"Why'd you do that?" I ask, staring at my brother in shock.

"He was going to tell Father. It was the quickest way of handling the situation."

"And how were you planning to explain the dead body to Christian?"

"That one's easy. I'll tell them I received anonymous intel that Freddie was selling insider secrets to the new elite." He bends down, pulling a handkerchief from his pocket, covering his hand before removing Freddie's gun and curling his dead fingers around it. "I'll say I confronted him, he pulled a gun on me, and I shot him in self-defense." He stands, wiping his hands down the front of his pants. "Father won't care. Guys like Freddie are dispensable. He'll have him replaced by morning."

His casual dismissal of murder has alarm bells ringing in my ears. "And what about me? How were you planning to explain me?" I ask.

He takes my hand, lifting me over Freddie's prone form. "I wasn't. You'll need to exit the back way. You'll come out at the side of the main entrance. Just walk around the building, and if anyone asks, you were taking some fresh air. Say you were concerned about Charlie."

He pulls me along with him, and I have to walk-run to keep up with him. No easy feat in these heels. "Drew, stop."

"No, Abby. There's no time." He punches a code in a keypad, and the door in front of us opens. "Go now. I'll tell one of the guys to meet you at the front door. Take out your gun and watch your back."

He pushes me out of the door. "Hurry and be careful."

The door slams in my face, and I stare at it, wondering if I just imagined my brother shooting a man in cold blood and not even batting an eyelash.

"Kai," I whisper as I remove my gun, holding onto the rail with one hand while I ascend the steps.

"He's a little busy right now, Abby," Rick says. "I heard, and I'm on my way to the front entrance to meet you."

"Is he okay?" I ask, reaching the top and looking left and right.

"Let's just say you're missing the show of a lifetime. Dad, Kai, and Christian are all shouting and shoving one another. I think Kai's actually enjoying himself. You know how much he hates those pricks."

I snort out a laugh, swaying on my heels, as I walk awkwardly over the gravel under foot. I clutch onto the wall to help keep my balance.

"Hey, baby," a voice says on the other end of the earpiece. "Where do you think you're going?" Rick switches off the feed, and I'm glad because Isabella is every bit as annoying as her younger sister. I've watched her blatantly flirt with my father all night, and now he's disappeared, she's turning her attention to her date.

Disloyal bitch.

A noise behind me sends butterflies racing through my chest. Blood thrums in my ears as I turn around, raising my gun and surveying my surroundings. But it's dark as shit, and there are no outside lights around this part of the building for a reason. I attempt to pick up my pace, but it's challenging in the dark, on stiletto heels, with stone underfoot.

An ominous sense of dread washes over me, and adrenaline flows through me like lava. I'm on high alert as I totter toward the front entrance, holding onto the wall with one hand and my gun with the other, feeling eyes watching me. I'm afraid to speak into my earpiece because, if someone *is* watching me, I don't want to give that up unless I have no choice.

I rush toward the doorway, almost taking a tumble in my eagerness to get back inside.

"Ms. Abigail." Jeremy, one of the new guards hired recently, nods. He opens the door for me, and I fall inside gratefully, cursing my stupid heels. I slip my gun back into the strap on my thigh, bending down just inside the hallway to rub at my sore feet. I glance left and right, wondering which way brings me back to the party. The music from the dungeon is muted, and I can't decipher which direction to go. The last thing I want is to take the wrong turn and end up in those hidden rooms Charlie warned me about.

Thoughts of Charlie bring a pang to my chest. Father is doing God knows what to him right now, because he sacrificed himself to save me a beating. I'm not sure it works like that. That Father won't punish me anyway.

"Drew," I whisper. "I don't know which way to go."

Radio silence. "Drew!" I whisper louder.

"Abby."

"Kai."

"Where are you?"

"I'm at the front entrance, but I've no clue how to get back downstairs."

"Stay put. I'm coming to get you."

"Hurry."

The door creaks behind me, and my blood pressure skyrockets. Every nerve ending in my body is on high alert as a heavy footstep lands on the tile floor. My heart is slamming against my ribs as I slowly ease my dress aside, reaching a hand underneath, wondering why I thought it was a good idea to put my gun away.

"Hello, Abigail," a voice I know says at my ear as an arm wraps around my waist from behind. Cool metal presses against my neck, and I go rigidly still. "I think it's time you and I got properly acquainted, don't you?"

CHAPTER TWENTY-FIVE

"Let me go or I'll scream," I threaten, hating how my voice quakes a little on the end.

"Scream," Denton Mathers says, "and I'll slit that pretty throat." He presses the edge of a knife into my neck. A tiny sting confirms he's drawn blood and that he means what he says.

"You won't get away with this, Denton." I say his name on purpose, knowing someone will hear me.

He laughs as he turns me around, forcing me to keep pace with him as he walks down the dark hallway. "We both know I will. Who do you think sent me to get you?"

That fucking bastard. Taking Charlie out of the room was nothing more than a move on a chessboard. Father wanted him out of the way so he could get to me.

"Where are you taking me?" I ask as he shoves me down the hallway, taking me farther and farther from the music and the party.

"You want to know what it means to be an elite wife? You think you are ready for it? You think you can give us the proverbial finger by turning up dressed like that? You're about to discover what it really means to be a part of this world."

Keeping the knife at my throat, he lifts his free arm, kneading my breast through my corset top. "Your father's guy did a fantastic job on your tits. I can't wait to fuck them."

Vomit inches up my throat, and blood is thrumming wildly in my ears as my pulse beats out of control.

He forces me into an elevator at the end of the hallway, pushing the button for the basement with his free hand. The knife never leaves my throat, and I'm terrified to move a muscle. He loosens his pants, grabbing my hand and sliding it into his boxers. I shake all over as my hand touches his hard, warm flesh. "You make me sick," I whisper.

"You make me horny." He shoves my hand down lower, gripping my wrist tight as he forces my hand to palm the side of his cock. "And you deserve this for being a little cock tease."

I won't plead or ask him to stop because nothing I say or do will stop him. It will only amuse him and make this even more fun. I've been around enough of these elite bastards to know that turns them on.

"Charlie will make you pay for this."

He snorts as the elevator pings. "Charlie is a little boy thinking he's playing in a man's world, but he is outnumbered and outmaneuvered. If you're counting on him to rescue you, you'll be disappointed." He removes my hand from his pants, dragging me out of the elevator by the wrist. We are at the top of the room, and the black curtain concealing the elevator to the house is on the right-hand side.

Denton bypasses it, bringing me to another door on the left. My heart is trying to beat a path out of my chest as I watch him type in the code. "Three six four five," I whisper softly, hoping someone picks it up. I can scarcely breathe over the massive lump in my throat, barely hear over the pounding in my ears.

He pushes me into another corridor, and as the door clicks shut behind us, it feels prophetic.

"I'm putting the knife away now, Abigail, because I don't want to embarrass you in front of all these important people. But know this. There is no way out of here without capture. If you try, it will only make things much worse for you." He places his lower hand on my back, steering me forward.

"What is this place?" I ask even though Charlie already told me. I need to say it aloud, to ensure the guys have enough clues to find me before this shit goes south.

"This is the inner sanctum. A safe haven for high-ranking elite to let down their hair and enjoy the many pleasures your father has organized for them." He presses a circular red button on the wall, and it parts, revealing a succession of glass windows. Bile swirls in my mouth as I look into each room, watching various men abusing women.

Panic gives rise to anger as we walk down the long corridor, and I see the same doped-up expression on the young girls' faces.

There are older women here too. Some I recognize from the party. Some look like they are willing participants, but others look terrified, some are crying, and others are screaming and beating off men to no avail.

Denton chuckles. "Does that offend you, Abigail?"

"How would you feel if that was Alessandra or Isabella?" I ask, pointing to a room where four men are taking turns with a small, thin girl with underdeveloped boobs. One man is holding her wrists up over her head while the other two grope her body as the large man with the protruding belly rapes her.

"Disgusted they weren't getting into the spirit of it more," he says, shrugging. "But I don't have to worry about either of my girls. They both fuck like pros."

I really hope the guys are hearing this.

"See for yourself," he adds, pinning my hands behind my back as he opens a door on the right-hand side.

This room is a large square, decorated in black and gold, with dim lighting and copious couches and beds littering the space. Every place I look, I see naked bodies and fucking. There are no kidnapped girls in here, and the only sounds are mutual moaning and groaning. Denton drags me through the room, and my heart rate elevates to heart attack territory.

Why the hell is no one speaking to me? Where are the reassurances from my guys that they are on the way to get me? I briefly worry that I somehow deactivated the communication chip, but it was fully functional when I came back into the house and he … Oh fuck. Shit. Denton grabbed my boob, and maybe he deactivated it. But that was *after* I'd said his name, so the guys have to know I'm in trouble.

But they might not know where you are.

And my hands are secured in Denton's tight grip so I've no way of checking the communication chip without risking discovery. However, it feels warm to the touch, and Sawyer said that meant it was active, so I'm confused. It could be that my body temp is elevated, thanks to the mix of adrenaline and fear coursing through my system, or it means the chip *is* active.

But if that's the case, why is no one speaking to me?

Panic explodes in my chest when I see them.

Trent and Alessandra.

As naked as the day they were born. Fucking like wild animals on the floor. It's no surprise he doesn't warrant a private room, and I'm guessing the other guests in here aren't important enough to warrant one either.

"Trent." Denton stands over the fornicating couple. "I have a present for you." He shoves me forward.

Trent slams his cock into Alessandra, and she digs her nails into his ass, moaning as she grins at me.

"Fuck yeah," he pants, glaring at me as he fucks the woman underneath him. "I've been waiting a long time for this."

"Not yet," Alessandra rasps, thrusting her hips up and digging her heels into his ass.

"Don't worry, baby," Trent purrs, leaning down to drag her nipple between his teeth. "I'll finish fucking you first."

"You should take her ass," Denton says, as if he wasn't giving the bastard advice on how to fuck his daughter. "It's nice and tight, and I've prepared her well."

I can't keep the horror off my face, and all three of them laugh.

"You're right, Trent," she says. "She is a stuck-up frigid bitch. I want to watch you break her down."

"Baby." Trent yanks her legs up to his shoulders. "I think we're engaged to the wrong people. We should swap, because you feel like silk on my cock and I love your way of thinking."

And what a stellar idea that is. *Thank you, Trent.* I smother a smile. I'm sure Drew could use the virginity clause to present an argument for breaking off the engagement to Alessandra.

Although Father turned a blind eye with Jane, it was because they kept the fucking behind closed doors. Alessandra is Drew's fiancée, and she's fucking another woman's fiancé in front of an audience of elite. That should be grounds to extricate him from her.

Although my situation isn't humorous in the slightest, I can't disguise the smirk that graces my mouth. "I can think of no other couple more deserving of one another," I say. "The skank and the manwhore. What a match made in heaven."

Denton chuckles. "I like your fire, Abigail, but only under carefully controlled conditions." He grabs the back of my head, yanking the pins out of my hair. Strands fall out of my chignon, and he tugs on them hard, yanking my head back.

"I say we fuck her in here," Trent suggests. "Humiliate her in front of everyone."

"Your father has other ideas in mind," he says, and a shudder whips through my body.

"Oh look. She's shivering in anticipation already," Alessandra laughs, emitting a guttural moan, as Trent pivots his hips, drilling deeper inside her.

Denton reels me back, heading toward the door. "Don't wait too long," he says in parting to Trent. "Or you'll miss all the fun."

He wrestles me out of the room, while my mind is whirring. I need to get my hands free to check my chip and get to my gun or my knife. I will my errant pulse to calm down, because I can't pull this off unless I'm in control. But it's fucking hard.

Because I'm scared shitless.

Especially when he pulls me into the room at the end of the corridor and I see who is lying in wait. All the blood drains from my face as I look at Charlie. He's tied to a chair in the middle of the space. His shirt is off, and his chest is awash with blood. A handkerchief is stuffed in his mouth, so I can't hear what he's saying, but I know he's not happy. Panic blares from his eyes as he attempts to stand in the chair, but it's bolted to the floor, so it's futile.

"Did she give you any trouble?" Christian asks, removing his shirt in slow motion.

"None." Denton slips his hand down the front of my dress, his fingers moving dangerously close to the chip, and I stop breathing. He rubs his thumb over my nipple, and I fix my face into a neutral expression, not wanting to give them the satisfaction of knowing how panicked I am.

Charlie's eyes are full of apology.

"Bring her to me," Christian says, folding his shirt on the desk and reaching for his pants.

The door swings open. "What did I miss?" Trent asks, sauntering into the room with a shit-eating grin on his face. There's no sign of Alessandra, and given how fast he got here, and the fact he's naked, I'm guessing he left her high and dry and, now, she's sulking.

"You're just in time," Christian says, grabbing me forward and pushing me to my knees. "From what I've heard, Abby gives great head."

Father and son share a conspiratorial look, and I know Trent has told him everything that transpired between him and me. Hell, he probably had cameras in his bedroom. Thank fuck, I never had sex with him.

"I'm about to experience it for the first time."

My eyes dart to Charlie's in alarm before resolve sets in. If that asshole puts his cock in my mouth, it won't be coming out intact. I will maim him. Butcher him so badly he won't be able to use it again without surgery. I'll bite it so hard he'll have PTSD every time a woman drops to her knees before him.

If this goes down, I want to know I fought every step of the way. Because otherwise there's no fucking way I'll survive this with my sanity intact.

Christian grabs my chin. "Don't look at him. He can't save you. He never could." He jabs his finger in Charlie's face. "This is your fault. All you had to do was share."

"We're married. Why the fuck should he share?!" I screech, trying to buy myself some time. My hands are free now, but my heavy dress is covering my thighs, and the material is pinned under my knees. If I try to go for my weapons, they will notice and disarm me, so I can't strike now.

But I also don't want that pervert's dick in my mouth.

I almost puke at that vile thought.

The good thing about the voluminous dress is it hides my feet, and I slowly maneuver my heels off, focusing on doing it discreetly so they don't notice. It also helps distract me, keeping a light lid on my terror.

"Because it's the elite way," Christian replies. But he's spinning half-truths, because Charlie's dad kept his mom protected from this, and he can't be the only one. "Thanks to his disobedience, we aren't just going to fuck your pussy. We'll fuck your mouth and your ass too so Charlie gets the message that you are ours to do with as we please." Christian smirks, dropping his pants and boxers. "You like a hard dick up the ass, don't you, Abigail?" He strokes his cock. "Your mother was never fond of anal, but that didn't stop your father and I from taking her there." His eyes flash with dark lust. "Those were the good ole days."

"I'm sorry we weren't better acquainted back then," Denton says. "It sounds like I missed out on good times."

The men clearly only know one another via Parkhurst and have only grown close in recent times if that comment is to be believed.

I recall the intel the team has built on Denton. He's a descendant of one of the founding fathers from Alabama and the most prominent elite member in that state. He runs a global engineering firm and is a big philanthropist with strong connections within government and politics. He's a formidable force, so it's no surprise Father has aligned with him. Uniting our families through marriage is a smart elite move, and it will boost his profile to have both his children married to the offspring of founding fathers.

The Alabama connection sparked fireworks inside me, and I've been trying to uncover evidence of any ties with my deceased aunt or Wesley Marshall, Cam's uncle, but so far there is nothing connecting them.

But it can't be a coincidence they are from the same state.

Both men ogle me, and bile collects in my mouth. I frantically scroll through my mind, grappling for options to get me out of this, because it seems obvious I'm on my own here.

"Don't worry, Mathers." Christian slaps him on the back as Denton removes the last of his clothing.

Charlie's muffled screams are background noise as he thrashes about in the chair. His eyes are trained on Christian, and Christian is staring at him with a smug look.

"There are plenty of good times ahead," Christian adds, grabbing his cock and pumping it slowly as he smirks at me. My stomach heaves, and I can't believe after all our planning that I am still here. We knew something like this could happen, but we thought we had covered all our bases.

In the end, it was far too easy to get to me.

I work hard to fight the trembling overtaking my body. My chest tightens, and I'm struggling to maintain my composure. The prick notices too, grinning as he moves toward me. "Open your mouth nice and wide, Abby."

I do the only thing I can—I hesitantly open my mouth.

"Good little slut," he says, pumping his cock faster, and I almost puke all over the place. When he's close enough, with his cock all up in my face, I make my move, shoving him forcefully in the stomach as I simultaneously push to my feet. Christian stumbles back, slamming into the desk, as a string of expletives leave his mouth. "Get her!" he roars as I race around the desk, fumbling with the layers of my skirt with shaking hands. Trent rounds one side of the desk while Denton comes up on the other side. Christian straighten ups, pinning hateful eyes on me as he stalks toward me.

Charlie kicks out with one leg, hitting him in the shins, and he goes down, hollering. I'm not sure how Charlie got one leg free, but I hope he figures out how to untie the rest of the binds because things aren't looking too hot back here.

Trent makes a grab for me, and I dart back out of his reach. A ripping sound echoes throughout the room as the side of my corset top comes undone. "You're not getting away from me this time, Abby. I'm going to fuck every hole until you bleed."

"Come here, you little bitch," Denton says, just as I finally manage to wrangle my knife free.

I brandish it in front of me. "Don't come near me, or I'll fucking kill you."

Trent laughs, and mirth flashes in Denton's eyes as they slowly inch toward me on either side. I'm trapped, and they fucking know it. One on one, I might stand a chance, but outnumbered like this, I'm a sitting duck.

I slash at the layers around my legs, watching bits of taffeta drop to the ground, and then, I jump up onto the desk, evading both sets of arms that make a grab for me. Clearing the other side of the desk, I race toward the door and I'm almost to it when a hand snags my ankle. The knife flies out of my hand as I lose my balance, crashing to the floor, face-first. Ignoring the splintering pain ricocheting through my skull, I angle my body and reach for my gun the same time I'm spun around onto my back.

I don't stop to think. I aim the gun and fire, and Denton emits a loud roar as the bullet embeds in his thigh. Blood oozes out of the wound, flowing everywhere, and he pins me with murderous eyes. Christian crawls up my body, and I aim my gun at his chest, pressing my thumb on the trigger just as it's yanked from my hand from behind. I hadn't noticed Trent creeping up on me, because I was too concerned with the two men in front of me. The gun goes off, the bullet lodging in the wood paneling.

Denton is howling in pain, clasping his hand to his thigh, trying to stem the blood flow. Christian straddles my hips, placing his hands around my throat as Trent empties the gun chamber, tossing the gun and the remaining bullets on the chair to his left. "You really shouldn't have done that, Abby. You can't shoot a high-ranking elite and expect to get away with it," Christian growls, squeezing his hands tighter around my throat. Black spots mar my vision, and all I can think is he's going rape me and kill me.

My fight instinct kicks in, and I buck my hips up, trying to throw him off, but he's too heavy and my body's panicking, my lungs constricting as my oxygen supply dries up.

"Move off her," Trent says. "You promised me I could fuck her first, and I can't get to her with you sitting on top like that."

Christian slides off me, still keeping his hands around my throat, as Trent moves to my feet, smiling smugly as he traces his fingers up my legs.

CHAPTER TWENTY-SIX

Kaiden – a few minutes earlier

"Get the fucking door open, Drew!"

"I'm fucking trying," he shouts, his fingers punching in the code again. "He must have changed this code. Shit." He rests his forehead against the wall.

"Guys!" Rick catches up to us, almost out of breath. "I heard Abby whisper something before the communication went dead. Three six four, I think."

Drew explained how his father has some form of blocking technology in use on the rooms in the back so no one can record anything that goes on in there. It's why the feed went dead the second she stepped foot inside. Before that, when she'd been out in the quiet corridor with Mathers, we'd all been too afraid to speak to her in case he overheard.

It killed me not being able to reassure her.

But Abby is smart, and she knows we'll get to her somehow.

"It's a four-number code," Drew barks.

"Then start trying numbers!" I snap, yanking strands of my hair. Hunt, Lauder, and Xavier are on their way, along with the four security guys I hired a month ago to help protect us and Abby. But I fear we're all too late. "Hurry the fuck up!" I hiss. I'm terrified of what they're doing to my wife behind this door. I thought I was doing the right thing creating a distraction but all it did was get me, Dad, and Rick kicked out.

After a few carefully chosen words on my behalf, Dad wandered off in search of Patrice, while we listened helplessly to Abby getting taken. We lost precious time sneaking into the building via the back entrance, not realizing Drew was busy getting rid of a body, meaning Abby was all alone.

I kick the wall in frustration as Drew continues punching in numbers, to no avail.

If they've hurt her, I will fucking murder every single one of them.

A loud bang from the back of the room momentarily startles me. Screams and shouts ring out as a secondary bang follows it, joined by a crackling sound that has people running toward the exit. "What the fuck is that?"

"I told Shandra to grab a few of the others and create a diversion that would get everyone out of the room," Rick says.

"Whatever she did, it's working," Chad says, watching people rush from the room as a third bang reverberates around the emptying space.

"Thank fuck," Drew shouts as the door finally opens. "Look sharp, guys," he says, drawing his gun up. I flip the safety off as Rick and Chad do the same.

Drew races into the corridor, holding up a hand when he reaches a control panel mounted to the wall. He taps in the code again and a couple of other buttons, before jerking his head to the side. "Come on."

We take off running down the long dark corridor.

"How likely are we to be ambushed?" I inquire.

"I just locked every room but my father's private room. There is an override button inside each room, but it's on a timer. We have five minutes before they all come after us," Drew explains. "And I fucking hope he took her to his room."

A gunshot goes off, quickly followed by another one, and my heart lodges in my throat. Panic claws at my insides, and I pray it was Abby who fired those shots and not the other way around. I push my legs harder, sprinting alongside Drew. His face matches how I feel on the inside.

We reach the end of the hallway and the only other door in this section of the dungeon. I'm expecting to have to break the door down, so when Drew turns the handle and it freely opens, I'm surprised.

My eyes are black orbs of hate as I lock eyes on Trent Montgomery. He's buck-ass naked, crouched at Abby's feet, his hands trailing up her legs. Drew aims his weapon at Christian Montgomery, his finger curling around the trigger. "Get the fuck away from my sister."

Christian has his hands around Abby's throat, and I aim my gun at his forehead. Her eyelids are fluttering, her skin pale, and it's clear she's struggling to breathe. My finger twitches on the trigger. "Don't, Kai," Rick says, cautioning me to keep my cool.

If I shoot him, as I want to, they will call the cops and have me hauled away for murder. I've no doubt about that. All that will do is leave Abby more vulnerable and exposed, so I force myself to rein in my murderous rage.

Charlie is half-tied to a chair with a gag in his mouth, pinning frantic eyes on me. He's been beaten, and it's clear the intent was to violate Abby and force him to watch.

"I wouldn't do that," Christian warns, yanking Abby upright so she's shielding him. The pervert is naked too. As is Denton Mathers. He's groaning in pain, clutching his leg, his fingers coated in blood. A flash of silver glints, and Christian raises a knife to Abby's throat.

Her head is lolling back, her body limp, and she's barely conscious. Her dress is torn in several places, her legs are covered in blood, and there's a trickle of blood from a small cut in her neck.

My blood boils and my fingers twitch with the need to inflict pain. But I hold back. Because that psycho nutjob has a knife to the throat of the woman I love. One false move and she could die.

"Drop your weapons. Now. Or I'll slit her throat," Christian demands, and he's not fucking around.

The four of us drop our weapons without hesitation.

The asshole smirks, yanking Abby to her feet and kicking our guns aside. "Your father will be most disappointed in you," he says to Drew, inching around us, continuing to use Abby as a shield, keeping the knife pressed to her flesh. A fresh line of blood oozes from a new cut, and I want to lunge at the bastard and gut him from the inside out. "Trent. Grab Denton. We're moving our party upstairs." He shoots me a malevolent grin, and I dig my fingernails into my palms. "We'll return her to her husband tomorrow," he says, setting his gaze on Charlie for a second. "If you attempt to intervene again, I will enjoy slicing through her soft skin." He presses the knife to her throat as he backs up toward the open door, and a whimper falls from Abby's mouth.

"What the hell do you think you're doing?" a gruff voice snaps, and I whip my head around in time to see Michael Hearst glare at his best friend.

"Don't start getting sentimental now, Michael," Christian says. "Unlike your son-in-law, we were going to share."

Hearst's nostrils flare. "Remove the knife from my daughter's neck now, Christian, or I'll put a fucking bullet in your son's head and then one in yours."

They face off for a couple of tense seconds, and then, Christian removes the knife and steps away from Abby. Hearst grabs her elbow, barely keeping her upright, and I want to go to her so badly it almost kills me.

Denton winces in pain, and Hearst stares at him. "What the fuck happened to you?"

"The bitch shot me," he says, and a surge of pride filters through me.

A flash of pride flares in Hearst's eyes before he chuckles. It enrages me. His so-called friends were going to rape her, and he's laughing. I contemplate reaching for my gun, wondering how many of them I could take out before they kill me. But I won't risk it. Because Abby needs me, and as much as I want to end all these bastards, I dampen my murderous thoughts, because their time will come. "Drew, untie Charlie," he commands, and Drew moves to Barron's side.

"We need to have a conversation, gentlemen, about what is and isn't acceptable when it comes to my daughter," he says to Christian and Denton. He narrows his eyes as he looks at Trent. "I thought I made myself perfectly clear, Trenton. Abby is of-limits to you. Permanently. You had your chance, and you blew it. Focus on your new fiancée."

His gaze flicks to me, Rick, and Chad. "Your presence here is no longer required. I thought my guards made that perfectly clear when they threw you out on your ass."

"I will leave when Abby leaves," I spit, folding my arms and glaring at him.

"You don't get a say. You're not her husband. Charlie is."

Hah. That's where you're wrong.

"She's leaving with me," Charlie says, hobbling toward us, supported by Drew. He shoots a lethal look at Christian, Trent, and Denton. Denton is bitching and sobbing like a baby, and I wish I could record this moment, because it's too pathetic to be believed unless you're seeing it.

"You are in no condition to support Abby right now," Drew says to Charlie, propping him up higher on his body. "Chad, can you take Charlie, and I'll take Abby," he adds. I know he's doing this to keep Hearst from getting suspicious, but I want to be the one to carry my wife to safety.

But I push my own wants aside, focusing on just getting her out of here. Drew lifts Abby, cradling her to his chest. Her eyes are fully closed, but she's alert because she grips onto his shirt, nestling in closer to her brother.

"Your behavior tonight was intolerable, Kaiden," Hearst tells me as I move to go past him. "You need to think about how this reflects on your father. He's been given a second chance, but he doesn't get a third. This is your last warning."

I shove him out of the way before I punch his fucking lights out.

We walk down the hallway in twos, and I'm itching to take my baby in my arms. When we step outside into the main room, it's been completely cleared. Drew leads the way, bringing us out through a different exit. By the time we make it to the elevator, I'm all out of patience.

"Give her to me," I demand, opening my arms.

"She isn't yours anymore," Charlie says, bent over, his face contorted in pain, his breath oozing out in spurts. He's in pretty bad shape. Couldn't have happened to a more worthy recipient. "She's mine."

"Go fuck yourself, Charlie." I pin determined eyes on Drew, ignoring the look he's giving me. I couldn't give two shits about the charade right now.

I want to hold my fucking wife.

I need to be the one to take care of her.

Drew sighs. "I hope you know what you're doing," he murmurs as he carefully deposits Abby in my arms. I fully support her body, holding her up, and she clings to me, emitting a relieved sigh.

The elevator pings, and we step inside. I carry her close, inhaling her smell, thankful to finally have her in my arms.

Charlie glares at me. "This changes nothing."

"Like I said." I glare back at him. "Go fuck yourself."

"Kai," Abby whispers, and it's the sweetest sound in the world.

"I'm here, baby." I inspect her face closely as she blinks her eyes open. Her lower lip trembles, and a sob rips from her mouth. "It's okay, sweetheart. You're safe now. I've got you."

"Don't leave me," she begs, clinging tighter to my shirt.

Out of the corner of my eye, I notice Charlie flinching.

"I'm going nowhere," I tell her, pinning Charlie with a deadly look. "You're staying with me." My look dares him to challenge me. There's no doubt if he wasn't hurting he would fight me.

"Kai." Abby nuzzles into my neck, and I wonder if she's aware of her surroundings. "I love you."

Drew grimaces, because the ruse is most definitely up now. Unbridled pain flashes across Charlie's face before he locks that shit down. I know he loves her, and I also know he tried his best to protect her tonight. I can begrudgingly admit that.

But he failed.

We all did.

And she ended up hurt again.

Well, I'm putting a stop to it now.

Hunt confirmed it before we left, but I haven't had any time to tell Drew or Abby.

Abby will protest if she finds out what I'm planning to do, which is why I'm not telling her until after it's done.

She's my wife, and it's my job to protect her and keep her safe.

I know she wants, *needs*, to direct this thing. Because that bastard has hurt her over and over again.

I get that.

But she needs to realize she isn't alone.

That sometimes others know what is best for her.

And on this occasion, I'm doing what I must do to ensure nothing like tonight ever happens again.

CHAPTER TWENTY-SEVEN

Abby

"Kai, I'm fine. I promise," I say, hating how raspy my voice sounds. Truth is, my throat hurts like a bitch, and I'm shaking all over from the aftermath of my near miss, but I don't want to worry him any more than he already is. His face is twisted in pain, and I know tonight put him through the ringer as well. Apparently, I fell asleep in the car on my way to Lauder's place a couple hours ago. Which is why I'm still wearing my ripped wedding gown. Drew stayed behind to help Charlie, but I've still got five strapping guys hovering over me, all wearing troubled expressions.

"Can I get you something to eat or drink?" Jackson asks, kneeling in front of me.

"How about some hot sweet tea?" Sawyer inquires, arching a brow.

"Do you need any pain pills?" Rick asks, frowning. "And I really should check you out."

"How about tequila?" Xavier says. "Or a whiskey for the shock."

"Guys." Kai shoots them the evil eye. "Stop crowding her."

"It's fine." I push off my elbows on the couch, straightening up and biting down on my lip to avoid whimpering as pain shoots through my hip bone. I took quite a nasty fall, and I'm guessing I have the bruises to show for it.

"How about a warm bath?" Kai suggests, and I nod, because soaking my aching muscles in the tub sounds perfect. But I'm caked in Denton's blood, and I really need to scrub myself clean first.

Rick follows us, but the others give us space, as we leave the room. Kai carries me upstairs to his bedroom, setting me down on the bed. "I'll start the bath, while Rick checks you out."

I nod, holding still as Rick checks my vitals, examines my throat, and asks me a few questions. When he's happy I don't need medical intervention, he slips quietly out of the room, and I'm glad he didn't ply me with sympathy or pepper me with endless questions, because I can't deal with that right now.

Kai steps into the room, lifting me off the bed and carrying me into the steam-filled scented bathroom. Silently, he helps me out of my ruined dress. I grab the USB sticks from the side panels, handing them to him. "Xavier and Sawyer will want those."

He nods, placing them on the marble counter. "I'll ensure they get them."

"I want a shower first," I explain, reaching for the shower door. "To get clean, and then I'd like to soak in the tub."

"Okay, babe. You need me to hold you in the shower?" he asks, leaning in to switch it on.

I shake my head. "I'm covered in that bastard's blood. I don't want any of that touching you."

His jaw locks tight. "Our long game better work, Abby, because those bastards are not getting away with any more shit." The vein in his neck pulses, and his body is chock full of tension.

"It will work," I say even more determined to bring them all down.

"Fuck, baby." He pulls me close, resting his forehead against mine and closing his eyes, as his hands rest gently on my waist. He's shaking all over, and his chest is visibly heaving.

"Hey." I touch his face. "I'm okay."

He opens his eyes, and there's so much emotion brimming in his gaze. "I can't watch them hurt you anymore. I can't stand by and do nothing, Abby. I just can't." His voice cracks, and I want to wrap my arms around him and soothe him, but I'm covered in blood. "I need to protect you from them, and I haven't been doing a good enough job."

I caress his cheek. "None of this is on you, and what I need now is you to hold me and love me and help me put it behind me." I hold his face more firmly. "They didn't win tonight, Kai. I fought back, and you all came for me. They didn't get what they wanted."

"How are you so strong?" He kisses my cheek. "You are so brave, Abby. And every day I find more reasons to fall deeper in love with you."

I stretch up and kiss his lips. "That right there. That's what I need." I sigh. "But first, I need to get clean." He moves aside, and I step under the water, closing my eyes as the shower washes away every trace of them.

When I get out, Kai carries me to the tub, gently placing me in the water. A contented sigh slips from my mouth as the warm water caresses my aching muscles.

"Can I join you?" he asks.

"Please." I smile, happy to be with him, despite what went down tonight. I watch him stripping out of his clothes, admiring his beautiful body, feeling the usual stirrings of lust, but I'm not able to act on anything. Because I feel like I've just gone ten rounds in a boxing ring and my psyche has taken another battering.

I shudder uncontrollably as the events of tonight return to haunt me, remembering how close of a call it was. Thank God, I fought back and delayed them long enough for my brother, my friends, and my love to rescue me. I daren't even think about how awful things would've been if they hadn't arrived in time.

Kai gets in the tub behind me, pulling me back into his chest, and I lean my head against him, holding onto his strong arms, needing to feel protected.

I came so close to complete and utter destruction tonight. I've been broken so many times, but this would have been my final undoing. I squeeze my eyes closed, remembering Christian approaching with his cock in hand, and bile floods my mouth. I shiver again despite the warmth of the body behind me and the soothing water swirling around me.

"Abby." Kai presses a kiss to the top of my head. "Were we too late? Did they—"

"No," I cut across him, quick to reassure. "It hadn't gotten that far."

"Do you want to talk about it?"

My initial instinct is to say no, but if I store this grief up inside, like I've done so many times recently, I'm giving them power over me. Because every time I think of it, I'll feel violated all over again. I want to tell my husband. To reinforce my earlier words. They didn't win tonight. We did. Because I got away, and they didn't get to hurt me in all the ways they planned. "Yes," I say, and I begin telling him what happened.

He listens attentively, never interrupting, running his hands up and down my arms and pressing kisses to my head and my temple, supporting me with his touch and his silence, letting me expunge it from my soul.

Silence descends when I finish, and I know Kai has got to be feeling all manner of emotions, but he doesn't vent, because he's focused on me, and he's not the only one finding new reasons to fall more passionately in love.

"I hate that happened to you, and I wasn't able to prevent it. I'm sorry I wasn't there to stop it."

"It's not your fault. You were all trying to protect me. I know that. If anything, tonight has taught us that no matter how much we plan they still have the ability to outmaneuver us."

"Do you believe your father?" he asks, adding some soap to a sponge. "Or did he set it up and he reacted like that to cover his ass?"

"I don't know," I honestly admit. "He wanted to punish me for tonight, and this might have been his way of doing it." Although, given how he was attempting to grope me on the dance floor, I think he would much rather have been the one doling out my sentence. "Denton insinuated he was behind it, so perhaps, he was planning on joining them and he improvised when you guys showed up."

Kai rubs the soapy sponge up and down my arms and it feels wonderful.

"Well, it won't happen again. You are safe, at least until the vote."

I frown, angling my head around so I'm looking at him. "How?"

"Earlier tonight, Xavier and Hunt unscrambled the video recordings from your house on Christmas Day."

"What?" Excitement bubbles up inside me.

"We have it all. Him killing Charles Barron. Me tied to that chair. Him threatening you into marrying Charlie." He runs his fingers along my cheek. "We could try and use that to take him down."

I shake my head. "It's not enough. He has too many judges, cops, and authority figures in his pocket. We can't risk it. It's why we must hit him from several angles. To ensure he's taken down. And it's not just about him. We need to fuck up the order. To throw Parkhurst into chaos. To try and do something about the kids he's kidnapping. We can't be selfish."

"I love how in tune we are," he says, pressing a kiss to my head as he moves the soap lower. "Because those were my sentiments exactly, with one small difference."

"What difference?"

"Don't be mad," he says, and my hackles are instantly raised. "But I did a thing."

"A thing?" I screech, turning around fully in his arms so I'm looking him straight in the eye. "Spit it out, baby. What have you done?"

"We sent a warning to the bastard along with a snippet of the tape. We told him to lay off you, or it would be sent to the council and the national media as well as the authorities."

I jerk up onto my knees, ignoring the stab of pain the motion produces. "Why the hell would you do that?! Now he knows we are on to him!"

He cups the back of my head. "I know it's risky, but he needs to understand we are serious about the consequences if he or any of his cronies attempt to hurt you again."

"He will fucking kill you, Kai!" Tears prick my eyes, and I can't believe they did that.

"He won't risk anything until after the vote, so that buys us some time."

"And then what?" I gently ask. "Then he'll come after you for this."

"He is not above the law, Abby. He might be protected within the order, but if we released that tape nationwide, the authorities would be forced into action. It doesn't matter how many cops he has in his pocket, that video clearly shows him committing murder, and there would be a public outcry if nothing was done. We are stripping him of everything at the vote, so it won't matter anyway. He's screwed, and he'll be in jail so he can't get back at me. Right now, protecting you is what's most important, and I won't apologize for doing it."

"So, what does it mean for us now?"

"I pretty much showed my hand tonight," he admits, and my heart stops beating for a couple seconds. "Your father knows I still care about you." He stretches up, pecking my lips. "And you told me you loved me in the elevator in front of Charlie too."

"Oh fuck." I have no recollection of that.

"The game is up with Charlie, but I still don't think he'd do anything to hurt you. He's guilty as hell after how things went down tonight, and you can use that to buy his silence. That and the fact we have the tape." He kisses me softly again. "I'm done living without you, Abby. I want you back in my life and in my bed." He pulls me down on top of him. "We can make a deal with the bastard. You agree to maintain the charade with Charlie in public, and in return, we get to do what we want behind closed doors. If he doesn't like it, we threaten to release the recording now."

"He'll want to negotiate," I say. "He'll want that tape, and we'll have to find somewhere secure to store it, along with backups, because he'll try everything in his power to steal it back from us."

"We already have that all figured out," he says. "And it's under control. Don't ask me to tell you, because it's safer if you don't know."

"Kai." I sit up, slanting him with a warning look. We agreed no more secrets, and he's not starting this shit again.

"No, baby." He holds my face in his hands. "There are some occasions where I get to overrule you. It's my job as your husband to take control when you need to let someone else take care of you. This is one of those times, so please don't fight me on it, because tonight has tested every limit I've got. Have you any idea how badly I wanted to slaughter every fucking bastard in that room tonight? How fucking terrified I was for you?"

"I know, babe," I say, resting my head on his chest. "Because I was feeling those emotions too." I'm worried about the consequences of what he's done, but I can't deny how happy it makes me feel that he's taken charge and he's arranging it so we are back in one another's arms.

"Can't sleep, huh?" Jackson asks, as I saunter into the kitchen a couple hours later, yawning.

"I slept fitfully," I admit, scrubbing my eyes as I head toward the coffee pot. You'd think being back in Kai's arms, getting to sleep snuggled up against him in bed, would induce the best sleep ever, but I couldn't shut my brain off. I'm too wired over all the what-ifs.

"Let me get that." His hands land on my shoulders, and he maneuvers me onto a stool.

I prop my face in my hands as I watch him pour two steaming mugs of coffee.

"I know why I can't sleep, but what about you?" I ask, glancing at the clock on the wall. It's twenty to five in the morning.

He shrugs, sipping his coffee, and I understand if he doesn't want to say. But I've wanted to ask for a long time, and the opportunity has never presented itself. "The elite did something to your sister, didn't they?" I softly ask, promising myself I'll drop it if he doesn't respond.

His entire body stiffens, and I reach out, placing my hand over his. "It's okay, Jackson. I'm sorry for prying."

His head hangs, and his eyes lower to the table. Silence descends, and it's uncomfortable. "When Kai told us what happened tonight," he says, in a low voice, lifting his chin. I'm startled to see tears in his blue eyes. "It brought it all back," he admits, pretty much confirming my suspicions. "And, I—" He sighs heavily. "Fuck. If anything happened to you." He stands, pulling me into his chest, and I wrap my arms around his waist, resting my head on his chest. He's wearing a white T-shirt, but heat rolls off his body in tight waves.

"I'm so sorry, Jackson." I hope someday he's able to tell me about her. But if those bastards got a hold of her, I can only imagine the horrors she endured.

"I've spent all this time since her death fighting my feelings, but I can't do that anymore because it's killing me inside." He tips my face up and our eyes meet. "Your strength and your determination to bring them down has encouraged me to start facing up to it." He smiles, and my heart hurts so bad for him because he's not hiding behind his humor. I'm getting an up close and personal view of the real Jackson. "I've failed my sister. I've let myself down. And I'm done being that guy."

"I happen to think that guy's pretty great," I say, peering earnestly into his eyes. "And don't be too hard on yourself. Everyone handles grief differently, and the mind can only process what it's capable of processing. I didn't know your sister, and I didn't know you when she was alive, but I know you loved her very much. I know you were an amazing brother. And I definitely know you didn't fail her." I clasp his wrist. "So, whatever you're saying to beat yourself up, stop. When you're ready to deal, we'll do it together." Renewed determination fuses through my veins. "And whoever is responsible, we'll make sure they pay."

CHAPTER TWENTY-EIGHT

"I need to get my things," I say the following morning, stretching my arms up over my head as I yawn. I finally crawled back under the covers at six thirty a.m., snuggling contentedly into Kai's welcoming arms. At some point, he got up, returning with a tray laden with food. My tummy is full after a plateful of delicious eggs and bacon, and now, it's time to get moving.

"I'll get them," he replies, pinning me with a look that says he means business.

I swing my legs out the side of the bed, moaning as pain spreads up one side of my body. "I need to talk to him, Kai."

"It can wait until you feel better."

"I know Charlie. He'll only show up here if I don't make an appearance today."

"So, let him come here. It's safer than you going there."

I stand and walk around the bed toward him. "I'm going to him. That way I can kill two birds with one stone." I peck him on the lips. "Come with me if it makes you feel better."

He scrubs a hand over his prickly jaw. "What if he tries something?"

"What's he going to try, Kai?" I shrug. "It's clear whatever deal he had with my dad has broken down. They beat him and tied him to a chair last night. I don't think he'll be feeling charitable toward them."

He sighs. "Okay."

I look up at him. "Okay?" I wasn't expecting him to concede so easily.

"There's no point arguing when we both know you're going to do it whether I approve or not."

My smile is wide. "I'm glad you know me and that you're willing to compromise."

He playfully swats my butt. "It's less about compromise and more about saving myself a pointless headache."

An hour later, we are on the road. Sawyer and Jackson are in the back while Kai drives and I'm riding shotgun. Xavier, Rick, and Drew are on standby in case we need to call in the cavalry, but I really don't think that'll be necessary.

Kai parks directly in front of the Barron mansion, turning to face me. "I'm coming in."

"No, you're not." I slant him with a warning look as I secure the earpiece in my ear. "That will only end in bloodshed." I check my gun has the safety on before slipping it in the back waistband of my jeans. Then, I pull Kai's sweater down over it. I had left a few items of clothing at Lauder's place previously, but I had no tops. I'm sure turning up in Kai's clothes will be like waving a red flag in front of Charlie, but it was that or show up in my black bra. I yank the sweater down at the top, securing the communication chip to my lower chest where it's out of sight. I press down on it to activate it as the guys slip their earpieces in.

I lean across the console and kiss his antsy mouth. "He won't hurt me, but if you hear anything you don't like, just come get me."

"I don't like this at all, and if he says anything even remotely threatening, I'm barging in there."

I kiss him again. "I'm counting on it, caveman."

"Charlie?" I call out as I close the front door behind me. There's no reply, and I wander to the kitchen, but he's not in there. The house is spookily empty and quiet as I make my way from the kitchen to the basement. I'm guessing Lillian is out and Elizabeth is squirreled away in her bedroom, as usual.

Quietly opening the door to the basement den, I discover Charlie lying on the couch in sweats and a plain white T-shirt, watching TV. A plaid blanket covers his lower half, and his feet are bare. "Hey," I softly say as I walk across the room.

He jerks around, grimacing and wincing in obvious pain.

"Can I get you some pain pills?" I ask as I round the couch toward him. "Did you call the doctor to check you out?"

"Don't do that," he says, his face contorting further as he attempts to pull himself upright.

"Do what?" I question, tentatively sitting down at his feet.

"Pretend like you care," he hisses. "It's clear now that I was fucking played."

There's no point lying. "You left me no choice."

"I did it all for you, Abby. And it was for nothing." A cold look washes over his features, matching his chilly tone.

"It wasn't for nothing." I lean toward him. "I still care about you, Charlie. I care about you a lot even though you've hurt me."

The indifferent mask drops away, and anger blazes in his eyes. "Don't fucking lie," he roars, sitting up straighter, and wincing. "You don't fucking love me! Not in the way I love you."

"I can't force myself to feel things that don't exist." I shoot him an earnest look because I'm being completely up front with him. "If you'd taken the time to properly talk to me, instead of siding with my father, then all of this could've been avoided." I get up and sit down beside him. "I still love you as a friend, Charlie. You have been in my life for as long as I can remember, and I know this isn't you. I know my father manipulated you. Using your feelings for me to screw with your mind and—"

"Don't be naïve, Abby," he sneers, and his alternating mood swings are giving me emotional whiplash. "This is bigger than your father, and we both know it."

I frown. "What do you mean?"

He shakes his head. "It doesn't matter now, because I've failed." His features soften temporarily. "I failed you last night, and I'm so sorry." The mask is gone, and pain is etched across his face. "I thought I had it handled, but I was outplayed." He barks out a bitter laugh, but I see the vulnerability behind his reaction. "Everyone is fucking playing me, and I'm so far out of my depth it isn't funny." A muscle ticks in his jaw, and his chest heaves up and down as he glances at the ceiling. I give him a couple minutes to gather his thoughts. When he bends his head, looking directly into my eyes, I see a lost little boy who has finally realized he epically fucked up.

I see the Charlie I know and remember, and my heart hurts.

He cups my face, pinning me with those beautiful green eyes. "All I've ever wanted is to keep you safe, but I can't protect you from them. Last night proved that." I place my hand over his hand on my face. "Not alone."

"So, come back to us. Be on our side." I thread my fingers through his. "On *my* side."

"Abby, no!" Kai whispers in my ear. "He can't be trusted."

"And watch you all over Anderson?" Charlie asks, shaking his head as a harsh quality replaces the previous tenderness of his expression. "I can't do it." A cold veneer shrouds his face, and he yanks his fingers from mine. "I gave up everything for you, Abby," he deadpans in a voice devoid of feeling. "I fucking sacrificed my own father for you. He told me you'd never love me, and I repaid him by keeping quiet when they told me he was a pawn." A look of disgust appears on his handsome face. "I didn't know your father was going to murder him in front of us, but I might as well have put the trigger in his hand."

A strangled cry bounces off the wall, and we both whip our heads around. Elizabeth is slumped against the doorway, her eyes wide with shock as big fat tears roll down her face.

I never wanted her to discover the truth, and now, she's found out in the worst possible way.

Poor Elizabeth. And poor Charlie.

"Fuck!" Charlie shouts, pushing awkwardly to his feet as concern splays across his face. He sways unsteadily, and I jump up to help him, but he swats my hand away. "I don't want or need your help," he snaps. "All you have done is destroy my life." His cold, dead eyes bore a hole in the side of my skull as he glares at me. Whatever vulnerability he allowed me to see is securely locked away now.

Elizabeth's sobs grow louder, and I walk toward her, but Charlie grabs hold of my elbow. "Get your shit and get the hell out of my house and out of my life."

"Your mom is upset and—"

"And she's no longer your responsibility," he confirms, cutting across me.

"We are still married," I lie. "And we'll have to keep up appearances in public. It's too risky for all of us if we don't."

"That is the least of my concerns right now." His mask drops again for a split second, and I spot real fear on his face. "Just go, Abby. Go to him and stay the hell away from me because I am fucking done wasting any more time on you."

259

I grab the essentials from my bedroom, including the album of sketches Kai gave me, and hotfoot it out of the Barrons' house with the sound of shouting echoing behind me. Charlie and his mom are really going at it, and I hate leaving them both when they are in pain, but he made his intentions very clear, and if I try to intervene, it might only make things worse.

Kai gets out of the car, coming toward me. "Is that everything?" he inquires, taking the large bag from me.

"No, but it's enough. I'll get Drew to grab the rest of my stuff during the week."

Kai shepherds me to the car, dropping my bag in the trunk while I climb into the passenger seat.

"That went better than expected," Jackson says as I pull the door shut behind me.

"He hates my guts now," I say, "which could be a good or a bad thing." A tight knot forms in my chest.

Kai climbs behind the wheel. "His mom overhearing is a good thing because it means he'll be preoccupied trying to fix things with her. He's already busy with the business, so that means less time to plot against you or us. I think that was the best result we could have hoped for."

I slouch in my seat, propping my feet up on the dash. "I don't like leaving him alone to face that," I truthfully admit.

"It's exactly what he deserves," Kai retorts, kick-starting the engine and flooring it out of there. "Don't forget what he did to you. To us."

"I know, but he's not all bad."

"Charlie Barron is fucked in the head, Abby," Sawyer says. "And you shouldn't feel guilty. He brought all this on himself."

"He doesn't have anyone," I murmur.

"Because he's isolated himself from everyone," Kai says, looking at me with a puzzled expression. "And it's his own fault for trying to take something that was never his."

Kai will never agree, but I can't help feeling sympathy for Charlie, because he's all alone now. His mom might not ever forgive him for the part he played in getting the love of her life killed. Although, she should really vent all her frustration in my father's direction, because he's the one who committed murder. I'm guessing she'll want to shield Lillian from the truth, but Charlie's sister is smart, and she's bound to pick up on the tension between them. If it comes down to a choice, I think she'll choose her mom's side.

He's no longer on speaking terms with Trent or Drew, and he's just thrown me out on my ass.

Meaning he literally has no one.

He hurt me, and he hurt Kai.

And he helped set everything in motion.

I have every reason to hate him, but I just feel sorry for him.

Charlie is a product of his environment and his upbringing, and I wonder if there is ever any way back for him.

I'm sad for my friend.

For the guy who has always had my back even if his motives weren't always pure.

"Babe." Kai lands his hand on my thigh as we emerge from the driveway out onto the open road. "I love how passionately you care, but Charlie Barron dug that hole he's in, and he has no one to blame but himself. As long as he leaves you alone, I consider this a win."

I gulp over the messy ball of emotion in my throat as I place my hand over Kai's. "I know it's a win, and I'm happy I'm back with you, but I can't help how I feel."

"You have a big heart, Abby," Jackson says. "Don't ever change."

"Shit," Sawyer says, sighing, and three sets of eyes turn in his direction. "Drew just texted. Your father has shown up at our place. He's demanding a meeting."

"Crap. He's probably mad Drew is there." I'm always worried about Drew ending up bearing the brunt of all this. He's still not off the hook with the bastard.

"I informed your father in the message that you were living with me," Kai says, and my eyes pop wide. Kai really threw caution to the wind, and I seriously hope he doesn't end up regretting his ballsy move. "Drew can say he was checking up on you." He takes his eyes off the road for a second to glance at me. "Don't worry. He'll be fine."

"He's got some balls showing up there," Kai adds. "But I'm glad he appears to be taking our warning seriously." He sends me a triumphant smile I don't share. "Now, it's our turn to lay down some ground rules."

When we return to the house, Drew and Rick are with the bastard in the formal living room. I'm guessing Xavier is keeping out of sight, because he doesn't want Father discovering his identity. I'm hoping he had time to set up surveillance so this conversation is being recorded. Kai keeps a tight hold of my hand as we step into the room. He shoots daggers at my father, not hiding how much he hates him.

"Abigail." He stands. "I came to see how you were."

I snort. "Cut the bullshit, Father. We all know why you are here. You want to negotiate, so just spit it out."

He takes a step toward me. "Abigail, I—"

Kai moves in front of me, keeping his hand threaded through mine. "Don't come any closer, or I'll blow your fucking brains out. You don't get to speak to her or touch her. You have something to say, you say it to me."

"I've got to hand it to you two," he purrs. "You almost had me fooled, but you let your emotions get in the way. You should never show your hand so blatantly, Kaiden. It's a rookie move."

"I don't give a damn what you think, you perverted fuck," Kai says. "All I want is you to stay away from Abby and to ensure those fucking assholes you call friends get the memo too."

"You are so much like your father," he calmly replies. "And look where loving a woman got him."

I grab fistfuls of Kai's shirt, sending a silent warning to keep his cool. Because the bastard wants to wind him up. "I am nothing like my father," Kai says in a lethal tone. "Because he's always been a selfish prick who was too arrogant to see what was right in front of him. Trust me, I won't make the same mistakes." He pulls me around to his front, bundling me into his chest and wrapping his arms around me. "I love your daughter, and I will go the ends of the earth to protect her. If you think my threat is empty, then you're the fool. If you even breathe funny on her, I'll send that video to every major news outlet worldwide. Not even the elite could save you from the fallout."

"Once I am elected president," he says, "I will permit Abigail to seek an annulment of her marriage to Charlie, and I'll give you both my blessing and my word that you are free to do as you please provided the shares in Manning Motors are transferred back to me and all copies of the recording are also in my possession."

"And in the intervening period, you will keep away from her and keep those other bastards away from her," Kai adds.

"You have my word," he says, and I smother a snort. He's so full of shit. No one is buying this, and it's the most ridiculous charade, but at least it buys us some time to implement our plan.

"Fine. We have a deal," Kai confirms, and I know he's deliberately letting Father think he's weak by not arguing the point further.

"Abigail will have to act as Charlie's wife in public until then. I don't care what you do behind closed doors, but there can be no indication the marriage isn't real."

"I'm not the one you must convince," I say, turning around in

Kai's arms. I can barely tolerate looking at him, but I fake it, schooling my lips into a neutral line. "Charlie doesn't want anything to do with me now."

"You leave Charlie to me." An evil grin spreads across his mouth, and my stomach twists painfully.

"You won't hurt him, Elizabeth, or Lillian," I say. "They get the same protection as me."

He shakes his head slowly. "To think I was actually proud of you last night over how well you defended yourself," he says, tut-tutting. "And then you have to go and let emotions get in the way."

"It's called compassion, not that I expect you to understand because I doubt you've experienced any normal human emotion ever in your life."

He looks through me, not even dignifying that with an answer.

"And I have one other condition," I say.

"That's not how negotiations work."

"I don't give a flying fuck how your usual negotiations work," I hiss. "This is how this one is going down unless you want us to out you as the cold-blooded murdering, sadistic bastard you are."

Drew shoots me a warning look, and I force myself to calm down. "Alessandra publicly embarrassed Drew last night. You will arrange it so Trent and Alessandra are engaged, and Shandra will become Drew's new fiancée."

Shock splays across Drew's face. I knew he'd never ask for himself, and while we have the bastard by the balls, we might as well squeeze as much out of him as we can.

"It's not that simple," he replies.

"Oh, please. Of course, it is. The elite have no regard for women. We're interchangeable, so this should be a cakewalk." He purses his lips, and I enjoy watching him squirm. "I don't care what you have to do or say to make it happen, just make it happen. That bitch is poison, and I want her a million miles away from my brother."

His wry smile rubs me up the wrong way, and I've had enough of his toxic energy polluting our airspace. "And this conversation is officially over, so get the fuck out of our house."

Oh, he doesn't like being spoken to like that. Not one little bit. My inner minx is throwing a party.

He's fuming, but he's doing a good job of hiding it. "Drew," he tosses over his shoulder. "I'll wait for you in the car. Don't be long."

He gives Kai and me the evil eye as he walks out of the room, followed by Rick, who is quick to chaperone him to the door.

"Thanks for that," Drew says, standing and smiling. "At least Shandra is pleasant to be around."

"And she's very easy on the eye," Jackson adds, grinning.

"I wouldn't know," Drew says, completely serious. "I only have eyes for one woman, and it's not her."

My heart aches for Drew, and thoughts of Jane enter my mind again. When all this is over, I'm going to track her down, because I hate seeing my brother so miserable.

"What's going on?" Kai asks, directing his question to my twin.

"We've been summoned to Parkhurst to explain how Denton Mathers got shot," he replies.

What a fucking joke. He gets to almost rape me without consequence, but they're making a big deal out of the fact he got shot? Typical elite bullshit.

"Will this be a black mark against Father's campaign?" I inquire.

Drew shakes his head. "He'll wriggle his way out of it. He'll blackmail Denton into withdrawing his complaint, and it'll get buried."

"How long will you be gone for?" Kai asks.

"Two nights, max," Drew replies.

"Is that enough time?" I ask Sawyer, being vague on purpose

because I want to be careful with that bastard in the vicinity.

"I believe so."

"This is the perfect opportunity," Drew whispers. "Because Christian, Trent, Charlie, and Denton have all been requested too. You have the list of elite targets, and there's enough time to work out a plan. Go for it, so we can get ready to really nail the bastard to the wall."

CHAPTER TWENTY-NINE

"That was easy," Xavier says, when I return from the dungeon to my old bedroom the following night, having given the new guard on duty down there a glass of iced tea laced with the sleeping potion I've used to drug Charlie.

"It helps that we have eyeballs on him to ensure he drinks it," I add, watching the new guy sipping from the drink via the live feed on Xavier's tablet.

Thanks to the intel I acquired from Father's computer, the guys broke through the firewall into the security system. We don't even need to call the safecracker dude in, because the infrared security is all digitally monitored and controlled, and Xavier now knows how to deactivate it. The only thing we aren't sure about is whether it will emit any alarm once it's disabled, so knocking the bodyguard out was important for more than one reason.

"And you're sure the camera system in the house is separate to the system in the dungeon," Kai asks, folding his arms across his chest.

"Yes," Sawyer replies. "They are completely separate systems. Xavier has already uploaded a fake feed to the system in the house, so they won't see us sneaking down there. It's why no one discovered Abby wandering around the house. All we have to worry about is bumping into any guards patrolling inside."

"It's the middle of the night," I say. "And whoever is on house duty is most likely dozing in front of the TV or already passed out. I didn't bump into anyone." Although, I had a story concocted about needing something from my old bedroom if I'd been discovered. "Everyone is away, and the staff is sleeping, so they won't be expecting any trouble. Especially when we snuck in through the tunnel, so they have no idea we are here."

"And if we are discovered," Rick says. "We're ready to deal with them." He pats the gun strapped to his hip. We are all carrying because we're taking no chances. It's been mutually agreed that anyone who finds us must be taken out. I don't like thinking about it too deeply, because these men are only doing their job, but there is too much at stake to leave witnesses.

Let's just hope we don't run into anyone.

We spend another twenty minutes anxiously watching the guard on the feed until the drugs take effect and he slumps unconscious to the floor.

"Showtime," Jackson says with a muscle popping in his jaw. He's been unusually quiet tonight, and strain literally oozes from his pores. I know this must be hard for him, but I love him for wanting to come tonight even though no one would blame him if he wanted to sit it out.

Xavier stays behind to monitor our progress through the house and to disable the security system at the last second. Rick is staying with him, to keep watch on the corridor outside my bedroom, just in case anyone appears. Xavier's role in this is crucial, plus we need access to my bedroom to exit via the tunnel. Sawyer, Jackson, Kai, and I will break into the vault and locate the files we need. We're using the earpieces again to stay in constant communication.

We move stealthily through the house, and in next to no time, we are downstairs, pushing past the immobile guard, spread-eagled across the floor in the hallway. Using the code Drew gave us, we enter the bastard's office, waiting for Xavier to shut down the main system before stepping inside the elevator that takes us to the vault in the hidden lower level of the basement.

It's eerily quiet when we step out into the narrow hallway, and the only sounds are our collective deep breaths. Our feet squelch on the shiny floor as we edge toward the only door down here. I curl my hand around the door handle, drawing a brave breath. "Disable the infrared system now, Xavier," I instruct.

"On it."

A piercing alarm rings out, and my eardrums silently protest.

"Shit." Kai shares an anxious look with me. "Please tell me that's only going off down here."

"It is," Xavier confirms. "I'm watching the hallways in the house, and there isn't a sinner in sight. The system is set up so a warning communication is issued when the alarm goes off, but I stopped it, so no one is aware you are down there. I'll keep you posted if that changes."

"Okay," Kai says, pulling my hand away from the door and nudging his way in front of me. "We're going in now."

Sawyer pulls me back behind him, pushing me into Jackson's body. "Stay here and let Kai and me check it out first."

My initial instinct is to pout and protest, but it's cool that my husband and his friends want to protect me. That they are willing to put themselves at risk to ensure my safety. Only an idiot would argue against that.

Jackson wraps his arms around me from behind. "I'm glad you're letting us take care of you. No one wants to see you hurt again."

The guys enter the room, and I'm too preoccupied watching them to even respond to Jackson's statement. Or to point out that I don't want to see any of them hurt either.

Anyway, it's a moot point. Because the coast is clear and Kai is back, taking my hand and leading me into the room.

It's a large open-plan room, split in two by a small seating area placed in front of a large wall-mounted screen. "That must be where he plays the home movies," I ponder out loud, shouting to be heard over the ear-shattering chiming of the alarm.

"Over here, guys," Sawyer hollers and we walk to the row of silver drawers running from ceiling to floor. "They are alphabetically organized," he says, grinning. "Thank fuck for your father's OCD."

I'd split up the target list into four separate lists last night, also organized alphabetically so it should make this easier to locate the correct files. I quickly distribute the lists to the guys, and we head in separate directions to track down our pile.

We work silently and speedily, everyone understanding the urgency of the situation. We can't risk detection, so we need to get in and out fast. I locate my first target and pull open his drawer. The recording is on a small disc, and I slip it into the small backpack I have strapped across my chest. Curious, I flip through some of the papers in the drawer, my eyes growing wider as I explore. "There is so much evidence in here," I say to no one in particular. "He has financial records, details of their families, tons of surveillance footage, and all manner of shit on these people."

"I know. It's the same in this drawer. He must have a team of PIs on his payroll," Sawyer says.

"We need to stay focused," Kai reminds us. "As tempting as it is, we can't take any of that stuff. We need to grab the recordings and copy them asap. Don't get distracted."

Ten minutes later, we have half the video files we need and Sawyer walks to the couch, dropping down onto it with the bag and some high-tech digital device to begin copying them. The three of us continue searching for the rest of the files while he works away, dropping them over to him in batches.

I stumble across a name that isn't on the list, but I can resist looking. From the myriad of evidence stored in this drawer, I can tell Father has been compiling ample evidence. A massive grin spreads across my mouth as I snatch up the recording and walk over to Sawyer. "Copy that one too." He looks at the name, arching a brow. "It should make for interesting viewing."

A half hour later, we are done, and I'm on edge as we conduct one last inspection of the room making sure nothing is out of place and that we're leaving no evidence behind.

Kai pulls the door closed behind us, informing Xavier so he can reset the alarm. My ears rejoice when the blaring alarm stops ringing, and everyone sighs in relief.

"Thank fuck for that," Jackson says, rubbing at his temples as we race along the corridor toward the elevator. "My head is throbbing from the noise."

"Stay alert," Kai warns, as the elevator opens into Father's office. But it's as we left it, and the guard is still conked out on the ground, his chest heaving as loud snores rip from his mouth.

"Give it to me," Kai says to Jackson, flipping his palm up. Jackson removes a slim rectangular box from his back pocket, handing it over without question. Kai opens it, removing a needle and a syringe.

"I still hate this," I mumble, remembering the argument we got into last night with them and Rick. Xavier and I were vehemently against shooting the guy full of heroin, but it was four against two, so we lost that battle. If Drew had been there, I know he would've voted for this plan too.

"Would you rather we put a bullet in his skull?" Kai says, eyeing him as he crouches over the unsuspecting unconscious guy.

"Of course not, but this could kill him too."

"It's not a lethal dose, and Rick got it off a reputable source so it's as pure as you'll find anywhere in Boston. He'll be strung out when the shift changes, and he'll be fired. Even if he attempts to mouth off, no one will believe him. And if your father is suspicious and he checks the camera feed, he won't find anything amiss. We're covered, but only if we do this. Otherwise, he'll blab to everyone that the boss's daughter gave him an iced tea and that's the last thing he remembers." I look away as Kai prepares to inject the needle into a vein in his arm. "I don't like it either," Kai adds. "But this needs to happen."

We leave the guy on the floor after Kai has shot him up, returning to my old bedroom with everyone constantly looking over our shoulders.

"That was almost too easy," Sawyer admits when we exit the tunnel into the woods, heading toward the SUV.

"Don't fucking jinx us, man," Jackson says, slapping him on the back.

"It was easy because we planned well, we have mad skills, and we're fucking badass," Xavier says, smirking like the cat that got the cream.

Sawyer rolls his eyes. "Even the best laid plans run into unforeseen obstacles."

"Relax, man." Kai wraps his hand around mine as we walk the last few feet to the car. "We pulled it off, and we're walking away with enough evidence to bury the bastard and a lot of the high-ranking elite. This is a good day." He swings me up, spinning me around.

"Don't get too cocky," Sawyer says, bringing us back down to earth. "Never forget who we are dealing with."

CHAPTER THIRTY

When we get back to the house, we all collapse into bed despite the temptation to check out the tapes. We need to grab some sleep because we've got school in the morning. Although we all have enough credits to graduate early, we need to go about business as usual so as not to draw attention.

Getting to sleep beside Kai again is heavenly, and as I snuggle into his side, sliding my leg between his, it doesn't take long to fall into a deep sleep.

I'm woken the next morning with wandering hands roaming my naked body. Kai brushes his lips against my inner thigh, and I jerk under his expert touch. "Good morning, baby," he murmurs across my heated skin before his tongue flicks out, licking a line up and down my slit.

A needy moan escapes my lips. "It *is* a good morning," I agree, arching my back as his tongue works in tandem with his fingers inside my pussy. He has magic fingers and a magic tongue, and I'm already so wet for him.

"I need to be inside you, firecracker," he says, surging to his knees.

"I'm not complaining," I say, pinning him with lust-drenched eyes.

Wasting no time, he parts my thighs wider before thrusting inside me in one confident move. I instantly perk up. My mind might still be sleepy, but my body is fully awake, and he slides in and out of my slick channel with ease. Circling my legs around his waist, I dig my heels into his ass and lift my hips, meeting him thrust for thrust. His lips glide up and down my body, worshiping every inch of bare skin as he rocks me into oblivion.

After we've showered and dressed in our uniforms, we make our way downstairs holding hands.

Xavier and Sawyer are in the kitchen, heads bent over their laptops, furiously tapping away.

"Morning!" I say cheerily, and Xavier lifts his head, blowing me a kiss. Kai deposits me at the kitchen table before moving to the coffee pot. "How long have you guys been up?"

"Not long," Sawyer says without looking up. "We're just checking the camera feeds from Chez Manning to ensure everything is good."

"And is it?" Kai asks, handing me a mug before claiming the seat beside me.

"Yep," Xavier says. "Your friend downstairs was carted off in an ambulance at six a.m., and I'm watching email communications between your father's head of security and the company he used to recruit him. He's toast. I think we got away with it."

"Sweet," Jackson says, ambling into the kitchen in his gray school pants and nothing else. His hair is all messed up, and he's sporting a thin layer of scruff on his chin and cheeks.

The doorbell pings at that exact moment, and we all share a look. "You expecting anyone?" I ask.

"Nope," Jackson says on a yawn.

"I'll get it," Rick says from the doorway, also yawning.

"Hold up," Sawyer says. "Let me check with security." He calls the guard on duty at the door, nodding at Rick as he listens to whatever the guy is saying on the other side.

Rick dumps his duffel bag on the ground before walking in the direction of the front door.

He returns a couple minutes later with Shandra in tow.

"Hey." She smiles, looking a little unsure as she steps into the room. "I just wanted to drop by and check up on you before school."

"I'm good," I say, ignoring the dull ache in my side. The skin on my hip is every shade of blue and purple known to mankind, but there's no permanent damage so I can't complain too much.

"You want some coffee?" Jackson asks, holding up the pot.

Shandra's eyes are out on stilts as she tries her best not to ogle his impressive upper body. "Sure," she splutters, and I smother a grin.

"Have a seat," I offer, pulling the empty chair beside me out for her.

She slides into it, shooting me a grateful smile. "I still can't believe all the shit that went down Saturday night."

"Just a normal night among the elite," I quip even though there's nothing even slightly humorous about it.

"Chad told me what happened," she adds in a quieter voice. "Are you okay?"

"I'm fine." I lean back against Kai, holding onto his arms as they encircle my waist.

Her eyes pop wide. "So, it's true? You've left Charlie and moved in here?"

"Who told you that?" I ask, narrowing my eyes.

"Drew!" she blurts. "He, ah, also told me what you did. Requesting Alessandra and I swap fiancés, and I can't thank you enough."

"Don't thank her yet," Kai says. "Not until you get the official word."

Jackson hands her a coffee.

She beams at him. "Thanks."

"You want toast, beautiful?" he asks me, and I nod.

"That would be great, thanks, but do we have time?"

"We have time," Kai says, pressing a kiss to that sensitive spot just under my ear. "You need to eat."

Having to wait until the end of the day to watch the recordings we stole is sheer torture. While I know it will make unpleasant viewing, I'm still anxious to watch them.

To know they are legit.

That we have concrete evidence now to properly implement our plan.

Those are the only thoughts going through my mind all day, and school seems to last forever. But, finally, the last bell dings, and we are on our way back to the house.

To keep up the marriage charade, I drove myself to and from school although the guys insisted on trailing me all the way. Kai and I agreed we need to continue ignoring one another in public, but he still managed to steal a few kisses here and there, as usual, and there's no denying we are both happier now we can be together in private.

"Where should we start?" Xavier asks after we've all eaten and changed and reconvened in the living room where he has everything set up. Rick and Drew are missing, because the former had to return to Harvard this morning, and Drew is at Parkhurst, but we agreed not to delay, because this shit can't wait.

"With this one," I say, slapping the Christian Montgomery recording into his hand.

Christian hadn't been on our target list of blackmailed elite, but when I spotted the file, it was too good an opportunity to pass up. It makes sense that the bastard would have a file on his best friend because his motto is to never trust anyone and to keep your enemies close. I'm salivating to see what he's compiled on Christian and hopeful it's something we can use to take him down too. Xavier inserts the file into the driver, but I place my hand over his. "We need to wait for Shandra. She's only five minutes away."

"Are you sure it's wise to let her sit in on this?" Sawyer asks.

"She's going to be Drew's fiancée, and we can't shield her from this shit." I plop down onto the couch beside Kai, and he immediately tucks me under his arm. "Knowledge is power, and she needs to know what she's involved in."

"How much do we want to tell her though?" Xavier says. "Charlie may've had a point. She was Trent's fiancée. Maybe the whole Trent and Alessandra fucking scene was a trap. Trent knows you. It's not a huge stretch for him to guess you'd request this. She could be his spy, and now, she's slap bang in the middle of our lair."

"She's firmly anti Team Trent," Kai says. "We can trust her."

I twist around in his arms, eyeing him suspiciously. "Why do I get the sense that is not just an observation?"

He shifts a little and his tongue darts out, wetting his bottom lip. Ignoring the fact I wish I *was* that tongue, I narrow my eyes farther. "Out with it." I fold my arms across my chest, daring him to lie.

He drags his hand through his hair. "I did it to protect you." I work hard to keep calm. "I hated that I couldn't be by your side to protect you myself, so I did a few things. I've had a bodyguard following you around in public, and I spoke with Shandra and asked her to stick close to you."

I hop up. "She's only been pretending to be my friend?" I screech, incensed even though another part of me is happy he went to such lengths to keep me safe.

"I haven't been pretending," she says, walking into the room at the perfect moment. She drops her purse on the coffee table. "I've always liked you, Abby, but you were hard to get to know because of the whole elite bullshit rules." She unbuttons her coat, draping it over the side of the couch. "I thought being engaged to Trent would pave the way for us to be friends. But the asshole was vehemently against it. Kai overheard us arguing about it at school, and he approached me later, suggesting it would work to our mutual benefit if we became friends." She stands directly in front of me, and there is zero remorse or regret on her face.

"How much was real?" I ask, because I need to be sure.

"Nothing I have said or done has been fake or coerced. Having you as a friend has helped me process the clusterfuck of feelings I'm dealing with. I've been forced into this world kicking and screaming." Her eyes plead with me for understanding. "I've needed you as much as you've needed me, and I hope this won't come between us." She glances at Kai briefly. "I was planning to tell you about my conversation with Kai, but the right opportunity never arose. I don't want there to be any secrets between us."

"This doesn't exactly help me trust you," I honestly admit.

"I know you have trust issues, and for good reason. But I swear I have no ulterior motives. I fucking despise Trent. You deserve the Nobel Peace Prize for putting up with him as long as you did. Never in a million years would I ever side with him. His bastard father screwed over my father, which pulled me into this life, and I hate the Montgomerys with a passion unrivaled." Her eyes shine with anger, and I just know she's telling the truth.

"Okay. I'll take you at your word, but if you're lying, I'll put a bullet directly between those pretty eyes."

I'd never go there, but I'm in a bit of a belligerent mood now, and I want to push her and see how she reacts.

"I'd expect no less," she says, knotting her hands in front of her.

I stare her out of it for a few seconds, and I'm betting Jackson is hard as a rock watching our tense standoff.

"Okay." I nod, giving her the benefit of the doubt.

Her shoulders relax, and she smiles. "So, we're good?"

I return her smile. "We're good." I could cling to the suspicion simmering under the surface or embrace her at face value. With everything else we have going on, accepting her explanation as the truth is the obvious choice.

I have enough people I mistrust, and I'd rather not add someone else to the list.

So, I'll accept her friendship, but all bets are off if she *is* playing me.

"What is it we are looking at?" she asks me.

"My father has a whole vault of evidence he uses to blackmail high-ranking elite members into supporting his campaign for presidency. We broke into his vault and stole some of the tapes. We're watching them to see what's on them, and we're going to use it to approach these men and get them to switch allegiances."

Shock splays across her face. "Ho. Lee. Shit."

"It's not going to be pleasant." I take a few minutes to recap what I've seen in the dungeon and what we know from Drew about the young girls being abused down there.

"Oh my God." She clasps a hand over her mouth.

"They are the sickest, most depraved bastards, and we're planning to take them down." I'm not elaborating any further because that's as much as she needs to know for now. "Are you with us?" I ask.

"I'm in." She doesn't hesitate. "Whatever I can do to help, I'll do it."

We spend the next five hours watching bits of every tape. It's all any of us can stomach. The scenes are scarily similar.

Men abusing young girls and boys. Men fucking men. Men submitting to other men and being physically and verbally abused. Men giving in to their darkest desires, using all the facilities and tools the dungeon has to offer. A few of them show men killing their sexual partners in some form of twisted sex fantasy.

A lot of these high-ranking elite are prominent figures in the world of business and politics. Drew and I had scrolled through the names at our disposal, choosing the best targets, and Father hasn't let us down. If any of these recordings got out, their careers would be ruined, their reputations in tatters, their families torn apart and they'd definitely kiss their freedom goodbye. I don't care how well connected the elite are, there is no way those men would avoid jail time with such incriminating evidence.

No wonder they are all scared to cross him.

"Fuck it. I need a drink after that," Jackson says, stalking to the liquor cabinet, looking like he's about to puke. The old Jackson would have pulled out a blunt and smoked his brains out. I'm not sure switching his addiction to alcohol is much better, but we all need a drink or ten after tonight's harrowing session.

"You want something, babe?" Kai asks, and strain is evident in his tone and on his face.

"Vodka. Thanks," I say, not even attempting to hide the tears cascading down my face.

"Hey." He kneels in front of me, taking my hands in his. "We're going to fucking end those bastards."

"It can't come soon enough," Shandra says over a sob. Our pained tearstained eyes meet in joint understanding.

"I say we hire a fucking hitman to take them all out," Xavier says, as a myriad of emotions flit across his face.

"The thought had crossed my mind," Sawyer says.

"Fuck hiring a hitman," Kai says. "Let's just fucking take the assholes out ourselves."

No one responds to his statement, because we all feel the same way but know it's not possible. As much as no one wants to admit it, we need those disgusting, depraved, sick individuals to help us take down the bastard and send cracks splintering throughout the order.

"We are definitely sharing those recordings the day of the vote," I say, more determined than ever.

"Hell yeah," Xavier says as Kai climbs to his feet. "I'll time it so the files are sent to the local police and the FBI at the same time."

Kai stands, rubbing his thumb along my jawline. "Let me get you that drink." He looks at Shandra. "Can I get you anything?"

"I'll take a beer."

She sits beside me, and we're both quiet, watching Kai and Jackson get everyone drinks. They're not speaking either. Everyone is feeling so many different emotions, and it's hard to put it into words.

Xavier and Sawyer are quietly arguing about something with their heads buried in their laptops.

"I had no idea, all these years at school, that, that … those horrors even existed, let alone so close to where I live," Shandra says, visibly shuddering.

"I've always known how nasty this world is, but I didn't realize that was happening right under my nose," I say, turning to face her. "I slept in my bed night after night, ignorant of what was happening a few floors below me. It makes me sick."

"They've got to be stopped."

"They will be. And we're the ones to do it."

We stay up for another hour, knocking back a few drinks. Conversation is minimal, interspersed between bursts of outrage as we all try to process. Everyone is in shock after what we've just watched, and the mood is solemn. I wave Shandra off at the front door and then follow Kai up to bed.

"You okay?" he asks the instant I step foot in his bedroom. He walks toward me in his boxers.

"I'm okay," I whisper, falling into his open arms. His heart beats steadily under my ear as I rest my head on his chest. "I just want this to be over. I want to see justice for those girls." I look up at him. "Are we crazy waiting another couple months to do this? How many more girls will suffer in the meantime?"

He brushes hair back off my face. "How many more will suffer if we don't plan and execute this carefully?" he replies. "If we don't succeed, countless others will fall victim to the elite. We stick to the plan, and it will work."

I nod, because I know he's right, but I feel so utterly helpless right now, and I need him to distract me. Lifting my head, I run my hands up his chest, swirling my finger around the intricate patterns inked across his skin, trailing my fingers up to his face and along his jawline. He shivers under my touch, closing his gorgeous brown eyes as he succumbs to my caress. I drag my nails gently through the shorn sides of his hair, tracing the skull tattoo with my thumb, before stretching up on tiptoe and pressing my lips to his.

"Make love to me, Kai," I whisper, staring deep into his eyes when he opens them. "Like you did the first night we met."

Usually we fuck hard and fast, like we can't get enough of one another. But that's not what I need tonight.

I slide my hand down the gap between our bodies, palming the growing bulge in his boxers. "I need to be reminded that sex is an act of intimacy between two people who love one another." I press my lips to his chest, right over the place where his heart beats wildly in anticipation. "I want to feel all of the pleasure and none of the pain."

He scoops me up into his arms without hesitation. "It would be my honor, Mrs. Anderson."

CHAPTER THIRTY-ONE

Kai is true to his word, making slow, sensual love to me, just like that first night in the cabin. My body, mind, heart, and soul are consumed by him, and it's exactly what I need to wash away the horrors invading my mind after watching those tapes.

He thrusts slowly inside me, kissing me deeply as we rock together, and I've never felt closer to any other person than I do in this moment. His fingers are like feathers gliding along my heated skin. His caress reaching soul deep. His touch is everything, and I give in to it, absorbing every sensation he coaxes from my body. My climax is building at a steady pace, but I don't want to come yet.

I want to stay here like this with him for eternity.

Feeling every stroke of his cock as he pushes carefully in and out of me.

My hands roam his back and his ass as his lips move to my neck and lower to my collarbone. His tender kisses send tremors of bliss ricocheting all over my body, and my heart is so full. "I love you," I rasp, as tears of pure, unbridled emotion pool in my eyes.

He lifts his head, brushing my tears away with his thumb as he continues rocking into me. "I love you too, and this is everything, baby."

I wrap my legs around his waist, pulling him in deeper, as I clasp both sides of his face. "Don't ever leave me, Kai, because I would die without you."

"I will never leave you, Abby. Not even in death. I will always find my way back to you."

Tears leak out of my eyes, but, for once, they are happy tears.

We continue loving one another, without urgency, until we fall off the ledge together.

I'm lying flat on my back beside Kai, with our fingers interlinked, and I've never felt more at peace or more secure. His love supports me in so many ways. I turn to face him, resting my hand on his chest. His skin is warm and clammy to the touch but not in an icky way. "You are my world, Kaiden Anderson," I tell him. "And I love you so very much." I lean down and kiss his lush mouth softly and slowly.

He pulls me in closer. "It's cheesy to admit this, but you fucking complete me, Abby. I never want to stop feeling the way I feel when I'm with you."

"You are such a closet romantic," I tease, as his belly emits a loud rumble. He moves to get up, but I push him back down on the bed. "You are always looking after me, now it's my turn." I swing my legs out of bed, swiping his shirt from the floor and pulling it on. "I'll make us something to eat and bring it up."

He sits up, and I love how his abs flex and roll with the motion. My tongue darts out, and I want to lick every groove and indent. But it will have to wait for round two, as I'm fucking starving too. He pulls me down for a searing-hot kiss, and I'm struggling to see straight when we finally break for air. "I love seeing you in my clothes. You are sexy as hell, baby," he says, sliding his hand up the outside of my thigh. "Hurry back, because I'm not finished loving you."

I dart out of the room like a ninja on skates, and his loud laughter follows me down the stairs.

I make us some chicken wraps and load the tray with a couple bottles of water and some chips before making my way back upstairs.

"What—" I start asking when I reach the landing, spotting Kai standing in the doorway to his room in his boxers. His brow is puckered, his head cocked to one side. A loud moan, followed by the sound of something banging against a solid surface cuts me off mid-sentence. My eyes widen as I pass the tray to Kai.

He jerks his head in the direction of Sawyer's room. The door is slightly ajar. Not enough that we can see anything. But enough that we can hear.

"Fuck, yes," a familiar voice shouts, as the banging picks up in intensity. "Fuck that ass hard, Hunt."

Thank fuck, Kai is holding the tray now because I'm one hundred percent certain the contents would be all over the floor if I'd still been carrying it.

"Oh. My. God," I whisper, as a grin forms on my mouth.

Kai wiggles his brows. "This has been in the cards a while," he admits.

"I agree. The sexual tension between them is off the charts."

"Hell, yes. Harder, Hunt," Xavier roars, and a door down the hallway opens.

Jackson pops his sleepy head out. "What the fuck is going on?"

"You don't want to know," Kai deadpans, just as Xavier lets out another primal moan.

Jackson's head snaps up, and a huge grin spreads across his lips. "About fucking time." He rubs his hands gleefully. "I can't wait to throw shade at Hunt for this." He chuckles, and I roll my eyes. His eyes drift to the tray, growing big. "Any of that for me?"

"What do you think, asshat?" Kai says.

I take half a wrap and put it on Kai's plate. Then I load some chips on the other plate and walk to meet Jackson. "Here." I hand him the plate, kissing his cheek. "I won't eat all of my mine."

He messes up my hair. "Thanks, beautiful."

"Cute PJs," I tease, glancing at his blue-, gray-, and white-striped pajama pants.

"I grabbed the first thing I found on the floor," he admits, popping a chip in his mouth. "Didn't think Anderson would appreciate me wandering around butt naked." He smirks at Kai.

"You got that right," Kai says. "The only cock Abby's seeing around here is mine."

Sawyer lets loose a string of expletives as Xavier moans and grunts. "Fuck yeah, baby!" Xavier shouts. "Pound that ass." Jackson and I convulse in a fit of laughter, and I've pains in my stomach I'm laughing so much.

"And I've heard enough." Kai lifts his shoulder. "Come back to bed, babe." His eyes lower to the tray. "I'm eating this first, and then, I'm devouring you." His eyes darken with lust. "And you can scream the fucking house down this time."

"Sooo," I say, dragging the word out the following morning in the kitchen. "You and Xavier, huh?" I quirk a brow, fighting a giggle as Sawyer's face pales.

"I'm not discussing him with you," he says, immediately going into lockdown mode.

"Fuck yeah, baby. Pound that ass!" Jackson says in Sawyer's ear, mimicking Xavier's voice, and I almost lose my stomach contents.

"We could all see it coming," Kai says, leaning back in his chair and patting his lap. I drop down onto him, wrapping my arms around his shoulders.

"There's no shame in admitting you are hot for one another," I say, taking Kai's cup from his hand and drinking his coffee.

"I am *not* hot for him," Sawyer says through gritted teeth, stabbing at the buttons on his tablet.

"What did I miss?" Drew asks, appearing in the kitchen doorway.

I slam the mug down on the table and hop up, racing toward my brother. I throw myself into his arms. "I wasn't expecting you back until tonight."

"The bastard had meetings today, so we flew back on the jet," he says, yawning.

"Well, how did it go?"

"It's fine," he says, slinging his arm around my shoulder and steering me back to the table. "He got Denton on his side, and he concocted some bullshit about a bodyguard accidentally shooting him."

"And what about the engagement swap?" Kai asks, holding out his arms for me.

"All done." Drew grins. "I'm officially free of the she-devil."

I sink onto Kai's lap again, facing my brother. "Thank fuck for that. Her and Trent are a match made in hell, and they so deserve one another."

"He's fucking ecstatic," Drew admits, accepting a mug of coffee from Jackson.

"Morning, hot stuff," Xavier says, eyeballing Sawyer as he saunters into the kitchen with a shit-eating grin on his face.

"Don't start with me," Sawyer says, frowning. "I'm seriously pissed right now."

"Over moi?" Xavier says, propping his elbows on the counter and leering at Sawyer.

"They all know because your mouth is too fucking loud!" Sawyer hisses.

"That's not what you were saying about my mouth last night," Xavier retorts, winking.

Sawyer audibly sighs, and his eyes close for a brief moment. Gathering up his things, he stands, clutching his tablet and paperwork to his chest. His gaze jumps between us. "Xavier and I hooked up. It was a onetime thing, and it's no big deal." He prods his finger in the air. "And if any of you gives me shit, I'll fucking walk and you can find another lackey to do your donkey work for you." Sending all of us a glare, he stomps out of the room.

"I thought getting laid would remove that giant stick up his ass," Xavier says, grabbing an apple from the fruit bowl. "But I can see I still have my work cut out for me." He waggles his brows before biting into the fleshy apple. "It's just as well I always rise to the challenge," he adds, and Jackson chuckles.

Kai rolls his eyes, while Drew looks at me. "I go away for two nights and miss all the drama."

The next week is busy with school and figuring out the next stage of our plan. Chad and the gang have finished their investigative work, and we have all the intel we need on the board members and the elite members we targeted, so their role in this plan has come to an end.

Drew and I meet the three board members he's been warming up the last few weeks, and it's a hugely successful meeting. We took a calculated risk and informed them of what goes on in the basement dungeon of our house and how we believe it's only a matter of time before the authorities swoop in and arrest Father. We impressed on them the urgency of separating the business from his actions and how there is little time to waste. They were particularly pleased to hear we have no plans to fulfill an active role in the business at this time and how we will allow the board and senior management team to continue to operate as they currently are. The only change will be the appointment of a new interim CEO until Drew has graduated college and is ready to take the mantle.

They agreed to work with us, behind the scenes, and they promised to secure their other colleagues' agreement. As soon as they have spoken with every board member, and gotten the green light, we will hold a group meeting where they will be required to sign nondisclosure agreements and new contracts.

It's like I thought.

They hate Father's guts, and he hasn't built any loyalty within his team.

Thankfully, because it makes our job easier.

The other progress we make is with the doctors on staff at the Parkhurst medical facility. There are only five on payroll, and Xavier was able to infiltrate the firewall and hack into their system undetected. He found two doctors noted as attending physicians on my file, so we have a manageable shortlist. Sawyer and I stayed up late over the weekend, researching both men, and we feel pretty sure we have our guy.

Dr. Tom Collingsworth has only been working at Parkhurst for four years. He took over from his late father after he passed. He has a wife and two young daughters, and they live in a sleepy town fifteen miles north of Parkhurst. As well as providing medical services to the elite, he owns his own doctor's clinic, servicing several neighborhoods. He donates to several charities, most of them focused on women's health or mental health charities, and he goes mountain biking every Tuesday and takes his family to church religiously every Sunday.

Maybe because he's atoning for his sins.

Or maybe it means he has a conscience and he's the doctor we are looking for.

We won't know until we talk to him.

Which is currently the hot topic of conversation around the dinner table.

Xavier and I made a massive pot roast, and we are debating how to approach the good doctor as we tuck in.

"You returning to Wyoming is risky as fuck," Drew says. "Because I'll be at the annual Parkhurst meeting, and I won't be able to protect you."

Drew, Trent, Charlie, Christian, and Father are leaving on Monday for the week, which means it's the only time we can do this. Our plan is to go to Wyoming, kidnap the doctor, and force him to talk to us

"I'll be with her," Kai says.

"*We'll* be with her," Jackson adds, stabbing Kai with a serious look.

"And I'm not getting left behind," I say, spearing a carrot with my fork. "If Mom is still alive, I want to be right there in that room when he admits it."

"I know," he quietly says, nodding. "But the elite can't know you are there. Father can't know you are there."

"Which is why we're driving," I say. It's over a thirty-hour trip, which means it'll take us three days to get there, but we can't risk flying because that leaves too much of a trace.

Drew shakes his head. "That won't work. You'll be missing from school for a week, and he'll find out."

"So, we'll lie, and I'll say Kai took me on vacation.

"He'll be suspicious as fuck." Drew looks contemplative as he sips from his glass of water.

"What about James Kennedy?" Sawyer asks. "He mentioned he could falsify travel logs, and the Kennedys weren't opposed to helping us before." He eyeballs Kai, who already has his cell in hand. "Ask Rick to ask them."

"I'm already on it," he says, bringing the phone to his ear.

The Kennedys are infamous around Boston thanks to Kennedy

Apparel, the fashion design empire Alex Kennedy owned and managed until a few years ago. And they have seven superhot sons who regularly make headlines on all the gossip sites. Rick is at Harvard with Kyler Kennedy and his wife Faye, and they've become good friends. When Rick needed to get Joaquin and Harley out of Connecticut without our father knowing, James Kennedy flew in on his private jet and got them safely out of there.

Here's hoping he can come through for us again.

The rest of us eat while Kai talks to his brother. When he hangs up, he says, "Rick is meeting Kyler later, and he'll ask him."

"Okay," I say, finishing off my dinner and pushing my plate away. "Let's park that aspect for now." I look at Drew. "How are you planning on approaching the elite without Father knowing?"

There are twenty elite members to win to our side, and Drew is the only one who can handle this part. I can't be involved because they hold such little regard for women, and my presence could be more of a hindrance than a help. So, Drew will have to be persuasive as fuck because it's all on his shoulders. I'm worried Father will catch him in the act and kill him.

"The main Parkhurst facility is huge, and there are tons of different recreational areas and private rooms. I'll be using the secure network Xavier established for me to reach out to them this weekend and schedule appointments. I'll vary the locations and the times, and I'll ensure they coincide with meetings Father has scheduled. I'm not going to lie and say it's risk-free, but I'm confident I can do this under the radar. He won't find out."

"And you think they'll agree to this?"

He nods. "I do. They all hate him. Handing over the evidence he's been lording over them will swing the power back in their favor."

"I've copied all the recordings three times and backdated the production dates so that should convince them you are handing over all the evidence," Xavier says, talking in between eating.

"And these men have enough power to convince his other supporters to abandon him?" Kai asks.

Drew nods. "Absolutely. These men will do all the work for us and be happy to."

"What about Atticus?" I ask, because he's going to be at the meeting too.

"Rick and I have played him perfectly," Kai admits. "He's already fucked Patrice, and we have it on tape."

I slap his arm. "You never told me!"

"It actually just slipped my mind," he says. "It happened the night of the wedding party, and I was more concerned with looking after you."

My temporary anger flits away. "It's okay." I place my hand on his knee, rubbing it. "So, what's the angle?"

"They have history of clashing over the same women, so we thought it apt that he'd make a play for Patrice, and it's one more thing we can use to discredit your father at the vote. It will embarrass him further."

"Plus, it will be frowned upon by the council and cast your father in a bad light at a time when he's supposed to be on his best behavior," Drew adds. "And betraying your sponsor is seriously frowned upon."

I wish we had the proof we need to confirm Atticus killed his wife Emma, but without it, we can't make that allegation stick. We can discredit him in front of the elite, and most likely get him permanently banned for life, but that's not justice served. Still, we need to choose one battle at a time, and we all agreed Michael Hearst needs to be taken down first.

"I can't believe she was so ready to open her legs for your father," I admit, even though it seems some women within the elite have no qualms about fucking any of the elite men. She's engaged to, potentially, the most powerful—and arguably the most evil—man among the elite, and one would think she'd be smarter than to fuck a guy he has bad history with.

"She was seething that night," Kai says, grinning. "Rick was working Isabella like a pro, encouraging her to flirt outrageously with your father, and Patrice was fuming he flirted back. When Michael and Christian left the room with Charlie, Rick enticed Isabella away without anyone noticing, and I convinced my dad that she was off fucking Michael. A few choice words planted the idea in his head, while Rick worked on planting the same idea in Patrice's." He shrugs. "It was as simple as that."

"You need a degree in manipulation to keep up with all the betrayals and backstabbing," Xavier pipes up. "We could make a fortune if you turned all this into a screenplay," he adds. "Think of how much money we'd make."

"We already have tons of money," Sawyer says. "And there's no way any network would air this shit. It's way too dark for mainstream television."

"I think you just love arguing with me for the sake of arguing," Xavier says, and I tune them out as they kick off again. It seems hooking up hasn't made a blind bit of difference to their usual dynamic. They're snapping and sniping at one another as normal.

"What's up, babe?" Kai whispers in my ear as his warm hands knead the corded muscles in my shoulders.

"What if it's not true?" I whisper, angling my body into his. "What if we're wrong and I've been quietly hoping for nothing?"

"There is nothing wrong with having hope, but you need to prepare yourself too. We don't know what this doctor will tell us, but whether it's good news or not, you know I have your back."

I stretch up and peck his lips. "That's why I know I'll survive this even if it turns out not to be true."

CHAPTER THIRTY-TWO

J ames Kennedy came through for us in the end, and that's how we find ourselves lurking in an alleyway, just off the parking lot of the doctor's office in a small town in Wyoming, freezing our butts off, Tuesday night. James is staying at a hotel in the nearest big city, and he's on standby to fly us back to Massachusetts either later tonight or tomorrow morning. It all depends on how successful our abduction and interrogation of Dr. Collingsworth are.

"Fuck, my balls are like blocks of ice," Jackson says, rubbing a gloved hand up and down his crotch.

"I've lost all feeling in my legs," Sawyer supplies. "It's that fucking cold."

"What a pity Xavier isn't here to warm them up for you," I tease, snuggling back into Kai.

"That shit is getting real old," Sawyer says, glaring at me.

"Oh, come on, you secretly love it," I joke.

He doesn't.

He hates that we've been yanking his chain since their hookup, but it's so fun. Besides, I desperately need distracting right now because I'm a bag of nerves as I wait for the doctor to step foot outside.

Sawyer flips me the bird, and I laugh.

"Maybe next time, you'll remember to close the door," Kai deadpans.

"There won't *be* a next time," Sawyer repeats, for like the umpteenth time.

"Tell that to someone who believes you," Rick says, grinning. Even though he's knee-deep in assignments, he insisted on coming with us, and I'm happy he's here. There is strength in numbers.

Xavier had to stay behind because he's delivering an important presentation that counts toward his graduation and he couldn't reschedule it despite his best efforts. He hates missing out, but at least he can keep an eye on things back in Rydeville.

Shandra wanted to come too, but both of us absent from school on the same day might raise flags, and my vacation cover story wouldn't hold up if she's on the MIA list too. At least this way, with Shandra and Chad holding the fort at school, and the well-timed fake text I just sent her, we are giving substance to our cover story should we need it.

"What the fuck is keeping him?" Kai growls, burying his face in my hair. "I thought the office closed at five?"

It's now five thirty-seven, and we've been out here an hour already. I managed to avoid snow the last time I was in Wyoming, but with the icy chill in the air, I wouldn't be surprised to see snowflakes form in the dark nighttime sky.

"There are still a couple cars here," I remind him. "He is obviously seeing some patients after hours."

Forty minutes later, the good doctor finally makes an appearance. We'd looked up photos of him online so we could identify him easily.

"Showtime," I murmur, wrenching myself away from the warmth of Kai's arms.

"Be careful, babe," Kai says, squeezing my fingers as I reach back for my gun. It's tucked into the waistband of my jeans, hidden under my bulky jacket. Ensuring the safety is on, I clasp the gun firmly, keeping it out of sight behind me as I stride forward with purpose, exiting the alleyway.

The doctor is almost to his car when he spots me approaching. I'm all bundled up in a puffy jacket and my hair is half hidden under my wooly hat, so he doesn't recognize me at first. My boots are heavy as I stomp toward him with every nerve ending on my body on high alert. "Dr. Collingsworth. I've been waiting for you."

He frowns a little until I'm up close, and all the blood drains from his face. "You shouldn't be here," he whispers, looking frantically around as he fumbles with his car keys.

"I know you know who I am," I calmly state. "And I'm not leaving without answers."

"Go home, Abigail," he whispers. "This isn't safe for either one of us."

"I want the truth."

"They will kill me if I talk to you," he blurts. "You're Hearst's daughter. You know how this world works."

"It's better if you come quickly then," I say, producing my gun and discreetly aiming it at his body. "Before anyone notices." Out of the corner of my eye, I spot the guys moving in our direction.

The keys slide from his fingers, hitting the cold ground. "They have spies all over town," he pleads, a wild look appearing in his eyes. "They'll hurt my family if—"

"Just get in the car, and drive through town as you normally would," I say, nudging his hip with the gun because he needs a little persuasion.

"We'll hide in the back seat," Kai says, crowding him on the other side, "and our friends will be accompanying us in a separate car," he adds, as the others hurry around the corner to where they parked the rental Xavier reserved for us in a fake name. "Pull any shit and you'll be sorry."

"Shit." Strain is evident in the doctor's stormy hazel eyes. "This won't end well."

"Get in the fucking car," Kai snaps, losing his patience. "Before you get us all killed."

He slides his long legs behind the wheel as Kai and I duck into the back seat, cowering on the floor, keeping hidden. I train the gun on him in case he tries anything. Even though the man seems as harmless as a fly, I've learned not to underestimate anyone. "I have my gun on you," I say, because he can't see from his position. "Try anything and I'll shoot."

"Where am I going?" he asks, a few minutes later as we reach the town border. "Keep driving straight," Kai says, checking the map on his cell. "You'll be taking a left turn about six miles ahead. I'll warn you before we come to it."

Deathly silence is heavy in the air as we drive toward our destination. I stare at Kai, and he holds my gaze, reassuring me with unspoken words.

"Call your wife," I blurt. This guy is a creature of routine. The last thing we need is her calling the local sheriff when he fails to return home. "Tell her you went for a few beers with a couple old college buddies who are only in town for the night. Tell her not to wait up for you."

His Adam's apple bobs in his throat. "She'll never believe it," he says. "I'm a one beer kind of guy."

"Well, then, tell her whatever you tell her when you're up at Parkhurst late performing illegal operations on kidnapped patients who've been locked up against their will," I snap.

He wets his lips as his finger hovers over the keypad on his cellphone.

"Put it on speaker," I command.

"And don't try to send her a hidden warning," Kai adds. "Because we know where you live. Nice neighborhood up there in Linwood. I bet Missie and Callie love swinging off the climbing frame in the playground across the road from your six-bed six-bath two-story house."

"Please don't hurt my family," he begs.

We would never hurt his family. Not in a million years. But he doesn't know that, and he needs to believe they're in danger, or he won't tell us what we need to know.

"Cooperate and your family will be safe. Pull any stunts, and you put them at risk," I say in a monotone voice devoid of outward emotion.

He makes the call, and we listen as he feeds his wife a pile of bullshit about why he won't be home until late tonight.

"She doesn't know," I say when he ends the call.

"I've tried to shelter her from Parkhurst. My father did the same with his wife—my mother—and my sisters don't know anything about it either."

"What *do* the locals think Parkhurst is?" I ask.

"A large private pharmaceutical and medical corporation servicing high-end, wealthy clients."

I snort. "Figures." I'm sure they have covered their tracks well.

"Most people around here don't pry because Parkhurst donates huge sums to the local community, and they'd hate to see them move out of state."

We don't talk after that until we get to the turnoff, and Kai directs him to the abandoned warehouse Xavier and Sawyer located in a neglected part of the outer suburbs. The guys are already there when we pull up.

"Stay put," Kai warns him, snatching his cell and keys before helping me out of the car.

"What's Drew's ETA?" I ask as we approach Rick, Sawyer, and Jackson.

"He says he won't be able to get away for a few hours yet," Sawyer confirms.

I nod, expecting this reply. "Let's get the doctor inside and make him sweat so he's good and ready to spill his guts by the time Drew arrives," I say, tossing a glance over my shoulder. Drew is taking a risk sneaking out of Parkhurst to meet us, but there's no way he wants to miss out on this, in the same way I wasn't taking no for an answer.

Rick and Kai manhandle the doctor on purpose, shoving and pushing him into the derelict building. The roof is splintered in several places, and the whole space reeks of mold and dead, decayed things. A shiver works its way through me, and I avoid looking too closely at the debris cluttering the floor as I step over it.

The guys plonk the chair down in the center of the space, and Sawyer ties the doctor to it with impressive speed and skill, making me wonder if he's done this kind of thing before.

I know so little about their lives in New York before they came here, except for what I've gleaned from Kai and the gossip mill in school when they first arrived at Rydeville High. I'm hugely curious about Sawyer's background, because he's notoriously cagey with details.

"Abigail." The doctor pins me with pleading eyes. "I wasn't the one who hurt you. I tried to help you. I—"

"Stop." I hold up a hand. I want to know so badly, but my brother is owed the truth too, and he's risking a lot to come here, so I'm waiting for Drew. "We need to wait for my brother."

His face pales. "Drew is coming here?" His voice elevates a few notches.

"Yes." I watch fear crawl up his neck and over his face.

Interesting.

I know Drew hasn't had any dealings with him before, so I've no clue why he appears terrified of my brother. Not for the first time, I wonder what the guys have been forced to do in that hellhole. "He won't hurt you, provided you tell us the truth."

"If I tell you, they'll hunt me down and kill me before doing unspeakable things to my family. I've seen it before." He thrashes about on the chair. "Please, Abigail. Just let me go, and forget about this. Nothing good can come from it. I've done all I can. Anything else and I risk the safety of my family. Please."

We're not going to let anything happen to his family, and we've already discussed protections we can put in place. But I'm not getting drawn into that now. For now, the best course of action is to leave him tied up, contemplating his options, while we wait for my twin to arrive.

CHAPTER THIRTY-THREE

"Where is he?" Drew asks, shuddering as he steps foot into the smelly, ice-cold warehouse a few hours later.

"We left him stewing in there," I say, following behind my brother. "Rick, Sawyer, and Jackson took hourly shifts guarding him."

"He's shitting his pants," Jackson pipes up, coming up the rear. "Leaving him to freak out for a few hours was the right move."

"I can't be gone too long," Drew says, slamming to a halt in front of me just before we enter the main room where the doctor is being held. He turns to face me. "I want you to let me lead this," he says. "And I might have to do things you won't like."

I swallow back bile. "Do what you have to do to get the answers we need. Whether he was willing or not, he's participated in the abuse that goes on in the medical wing. My conscience is clear."

Kai laces his fingers in mine, squeezing them in support.

"I'd like a minute alone with my sister," Drew says. Kai nods, pecking my lips before following Jackson and Sawyer into the belly of the building.

Drew hauls me into his arms and we hug in silence for a few beats. "I'm scared," he whispers.

"Me too," I whisper back.

"I want to be right so badly, A, but I'm terrified I've gotten it all wrong."

"I really don't think you are, D, and you know I feel the same. But I understand, because I've tried not to have too much hope."

He tilts my face up, cupping my cheeks. "No matter what, we don't let what we hear derail us. We have a good shot at pulling this off, Abby, and we can't let our emotions get in the way."

"I know, Drew and, unfortunately, I'm quite adept at locking my feelings up inside."

"If she's alive," he says, in a choked voice, "you understand we can't do anything about it tonight."

"I know," I whisper. "I know we can't just barge in there and take her." It will kill me if our mother is only a few miles up the road in that Godawful place and we have to return to Rydeville, leaving her in those monsters' care, but we have come too far to throw it all away in a reckless emotion-driven act of selfishness.

"Are you ready to do this?" he softly asks.

I shake my head, and a single tear creeps out of the corner of my eye. "No," I whisper. "But I'm as ready as I'll ever be."

He wraps his hand around mine. "Let's go and find out once and for all."

The doctor visibly shakes as Drew and I stalk across the floor in his direction, our boots thumping loudly on the concrete as we advance. Rick removes a handkerchief from the doctor's mouth, holding a bottle of water to his lips.

The guys step aside as we approach, giving us space. The doctor gulps as his gaze jumps between us. "What are you going to do to me?" he rasps, his wild eyes bouncing around the room.

"We can do this the hard way or the easy way," Drew says in a lethal tone he's used a couple of times before. Like then, it sends icy chills ripping up and down my spine. "The hard way will mean you have a lot of explaining to do *if* you return home to your wife. The easy way means you walk out of here without a scratch." Drew tightens his grip on my hand as he eyeballs the doctor with a threatening look.

"If they find out I talked to you, I'm a dead man walking," he blurts.

"We can protect you," Drew says. "And we don't plan on doing anything rash with the information we learn here tonight. Everything will be planned to the finest detail because we take minimal risks when it comes to the elite."

"Why are you doing this?" he queries. "Your father will kill *you* if he finds out."

"Our father won't know about this unless anyone in this room tells him," I say.

Drew scoffs, and an ugly sneer grips the corners of his mouth. "I'm his heir. He won't kill me. Especially not over someone like you."

I sneak a glance at my brother, and I can't tell if he genuinely means that or he's reverted to evil-psycho-bastard mode as part of his role playing.

"It's none of your concern," Drew adds, drilling him with a dark look. "Worry about yourself and your family and let us worry about the rest."

"It's not like I have any choice," the doctor concedes, looking resigned. "But I need your word that if it comes down to it you'll get my family out of the country."

"You have our word," I say without hesitation. "We will protect your wife and daughters and see they come to no harm." I truly hope I'm not lying to the man.

Drew purses his lips, shaking his head at me. "We can promise you no such thing," he says, and I frown. "And I'm done listening to your inane questions." He leans over him, putting his face right up in his. The doctor tries to cower back, but there's nowhere for him to go. "You will tell us what we need to know, without any further protest, or I will beat you bloody until you are begging for death."

You could hear a pin drop in the quiet space. Kai, Jackson, and Sawyer share a look while Rick stares curiously at my brother.

Ho. Lee. Fuck.

In this moment, as I watch my twin coldly threaten the doctor with blazing intent and zero remorse in his eyes, I realize he has done a stellar job of hiding his dark side from me. I was a fool to think the damage inflicted on him in Parkhurst hadn't changed him. It's altered all of them in different ways—Drew, Charlie, and Trent.

"Okay," the doctor agrees in a shaky voice, looking like he's about to shit his pants. He glances down. "Could you untie my arms? They hurt."

"Like I hurt every-fucking-where after what was done to me," I spit out. So what if his arms are aching after a few hours of being tied behind his back? It's nothing compared to what was done to me.

"I wasn't the one who did that. I was on vacation when you were first brought in," he starts explaining as Sawyer unties the binds around his hands. "When I returned to work, I was shocked you were there. And I was appalled when I discovered Dr. Lacy had performed an illegal abortion and breast augmentation at your father's request." He wets his dry lips, looking at Rick. Rick uncaps the water bottle and hands it to him.

My eyes meet Kai's in shared pain, but I lock that shit up, hardening my heart and preparing it for what's next to come. But I tuck Dr. Lacy's name away to come back to. That man is going to get what he deserves.

"We were told Abby had had a hysterectomy," Drew says. "But we know that's not true."

"Your father wanted it performed, but I got there in time to stop it. I'm Dr. Lacy's superior, so it wasn't unusual that I threw him out of the operating room and took over."

"You inserted the birth control implant," I say although I already know our guesswork was correct.

"I did, because I needed to cover my tracks. It usually messes with menstruation for the first few months, so I was hopeful you wouldn't have any periods, and at least it protected you from pregnancy should you have unprotected sex."

"Why?" I ask. "Why didn't you do it? You're clearly terrified of my father, and the elite, based on your earlier reaction, so why didn't you just do what he'd asked?"

His features soften. "Because I looked at you and I saw my daughters. And I saw a beautiful young woman with her whole life ahead of her." He averts his eyes, looking at the floor for a few minutes. "I've done a lot of things I'm not proud of, but I couldn't go that far. I never wanted to work for the elite. It's my legacy passed down from my father and his before him. I couldn't say no even though I wanted to. I'm trapped, and I've had to do things that keep me from sleeping at night, but I could not take away any young woman's ability to carry children."

He looks me straight in the eye. "I knew there would be consequences. I've been looking over my shoulder ever since although I wasn't expecting *you* to show up. I was planning on leaving the US with my family once I had it all set up, and then I was going to send you an anonymous communication explaining what had happened and asking you to say nothing about it."

There's no doubt in my mind that every word he has spoken is the truth. And I understand what it's like to be forced to do things to survive. I've done things I'm not proud of too. I doubt they are on the same level as him, but he has risked a lot to do this for me.

"Thank you," I say. "Thank you for saving my future babies."

"Did Dr. Lacy do an egg extraction?" Rick asks.

The doctor shakes his head. "No. I stopped that too. We had some redundant eggs in storage, and I took some of them and falsified the records, in case anyone went checking."

Bile fills my mouth, but I don't ask what happened to the woman they belonged to, because I can't get distracted, and his explanation is quite likely going to make me want to throttle him.

"You seem like a risk-adverse kind of guy to me," Drew says, leaning down over the doctor again. He flinches, clearly terrified of my brother, and for good reason, it seems. "And while I'm grateful you did my sister a solid, I'm not buying the explanation." Drew squares up to the man, and he's trembling all over in a way that has nothing to do with the arctic temps in this place. "Why did you really do it?"

"I told you," he squeaks, as sweat beads on his brow. "Not all of us who work there are monsters. A lot of us are forced into it, and they use blackmail and coercion to keep us on side, but I have a conscience, and I couldn't do that to a young woman."

"And?" Drew's look is glacial as he stares into the man's eyes.

The doctor exhales heavily. "If I tell you this, you've got to promise me you won't act recklessly."

Butterflies stampede across my chest, and I pin panicked eyes on Kai. He's across the space, holding me against his chest, in the blink of an eye.

"You don't get to make demands!" Drew snaps, straightening up and sharing an intense look with me.

This is it. The moment of truth.

I exhale heavily, nodding.

Drew returns his focus to the doctor. "Is she alive?" His voice is hard, his expression tight, but I know he's reining in his emotions on purpose.

The doctor's eyes pop wide. "You know?"

"Please." I drop to my knees in front of him. "Please tell us. Is she still alive? Is our mother a patient in Parkhurst?"

Drew and Kai stand behind me, one on either side, as blood thrums in my ears and a silent screaming takes up residence in my skull.

The anticipation is killing me and I. Need. To. Know.

"Yes," he says, and a sob rips free of my throat.

Tears roll down my face, and I clutch onto Kai's hand as he leans in closer to me.

"She's alive?" Drew asks again, in a clipped tone.

"Your mother is alive and well. Or as well as anyone can be in that place." He slants remorseful eyes at me. "She has sympathizers in the facility, and she's the one who found out you were brought in. She discovered what they were planning, and she caused bloody murder every day for a week until I was called back early from vacation to handle her."

"She's the woman in C9?" I say, and he nods. "Oh my God." Tears stream from my eyes, and I reach up and clutch Drew's hand with my free one.

"She earned a week in solitary for attacking one of the other doctors," he said, "but she did it on purpose because there is less security in that part of the building. When I arrived, she begged me to help you. To stop what that bastard Hearst was planning. Your mother is a very persuasive woman, and it didn't take much for me to agree. I knew the risks I was taking, but I knew in my heart it was the right thing to do."

"She visited me, didn't she?" I ask in a whisper.

A smile ghosts over his lips. "I snuck her up to your room through the back hallways so she could see you. I've never seen her face light up like it did that night."

I stand, clinging to my stoic brother. Drew is giving little away, but I know he's feeling this as much as me. He's just better at hiding it. Kai untangles his hand from mine, but he doesn't stray far. "How is she?" Drew asks. "Does she know I'm at Parkhurst regularly? Does she know what's going on in our lives? What our father is up to?"

"She doesn't know everything, because we're largely cut off in the medical facility, but she knows enough. She's been begging me to find a way to help her escape, especially as your eighteenth birthday approaches, and I've been trying to devise a foolproof plan, but we don't have the contacts or the means to get her out of the state safely. I haven't wanted to make a move in case I jeopardized her life and mine."

"We?" I ask.

"I have a few trusted colleagues in the facility who feel the way I do. What's been done to your mother is disgusting, and for years, no one believed her when she told us who she really was and how she came to be in there." He shakes his head. "Your father is a truly evil man."

Tell me something we don't know.

"And, mentally, how is she?" I ask, because I remember the zombie-like expressions and apathy of most of the patients.

He pauses for a few beats before answering. "She has her good days and bad days. She was subjected to a lot of questionable treatment until I arrived at Parkhurst. She's stable, but there's no denying there are long-term effects as a result of what she's endured."

"Does he visit her?" Drew asks.

The doctor shakes his head. "Not that I'm aware of."

Of course, he doesn't. Out of sight, out of mind. I'm still in shock, and I'm not sure it's fully sunk in. "Mom isn't dead, Drew," I whisper, clutching onto my brother's arm and smiling at him through tear-sodden eyes. "We haven't lost her."

"We're going to get her out of there, A. You're going to get to kiss and hug her again," Drew promises. Tears cling to his lashes briefly, before he composes himself.

"How?" the doctor asks.

"You don't need to be concerned about that," Drew says, his voice resonating with confidence. "But we'll need your help and the help of your colleagues."

"We want to help, but we're afraid," he truthfully admits.

"Don't be," I say, sniffling. "Because in a couple of months, lots of things are going to change. We just need you to take care of our mother in the meantime."

It kills me to think of her in there for that long, and the urge to race to Parkhurst and bust our way into the medical facility, come hell or high water, is riding me hard, but I won't risk her life like that. And I won't risk everything we have planned.

"Can we count on you to keep our mom safe?" Drew asks.

"I've been keeping her safe for the four years I've been a doctor at Parkhurst."

"Good." Drew straightens his shoulders. "You'll be contacted for the pertinent details, and I need you to start noting all schedules. Meds, rotations, schedules, deliveries etcetera."

The doctor nods. "I can do that."

"Then we'll see to it that no harm comes to you or your family and that same protection applies to your colleagues and their families if they're willing to help us," Drew confirms.

"You will be free of the elite and comfortable for life," I add, "and you can start being the man your wife and daughters believe you to be."

CHAPTER THIRTY-FOUR

The next couple of months are some of the worst torture I've ever endured. Knowing my mother is alive and that I can't go to her is killing me. I know it's getting to Drew too. But we get regular updates from Dr. Collingsworth via a secure line Xavier set up, and we've been writing letters back and forth to Mom. Xavier offered to set up a video link, but we declined. We're fearful of doing anything that might be traced, and neither of us could bear to see her again for the first time after ten years where we couldn't hug her and kiss her and tell her to her face that we loved her.

So, we are trading correspondence.

Dr. Collingsworth burns all our letters after Mom reads them because we can't risk them falling into the wrong hands.

The first time we got individual letters from her, we sat on the floor in Kai's and my bedroom, staring at her neat handwriting on the plain white envelopes for at least an hour before either of us could pluck up the courage to open them.

And then I spent hours shedding happy tears, reading her loving words through blurry eyes, with a happy ache slicing through my chest. It's clear from the way some of her letters are worded that her mind is not altogether there, but it's a testament to her strength of will that she's survived ten years in that place.

We're more determined than ever to get her out of there, and finally, all our planning and preparation is coming together.

These past two months have been both difficult and easy-breezy. Easy because I'm living with my husband and I'm more content in my relationship than I've ever been in my life. Every day, Kai and I grow closer, and it's got to the stage where I can't imagine what life was like before he barreled his way into mine.

I've seen little of Charlie except for a few functions the bastard made me attend with him. All events were hell, because Charlie is giving me the cold shoulder, and he's completely closed himself off to me. I've tried to reach out to him, as a friend, but he's not interested, and I'm not going to force him to talk. There is a lot of hurt and regret between us, and I know regaining a friendship won't be a walk in the park, but I'm hopeful we can get back to where we once were.

I've reached out an olive branch.

Now the ball's in Charlie's court.

Father has kept his distance, and he hasn't made any demands on me or Drew, which should make me happy, but it just makes all of us uneasy and scared shitless. He's not one to take things lying down, and we're all on edge, constantly watching our backs, waiting for him to strike. I'd like to think he's distracted and concerned enough about the recording to have legitimately backed-off, but he's a twisted, unpredictable bastard, and we can't assume anything.

Atticus was voted back into the elite, but it was no cakewalk either. A lot of high-ranking elite were opposed to letting him back in, but Father pushed for it, no doubt resorting to his usual blackmail tactics to achieve his goal. Rick and Kai were applying subtle pressure, convincing Atticus to threaten the bastard with a renewal of his legal suit against him and Christian if he failed to pull off his end of the bargain.

Atticus is living at his old house in Rydeville again, but we go out of our way to avoid him where possible. Harley and Joaquin are living by themselves in the New York apartment during the school term, returning to Rydeville during breaks.

All the board members at Manning Motors have signed NDAs and new contracts that come into effect the day of the Parkhurst vote. We've managed to keep it a secret, but it's just another thing that keeps me tossing and turning at night.

Drew successfully turned our target list of high-ranking elite against the bastard, and it took little effort on his part. They welcomed the opportunity to stab him in the back, and we've been assured that the vote will not go his way tomorrow.

Everything is lined up, and we've gone over our plans excessively, trying to second-guess all obstacles and things that can go wrong. It's a rock-solid plan, but I still haven't been able to eat or sleep for the past week.

Everything hinges on tomorrow, and I'm beyond anxious.

Charlie's hand clamps down on my quivering thigh as we ride in a limo from the private airfield in Wyoming to Parkhurst. This is my first time in the main facility, and having to sleep there overnight, in a room with Charlie, is making me all kinds of nervous. It helps that Drew and Shandra are traveling with us now and staying in the hotel suite next to ours. And Kai and Rick will be staying there too. Xavier, Sawyer, Jackson, and the security detail who have been our perpetual shadows these past few months are staying in a house we've rented a couple miles away.

Everything needs to be timed to perfection tomorrow so the fireworks go off in the sequence we've planned, and even one minor hiccup could really screw things up. Which is why I'm so on edge.

Failure is not an option, but success isn't guaranteed either.

"Relax," Charlie says. "Your constant leg jerking is driving me nuts."

"Do you blame me for being nervous?" I ask, arching a brow. "Or have you forgotten what they did to me the last time I was here? And what they tried to do to me the last time there was a big elite event?"

"Of course not." His features soften momentarily. "And I will never forget that night as long as I live." His customary blank expression is back on his face, and while he's not giving much away, his brief thawing is the first hint that he's not completely immune to me after all.

"Things are different now," Drew says from his seat across from me. "And no one would dare try anything like that this weekend." We both know that's bullshit, but we've just got to get through tonight, and then the balance of power should shift.

If everything goes to plan.

If it doesn't, it'll be a free-for-all, and I shudder to think what punishments will be meted out if we fail in our mission.

Shoving those hideous thoughts aside, I focus on my brother. He's holding Shandra's hand and she's leaning into him, admiring the sharp line of his jaw. I've watched them grow closer these past few months with a little unease. Don't get me wrong. I'm glad Drew isn't with that witch Alessandra anymore, but it's hard seeing him looking all loved up with someone who isn't Jane.

Even if it's for show.

Which I *think* it is.

And even if Shandra has become a good friend.

"What time does the engagement party start at?" Shandra asks.

"The invite said eight," I confirm, glancing out the window as the landscape flashes past in a blur.

"And who will be there?" she asks, looking at Drew.

"All the high-ranking elite, including the council members and their wives and any children who are members," he says.

"It will be boring as fuck," Charlie says. "Especially for you," he adds, staring at me coldly. "I can't imagine how torturous it must be being forced to keep my company instead of *his*."

"Don't do that, Charlie."

"Why the hell not, Abigail?"

"Because this weekend will be hell if you're going to act like a toddler throwing a temper tantrum." I deliberately lower my voice even though the privacy screen is up, and the sound is muted back here. I'm not taking chances. "You know I'm with him now, and I've tried to talk to you on several occasions about our situation, but you haven't wanted to know."

"Because I was fucking hurt and dealing with a ton of shit," he hisses.

"This is hardly the ideal time for a heart to heart," Drew calmly says, shooting him a warning look. "I'm sure Abby will have no issue talking it out with you when we get back to Rydeville, but discussing it at Parkhurst is risky for everyone, especially my sister." His eyes stick to Charlie's. "Unless you've decided you don't care for her at all anymore, and that her safety doesn't matter to you now, and if that's the case, you and I have a big problem, buddy."

A muscle pops in Charlie's jaw as he turns his head, staring out the window, refusing to reply, and avoiding all further conversation.

It doesn't exactly leave me feeling all warm and cozy.

My gut balls into tight knots when we arrive, and Charlie helps me out of the car, keeping a firm hold of my hand as we walk up the steps toward the entrance.

It's not at all what I was expecting.

I thought it would be an old-fashioned building with an old-world grand interior to match, but it's a modern build, five stories high, composed of cream Italian stone with high windows. Glass balconies surround the exterior of the residential quarters which are located on the third, fourth, and fifth floors.

Inside, the lobby is a large open-plan rectangular shape with gray and pink velvet couches and chairs dotted around the bright, airy space. Overhead, massive chandeliers shine incandescent light on the room below, highlighting the expensive vases filled with scented in-season blooms and the exquisite artwork adorning the walls.

Charlie walks us to the reception desk, and we're greeted by a tall, thin older woman with dark reddish-brown hair. "Mr. Barron." She smiles warmly at Charlie, deliberately touching his hand as she passes a pen and card to him to sign. "How lovely to see you again."

"Nice to see you too, Marina," he says, scrawling his signature across the card and handing it back to her. "This is my wife, Abigail," he adds, casting a cursory glance my way.

She turns sharp eyes on me, and the edge slides off her smile. "You're very welcome, Mrs. Barron. First time here, right?"

"Yes." I give her my best fake smile.

"I hope you enjoy your stay. And if you'd like a recommendation, I'd try out the purple recreation room. It's Charlie's favorite." You would never know she's digging a knife in my back by the pleasant smile plastered on her face, but only an idiot would fail to pick up on her meaning.

"Do you like your job, Marina?" I ask.

Her confident smile falters a little. "I love my job."

I deliberately look her up and down in a blatantly derisory manner, channeling my inner bitch. "Then I suggest you avoid telling other newly married brides in a none-too-subtle manner that you've fucked their husbands, and in which rooms too." I lean in close, inspecting her name badge on purpose. "Before I became Abigail Barron, I was Abigail Hearst-Manning."

All the color drains from her face.

"So, you know who my father is, and the kind of power he holds around here. Try to piss me off again and you'll find yourself out of a job. And that's your only warning." She's lucky I'm strung out about tomorrow, or I'd have her fired on the spot.

"I'm very sorry, Mrs. Barron. I don't know what came over me."

I dismiss her with a wave of my hand, refocusing on Charlie. "Are we done here?"

His lips twitch. "We're done." He looks at a pale-faced Marina. "I assume my usual room is ready?"

"Actually, Mr. Hearst requested you to be moved to the presidential floor."

Charlie's eyes burn with indignation as he thrusts the key card back at her. "I want my usual room. Fix it on your system." Marina looks like she wants to argue but glances at the thunderous look on Charlie's face and my bored face and thinks better of it. I tap out a quick text to Drew, warning him that Father has most likely requested to move his room too, so he sticks to the original arrangements. I need the comfort of knowing my brother and friend are close by should I need them.

Ten minutes later, Charlie opens the door to a lavish room, and I step inside, relaxing a smidgeon until I spot the king-sized bed I'll have to share with him. I could protest and sleep on the couch, but I need to bring my A-game tomorrow, and I haven't been sleeping well as it is.

My cell pings, and I remove it from my purse as I kick my stiletto heels off.

After months of living in jeans and Kai's sweatshirts, being forced to dress the part of an elite lady again is so stifling I can barely breathe. A smile crests over my mouth as I spot his gorgeous face smiling back at me from my screen. I press the button and accept Kai's call, walking into the bathroom and shutting the door. "Hey, babe."

"You okay?"

"I'm fine. Father tried to move our room to a room beside him, but Charlie was having none of it."

"Good. You've still got the tracker in your cell, your purse, and your shoes, right?" he asks.

"I do." I didn't protest it was over the top when Xavier insisted on it yesterday, because the truth is, we need to be over the top with everything to ensure we're safe. The guys all have trackers in their cells and shoes too, and we all have the tracking app on our phone. Tomorrow, we'll use the earpieces so Xavier, Sawyer, and Jackson can hear everything going on from the comfort of their rental car which will be parked on the road outside here. Sawyer checked with his father, and the devices should still work at this distance.

"Is she there yet?" I ask, a scowl immediately appearing on my face at the thought of Giselle.

"I haven't seen her, but she sent me a text to say she was here," he confirms. He hasn't heard much from her since the wedding party, when he made it clear he had no interest in her after she let Trent finger-fuck her on the dance floor in view of others. Atticus could've used it as an excuse to get Kai out of chaperoning her this weekend, but we figure the devil you know is better than the one you don't. Giselle isn't a threat. She's more of an annoying gnat. But one we can swat away when we've had enough of her.

Trent and Alessandra, on the other hand, are a force to be reckoned with. Tensions have been high at school with a clear divide among the elite. Trent finally seems to have met his match, and the way those two paw at one another each lunchtime confirms it. Yet he hasn't made any move to retaliate, and I'm not naïve enough to think Father's warning actually did anything but make him more determined. We continue to trade barbs and insults, but he hasn't physically made any move, and that's another reason to be nervous.

320

"Don't worry about her, babe. She's nothing," Kai says, reassuring me.

"I know. And I'm not. She's probably the only thing I'm *not* worried about."

"We are well prepared," he says in a low tone. "And it's going to happen."

"We just have to get through this damn engagement party first."

My face hurts from smiling, and my feet are already killing me, and we're only an hour into this monstrous party. It's typical of the bastard to throw an extravagant engagement party the night before the big vote. If I didn't know better, I'd say he did it to distract himself from feeling nervous. But to experience nervousness, you have to feel emotion, and that bastard is incapable of feeling anything.

However, he definitely looks on edge tonight. I wonder if he's heard whisperings of discontent or he knows what's about to go down. Everyone involved understands the need for secrecy, but the bastard has ways of uncovering the truth.

On this occasion, I hope we've completely hoodwinked him as I want to watch the realization dawn on his face when the revelations start hitting.

"Want another drink?" Charlie asks when he finally breaks free of conversation with a short, stocky man sporting a trimmed mustache and a leering expression every time he glances my way.

"I'll just have a water," I reply. There is no way even a drop of alcohol is touching my lips around this place. He walks me over to where Drew and Shandra are chatting with Rick and Isabella. Kai is with Giselle over on the far side of the room, huddled in a group with Atticus and several men, loudly conversing. His back is to me, and I'm sure he's desperate to check up on me, but we both agreed neither of us would take any risks this weekend.

"Stay here," Charlie says. "I'll be back." He hasn't left my side all night, and despite his lack of response in the limo earlier, I know Charlie won't let me come to any harm. Our relationship may have broken down, but you can't get rid of feelings overnight, and we have a whole heap of unresolved feelings for one another that will need to be confronted at some point.

"Your father is looking very handsome tonight," Isabella says, not disguising her interest.

The bastard *is* handsome, and he takes good care of himself, but it's all fake, like his personality, and that makes him the most unattractive person in the room.

But Isabella is like a dog with a bone when it comes to him. She's continued to flirt up a storm at events, ignoring the daggers Patrice sends her way. Which is laughable really when you consider she is regularly screwing Atticus behind my father's back. I've no doubt Isabella sees herself as the new president's wife, but she seems not to have gotten the memo that this is their *engagement* party. Although, in this world, that doesn't really count for a lot.

Rick has been having a ball winding her up about him every chance he gets, and Kai is continuing to whisper in his father's ear. Really, it's way too easy to manipulate certain people and they deserve everything coming their way.

Patrice catches my eye and I wave her over. Might as well have a little fun with this.

"Patrice, you look stunning as always," I say, buttering her up. "That shade of green really suits your coloring."

Blech.

She smiles graciously, but her attention span is limited because she's giving Isabella some serious side stink-eye. "Isabella was just saying how handsome Father is," I innocently say, as Shandra fights a smirk. "And I've got to agree you make a beautiful couple."

Patrice's claws, predictably, come out. "I'm sure she did. But she'd say that about any man in a position of power, irrespective of how he looked. Isn't that right, dear?"

"Worried much?" Isabella grins.

"Desperate much?" Patrice retorts, and I just step back and watch it all play out beautifully. They are both so riled up after months of this game that it doesn't take much to ignite the spark.

"You've always had a devious streak I've admired," a deep voice says in my ear, and panic instantly flares to life inside me.

Drew makes a move to come to my side, but I caution him with a warning look. The last thing I want Christian Montgomery thinking is that I'm scared of him.

Even if I am.

I still have nightmares about his hideous cock and the feel of his hands on me.

Christian doesn't make any uncalculated moves, and I want to know what he's up to. "What do you want, Christian." My voice is glacial, and I don't turn around to look at him.

"I wanted to thank you," he whispers in my ear, and my skin crawls like a thousand fire ants are scratching me.

"I'll bite," I say, watching Charlie frowning from his position at the bar.

"You have made this too easy."

All the tiny hairs lift on the back of my neck, and acid churns in my gut.

"Not that it excuses what you tried to do," he continues, "and I've a long memory and limitless patience reserves, so I can wait it out, but something tells me I won't have much longer to wait."

"Get the fuck away from her," Charlie says, pulling me back from Christian.

"I'm going," he says, with clear amusement in his tone. "But only because it won't be long before she's mine to do with as I please."

And with those awesome parting words, he walks away, leaving me shaking in fear at the thought he has something big planned for me.

CHAPTER THIRTY-FIVE

"Are you nervous?" I ask Father the following morning when we are all convened in the presidential suite over breakfast, just before we head down to the auditorium where the vote will take place.

"Nerves are for the weak." He puffs out his chest. "Today is just a formality." Patrice flicks a piece of lint off the pocket of his jacket. "I've spent years working toward this goal, and everything is lined up to slot perfectly into place." He drains his freshly squeezed orange juice, looking predictably smug.

His arrogance and his cruelty were always going to be his downfall.

I take Charlie's glass and stand. "I'll get you a refill."

Father thrusts his glass at me, and I fake a lip bite, taking it as my mouth pulls into a thin line. "Good girl." He pats me on the ass as I turn away from the table, and it's the first time he has laid a finger on me in months.

It was a blatant move.

A warning that after today everything will change.

I want to grab the coffee pot and empty it over his perverted head, but that would defeat the purpose, so I swallow my pride and ignore his groping. I take my time filling both glasses with fresh juice as Drew distracts the bastard with questions about how the vote will go.

"After the outgoing president makes the opening speech, and the introductions, the public vote will take place," he explains as I hand him his fresh glass of juice.

I hand Charlie his juice refill, smoothing a hand down the front of my black pencil skirt, ensuring the small handgun strapped to my inner thigh is still hidden. I smile at Charlie as I slide back into the seat alongside him. "What was that all about?" he whispers.

"He believes he's back in control because Kai made a deal that we would hand over the recording from Christmas after the vote."

Charlie arches a brow, drilling Father with a poisonous look when he glances our way. He's still pontificating, and he really does love the sound of his own voice.

"That doesn't sound like a smart move on Kaiden's part," Charlie whispers in my ear.

"We had our reasons," I cryptically admit, and that's as much as I'm prepared to say. I have no clue which team he's supporting, if any, and I can't let my guard down around him.

"How many times have you been told it's rude to whisper at the table," Father barks at me.

"I apologize, Father." I almost choke over the words as they leave my mouth.

"I hope you enjoyed your little rebellion these past couple months, because after today, everything is going to change."

"We had a deal," I remind him, even though I am in no way surprised he's reneging on it. It's what we've all been expecting.

"I don't negotiate with punks," he supplies, grinning, and I work hard to fight my own grin. His predictability was inevitable, and he's sitting here, gloating and acting all superior-like because he thinks he has all copies of the Christmas Day recording in his possession.

But only because we want him to think that.

For months, he's been searching for it, and it wasn't that difficult to drop a few breadcrumbs. His PI took the bait, retrieving the box with the recordings we'd hidden in the earth under the old oak tree on the grounds of Chez Manning.

He believes he has the upper hand, and I'm not going to dispute it. We want him to feel supreme confidence as he walks into that room, thinking he has everything under control. Which is why we also threw Atticus and Patrice under the bus last night.

Xavier sent an anonymous email to Father's private account with video evidence of their betrayal. I'm certain he has something planned for Atticus, especially if the bruising around Patrice's neck this morning is any indication. Oh, she's done a good job of disguising it, but I saw the marks before she tied the silk scarf around her throat. She's as timid as a mouse at the table, jumping every time his loud voice booms around the room. Whatever punishment he doled out has scared her into submission, but I highly doubt he is through with her yet.

And I don't need any proof to know he fucked Isabella last night. He probably forced Patrice to watch while he did it too. That's exactly his M.O. I imagine he will keep Patrice around long enough to break her, and then he'll toss her aside in favor of the younger, hotter woman.

Or, at least, that's what he would do if he was free to do it.

But he'll be behind bars if we have anything to say about it.

I enjoy the gloating look on his face, knowing it'll be wiped off soon enough.

He thinks everything is lining up perfectly, but he knows nothing.

The evidence we provided gives him a legit reason to throw Atticus out of the elite, and he won't have to worry about any lawsuit after today—when he believes he'll hold the most important role within the order and the elite at large—so he feels justified in his good mood.

Drew and I share a surreptitious look, but neither of us is cocky because there is still a lot that could go wrong. Let's just say we are quietly optimistic.

We enter the auditorium as a group, and men crowd around Father, slapping him on the back as we make our way down the steps toward the front, but it's all for show. Father takes his place in the first row in front of the podium, while Drew exits left to join the other elite members on the far side of the space.

There are a little over five hundred elite members here today, and two hundred of those are voting members. Add family members to the mix and there is over one thousand people in this big auditorium. Enough for me to worry about all the ways this could go down, harming innocents in the process. A lot of the elite family members are forced into this way of life, like we have been, and there are plenty of people in this room who will enjoy seeing the order thrown into chaos and some of these sick bastards thrown into jail.

Charlie kisses me on the cheek. "I know I didn't say anything yesterday," he whispers, "but I do still care about you, and I won't let you come to any harm."

I lift a neat brow.

"I know the way your mind works, Abby, and I know what was in the works before I switched allegiances." He holds my hands firmly in his. "Whatever you have planned, please be fucking careful."

"You won't stop us?" I whisper.

He shakes his head. "I've made grave mistakes, Abby. Mistakes that have cost me my family and you, but I'm done making bad decisions and choosing the wrong side." He looks over his shoulder at Father. He's sitting beside the other candidates looking like the cat that got the cream. Charlie looks back at me. "I trusted the wrong people and allowed my mind to be swayed." His features harden. "I hope you make him pay."

"What was that all about?" Shandra whispers when I take my seat on the edge of a row with her to my right.

"I think Charlie might have finally come to his senses," I say as a dark shadow looms over me.

"Move," Alessandra snaps, tossing her long dark hair over one shoulder while planting her hands on her curvy hips.

"Only if you ask nicely." I grin up at her.

"I will yank you up by the hair and enjoy every second of it," she retorts.

I flash her an even wider grin. "Yeah, I don't think so. Your daddy told me what a dutiful daughter you are." I stand, leaning into her ear. "How you spread your legs and your ass for him and numerous other men." Her nostrils flare and her fists clench at her sides. "I'm guessing he wouldn't be pleased if you made a scene at such an important event, but feel free to test my theory."

I step out, and she deliberately shoulder checks me as she pushes her way into the row. She's poured into a bodycon dress that is better suited to dancing than a formal elite event but judging by the way Trent is panting in heat, I'd say he had a hand in what she wore today.

I fix the collar of my white silk shirt, adjusting the strand of pearls around my neck so they are perfectly positioned. My hair is in an elegant chignon, matching my classic straight black skirt, and white silk blouse combo. I'm wearing heels but not skyscrapers because I don't want to risk taking a tumble when I make my way up to the stage.

Adrenaline flows through my veins and a flurry of butterflies are idling in my chest as I sit back down, hoping the formalities kick off soon.

When everyone is seated, the current president calls for quiet and the ceremony begins. A screen lowers behind him, and a bullshit presentation lauding the legacy and achievements of the elite plays for ten minutes, while I fight boredom. When that ends, the president jumps right into his speech.

The man is clearly in ill health, leaning heavily on a walking stick and wiping his mouth with his handkerchief every time he coughs. Every second of his speech feels like hours, and a trickle of sweat rolls down the gap between my breasts. From my position, I can see Drew, Rick, and Kai sitting in the second row on the left. We tested our earpieces out first thing, and I know the guys are listening from outside. Xavier has successfully infiltrated the IT system, and he's primed and ready to get this show on the road.

"Now to the business of the day," the president says, spitting into the mic as he breaks out in another coughing fit. "The election of a new president to reside over the council and oversee the running of the elite nationwide. All candidates, please rise."

The five men stand in the front row as a round of applause breaks out around the room.

When the clapping has stopped, the president continues explaining the process. "Each candidate's name will be called out individually, and I will invite a show of support. Voting members will raise their left hand while simultaneously pressing the button on the digital keypad to register their vote."

Drew previously explained how all members over the age of eighteen have automatic voting privileges. The raising of the hands is a nod to the old traditions, while the little digital pads on the arm of each member's seat allows for fast computation of votes.

"When all the nominations have been called, and the votes tallied, the candidate with the majority votes will be announced as our next president. All the results will be displayed on the screen," he adds, waving his hand behind him. "A minimum of fifty votes is required to be eligible. In the event no candidate receives the minimum entitlement, the voting process will be halted while the council discusses how to proceed."

He waffles on for another few minutes before calling for absolute quiet.

And then it begins.

One by one, the candidates' names are called, and I'm on the edge of my seat as I wait for the bastard's name to be announced. The cage restraining the butterflies in my chest has broken apart, and those beautiful creatures are running amok inside me. I wipe my sweaty palms down the front of my skirt, while Shandra grips my arm in a silent show of support.

Father's name is called out last, and at this stage, no other candidate has received the minimal entitlement. Father is preening as he stands, probably believing he's won more than his expected number of votes.

"Get ready," Drew whispers through the earpiece. I wet my dry lips and fold my hands in my lap to stop fidgeting.

"Those in support of Michael Hearst for president, please raise your hands and register your votes now," the president says, and an eerie lull sweeps over the room.

Not a single person raises their hand, and Father's brow puckers as he looks around the room.

The president clears his throat. "All those in support of Michael Hearst for president, please vote now."

No one moves a muscle, and panic flares in the bastard's eyes. He sways a little on his feet, and I can detect the sheen of sweat on his brow on the projected image of him now displayed on the screen.

"It's working," Drew whispers.

"What is the meaning of this?" he shouts, his voice projecting around the room, the slurring of his words evident to all.

A tall, distinguished man with salt-and-pepper hair stands. I recognize him from his file photo. He's a respected senior judge from the state of Michigan and a man who was personally appointed by the president of the United States. He holds an elevated position within the elite, and he is someone a lot of members look up to, according to Drew.

We handpicked him for this role, because someone of esteem needs to kick-start this into gear. If Drew or I attempted it, we would most likely be hauled out of the auditorium and thrown in the dungeon which I know exists in the basement area of this building.

Judge Gregory Penn looks like an upstanding citizen in his pressed gray suit with his broad shoulders held high and a haughty expression on his face. He prides himself on his family man image, and he has a large family of three sons and four daughters.

He's also a perverted pedophile who loves raping young boys for his sick pleasure.

"Permission to approach the council and address all members," he asks.

The president frowns, totally oblivious to what is happening. He looks to his council members, and they nod. "Permission granted," he says before coughing into his handkerchief. He walks to the table on the stage where the other council members sit, dropping into the empty seat and mopping his brow.

The judge steps up to the podium, adjusting the microphone. He loudly clears his throat as a young man with a mass of shocking red hair steps onto the podium, looking agitated as he stands beside the judge, clutching a large white envelope.

Gregory Penn looks around the room before eyeballing my father who is clinging onto the side of his chair like he's about to keel over. "In this envelope is a signed petition from the majority of Parkhurst members demanding the denouncement and removal of Michael Hearst from our noble institution."

"That's preposterous," Father splutters, barely standing upright at this stage. The low dose of GHB I snuck into his juice will confuse him and slow him down so he can't easily defend himself or escape.

"On what grounds are you making this request?" the president asks, slipping his glasses on as the young man with the red hair hands him the envelope with the petition.

"False representation, blackmail and extortion, murder of high-ranking elite members, and behavior unbecoming of an elite," the judge says without batting an eyelash.

Hushed whispers whip through the crowd, and the president bangs his fist down on the table, instantly muting the room.

Alessandra pointedly looks at me, and there's no disguising the look of sheer glee on her face. My finger twitches with the need to flip her the bird, but I shoot her a disinterested look instead, knowing that will piss her off more.

"You have no proof!" Father slurs, almost taking a tumble.

"We call Drew Hearst-Manning to the stage as our witness," the judge says, and Drew stands. I rise, walking down the few steps toward the stage at the same time as my twin.

"Get back in your seat, Abigail," Father hisses as I walk past him.

I can't resist stopping in front of him. "You don't look so hot, Father. Perhaps you should sit down." I push his chest with one finger, and he collapses in the seat. I lean down over him, pouring every ounce of hate in my heart into my stare. "You should never underestimate women. Especially not the women in your life. I hope you get everything that is coming to you."

"You tell him, babe," Kai whispers in my ear. I smile broadly, and it's all for him.

Drew is waiting at the side of the dais for me, and the judge frowns as he watches us both approach him, clearly perplexed and unhappy because I wasn't part of the agreement.

But there is no way in hell I am sitting in the audience and watching Drew exact our revenge.

This retribution is *mine*, and it's all the sweeter knowing I'm sticking two fingers to the elite and their sexist bullshit, as well as taking my bastard father down.

After today, every man in this room will learn a valuable lesson— that hell hath no fury like a woman scorned.

CHAPTER THIRTY-SIX

Drew takes my hand as we step up onto the podium. The judge pins Drew with a sharp look when he nudges him to one side, allowing me in front of the mic. I bring it down to my level and wet my dry lips, willing my nerve to hold.

"You've got this, firecracker," Kai whispers. "Give them hell." Out of the corner of my eye, I spy Rick and Kai getting into position.

"Good morning. My name is Abigail Hearst-Manning. I am the daughter of Olivia Manning and Michael Hearst and sister to Drew. My father, and I use that reference in the very loosest terms, is a fraud and a manipulator, and he has spent years compiling evidence he has used to bribe key elite members into supporting his campaign for presidency."

Rumblings of discontent echo around the room, and behind me I hear someone getting to their feet. "Not only that, he has falsified records pertaining to his childhood to present himself as an orphan and ward of the state when he is in fact the illegitimate son of a failed businessman and a prostitute."

The crowd looks over my head at the images Xavier is projecting on to the screen.

"Every facet of the persona he has presented is fake. Even his engagement is a ruse, and he has no plans to marry Patrice. It's one of the reasons why she's been having an affair with Atticus Anderson behind my father's back."

Gasps ring out around the vast space, and I know Xavier has switched the feed to some stills from the footage we have of Patrice in bed with Kai's father. Most of the elite look mildly amused, because there is no shame or shock at this kind of usual behavior. But most family members are disgusted, and it shows on their expressions. While I'm sure many of them are accustomed to what goes on at Parkhurst, it's distasteful to have it so blatantly referred to.

Patrice jumps up, brushing past people in her haste to exit her row and get the hell out of here. I look to where Atticus is sitting, enjoying the panicked expression on his face. He has just realized how short-lived his elite return was.

"When my brother and I turn eighteen in two months, my father's shares in Manning Motors will divert to us." Drew hands an envelope to the president who is now standing directly behind me. "All board members have signed new contracts and statements of allegiance to us. Furthermore, they have publicly announced their separation from all actions and activities of Michael Hearst in a televised conference happening right now."

I glance over my shoulder at the screen, watching as the chairman of the board addresses an assembled crowd of reporters at Manning Motors HQ, explaining they have fired Michael Hearst as CEO and replaced him with an interim CEO.

Down in the front row, Father is struggling to get to his feet. Sweat pumps out of his brow, and he's staggering and swaying all over the place. The president comes up beside me, scowling as he looks at him. He takes control of the mic from me. "Guards, seize that man and bring him to me."

"But that is not his only crime," Drew says, taking control of the mic from the president.

Cries of outrage ring around the room as the footage from Christmas Day airs.

Now *this* is something the elite won't appreciate.

While blackmail and murder are commonplace, taking out a high-ranking elite member without justification and in such a cold, clinical way, *is* frowned upon. Especially when the man committing murder of a founding father is an illegitimate bastard only in the organization by virtue of marriage.

I so wanted to warn Charlie about this, but it was too risky.

"This footage was taken last December," Drew continues, "and it shows our father murdering Charles Barron, a high-ranking elite member and a descendant of a founding family from our hometown of Rydeville, in cold blood."

"And previously," I add, leaning in beside Drew as Kai and Rick edge closer to the stage. "He was instrumental in the murder of Emma Anderson, the wife of another founding father from Rydeville, although it was actually Atticus Anderson who killed his wife."

We debated whether to bring it up because we have no evidence, but we have enough evidence to support all our other allegations that we felt it was worth taking this risk. No one is going to focus on the one accusation we have no backing for, because they will be too caught up in the severity of all the other accusations.

"What?" Father blurts as he's dragged onto the stage by two guards.

"You were right to keep your enemies close, Father," I hiss as he's shoved into a chair and one wrist is handcuffed to the wooden arm. "It's a pity you lost sight of it though. Christian has known for years, and he's kept that from you." It took me a while to figure that one out, but Christian's comments last night confirmed it.

"This is bullshit," Father yells. "And I can explain. I didn't kill Emma Anderson, and I was forced to kill Charles Barron in self-defense. He's the one who pulled a gun on me."

"Liar!" Charlie roars from the crowd. "You murdered him because he was trying to stop you. To stop this."

More murmurings race through the crowd as Charlie approaches the podium.

"Order," the president commands, yelling into the mic.

"And my daughter lies about Manning Motors," Father continues, and I love the note of desperation in his voice and the panicked look in his eyes. For once, Michael Hearst takes a back seat, and his arrogant veneer has fallen away. But he wouldn't be who he is without trying. "Any contracts signed with the board are null and void because my daughter's shares are already entrusted to me by her husband."

"No, they're not," I say, as Kai jumps up onto the stage the same time Charlie approaches from the other side.

"I'm sorry," I mouth at Charlie before taking Kai's hand and turning to my father. "Because that wedding you forced me into on Christmas Day was not legal." I take the copy of our marriage certificate from Kai's hand and thrust it in the bastard's face. "I married Kaiden Anderson three days previously. He's my legally wedded husband, and he has already reassigned his shares to me."

Charlie almost falls off the stage in shock.

Father barks out a hoarse laugh, crumpling the paper in his hand. "It doesn't matter anyway, because those shares are still mine by reason of marriage."

More outraged cries reverberate around the room, and family members get to their feet, clasping hands over their mouths.

"Abby." Drew's strangled cry and his tight grip on my arm tells me this part of the plan worked out.

We didn't know if Sawyer and Jackson and the team of armed

guards had managed to get Mom out of the medical facility because we asked them not to tell us. Xavier got them fake IDs, which enabled them to breach the facility, and they worked with Dr. Collingsworth and his few trusted colleagues to smuggle her out. Neither Drew or I could risk getting distracted, and I've worked really hard to forget about that aspect of our strategy.

I assume the second part of that plan is already underway and that the doctor and his family are boarding James Kennedy's private jet to leave the US and go into protective hiding.

Atticus climbs to his feet. "Olivia!" he yells, looking like he's just seen a ghost. I suppose, for him, he has. Kai glares at his father, pinning him in place.

"No, they are not." Mom's voice is remarkably calm as she walks across the stage, supported by Sawyer and Jackson. She's wearing the black pants and green silky blouse combo I chose for her, but the clothes hang off her skeletal frame.

Kai wraps his arm around my waist, and that's the only reason I don't faint.

The second my eyes meet my mother's for the first time in ten years, it feels like coming home.

As if all the years of separation never existed.

As if her once lustrous dark hair isn't now graying, her curvy figure now rail thin, and her once flawless skin marred with lines.

I'm a little girl again, and I just want my mom.

Kai instinctively knows what I'm thinking, and he lets me go as Drew and I rush toward her simultaneously. "Mom!" I cry, flinging my arms around her gently the same time Drew does.

"My babies." Mom circles her arms around both of us, and we're all crying. Behind us, the crowd is talking more loudly, Father is shouting slurred obscenities, and the president is banging the table with his fist calling for order again.

Things are devolving fast.

And we still have tons more revelations to come.

"Let me look at both of you," Mom says, keeping a tight hold of us.

She cups my face. "My beautiful, strong daughter." She messes up Drew's hair. "My handsome, brave son." She presses a kiss to each of our foreheads in turn. "I love you both, so much, and we have lots of catching up to do, but first I need to say my piece."

"I love you, Mom," I say through my tears.

"I love you, too, and we're so happy you are out of that place," Drew adds.

"Thanks to you both." She takes our hands, bringing us with her as she walks to the president.

"Drew," the president says. "What on earth is going on here?"

"Please, sir. Just let us have this time. There is much more you need to hear."

He stares at Drew for a few tense moments. "Fine, but hurry it up. We still need to resolve the voting issue."

I'm not surprised he has little interest in this. Most of the elite are getting bored, because they have gotten what they wanted. Michael Hearst is discredited and he's about to be evicted from the elite permanently. Now, they want to go about their business as usual.

Except we're not allowing that.

Mom snatches the mic from the president's hand, shooting him a filthy look. "Good morning, ladies and assholes," she says to the crowd, and I smother a laugh. "My name is Olivia Manning. I'm the daughter of a founding father and descendant from one of the oldest legacy families in Rydeville. Michael Hearst tricked me into marrying him years ago, and when he discovered I was planning to escape with my children, he staged a car accident and locked me up in the medical facility here under false pretenses and under a pseudonym."

Mom walks right up to him, slapping him across the face. "Bastard."

"You look a hot mess," he slurs, and this time, I jump in and slap him. I've no qualms about the elite stopping us, because this is child's play compared to the torture they normally inflict on their enemies, and most of the men are now sitting up with more interest in their eyes.

"You do not get to speak to my mother like that." I yank his head back by his hair. "And you don't ever get to disrespect her, me, or Drew ever again. You will never see the light of day, because once the authorities get the file we've sent them, they will lock you up and throw away the key."

"And in case it's not obvious," Mom says, sliding her hand around my back. "I'm divorcing you, and any claim you have on Manning Motors will officially end once the ink is dry on the paperwork."

"Fuck you, bitch," he says, his head lolling back as I release him.

"You will never get to fuck me again," Mom says, baring her teeth.

"The only action you'll be getting is a cock in the ass in prison," I taunt. "And I hope they fuck you up so badly you wish you were dead."

"Can we move this along?" the president says. "We have heard enough. You are officially extradited from the organization and stripped of your elite status, Michael Hearst." He turns to the guards. "Remove him from the building."

Drew has a word in his ear, and he nods. "Very well."

The president holds up a hand, addressing the two guards. "He will remain here until the meeting has concluded, and then you can take him to the dungeon and lock him in one of the holding cells."

"El Presidente," a voice I'm familiar with says, and I whip my head around, narrowing my eyes at Denton Mathers. "Permission to approach the council."

Kai, Rick, Drew, and I exchange concerned looks.

"Yes. Mr. Mathers," the president says, wiggling his fingers at him.

I smirk as Denton makes his way to the stage with an obvious limp, feeling a surge of pride knowing I have caused him pain. He flashes me a wicked look, and I stare right through him, refusing to let him intimidate me.

"I'm sure you are as keen as the rest of the members to salvage the meeting and achieve the purpose we set out to achieve here today."

"Spit it out, man," the president says, his impatience showing as he coughs into his handkerchief again. I'm close enough this time to see the speckles of blood coating the white linen, and if we had any doubt, it's now gone.

"I would like to propose an alternate candidate," Denton says. "None of the other candidates here today received the minimal eligible votes, but we have a candidate in our midst who has earned the respect and trust of his fellow members the right way. I feel completely confident that this man is the man to lead the organization into the next era of prosperity."

He shoots me a sly look as footsteps resonate behind him.

This won't be happening. But we'll let them continue their charade.

He hands a sheet of paper to the president. "I believe the paperwork is in order with a nominator and a second supporter, which is all that is needed to formally announce Christian Montgomery as a viable candidate for president." His smug expression grows more confident. "Shall we take a vote?"

CHAPTER THIRTY-SEVEN

The president inspects the paperwork as another council member calls Christian to the stage.

"Standby, Xavier," I murmur.

Christian shoots me a gleeful look as he steps up onto the podium, flanked by Trent.

"No one can save you now," Trent whispers in my ear. "As soon as my father is declared president, we can do with you as we please." He glares at Kai. "A stupid piece of paper won't protect you. You will not be leaving here with him."

That's what you think.

I tug on Kai's hand, when a growl rips from the back of his throat, and urge him to ignore Trent and not rise to the bait.

"The paperwork is in order," the president announces. "And we will take a vote."

It's ridiculous how easy it is to nominate a candidate for the presidency. Drew had explained this before. The hard part is gaining support, and that's why most don't offer themselves up as candidates unless they are willing to work their butts off on their campaigns.

"Excuse me," I say, keeping hold of Kai as I angle in closer to the president. "We object."

Christian barks out a laugh, and Denton smirks.

"Young lady, I believe you've had your say," the president says, shooting me an irritated look before he glances at his guards. "You can escort everyone off the stage back to their seats."

"He poisoned you!" I blurt before anyone can remove me. I hear Drew instructing Xavier to play the recording through the earpiece. Kai hands me the medical report, and I thrust it at the president. "It's all in that report, signed by Dr. Collingsworth, the most senior doctor on your payroll in the medical wing."

The recording starts up at that very moment. "Listen to what he has to say," I implore the president, turning around to watch the doctor on the screen. We debated having him come here in person to make his statement, but it was too risky.

"Mr. President. I wish to make a statement to you and the authorities," the doctor says, "who have just now received a copy of this recording along with a number of files confirming criminal activities of several of your members."

Our original plan had been to transmit the blackmail tapes my father had on the high-ranking elite members, but the morning after watching the sick footage, we all agreed we couldn't show them in public, because this isn't a victimless crime.

The victims had been humiliated and abused enough already, and we weren't comfortable airing that footage in public. Also, there are several young family members in attendance today and the stuff on those tapes would scar them for life. None of us want to do that, so, instead, Xavier has just sent a video file to the local police, and the FBI are enroute here, thanks to Keven Kennedy and Lauder's father's interventions.

Mr. Lauder has some contacts within the FBI, and he was more than willing to help take down the elite. Kyler Kennedy spoke to his brother Keven—he's a field agent with the Boston FBI—and he helped set things up in a way that won't bring heat on us. DHL should be delivering the boxes of physical files to the police station right now, and I'm praying it doesn't take them too long to get here.

Because I know things are about to head south.

I refocus on the screen as the doctor continues. "Christian Montgomery approached me a year ago, threatening to kill me and my family if I didn't supply him with a slow-acting poison he could use on an enemy. At that time, I had no knowledge of the identity of the person he intended to use it on, but it was only after you attended the facility for tests, that I realized the person he was using the poison on was you."

The president sways on his feet, and Rick's hand darts out, helping to steady him.

Shouts and accusations ring out around the room as men get to their feet, shaking their fists and baying for blood.

The council is the most sacred structure within Parkhurst, and to take such action against the president is the most grievous crime of all, in their eyes. Dr. Collingsworth was smart enough to confide this knowledge in us, and it tied into the plans we had for Christian for today.

I've always wondered why Christian put up with my father's shit. Christian is a descendant of a founding family, yet he acted as my father's lackey for years. I knew there had to be a reason for it, and for the fact he let him believe he killed Emma Anderson.

We discussed it at length, and all drew the same conclusion—that he was biding his time until he could use it against him. Father wasn't the only one planning things on the sidelines. Christian was letting father do all the donkey work, and he facilitated it by poisoning the president, paving the way for Father to build his campaign, and then he was going to swoop in and steal it out from under him.

What he said last night confirmed that our confidence had been breached. That someone had told him what we were planning, and the arrogant son of a bitch just sat back and let it happen. We were doing his legwork for him, and he thought he could swoop in like a noble knight and rescue the vote and the council.

But he underestimated us.

Like most everyone has.

We have considered every angle, and we also caught a lucky break. Gregory Penn was the one who let it slip to Drew that the elite were switching their allegiance to Christian. It was a major fuck-up, which sealed his fate today. But we were coming prepared anyway.

We knew Christian and Trent were going to strike now, so we have all the evidence father compiled on him with us today, and it was also in the files delivered to the police station. Christian is going down too, and I'm only sorry I didn't think to grab Denton Mather's file from the vault as well.

But once Father is gone, we'll have full access to his files, and we plan to use them to completely shut the elite down for good.

"This is complete bullshit," Christian coolly says, smiling at the president. "Surely, you don't believe the words from a corrupt doctor who doesn't even have the balls to show his face here today." Christian snatches the paper from the president's hand, tearing it up.

"It's true!" Sylvia Montgomery says, approaching the stage with tears in her eyes. I was wondering when she was going to make a move. She and mom have been sharing looks ever since she reappeared. "I've overheard him bragging about it with others," she says, and I wince as she slurs her words a little. "Including him." She points her finger at Mathers. "It wasn't just Christian. He was in on it too."

Mom steps forward, grabbing Sylvia into a hug, and glaring at Christian over her shoulder. I lock eyes with Rick. "Can you get them out of here now?" I murmur. I want them gone before chaos descends.

"I've got this," Rick says, walking toward the women.

"This is utter nonsense," Christian says, sending a derisory look in his wife's direction as Rick and Sawyer usher her and Mom off the stage. Mom looks back at me, and I nod, telling her it's okay to go. Jackson and Sawyer filled her in on the way, so she knows the score, but I spot the terror in her eyes, and I get it. I don't want anything to happen to her, not after we've just been reunited, and she feels the same way about us.

"Go," I mouth. "We'll be okay. We love you." I nod at Shandra as she steps out of her seat to join them, urging her to leave with them too.

Christian is continuing in his attempt to pass this off as nonsense. "Fabricated by my wife who doesn't live in the real world. She spends most days drunk or high, and I should have placed her in the medical facility years ago."

We all know why he didn't. Because Mom was there. And he wouldn't reunite the best friends, even if it meant she was out of his hair.

Christian pins darks eyes on me. "And orchestrated by a little girl who thinks she can get up here and try to tell us, the *elite*, how to conduct our business. It's clear Hearst failed as a father, but don't worry, I will take the girl in hand and discipline her."

Kai growls, taking a step forward with his fists raised, but I hold him back. Christian Montgomery won't be anywhere near me to lay a hand on me.

Drew takes the file from Jackson, passing it to the president. "I assure you, the medical report and the doctor's statement is no word of a lie, but feel free to get another opinion," he says.

"And poisoning you is the least of Christian's crimes," I say, grinning. "That file contains a list of all his fraudulent financial transactions. For years, he has been skimming an additional ten percent off every transaction for services his company provided to Parkhurst and other elite organizations. The list of companies who have been defrauded are on the screen right now."

Most heads turn to the overhead screen, eyes squinting as they examine the names of the companies he took advantage of.

Cries of outrage echo around the room, and a red haze coats Christian's eyes as reality dawns.

No one in this room will support him now.

Not with the knowledge he was stealing from them and he poisoned their president in a blatant move to take his position.

Father throws back his head, laughing hysterically at the anger and panic surfacing on Christian's face. "Abigail, you little bitch," the bastard says, turning to look at me. "I hate your conniving cunt, but I've never been prouder than I am in this moment." He cocks an unfocused eye at Christian. "I knew you couldn't be trusted, and I've spent years compiling evidence of your corruption. I told you before if I go down, you go down."

The next few seconds happen as if in slow motion. Christian whips a gun out of the back of his dress pants, aiming it at my father while Trent yanks me back, pressing a gun to my temple.

A shot rings out at the same time a massive explosion rattles the walls. The podium floor shakes and my limbs tremble as I sway on my feet. Dust plumes rain down on us, and I scream as my ears splinter, a pounding, piercing pain ripping through both eardrums. Blood splatters my white blouse, and all hell breaks loose in the aftermath of the bomb and the shooting.

Father's head rolls back, and his blank eyes stare at me, as his limp body slumps in the chair. Christian grins manically as he pumps another bullet into Father's chest.

Fury crests the surface because I didn't want the bastard to die.

I wanted him to rot in a jail cell, and Christian fucking

Montgomery has just robbed me of that justice.

I scream in frustration, or at least I think I do, because I can't hear things properly. Sounds are muffled, but I hear faint screams as people dash from the auditorium, tripping over one another in their haste to get away.

The air is thick with dust, visibility is hazy, like fog, and I cough profusely.

On the stage, everyone is clutching their ears, and Trent's hold on me has loosened. Using it to my advantage, I reach around, grabbing hold of his dick and digging my nails in as I squeeze it hard. He screams out in pain, releasing me and dropping his gun as he cups his junk, moaning in agony. Ignoring the dull ache in my skull, I reach for the gun strapped to my thigh.

"Abby!" Kai shouts, but his voice is like a whisper in my ear. "Behind you."

Jackson emits a loud roar as he launches himself across the stage toward Christian. Christian's arm is elevated, and his gun is pointed.

At me.

Does he hate me that much he wants to kill me too? Because I've foiled his plans for elite domination, or he's pissed on his son's behalf? Or he's just a crazy psycho who loves shooting people?

A shot goes off, whizzing over my head, only missing me because Kai tugs on my ankle, pulling me to the ground in time. Jackson lands on top of Christian, and they wrestle for the gun. Trent grunts, struggling to his feet and reaching for his gun. Jackson is oblivious, still fighting with Christian, so he doesn't see Trent lift his gun in his direction.

"No!" I scream, turning on my side and raising my gun as Kai climbs to his feet, running toward his friend.

But my scream alerts Trent, and he spins around, pointing his weapon at me now and firing.

Drew's panicked shout tickles my sensitive eardrums, and I glance at my twin. His eyes are wide as he stares at me from the other side of the stage. Denton Mathers, whom he's fighting, seizes the opportunity, ramming his fist into Drew's face.

Time stands still as I turn back around, facing a smug-looking Trent.

Kai roars, turning around the same time Charlie barrels past him, knocking him to the ground.

I squeeze the trigger of my gun and pray it hits its target before the breath leaves my body.

But Trent's shot never reaches me.

Because Charlie jumps in front of me first, taking the bullet intended for me.

I crash to the floor on my back, Charlie's weight pressing down on me as warm liquid oozes all over my blouse. Kai shouts, crawling toward us as the doors to the auditorium burst open, and swarms of cops and FBI agents enter the room. In the same second Jackson grabs the gun from Christian's hand, Trent swings around, pointing his weapon at Jackson's back. My aim was clearly off, and my shot missed him, or he dodged it in time.

"Trent has a gun on you, Jackson!" I screech, hoping he can hear me through the earpiece.

Jackson whips around and shoots without hesitation.

Christian pales, staring wide-eyed at his son, looking indecisive for a split second before he slides out from behind Jackson and races toward the side door.

Trent's gun drops to the floor, and blood oozes out of a wound in his chest. His fingers splay over the blood leaking down his white shirt, while more blood spurts from his mouth.

Jackson looks over his shoulder, cursing as he spots Christian slipping into the back corridor. Raw pain is etched across Jackson's face, and I can almost see the wheels churning in his mind as he calculates whether it's worth giving chase.

Trent turns his head in my direction, and our eyes lock. A multitude of differing emotions splays across his face. Shock. Fear. Disbelief. Anger. He opens his mouth, attempting to say something to me, pointing his arm as blood pours like a river from his lips. His powerful body sways, and I watch as he falls to the floor with a resounding thud, seeing the exact moment the light vanishes from his eyes.

"Abby, fuck!" Kai's voice sounds distant even though he's right beside me. His fingers touch my cheek. "Are you hurt?"

"No." I shake my head even as my lungs constrict. Charlie is heavy on top of me, bleeding all over me.

Drew sinks to his knees. Blood drips down his face from a cut over his eye, and his nose is all busted up. "Abby. Are you injured?"

"Not me." I wrap my arm around Charlie, feeling fiercely protective. "Help him." I plead with my eyes, looking to Kai and Drew. Together, they gently lift him off me, placing him on the floor. I crawl to his side, pressing my fingers to his neck, almost fainting in relief when I feel the faint thrumming of his pulse under the tips of my fingers.

"He's still alive," I whisper with tears in my eyes. Kai rubs my back, but no one says anything.

Things have been fractured with Charlie for a while, and I've wondered if he'd completely lost his way.

But today, I know he hasn't.

That there is hope.

That the Charlie I know and love is still in there somewhere.

Because he risked everything to save me.

And I pray he pulls through, so I get to tell him how grateful I am.

CHAPTER THIRTY-EIGHT

Law enforcement officers swarm the stage, and paramedics take Charlie away on a stretcher. I want to go with him, because he has no one, but I don't want to leave Mom. Besides, the FBI is insistent on speaking to us, so I reluctantly let him go. Kai sends one of his security guards in the ambulance with Charlie, giving him firm instructions to keep us regularly updated, and I kiss my husband, proud of his selflessness.

A couple of armed FBI agents escort us upstairs to our suite. The female agent takes my bloody clothes as evidence, and we are all officially processed when a team of crime scene investigation personnel arrives. Then we are checked out by a team of medics, but we all only have superficial injuries with no permanent damage to our ears, thank fuck.

As soon as the formal shit is done, I grab a quick shower and get changed. When I step out of the bathroom, the whole crew is here, including Mom and Sylvia, along with four FBI agents and the local sheriff.

We sit down and tell them everything. Confirming what Keven Kennedy has already explained. Thank God for his intervention; otherwise, we might have found ourselves getting arrested. An FBI technical team is going through the CCTV footage from the auditorium, which will back up our version of events. However, we're well aware of how suspicious it looked when they first arrived. I was especially worried for Jackson, because he shot and killed Trent, but they accept it was self-defense.

Mom explains who she is and where she has been the last ten years. They have already sent a team to the medical facility, and the kidnapped patients are being processed and moved to a private government medical facility where they will receive the right kind of care.

While they are free, there is a lot of red tape to go through, especially since a lot of them are deemed to be dead, and most of those patients have been heavily medicated for years. They weren't as lucky as Mom to have someone on the inside who gradually weaned her off the drugs and then helped her hide it. These people will have to be weaned off their medication gradually and in a carefully monitored way.

The special supervisory agent in charge informs me they have arrested Dr. Lacy, along with the other medical personnel, and they are being held for questioning. With the evidence Xavier compiled on Dr. Lacy, I know he won't see the light of day ever again.

They are also trying to identify who set the bomb to go off in the auditorium, but I'm guessing it was my father, Christian, or Denton because they'd have insurance in place in case things didn't go their way.

They pepper us with questions, and we do our best to answer them. Kai has his arms around me the entire time, and Mom holds my hand on my other side.

It's late when we finish up, and we're all exhausted, but none of us want to stay here a second longer, so we pack our stuff up and head out.

Downstairs, officers mill around, and the entire facility has been shut down pending local and federal investigation. Elite members are being brought out in handcuffs and thrown in the back of large black vans.

Drew and I trade a relieved look, but it's somewhat short-lived.

"Fuck," Kai says, pulling me back into the lobby as we were just about to leave. "Can you turn that up?" he shouts to the girl behind the reception desk, and she raises the volume on the TV.

We crowd around it, and I go to Mom and Drew, placing my arms around them.

CNN is reporting from outside our house in Rydeville. What's gone down here today has been playing on a loop on all the TV stations because we sent a summary of some stuff to the major news outlets. We hung Judge Penn out to dry, and he's been the scapegoat for the elite. We couldn't risk sending everything to reporters, in case it damaged any criminal proceedings, but the scandal is enough to ruin the judge's life irrespective of any charges brought.

But that's not why Kai called us back.

The house I grew up in, the house Mom grew up in, is highlighted on the screen, engulfed in flames, the dark sky above the house coated in a foggy layer of billowing smoke that shoots upwards in a steady stream. The reporter explains that an explosion rocked the basement of the house and then a raging fire whipped through the mansion.

"Oh no." Mom's lower lip wobbles as she watches her ancestral home burn to the ground. I'm grateful I removed everything of mine from that house months ago and that all my personal possessions and mementos are safe, but poor Mom has lost everything of sentimental value. I hold her tighter, pressing a kiss to her temple as we watch.

"That fucking bastard," I seethe, instantly knowing Father is somehow behind this. He must have left instructions for someone to destroy the vault and burn the property should anything happen to him. "All that evidence is gone now. Goddamn it." Frustration trundles through me at the knowledge that most elite members are going to come out of this untarnished. "We don't even know where he was keeping those young girls, and now, we'll never find out."

The mood is somber when we make it back to the rented house a half hour later.

Mom is drained, and Sylvia is distraught now she's come out of her alcohol bubble and realized her son is dead.

She knew he was a monster, but he was still her baby.

Mom is doing her best to console her, but she's dead on her feet. Sawyer shows them to a guest room. Mom helps Sylvia undress and get into bed while I fetch them some hot chocolate. I give Mom some of my things, because she has nothing, hugging her close before I say goodnight.

When I return to the living room, everyone is drinking, and I happily accept the beer Kai hands me before sinking onto his lap and clinging to his warmth. Shandra is similarly situated in Drew's lap, and he's running his hand up and down her arm.

"I know it sucks," Xavier says, sitting cross-legged on the ground, trading a joint back and forth with Jackson. "But we should focus on the positives. We still did a lot of good today."

"I agree with Xavier," Shandra says. "What we pulled off today has thrown a spotlight on Parkhurst and thrown the elite into chaos. It won't be business as usual for them anymore, and they're going to be dealing with the fallout for a long time."

"But we haven't succeeded in ending them the way we'd hoped," I say.

"We made good progress today," Sawyer says, sipping his old-fashioned. "And no one says it has to end here. We've seen what we can achieve when we pool our efforts. We can continue the work we started today."

"That fucking bastard got away," Jackson spits out, his hands balling into fists. "I had the shot, but that bastard son of his fucking ruined it."

The FBI confirmed both Christian Montgomery and Atticus Anderson are MIA.

"But you took Trent out," Xavier says.

"He wasn't the main target," Jackson snaps. The weed isn't affecting him the way it usually does, and he's highly strung and clearly on edge.

"It's still one less asshole in the world," I say, and I mean it.

That bastard was going to murder me with no regrets, and Charlie got hurt in the process. I have no sympathy for how things turned out for my nasty ex–fiancé. Trent put me through years of torment, and he was hell bent on making my life miserable into the future so I'm not sorry he's dead. The choices he made in life led him to an early death.

His death also gets rid of Alessandra Mathers. The authorities confirmed that Denton, his wife, Alessandra, Isabella, and Giselle have been cleared to return home to Alabama. The women had left the auditorium the minute everything turned to shit, and although Denton got into it with Drew, he didn't shoot anyone or do anything they can hold him with. His high-powered lawyers rocked up to release him, and there wasn't anything more the police could do.

"Two," Drew says. "Dad's dead too."

"I know I should be happy about that," I honestly admit. "But I'm pissed Christian took that from me. I wanted to see him locked in jail."

"I wanted to beat his ass until he was inhaling blood," Kai says. "But it's better this way. Because he was a sly son of a bitch, and he might have wriggled out of a conviction."

"I'm happy he's dead," Drew says, sipping his beer. "I hope he's rotting in the fiery pits of hell." His facial expression softens, and he looks to me. "And we got Mom back. That's our greatest personal success today."

Happy tears prick my eyes as I nod, and Kai holds me closer.

Silence descends then, but it's companionable. It's been some day.

"Any news on Charlie?" I ask Xavier, after a few moments. I love how in sync my bestie is, because he'd already hacked into the hospital system before I asked him to.

"He's still in surgery," he says, confirming what Kai's bodyguard had already communicated.

"I should go there," I say.

"He's not your responsibility," Kai says, making a deliberate effort to soften his tone.

"He took a bullet for me, Kai," I say, peering into his eyes. "And he's all alone in the hospital. It doesn't feel right."

He thinks about it for a moment. "You're right." He nods. "But there's no point going tonight. He won't know we're there if he's in surgery. We'll go first thing in the morning."

Kai holds me close all night, and his warm arms lull me into a deep sleep.

He wakes me at seven a.m. with a soft kiss. "Morning, baby."

I yawn, stretching my arms up over my head. "Morning, sexy." I yank him down on top of me, licking a line up the side of his neck.

"You're killing me, babe," he says, propping up on his elbows. "I want nothing more than to bury myself balls deep inside you, but Charlie just came out of surgery. I thought you wanted to go to the hospital to be there when he wakes."

Screw morning breath. I grab Kai's head down to mine, smashing my lips against his mouth for a quick, hard kiss. "I fucking love you so much. You're one of the most selfless people I know."

"I love you too." A wide smile graces his mouth. "And you know what this means. We can make plans. We have a future. We can get a house, and go to college, and have babies." He caresses my cheek. "And I get to make love to you every morning for the rest of my life, so I can forgo this morning, because I owe Charlie."

Pain stretches across his face. "Have you any idea how terrified I was when I saw him point that gun at you?" He palms my cheeks. "I knew I couldn't get to you in time. My whole life flashed before my eyes. I thought I lost you." His voice cracks. "I still don't like Barron, but I will forever be in his debt, because I get to wake up with you every morning for the rest of my life, thanks to him." He straightens up, whipping back the covers. "So, get that sexy ass up and into the shower."

I hop up. "Only if you come with?"

Desire shimmers in his eyes. "I like your thinking, Mrs. Anderson." He scoops me up. "A quickie in the shower it is."

"Mr. Barron woke a few minutes ago," the pretty nurse says, trying her best not to stare at my man.

Kai is looking especially hot today, so I'll give her a free pass. He's wearing a fitted black shirt, rolled to the sleeves, with skinny black jeans and unlaced boots, and he looks fucking badass, and sexy as fuck. My pussy aches as I remember the possessive way he claimed me in the shower, but it wasn't enough.

It never is with him.

I always want more.

"But he's been through two surgeries, and he's going to be tired."

"But he's going to pull through, right?"

"The surgeon managed to remove the bullet, and it hadn't hit any major arteries. He was extremely lucky."

I'm not sure lucky is the word I'd use, but I'm just thankful he's going to be okay.

"Thank you for looking after him," I say, and her smile is genuine.

"It's my pleasure. What time are his mom and sister due to arrive?"

"They should be here in five hours," I confirm.

I called Elizabeth from the car on the way here and told her what happened. I don't know how things are between her and Charlie now, but she had a right to know.

I also spoke to her about her husband's death, pleading for forgiveness on Charlie's behalf. My bastard father killed Charles Barron, and it wasn't Charlie's fault. And she needed to know her son saved me last night and that he's not a monster.

He's broken and hurting, but he's not a bad man.

I would have called Elizabeth last night, but it was so late, and I knew I wouldn't be able to charter the Manning Motors jet until morning. Drew arranged things with the interim CEO, and the pilot, and they should be up in the air now.

The nurse leaves, and we hold hands as we pull up chairs beside Charlie's bed and wait for him to regain consciousness.

He wakes four hours later, looking around him in confusion. "Hey." I lean toward him, lifting the cup of water by his bed. "How are you feeling? Do you need some water?"

"What happened?" he rasps, frowning.

"You don't remember?" Kai asks.

Charlie's predictable scowl is almost funny. "What are you doing here?"

"I came with Abby. She was worried about you." Kai stands, glancing down at me. "I'll grab some fresh coffee. Take your time." He pecks my lips and turns to leave, stopping for a second and turning around. "You risked your life for my wife, yesterday, Charlie, and I won't forget that. If there is ever anything I can do for you, you only need to ask." His eyes glisten as he casts a glance at me. "She's my everything, and I would never have survived if I'd lost her, so thank you."

Charlie's Adam's apple bobs in his throat as he nods. Kai quietly leaves the room.

"Here, drink this," I say, holding the straw to his mouth.

He takes a few sips before pushing my hand away. "So, we were never actually married then," he says after a few beats of awkward silence.

"I'm sorry I lied to you."

"It's okay, Abby. I betrayed your trust. I get why you didn't tell me."

"I care about you so much, Charlie," I say, threading my fingers in his.

"But you don't love me."

I hate to beat on a man when he's already down, but I can't lie. And it's not as if this is anything new. We've already had this conversation before.

"I love you as a best friend, and I'd hate to lose you from my life, but I don't love you in a romantic way, Charlie. I am very much in love with Kaiden. He's the only one for me."

"He's a lucky man, and I'm not bearing any grudges." He squeezes my hand. "I want you to be happy, and I can see he makes you happy." Pain slices across his face, and I hate that I put it there. "And I'd like to think we can regain our friendship one day, but I don't know if I can do it."

Now I'm the one hurting, but I can't disregard his feelings. I don't trust myself to speak, so I just nod.

"I love you so much, Abby." Tears cling to his lashes. "And I got a taste of what my life would be like with you in it, and I loved every second of it."

I'm tempted to bring up the woman he screwed the night of our fake wedding, but there's no point dragging that shit up again. I think Charlie is in love with the idea of loving me, and it's only when he meets the love of his life that he'll realize that.

"I can't be around you knowing I loved and lost you. And I can't be around you with him." He wrenches his hand from mine. "I'm sorry."

A tear creeps out of the corner of my eye. "I understand. It sucks, but I get it."

"I appreciate you coming here. I really do, but I'd like to be left alone."

I stand. "I called your mom and Lil. They are on the way."

"Thank you."

I lean down and kiss his cheek. "Get well soon, and thank you for saving my life. Kai isn't the only one who won't forget." I cup his face. "If you need me, I'm here for you. Always."

Tears well in my eyes as I close the door to his room and step out into the corridor. Kai is slouched against the wall, holding two cups of coffee. He tenses when he sees me. "I don't care if he's in a fucking hospital bed, I'll fucking—"

I press my lips to his, cutting off his diatribe. "He didn't hurt me. I'm the one who hurt him." I press my face against his chest as he puts the cups down and wraps his arms around me. "I hate that I'm the cause of his pain, both physical and emotional."

"He'll be okay, babe." Kai runs his hand down the back of my head. "He just needs time."

We return to Rydeville different people but the same. The town is full of gossip over what went down in Wyoming and all the revelations that came to light. But we ignore it and them, returning to school as normal, focusing on our upcoming graduation and on building a new phase in our lives.

Mom has a bunch of medical issues, but Drew and I are supporting her through them. She has good days and bad days, but we are both there to help her.

Kai and I found a beautiful new modern build on the outskirts of Rydeville and moved in almost straightaway. I fangirled like crazy when Rick arranged it for Alex Kennedy to manage the interior design of the house. Kai teased me endlessly while she was overseeing the project, but I was too busy gushing to care. And we have a beautiful, stylish yet comfortable home, thanks to her amazing talent.

Mom wants to stay in Rydeville, because it's the only home she's ever known—even if the house she grew up in is a pile of rubble. We're working with her and an architect to build a new home on the grounds of the property she loves. In the meantime, she's staying with Drew in the house he bought a couple of miles away from us.

Kai offered for Mom to live with us, which only made me love him more, but Drew wouldn't hear of it, insisting he didn't want to live alone. But I know it's because he wanted to give Kai and me time to be newlyweds.

I've broached the subject of Jane with him several times, but he refuses to speak about her, and I don't know what's going through my brother's brain. I'm convinced something happened between Drew and Shandra, because she's been melancholy since we graduated high school last week. She hasn't said anything to me either, and any time I've asked, she's said she doesn't want to talk about it, and I respect her privacy, even if I'm curious as hell.

The fact there was something between them is one of the reasons I haven't reached out to Jane. The other is because Xavier hasn't been able to find her. Wherever she's hiding, it's clear she doesn't intend to be found.

"Where are we going?" I ask again as Kai takes the exit off the highway for Boston.

"You'll see soon," he says, glancing anxiously at me. He's been acting weird since we left home, and I've no clue what's up with him. I'm wondering if it's something to do with our plans to hold a wedding reception in Alabama at the end of August. If he's surprising me with something.

Turns out, he is.

But it's not what I was expecting.

"Why are we here?" I ask, looking up at the sign over my head with a frown. He's brought me to a cosmetic surgery clinic, knowing how I feel about that shit.

Kai reels me into his arms. "You know I love you and I find you sexy as hell," he explains. I nod, because he never leaves me in doubt. He tells me every day how much he loves me, and how sexy I am, and he worships my body like a man thirsting for air, so I'm supremely confident in his love and his attraction to me. "But I know how much you hate those boobs your father forced on you."

I suck in a shocked gasp as I realize what he's done.

"I would love you and find you sexy with big tits, small tits, wonky tits, or no tits." His brows knit together and he pouts. "Actually, scratch that last one. Cause that's like saying I'm into boys or some shit, and I'm strictly hetero, and I love boobs."

I laugh. "I think I get that by now," I tease.

"What I'm trying to say, *badly*," he admits, holding me closer. "Is that I'm okay if you want to get the implants removed."

"I'll have scars, and they might sag because the skin has stretched. They won't look like they used to."

He kisses the tip of my nose. "I don't care. As long as I have something to play with while I'm fucking you, I'm happy." His expression turns serious. "Anyway, the person I spoke to said they have procedures for that, too. But, honestly, babe, they'll be perfect because they're a part of you. I just want you to be happy and comfortable with yourself, and I see how you scowl at them and flinch sometimes when I touch them."

"Can you please stop being so perfect?" I tease, pressing a kiss to the underside of his jaw. "You're showing me up here."

"Don't deflect, and we both know I'm far from perfect. What I'm saying is I support you if you want to keep them or take them out." He looks up at the building. "Maybe it was wrong of me to arrange this consultation today, and we don't have to go in if you don't want to, but I just wanted you to know my thoughts on the subject, in case you were holding off on doing this because of me."

"You once told me you could live a thousand lifetimes and never be worthy of me," I remind him, lifting up to kiss his lips. "And now I'm saying the exact same thing back to you. My life might have been shitty these past few years, but I wouldn't change a thing, because it led me to you, and you are the best thing to ever happen to me."

"Ditto, babe." He kisses me slowly. "And I cannot wait to spend the rest of my life proving it."

EPILOGUE – Three months later

Abby

"Oh, Abigail." Tears instantly pool in Mom's eyes when she walks into the room. "You look so beautiful. Kaiden won't be able to keep his hands off you when he sees you."

"Ugh." Drew groans. "Did you have to go there. It's bad enough I suffer it every time I'm in their presence. I don't need to hear you condoning it."

"Shush." I slap his chest. "You're just jealous because I've stolen him from you."

Kai and Drew's bromance is back in full swing, and I love that they are the best of friends again. Even Jackson has warmed to my twin although Sawyer is still reserving judgment. I'm looking forward to seeing the guys today as they've been in New York since we graduated, and I've missed Jackson's flirty smile and Sawyer's grumpy face.

"All joking aside, I'm happy for you, Abby," Drew says, standing. He looks handsome in his crisp, white shirt and tan pants.

Our wedding ceremony is being held on the beach at Kai's Uncle Wes's place, and the reception is in a marquee erected in the grounds of his opulent mansion. Tonight, we're spending the night in the cabin where we first met, and my heart is so full. All our close friends

367

and family are here to watch us say our vows this time, and unlike my fake wedding party to Charlie, this time I've done it my way.

"You don't think it's too simple?" I ask Mom, inspecting my reflection in the mirror.

It's hot and humid in Alabama in August so I've opted for an A-line knee-length ballet-style white dress composed of delicate lace over tulle. The lace panel extends from my collarbone, down over the fitted corset-style top which gives my smaller bust a natural lift. My arms are bare, and there's a thin silk sash wrapped around my waist, tied in a pretty bow at the back.

My hair is in a half-up half-down style, curled in soft waves with flowers woven between the strands. My makeup is light and natural, and I'm wearing flip-flops. We told our guests to wear whatever they like, and I hope everyone has come casual and that it's as far removed from a formal elite wedding as you can get.

"It's classically elegant, and it suits you to a T," Mom loyally says. "Your natural beauty shines through, along with your happiness. You're glowing, Abigail, and it's clear marriage agrees with you."

"Kaiden agrees with me," I correct. "He completes me."

Mom looks a little nostalgic, and I wonder if she's thinking of happier times with Atticus, when he was the love of her life and she dreamed of marrying him.

It's ironic that I ended up marrying his son. Or maybe it was written in the stars.

Drew gags, and I flip him the bird.

"I'm in love, and I don't care who knows it. It's taken a lot to get to this point, and it's definitely a cause for celebration."

"It is, even if Anderson is completely pussy-whipped and proud."

"Language, Drew," Mom says, and we both laugh.

Holding my simple white and green bouquet, I walk down the makeshift aisle, which is a grass reed and shell path on the beach, with Mom on one side and Drew on the other. They are both giving me away today, and I couldn't be happier. Having Mom back in my life is the icing on the cake, and we're enjoying making up for all the time that was stolen from us.

A temporary decked area, surrounded by tall ornamental grass, has been built on the beach especially for today, and it's where the priest and my gorgeous guy wait. We decided not to do the whole bridesmaid and groomsman thing, because it would've just ended up with most of the wedding party involved.

So, Kai waits for me alone, beaming at me with emotion brimming in his eyes.

My smile is equally wide as I walk toward him, passing the few rows of seats on either side. Everyone is here. Jackson and Sawyer with their parents. Shandra and Xavier came together, and Chad is here with his new boyfriend. Kai's brothers all brought dates, and they look so handsome, proudly occupying the front row, alongside Wes and his wife, Ruth. I've gotten to know them the last couple of days, and I instantly warmed to both of them. They are lovely people, and they care about Kai a lot. They have stepped up in lots of ways over the course of the last few months, assuming legal guardianship over Harley and Joaquin now their dad is AWOL.

Atticus absconded overseas, as did Christian Montgomery, and there is an international warrant out for both their arrests.

Sylvia grabs hold of my arm as I pass, smiling expansively. "You look like an angel," she whispers. "And I'm so happy for you." Her eyes are bright, her cheeks flushed with health. Having Mom back has done wonders for the woman, and vice versa. That and the fact that bastard she was married to is now gone from her life. She spent a couple months in rehab when we first got back to Rydeville, and she's determined to lead a clean and sober life. She purchased a lovely condo fifteen minutes away from Drew's place, and she and Mom meet daily.

I press a kiss to her cheek, thanking her before moving on. I stop at the top row when I come to the wheelchair, bending down to hug Oscar. "Thank you so much for coming."

"I wouldn't miss this for the world, sweetheart," he says, clasping my hands.

"You look stunning, Abby," his wife, Julie, says, smiling at me.

"Thank you all for being here." I smile at Oscar's two beautiful daughters, and they give me shy waves. "It's all the more special because you are." We came so close to losing Oscar, but thankfully, he pulled through. He'll be in a wheelchair for the rest of his life, but we've seen to it that he's well looked after. They won't want for anything as long as we are around.

"You better not keep that handsome young man waiting," Julie says, looking up at Kai.

"Yes," I agree. "He's not known for his patience." We all have a laugh at Kai's expense as he wiggles his fingers at me.

I smile, looping my arm in Mom's and Drew's and stride toward the altar to my future.

Kaiden

"Are you happy, firecracker?" I murmur as we slow dance on the dance floor, surrounded by friends and family. The marquee looks beautiful with elegant floral centerpieces and lit tea lights on every table. The overhead hanging lanterns add a magical quality to a day that has been amazing so far.

"I'm so happy," she purrs, peering up at me with slightly dazed eyes. "Today was perfect."

I kiss her lips. "It was. This is the wedding we should've had the first time." I've already got enough happy memories from today to sketch another album for my wife, but I'm going to try and keep that a secret while I work on it, because I love surprising her.

"I loved our first wedding," she says. "But now we get to tell our kids we had two special days."

"I love hearing you say that," I whisper, because I spent weeks thinking kids were an impossibility. "And I can't wait until the time is right to start a family."

"Me too." She holds on to me tighter. "But I'm a selfish bitch because I want you all to myself for a few years first."

"I guess I'm selfish too," I admit, swirling her around. "Because I don't want to share you either."

"That's why we work, caveman." She stretches up, and I lean down, and our mouths collide in a searing-hot kiss that should be outlawed in public.

"I think it's time we retired for the night. What do you think?" My cock has been hard as a rock all day from looking at my sexy as fuck, gorgeous as fuck, wife. She has never looked more beautiful than she did today, and I plan to worship her body all night long.

"I thought you'd never ask," she says, cheekily squeezing my ass. "I've been dying for you to make love to me all day."

I laugh. "You're as horny as a dude."

She arches a brow. "And you're complaining?"

I lift her up, swinging her around, and she shrieks with delight. "I never said I was complaining. Just stating a fact." I place her feet on the ground, taking her hand as I lead her off the dance floor.

"It's your fault anyway," she murmurs. "Because you're too fucking hot for your own good. I just look at you, and I want to climb all over you."

"Fuck." I discreetly adjust the obvious bulge in my pants, hoping no one notices the monster erection I'm sporting.

We say our goodbyes, ignoring Lauder's crude innuendos and Xavier's crass teasing, racing across Uncle Wes's lawn and out onto the beach.

When we reach the door to the cabin, I scoop her up into my arms, carrying her over the threshold.

Someone has been in here today, because a myriad of soft candles is flickering in the bedroom and rose petals are strewn across the bed. A bottle of champagne is on ice along with two glasses and two pieces of the gorgeous wedding cake Olivia and Abby baked for today.

"Oh my God." Abby jumps into my arms. "You are so thoughtful."

"I'm tempted to take credit," I say. "But I didn't do this."

"Oh." She slides down my body, dragging me over to the bed. "My money's on Mom."

"Mine too," I admit.

It's been great having Olivia back in our lives, and not just because it makes my wife so happy. It also helps me feel connected to my mom. Olivia loves telling me happy stories of when they were growing up. Most of her mementos were destroyed in the fire, but we found a bunch of old photos in her sister Genevieve's things, and we spent hours reminiscing over a couple of bottles of wine that night. Whatever shit they did to Olivia at Parkhurst hasn't altered her memories of the past, and she was able to tell the story behind every photo. It's like getting to know my mom properly for the first time.

Abby spins around, circling her arms around my neck. "I want you to make love to me like you did the first night we were here."

"Was planning to," I say, pressing my lips to that sensitive spot just under her ear. I'm rewarded when she shivers all over. "Turn around, baby," I whisper, and she obliges. Slowly, I unbutton and unzip her dress, letting it fall to the floor with a gentle swishing motion. My hands wind around her body, palming her flat stomach, and I nuzzle into her neck, pressing feather-soft kisses against the elegant column of her neck. I unclasp her bra, letting it drop to the floor too, before gently cupping her natural breasts.

I love that she leans into my hands, not flinching or pulling away like she used to when she had the implants in. And she's perfect. Absolutely perfect, and I love every inch of her beautiful, supple body.

We shed the rest of our clothes, slowly and without talking. Then I carry her to the bed and lay her down underneath me. Her gentle moans reverberate around the room as I ravish every part of her with my lips and my tongue. My hard cock is bobbing against my stomach, pleading for release.

I take a mouthful of champagne and lean down to kiss her, depositing some of the amber liquid into her mouth as my lips press against hers.

"Mmm," she murmurs. "More."

I quietly chuckle, drinking a few more mouthfuls and sharing it with her. My lips leave a sticky trail along her body as I make my way down her silky-soft skin, sucking and licking her nipples and causing her to arch her back in pleasure as I kiss a line along her stomach.

Nudging her thighs apart, I lick her pussy from top to bottom, plunging my tongue into her wet warmth and suctioning on her clit when I sense her climax building. She falls apart under my mouth, and a surge of pride fills my chest as I watch her while my fingers and my tongue continue to milk her arousal.

I slide inside her gently, remembering the first time we did this here and how shocked I was to discover she was a virgin. It seems like a lifetime ago, because I can't imagine a time when she wasn't a part of my life. But it's only been sixteen months.

"I love you, Abby," I whisper against her lips as I rock in and out of her.

"I love you too, Kai," she replies, her hands roaming up and down my back and over my ass.

"Did you think that first night that we'd ever end up back here?"

"Never," she whispers. "But I couldn't forget you. Forget our magical night. I think, deep down, some part of me knew you were already a part of me."

"I never forgot you either," I admit, biting back a groan of pleasure as a familiar tingling starts at the base of my spine. "And I won't ever forget." I still for a minute inside her, needing to look her in the eyes when I say this. "Because fate led you to me that night, and I won't waste this chance we've been given."

"I'm yours, Kai, and you're mine," she says, tenderly cupping my face.

"For always." I kiss my wife's lush mouth, thrusting in and out of her as I imprint the words on my heart, knowing nothing or no one will ever tear us apart again.

THE END

Would you like to read the New York wedding bonus scene?
Copy and paste this link into your browser:
https://smarturl.it/SRbonusscene

JACKSON (Rydeville High Elite #4)

The devil came to me in disguise. Too bad I didn't notice until it was far too late.

Vanessa:
The devil doesn't always wear an evil mask.
Sometimes, he appears in the most beautiful form.
Like the super-hot bad boy with the dirty blond hair and a wicked glint in his blue eyes who swept in out of nowhere, stealing all the air from my lungs.
I thought he was my savior.
But he's my ruination.
And he's just taken a machete to my heart.

Jackson:
For years, my rage seethed under the surface. Hidden behind a cloudy haze of my poison of choice.
But now the fog has cleared.
And I'm out for blood.
I will annihilate those responsible for taking my sister from me.
Except *he's* not here, so I go for the next best target.
The woman he abandoned.
Until it suited him to drag her into this messed up elite world.
Sucks to be her.
Because when I'm done with Vanessa, she'll wish she was dead.

Preorder Now!

375

ABOUT THE AUTHOR

USA Today bestselling author **Siobhan Davis** writes emotionally intense young adult and new adult fiction with swoon-worthy romance, complex characters, and tons of unexpected plot twists and turns that will have you flipping the pages beyond bedtime! She is the author of the bestselling *True Calling*, *Saven*, and *Kennedy Boys* series.

Siobhan's family will tell you she's a little bit obsessive when it comes to reading and writing, and they aren't wrong. She can rarely be found without her trusty Kindle, a paperback book, or her laptop somewhere close at hand.

Prior to becoming a full-time writer, Siobhan forged a successful corporate career in human resource management.

She resides in the Garden County of Ireland with her husband and two sons.

You can connect with Siobhan in the following ways:
Author website: www.siobhandavis.com
Author Blog: My YA NA Book Obsession
Facebook: AuthorSiobhanDavis
Twitter: @siobhandavis
Google+: SiobhanDavisAuthor
Email: siobhan@siobhandavis.com

BOOKS BY SIOBHAN DAVIS

KENNEDY BOYS SERIES
Upper Young Adult/New Adult Contemporary Romance

Finding Kyler

Losing Kyler

Keeping Kyler

The Irish Getaway

Loving Kalvin

Saving Brad

Seducing Kaden

Forgiving Keven

Summer in Nantucket

*Releasing Keanu^*

Adoring Keaton*

Reforming Kent*

STANDALONES
New Adult Contemporary Romance

Inseparable

Incognito

When Forever Changes

Only Ever You

No Feelings Involved

Second Chances Box Set

Reverse Harem Contemporary Romance
Surviving Amber Springs

RYDEVILLE HIGH ELITE SERIES
Dark High School Romance
Cruel Intentions
Twisted Betrayal
*Sweet Retribution^*
*Charlie**
*Jackson**
*Sawyer**

ALL OF ME DUET
Angsty New Adult Romance
Say I'm The One *
*Let Me Love You**

ALINTHIA SERIES
Upper YA/NA Paranormal Romance/Reverse Harem
The Lost Savior
The Secret Heir
The Warrior Princess
The Chosen One
*The Rightful Queen**

TRUE CALLING SERIES

Young Adult Science Fiction/Dystopian Romance

True Calling

Lovestruck

Beyond Reach

Light of a Thousand Stars

Destiny Rising

Short Story Collection

True Calling Series Collection

SAVEN SERIES

Young Adult Science Fiction/Paranormal Romance

Saven Deception

Logan

Saven Disclosure

Saven Denial

Saven Defiance

Axton

Saven Deliverance

Saven: The Complete Series

^Releasing 2019

*Coming 2020.

Visit www.siobhandavis.com for all future release dates. Please note release dates are subject to change based on reader demand and the author's schedule. Subscribing to the author's newsletter or following her on Facebook is the best way to stay updated with planned new releases.

Made in the
USA
Lexington, KY